The GENTLEMAN'S CHOICE

Blake Rudman

A HellBound Books Publishing LLC Book
Houston TX

Dedicated to my beautiful daughter, Selah, as this book was written during COVID-19 when you were a magical hopeful thought soon to be a reality. You're a supreme blessing, and the world is your oyster.
Love, Dad

The GENTLEMAN'S CHOICE

Chapter One

The vibrator looked much smaller than it did on the show, but for Tracy Hickersley, that wasn't the most important thing at all. What did matter was, finally, after almost three long, frustrating months of waiting, she'd managed to get her hands on one of the vibrant pink sex toys that were featured every week on *The Gentleman's Choice*. It was the first such product tie-in the web show had attempted, and judging by the fact literally every online retailer had sold out within minutes—as had all the adult stores Tracy had visited weekly for twelve weeks—it had obviously been an incredibly successful launch.

Tracy had eventually hit lucky at Cherrie's Adult Emporium, which sat in the middle of an old strip mall on the edge of town; the store itself was a nasty little place with a small theater and viewing booths at the back. She recalled how the sickly reek of stale semen and cheap disinfectant had wafted through to the front of the store each time one of Cherrie's sad-faced patrons—every single one a man, all middle-aged or older; she'd guessed most of them to be married—made their way to what was purported to be a whole different, unpleasantly grubby world of glory holes and anonymous mutual relief.

Of course, Tracy had little desire to venture to the dimly lit, sordid world beyond the door that declared in faded-green Sharpie: "Absolutely NO Cross-Dressers." That had piqued Tracy's interest, and she couldn't help but wonder what the story behind that exclusion entailed. She had watched videos on *Pornhub* and the like where women—even some as young and attractive as herself— had enjoyed themselves among the desperate men in such places. But she'd gotten the distinct impression those scenes had been staged, even though they were advertised as "amateur." As with practically everything else on the internet, nothing in the wonderful world of adult entertainment was ever what it appeared to be. Even saying that, Tracy figured there would be some women who actually did get off from being ogled and groped by a bunch of random, sad, old men, but it sure as hell wasn't for her—although she was no stranger herself to getting down and dirty in front of the camera.

That, Tracy told herself, was something entirely different.

The girl in the sex store had been most helpful. Samantha, according to the neatly printed name tag, was young and covered in poorly but colorfully inked tattoos depicting everything from *Loony Toons* characters to dream catchers to large breasted, naked mermaids. She carried the acrid odor of weed about her; it clung to her clothes and long, dyed-black hair, and assaulted Tracy's nose every time the girl moved. Nonetheless, Samantha seemed cheerful enough and was only too happy to show Tracy what the demonstration model of *The Gentleman's*

Choice Magic Vibe could do—strictly on fingertips and the back of her hand, of course.

From the first touch of the vibrator's ultra-realistic latex skin, Tracy was hooked; the thing felt exactly like a human cock—even more so, apparently, if it was warmed under a hot tap as Samantha had advised. Tracy had *oohed* and *ahhed* as Samantha guided her hand through each one of the device's six stages of pleasure—from *gentle* to *stratospheric*; designed to emulate key stages of the female orgasm at the flick of the convenient rubberized button at its end. All the while, Tracy imagined the buzzing tip of the vibe upon her own body and was quite turned on by the time Samantha switched off the toy with the cheerful declaration that just one charge of the lithium-ion batteries was good for at least four earth-shattering climaxes.

The fact the thing cost a cent shy of eighty bucks—almost double the unobtainable internet versions—had done nothing whatsoever to deter Tracy from thrusting her credit card at the young girl the second the demonstration was finished. That the toy was approved by the renowned web show, *The Gentleman's Choice*—Tracy's favorite—was all the endorsement she needed. And besides, the extortionate price was most probably the reason Cherrie's still had a couple left on the shelf from their most recent delivery, and for that, Tracy would be eternally grateful. All in all, it had been a good day; Tracy had the whole evening off from work, the apartment to herself, and she was about to experience what the Magic Vibe promised to be the absolute best orgasms of her life.

Tracy settled back on her maroon couch, enjoying the silky feel of the velour as it caressed the bare skin of her back. She contemplated the compact, six-inch bundle of phthalate-free latex rubber, plastic, and intricate machinery that nestled among the unruly thicket of pubic hair between her thighs; it had been quite a long time since Tracy had dated, and she'd kinda let herself go a little—not that her evening's partner was about to complain.

Grabbing her laptop from the coffee table, Tracy brought it to life with a long, firm press of her thumb—the thing was getting old and the on switch was no longer as sensitive as it had once been. She placed the computer on the carefully positioned couch cushion beside her and watched as the screen flickered reluctantly to life and the hard drive whirred and hummed. In the brief moment the screen remained dark, Tracy caught sight of her naked body reflected there, and imagined her full, bare breasts and stiff, aroused nipples were once again being featured on *The Gentleman's Choice*.

Once the laptop was up and running, which felt like an absolute age to the growing impatience between her legs, Tracy clicked on the desktop shortcut that immediately plunged into the intriguing, sexy world of *The Gentleman's Choice*. The evening's episode had just begun, and Cole Gianni was introducing that week's contestant with a warm smile and a run-through of the highlights of his dates with the gal so far. It was a cheesy part of the show Tracy didn't really care for—she thought it made the show appear too manufactured and too much like *America's Got Talent* for shameless gold diggers and self-promoters, which was actually an accurate description of the proceedings, all things considered.

Cole, the show's host, looked just a bit older on screen than he did on the sexy toy's packaging, which Tracy chalked up to the manufacturers overdoing it with Photoshop when they'd designed the vibrator's box; either that, or they'd used some old publicity pictures. Actually, it was a bit of an insult to the show's host, in Tracy's opinion, as she thought Cole looked as breathtakingly handsome as he had when she'd been a season two *Gentleman's Choice* contestant four years before.

A noise startled her; it sounded like a key in the front door. Had she gotten her friends' schedules wrong and one of them had come home early? "Sandra? Is that you?" Twisting around to see over the back of the couch, Tracy lowered the computer's volume and listened for a reply.

Nothing. "J'Terrica?"

Hearing nothing more than street noise from outside, Tracy shrugged and upped the sound on her laptop. Then, she reached down between her spread thighs and clicked on the vibrator. It buzzed gently, and an instant shudder of pleasure and anticipation ran through her body; her skin prickled all over with goosebumps.

"Good evening, Cole," Tracy purred in perfect sync with the show's hot, young contestant. The gal's name was Jessica and she had, despite what Tracy considered to be a shitty attitude toward Cole, miraculously made it through to the fifth and final night of the week's show. And that meant Jessica and the deliciously sexy Cole would finally be having sex as the climax to their five-day stint together. And the sex would be full, unadulterated, entirely uncensored, and live on the internet for the show's myriad of subscribers

Perfect.

Tracy flicked her new, neon-pink toy up to its second setting and guided it with one hand to the left-hand side of her clitoris—it was a tad too sensitive at its tip after almost a week of neglect; Tracy knew from experience that to start there with a direct attack would be to risk putting herself through the damn ceiling.

The show's online audience had chosen a sexy spanking scenario for Cole and Jessica's final night together. Tracy guessed the viewers might just have selected BDSM from the delights on offer because of the girl's aloof attitude toward both the host and the show in general. And, although Tracy, personally, had voted for the crowd-pleasing orgy scenario, she was very much looking forward to seeing the snooty young miss with the teacup tits get her comeuppance.

In Tracy's racing imagination, she was the one about to clamber up onto that magnificent four-poster bed and spread her arms and legs, so Cole could strap her down by means of the harsh, leather cuffs that adorned each of the bed's thick mahogany posts. But it was Jessica's bare backside that awaited, with eager anticipation, the sharp crack of the cat o'nine tails she knew Cole would select from the wonderful collection of items upon the wall; her skin was already aglow with the man's handprints. The bitter sensation of jealousy dug at Tracy's conscience and threatened to take the edge off her pleasure; she'd been cheated out of her time with Cole and resented all of the contestants who had taken her place over the years. Tracy's friends said she was crazy living her love life vicariously through Cole Gianni and his countless dates, but she'd tried to re-create what she'd had with him with guys from dating sites, and not one had measured up; it was easier to be the voyeur and be with Cole in her imagination.

Besides, not even her closest friends knew the intimate things she'd shared with Cole during their four days together; much of it had been off camera. The star of the show was not supposed to fraternize with the contestants when they were not on screen; it was a rule the producer said he'd put into place to maintain the sexual tension. But that Cole openly defied that to spend time with her told Tracy he genuinely shared her feelings; they were in love, and nothing would come in the way of that. She'd gotten to know the man behind the smoldering, sex-driven Cole Gianni everyone else tuned in to see; the person Tracy knew—the *real* Cole—was sensitive, loving, and vulnerable. She had found out he was not from some far-flung European country as he pretended to be—his accent slipped almost the second the cameras were off him. He was more East Coast USA than Europe and definitely not of noble descent, a count, a lord, or even a prince. All of it was fabricated for the show's growing female viewers because, as Cole himself had explained to Tracy, what woman doesn't get weak at the knees at exotic European royalty?

They kept the exact whereabouts of Cole's supposed origins secret enough to keep it interesting and prevent people from looking it up on the internet; he had divulged to Tracy on their second day together that he was actually from Cochabamba in Bolivia and had not so much as visited anywhere in Europe.

In their more intimate moments away from the prying eyes of the cameras, Cole had alluded to some terrible secret he had run away from, which Tracy had seen buried deep in his eyes. He carried with him the dark, haunted look of a man being hunted, scared of the shadows, hiding behind the mask of the persona they had created for him on the show. He'd confided in her that the façade he wore for the show was the perfect guise for him, yet one he feared he might never be able to shed.

And Tracy had known then and there that, had they had more time together, Cole Gianni would have told her his deepest, darkest secrets.

And that was why, in her mind, Cole had not made contact with her at all after she left *The Gentleman's Choice*.

Jessica was being led to the four-poster bed, which was dressed with black satin sheets and an array of plump, matching pillows. Tracy knew the bed was most likely a set in the corner of a rental studio, although she'd heard the show was starting to use actual residences in the name of authenticity. But, nonetheless, it completely looked the part with dimmed lighting, flickering yellow candles, and the eye-watering array of whips, floggers, paddles, riding crops, and the old-style canes so often portrayed in period British boarding school dramas.

Jessica had been dressed for the occasion and titillation of the show's subscribers, of course. She wore a neck-high, tight red minidress, completely backless to expose her naked, perfectly toned butt. Cole's jaw had all but dropped open when the girl sashayed into the bedroom looking like some high-class escort girl all ready for her first trick of the night; Tracy had studied Cole's eyes as they fixed upon the rhythmic movement of Jessica's firm white ass cheeks as she paraded in front of him, and she remembered him looking at her in that way.

One of Tracy's fondest memories of her brief time on the show was working with the girls—and one token gay guy—to select the perfect clothes for each of the dates she was to enjoy with Cole. Naturally, every outfit had to be alluring and outright sexy for the benefit of the paying viewers: the ladies among the show's audience loved the inspiration that afforded for their own wardrobes, and the men loved to see seductively dressed contestants. So, dresses were suggestively revealing, skirts dangerously short, and tops scooped low in the front and back to show off as much skin as was humanly possible while still leaving just a little to the imaginations of the show's viewers.

Since her own appearance, over the subsequent years, Tracy had heard of some contestants complaining they felt objectified and demeaned by the skimpy outfits they were made to wear on the show. She thought that was a little hypocritical considering every girl knew exactly what they were getting themselves into when they signed up. And nor would they turn down a single cent of the prize money they were putting themselves on display to win.

A faint sound pricked Tracy's ears, only just loud enough for her to hear above the vibrator's buzzing, something like the faint tinkle of breaking glass. She gave a cursory glance over her shoulder and a quick look through the gap she'd left in the living room curtains; most likely it was the neighbors upstairs. Tracy found it surprising they were home so early, but they were often the source of odd noises, day and night.

"Bend over the bed," Cole commanded Jessica in that husky, baritone voice of his that was always filled with erotic suggestion; Tracy remembered well the effect Cole's deep voice and exotic accent had on her during her time on the show—even though she knew it was fake—and it really hadn't diminished any over the years.

Tracy looked on, rapt, as Jessica did as she was told with a compliant smile. The young girl's long, gym-toned legs strained, and her calves bulged in the impossibly vertiginous patent leather shoes that were held to her bare feet by nothing more than thin straps. Jessica pressed her sweet face against the silky, shimmering sheets, stretched her arms out in front of herself, and raised up her ass like some wanton wild animal in heat.

"Spank her, Cole," Tracy murmured as she double-clicked her vibrator's button to skip to level four; she was already way beyond the third level. Tracy let out a loud gasp as the tiny motor encased in the latex upped its game against her sweet spot. "Spank that rude bitch good and hard…"

As if on Tracy's cue, Cole delivered a hard, resounding slap to Jessica's left buttock. He turned to face the camera as he did so and seemed to relish the sharp cry of surprise and pain his hand had elicited in his date. Then, returning his attention to the pert ass presented for his delectation, Cole spanked the right cheek with equal firmness, and the imprint of his hand appeared immediately in a sensual, glowing red.

There would be sex on the show, of course—it was the final night after all—but as a seasoned viewer with inside knowledge, Tracy knew that wouldn't happen until Jessica's ass was suitably spanked and delectably striped. The show's subscribers would expect Cole to put on a spectacle of "punishing" Jessica to earn the money they paid each and every month to watch him act out the sexual fantasies most of them could only ever dream about; little did they know, as Tracy did, that Cole abhorred the BDSM they portrayed on the show. It was nothing like the real-life scene he'd experienced, and it denied the women any control; it was nothing more than inflicting pain for the titillation of the audience.

Even after so long, it still irked Tracy that she hadn't made it to Night Five. It meant she had missed out on going all the way with the gorgeous, charismatic host; she and Cole had gotten along famously throughout the four nights she was on *The Gentleman's Choice*—*dates* as the show liked to call them—and had enjoyed the kissing, fooling around, and heavy petting each of the nights required. But, because she had played a little hard to get and had not dropped her panties the second Cole had smiled at her, Tracy had been voted off after Night Four.

But, what really, *really* pissed Tracy off was she had only been playing the role the producer had told her to play—he'd even gone so far as to *guarantee* she'd be voted from the show on the *first* date if she refused to comply and, along with that, any hope of winning the ten grand prize. Not that it came as any surprise to Tracy to learn the unscrupulous people running the show were more than capable of manipulating the viewers' votes, but what had the producers dumb fucking idea done for her in the end anyway?

And it also rankled Tracy that she'd actually let the creepy producer guy finger-bang her while she sucked on his stumpy dick on the promise of her making it to Night Five. Maybe it would have been worth it if the prize money totaled a hundred grand like it did in later seasons. But for ten grand—to this day, the thought of it still stuck in her throat.

Of course, if Tracy had had her way, she'd have gone all the way with Cole Gianni; never mind the money, she had fallen completely in love with him, with the *real* Cole no one else ever got to know, and not the fake fantasy *product* the show had turned him into.

"Up on the bed now, Jessica." Cole's sexy voice drifted out from the computer's speaker, which managed to make even Cole's deep, resonant timbre sound a little tinny. "I'm going to spank your ass 'til you come for me."

"Oh, God, *yes*," Tracy groaned. She slid the toy deep inside her vagina, pressing the button as she did so; the accelerated vibrations radiated through her insides and brought with them waves of intense pleasure. "Make me come too, Cole, my love."

As she closed her eyes to relish the moment, something flitted in Tracy's peripheral vision.

"That you, J'?" Tracy's voice quivered as she called out to her roommate. She kept her eyes closed, not wanting to break the spell, and thought perhaps J'Terrica had let herself in and gone straight to her room to give a friend a little privacy.

If there was a reply, Tracy didn't hear it above the loud buzzing and the sound of Cole's sweet voice coming from the laptop.

"Are you ready for me, Jessica?" Tracy opened her eyes in time to see Cole look directly into the camera as he spoke. Before her time on the show, Tracy had been coached in breaking the fourth wall—the producer had explained it was kind of a signature move for *The Gentleman's Choice*, as it was meant to include the audience in Cole's adventures.

"Yes," Jessica purred, her soft, sweet voice muffled by the satin sheets. Cole brought the whip down upon her naked ass with such suddenness, such force, the harsh sound of leather on skin, accompanied by Jessica's shrill squeal of pain and pleasure, made Tracy jump a little. "Yes, *what*?" Cole demanded and made ready to strike his target once more.

"Yes, *Master* Cole," Jessica gasped as she wriggled and squirmed, crumpling up the once-pristine sheets with her legs as an array of angry red welts appeared on the smooth skin of her buttock.

Cole whipped Jessica again—twice—and Tracy was thrilled they had decided to go all *Fifty Shades* for the final night; the orgy scenes she so loved were commonplace on the show and, for as horny as they made her, Tracy was actually delighted the viewer vote had gone against her just this once. "Yes, *Master* Cole," Tracy repeated Jessica's line and slipped the Magic Vibe out of her body.

"I think we'll try the riding crop next, Jessica," Cole told his date with a lascivious look out of Tracy's computer screen. Tracy quivered as she imagined Cole was addressing her, and only her, and she was playing the part of Jessica.

"Thank you, Master Cole," Tracy gasped in perfect unison with the girl who Cole had so expertly strapped face down on the studio set bed.

Tracy's legs stiffened and her hips bucked upward as if to greet Cole as he mounted her in the dominating, masculine way she'd imagined he would have a thousand times on *their* fifth night together. To hell with the fact that millions of people would be watching every stroke, every thrust and grunt, every moan of pleasure; to hell with her puritanical father who had disowned his only daughter for displaying herself on the internet in perpetuity for countless men and women to pleasure themselves over like she was some cheap, slutty porn starlet. All that mattered in Tracy's fantasies was Cole making hot, sweet love to her—even though it was only in her imagination.

Engrossed in Cole's administrations to Jessica, a feeling of not being alone crept over Tracy; the noises and imagined movement had spooked her a little, even if it was probably only J'Terrica. It wouldn't be the first time her roommate had seen her masturbate—the girl was a habitual voyeur, and both she and Sandra had caught her peeping on several occasions. But what if she'd brought someone home with her and they were both watching?

Tracy was beyond caring at that juncture; her attention was focused on Cole, Jessica, and the pleasure sweeping through her own body.

As Cole went on to create a crisscross pattern of neat red stripes upon Jessica's peachy, nude derriere, Tracy pushed herself hard to meet the thundering climax that bubbled up inside of her; she imagined herself akin to some long-dormant volcano on the verge of eruption. The vibrator's packaging had not been wrong in its claim—Tracy had never felt pleasure so intensely powerful in her life, nor had she had ever felt so devilishly wanton and out of control while masturbating.

Cole had replaced the crop with a flat leather paddle. It had the word "SLUT" cut—mirror-image—into one side; the idea was the letters would be embossed upon the spanked skin and brand the recipient with the appropriate label. Jessica's cries and yelps turned quickly into groans of pleasure as the paddle came down swift and hard upon her already sore buttocks, and a thin sheen of sweat glistened in the deep, sensual dip of the small of her back.

The resonant smack of leather on flesh all but masked the soft shuffling noises Tracy heard coming from behind her. A smile spread her lips as she pressed her thighs tight together to embrace the vibrator as she welcomed her orgasm; in her heightened state of arousal, Tracy thought if J'Terrica—and even a complete stranger—*was* watching her, then she would embrace her inner exhibitionist and put on a damned good show for the girl. It would be a performance worthy of *The Gentleman's Choice* itself.

"Fuck me, Cole!" Tracy let out the scream that forced itself through her clenched teeth as she came hard in wave upon wave of hot, tingling pleasure. With her legs clamped firmly together, Tracy's hips bucked wildly as her bare toes dug hard into the blue fluffy rug beneath the coffee table. She pressed the vibrator hard against her clitoris with both hands to perpetuate the raw ecstasy coursing through her body.

Through her exaggerated performance, Tracy didn't once take her eyes off the screen as Cole abandoned the paddle and stripped himself naked to join Jessica upon the bed to fuck her like the magnificent stallion he was.

"I hope you're enjoying the show, J'Terrica!" Tracy couldn't help herself. "You should have joined—"

Then, in a heartbeat, as delicious climaxes pulsed through her body, everything suddenly went black for Tracy.

Before she could register what was happening, Tracy felt the rough scrape of burlap against her face and the sharp prick of a needle in the shuddering, sweat-dampened muscle of her bicep; a cold rush of liquid entered her arm and, in shock, she relinquished hold upon the vibrator, which slipped from between her legs and fell, buzzing, to the floor.

Fighting to catch her breath within the claustrophobic confines of the harsh canvas pressed against her face, Tracy had no chance of fighting back against whoever held it there as consciousness rapidly grayed around the edges, and her mind swam away.

As the drug raced around Tracy's body and closed down her brain, she managed at least a token flail of her arms, but her loose fists connected with nothing and quickly fell limp by her sides.

Chapter Two

"And… *cut*!" Skippy Webman barked into the microphone; his East London accent pinged off the walls of the tiny production booth.

"You do know we don't have to say cut… on account of the fact we're live streaming?" his assistant reminded him with a self-satisfied smirk. Sharon, Karen, or some such suitably uninspired name, was a short, dour-faced teenager Skippy had only hired because of her spectacular 38DD rack.

"I know that, but what else am I supposed to say when we're taking a break?" Skippy snapped back. Three days on the job, and not only had the girl spurned every one of his advances like some pissy, uptight dyke, she was already getting ideas way above her fucking pay grade and talking to him like he was a moron. "Don't you have tea to make or something?" He glowered at the girl, and his eyes danced on down to her spectacularly large breasts.

"Of course, *tea*." Sharon/Karen emulated Skippy's rough British accent perfectly and chuckled at just how clever she no doubt thought she was.

"Just piss off, will you?" Skippy growled and returned his attention to the screens.

"Whatever you say, boss." The assistant flounced out of the room, which was only illuminated by the glare of the half dozen screens Skippy had set up like it was a proper production booth for a proper TV show and not *The Gentleman's Choice*. Even after so many years of producing the show, Skippy still considered it to be nothing more than an internet-only porny game show and a means to an end. Stark, bright light from the hallway outside flooded in as Sharon/Karen—or could it have been *Carol*?—pulled open the door. With it came a welcome blast of fresh, conditioned air. Skippy was grateful for that, as the tart stink of his own body odor was actually beginning to offend him, let alone his assistant, who did appear most relieved to have tea to make.

Skippy did try hard to keep his three-hundred-pound bulk fresh with showers morning and night and gallons of industrial-strength deodorant, but it sure as hell wasn't easy in the unforgiving heat of Southern Texas. The arid, oppressive climate was as far removed from the temperate, gray weather of London as Skippy thought it was possible to get.

On three of the six screens in front of him ran the live footage of Cole Gianni and the show's latest contestant coming to the end of their schmaltzy, romantic horse ride. Skippy and Cole had blown a considerable chunk of budget on renting a remote log cabin in Fairfield Lake State Park, which sat conveniently between Houston and Dallas; they filmed segments of the show in and around both cities. The cabin was lakeside, of course, close enough to the horse-riding center and would provide the perfect location for the evening's entertainment after Cole and his new conquest had finished up riding the trail.

As for the week's contestant herself, Mai Ling was a nicely built, cutesy Asian chick from China or Vietnam or Korea—Skippy was just terrible with the minorities. She reminded Skippy of the petite, wide-eyed anime characters he used to jerk off to in his younger years, which had gone a long way toward securing her a spot on the show. She was one of the more malleable contestants they'd had in the six years he and Cole had been putting the show out, and she had those tiny Asian tits the viewers seemed to go wild for. There was something about Mai Ling that made Skippy promise himself to do everything he could to ensure the viewers' vote kept her all the way through to the fifth night; he certainly wasn't above fudging the figures to get his own way.

Yes, Skippy knew full well he was living vicariously through Cole and the show, and while Mai Ling was one of the increasing number who'd turned him down flat during the auditions, he knew he could at least look forward to watching Cole ride her naked ass on the show's final night.

Skippy viewed the screens with little interest. After so long producing *The Gentleman's Choice*, unless there was something *really* sexy going on, it didn't hold his attention for long. Cole and Mai Ling were riding their horses—a piebald gelding and chestnut mare, respectively—into the corral with Cole playing the true gentleman and doing the whole *ladies first* thing. Skippy liked to think his star's real motive was so he could watch the Asian gal's tight ass bounce up and down in her saddle. Not that Skippy could blame the guy, as she sure looked hot as fuck in the skintight faded Wranglers the wardrobe department had practically poured her into.

Although Skippy had called cut, which actually indicated the live segment of the show was done for the time being, the cameras still rolled over at the corral. That way, they'd capture filler footage for the montage they'd show as and when the girl left the show. The horse ride and picnic date were over at last with the final shot being just as Cole and Mai Ling made their way back along the track; the setting sun, bloated and orange-pink, made a spectacular background—Skippy was particularly proud of that one. They'd take an hour's break to show recaps and highlights of the date, which would whet the audience's appetite for the live feed of the couple cozying up by the fireside later that evening. There'd be a lot of kissing, a little groping, and Cole would have the chick at least topless by the end of the segment—Skippy had written the script, and Cole knew what was expected of him, so that much was a given; if he managed to get her stripped all the way naked, then all the better.

"What the…?" Skippy's attention was grabbed by a sudden movement on the screens. "Are you getting this, Eric?" he barked into the microphone at his lead cameraman as Mai Ling's horse reared up with its mouth wide open and eyes bulging. Of course, Eric was getting it, otherwise Skippy wouldn't be seeing it in the comfort of his little booth, but it was nonetheless a good "producer" thing to say.

Skippy hit another button, which patched him through to Cole's earpiece and microphone. "Cole! Get the fuck away from that!"

Mai Ling clung to her horse's reins for dear life; there was a look of horror all over her pretty round face, and somehow, she managed to stay in the saddle. Skippy was pleased he'd given in to Cole's insistence the girl be given some rudimentary instruction before the show, since she'd never ridden a horse before. It had actually made for some neat candid footage; Cole had played the macho man, leaning against the fence as he watched Mai Ling take instruction from the grizzled cowboy-type they'd paid a stupid amount of money to.

Even though there must have been at least a thirty-year age difference between them, the Asian and the roughneck cowboy had shared a definite spark and got quite flirty, which brought out a little of Cole's jealous streak; for all of his on-screen machismo and sexual confidence, Cole was a sweet, sensitive guy, insecure and terrified of rejection. Skippy figured that had a lot to do with what happened to the guy back in LA, and sometimes, it was good to pull Cole's jealousy strings. So, every now and then, he'd throw in a potential love rival on the show just to elicit a reaction from Cole; a couple times there had almost been a physical altercation.

And that made for some magical moviemaking.

"There's a snake!" Eric's voice came through the cheap speaker that made him sound tinny and distant.

"Then get the fucking thing on camera!" Skippy told him, and heard Eric instruct Pete, the second cameraman, to keep shooting Mai Ling's desperate attempt to keep her tidy little derrière on the goddamned horse. "Cole! Will you fucking answer me?"

"Quit panicking, Skip," Cole's voice came through loud and clear; he sounded eerily calm.

It took Eric a few seconds to focus on the snake. To Skippy, the thing looked to be a juvenile diamondback of little more than three feet long, and it was slithering away, scared, from the ruckus and dust the horse was kicking up with its flailing feet and terrified whinnying.

Skippy had made a point of learning all of the Texas snakes—venomous and otherwise—when he'd moved over from England; he hated the things with a passion and figured it was something he really ought to know.

"What *are you* doing?" Skippy screamed into the mic as Cole dismounted his gelding and raced toward Mai Ling's horse like he was some cut-rate John Wayne. "*Get away from that fucking horse!*"

Images flashed through Skippy's head of Cole taking a hoof in that handsome face of his, or the chest, or—God forbid—the balls. The idiot could get himself trampled, or the panicking horse might actually go all the way and kill him! The show had Cole insured, of course, but without him, it would be nothing more than a pale imitation of its former self.

If Cole died, what would become of *The Gentleman's Choice*? "I know what I'm doing, Skippy," Cole reassured him. "I'm not going to stand by and watch Mai Ling get hurt."

"Somebody go get the bloody cowboy!" Skippy snarled; did he really have to do *everybody's* thinking for them?

Mesmerized, unable to tear his eyes away from the impending disaster he just *knew* was about to unfold on the screens, Skippy could only look on as Cole stepped out in front of the panicky horse, arms outstretched like he was inviting the thing to go ahead and kick in his ribs.

"Oh, for fuck's sake, Cole," Skippy grunted. "*What do you think you're doing, you arsehole?*"

"Steady, girl." Cole was composed, collected, as if he'd done this a thousand times before. "Steady there… whoa now." Reaching up, he grabbed hold of the horse's reins just below the bit and mumbled something in Spanish; foam from the animal's mouth drenched his hand and ran down the sleeve of his red, wild-west-style plaid shirt.

The horse calmed a little and thumped its front legs back down into the dry, hard ground. A plume of red dust puffed up, which had the beast sneezing.

"Steady on there, girl," Cole soothed and moved his hand up to take hold of the throat lash with one hand while stroking the horse's nose with the other. Fidgeting, still spooked, the mare stomped her hooves and snorted at Cole. "Easy…"

Moving his hand up a little further, Cole looped his fingers through the cheekpiece and gently pulled the horse's nose to his chest.

"The cowboy's on his way, Cole—you can step away from the bloody horse now," Skippy said into the mic.

"It's okay, I got this," Cole whispered beneath his breath as he soothed the horse.

"*For fuck's sake*," Skippy growled; perhaps Cole *wanted* to get himself hurt so they'd be forced to discuss the future of the show? Skippy knew the guy wanted an out to try his luck in Hollywood again, but this was totally out of character, and he could see Cole looked genuinely scared. "You can get down now," Cole said to Mai Ling. "Nice and slow."

Mai Ling dismounted and took a few steps back from the horse; she was all dewy-eyed with admiration for Cole, her hero, who stood stock-still with the horse snuggled into him like some oversized puppy dog.

"That was amazing, my old mate," Skippy said into the mic; he knew Cole could hear him, but he didn't even glance into the camera. Eyes glued to the screens, Skippy let out the breath he'd been holding and shook his head to clear it of the gruesome images he'd conjured of his handsome meal ticket lying mangled in the dirt.

As things had turned out, Cole had played the dashing hero better than any number of Tom Cruises and had inadvertently guaranteed Mai Ling's undying devotion; who the fuck doesn't fall hopelessly in love with the man who just saved their life? Skippy allowed himself a moment of self-congratulation; he really couldn't have scripted the scene better himself.

"Make the most of the scene, Cole." Skippy quickly reverted to producer mode. "Get the fuck back into character."

"How did you do that?" Mai Ling reached out a tentative hand and stroked the horse's flank; the beast stood calmly next to Cole, no longer seeking comfort against his body.

"I grew up around horses," Cole told her with a smile Skippy thought came over on camera perfectly smug. "Back home on the country estate, we used to do it to impress the girls." He pursed his lips as if about to whistle, but from his throat came an uncannily accurate imitation of a snake's warning hiss. Startled, Mai Ling jumped back as the horse once again reared up on its hind legs with a horrified expression on its face.

"*What the fuck are you doing, Cole?*" Skippy yelled at the microphone. His heart pounded hard against his ribs— it had barely slowed down following the first scare Cole had put him through; Skippy sure as all hell didn't need to go through that amount of stress again quite so soon.

But, once more, Cole calmed the animal down with soothing sounds and well-rehearsed hand movements— much to the delight of his date, who appeared ready to swoon and drop her panties for him right there in the corral; he was back playing his role of the smooth, sexy Cole Gianni. "See." Cole smiled directly into Eric's camera to deliver the expected line that would have the female viewers glued to their screens. "All the girls back home used to go wild for this."

Skippy was delighted to see the cowboy walking into the shot. Taking the mare's reins from Cole's hand, he led the beast away. He gave Mai Ling a loaded smile, a tip of the Stetson, and a *howdy, ma'am* on his way by, but the girl only had eyes for the handsome young man who'd just saved her life.

Chapter Three

I t was daylight when Tracy finally opened her eyes. Head pounding, mouth feeling sour and stinking as if something had crawled into it and died, Tracy strained against what felt to be thin, nylon ropes digging into her wrists and ankles.

"Hello?" It was all Tracy could think of to say; her voice croaked out from her throat and sounded like something altogether quite alien in the empty room. "Is anybody out there?"

Silence.

Her eyes adjusted to the light and Tracy peered around the room. It appeared to be a spacious bedroom, complete with a California king-sized bed accented by polished oak nightstands on either side, a polished chrome stripper's pole, and red leather sex swing. A huge flat-screen TV dominated the wall opposite the bed, and dotted around the chintz-papered walls were artistic paintings and photographs depicting lewd sexual acts and erotically posed, entirely naked young men and women.

One of the pictures, a photograph blown up and printed in sepia on canvas to emulate something much older, was of a married couple in their sixties or early seventies. They were both completely nude and stood facing one another in an awkwardly posed embrace that Tracy thought was supposed to be a romantic cuddle. The couple's wrinkled, smiling faces matched those in the smaller silver frames adorning the nightstands; they looked happy, sexually aroused as if they were just about to get down to having sex in front of whomever was taking the photograph.

A hot wave of panic prickled the back of Tracy's skull; was she looking into the eyes of the people who had kidnapped her? They appeared so sweet, so… *normal*.

But wasn't that what everyone said about serial killers when they were caught?

Whoever they were, and whatever their motive for keeping her tied to a musty old mattress on their bedroom floor, Tracy knew they intended to do her serious harm.

Which meant she had to get the fuck out of there—and fast. But how?

Tracy fought hard to suppress the terror and abject feeling of helplessness that hit her hard as the drug-induced fog wore off; how could this be happening? How did they single her out—had they been watching her through her laptop's camera as she'd pleasured herself?

Why *her*?

Tracy's mind raced with thoughts that perhaps she was going to be trafficked; young, attractive White women disappeared all the time and spent the remainder of their miserable lives drugged and sold for sex. Or was she to meet with a gruesome death at the hands of the ostensibly sweet old couple once they'd had their way with her?

Naked, she was tied spread-eagle and supine to the single mattress that lay on the bedroom floor. Tracy felt alone, scared, and horribly vulnerable. The bedroom door was twenty—maybe more—feet away and closed, as was the slightly narrower door leading to what Tracy reckoned to be the end-suite bathroom. It gave her some comfort to know where the exits were, even though Tracy could see no way of breaking free from her restraints as the thin, faded-orange rope dug deeper into her skin with every movement she made. It reminded her of the stuff her daddy used to use to tie hay bales with back on the ranch where she'd grown up.

Tracy tried to relax her arms and legs to prevent the ropes cutting off the remainder of the circulation to her hands and feet; she'd need every bit of sensation and strength if she was to escape that damp, moldy mattress and the pervading reek of something unpleasantly rotten that was seeping into the room.

"Help me?" Tracy's dry voice bounced about the room. Her tongue stuck to the roof of her mouth. *"Please!"*

The door opened.

"My, we are a noisy little miss, aren't we?" It was a woman's voice. It sounded friendly, warm even, as its owner bustled into the bedroom. Dressed as a dominatrix, she wore a tight black leather pencil skirt that clung to the sensual curves of her thighs and ass, and a strappy leather, cupless corset top that left her high, heavy breasts exposed and swinging freely with every step she made in her spike-heeled shoes. The dominatrix's face was covered by an ornate feather mask, the type Tracy had seen worn at the New Years' parties she and her friends loved to attend; it covered all but the pair of piercing green eyes and bright ruby red lips, the latter of which glistened wet as if soaked in blood.

Tracy twisted her head to get a better look. It wasn't easy, given her predicament, as it put strain on the tendons in her neck and made her head thump so hard, bright flashes of light ignited behind her eyes.

"Make sure we get the establishing shot." The second voice belonged to a squat, stocky man who followed the dominatrix into the bedroom. He wore a red latex catsuit that covered him ankles to neck, and a matching leather gimp mask covered all but his eyes; there was a zipper across the mouth, which Tracy thought resembled a ragged silver scar. The man held a compact Sony video camera up to his eye, its lens pointing at Tracy; its little red LED light indicated he was filming her.

"Who are you people?" Tracy asked. "Why are you doing this to me?"

"Water?" The dominatrix ignored her captive's questions as if nothing had been said at all. "Would you like me to get you some, Tracy?" They knew her name.

"I'll go." The gimp was curt. Turning on his heels, he made his way across the plush beige carpet to the en-suite; all the while, he carried on with his filming.

Tracy was horrified to hear the dominatrix using her name in such a way—talking to her as if they were old friends. It made the whole scenario frighteningly familiar in Tracy's mind and gave her captors the distinct psychological advantage.

"I'm sure you're thirsty, sweetie, you've been asleep for *hours*." The dominatrix sounded strangely maternal—an odd juxtaposition to the severe, revealing BDSM outfit. There was a hint of kindness in her tone that provided with Tracy the slightest grain of hope she might just be able to engage and perhaps get out of her predicament alive.

Those hopes, however, were dashed the moment the gimp cameraman opened the en-suite door and a rancid, sickening stink spilled out into the bedroom.

"*Oh my God.*" The words spilled from Tracy's parched lips. She felt the stinging rush of acid bile at the back of her throat.

"Don't mind them," the dominatrix said with a sugary smile; her red-glossed lips parted to reveal perfect teeth. "They won't be joining us." With a glance over her shoulder, she followed Tracy's mesmerized gaze into the small bathroom where her partner-in-crime was busy filling a crystal-cut glass with water. Tracy immediately recognized the old woman from the pictures dotted about the bedroom, only her face was no longer smiling either the kind smile or the lascivious one on the canvas photo—it was slack, lifeless, her eyes glassy, fixed, and staring at the gray slate bathroom floor. The old woman was laid, along with her husband, in the white clawfoot bathtub; her head lolled over its side, and half of her sweet, wrinkled face was red with congealed blood. Someone had bashed in the back of her skull with such ferocity the gray pink crinkles of her brain were exposed and glistening at the back.

The husband's face was balanced on its chin an inch or two away from the old woman's, and it sickened Tracy to realize the killers had obviously taken the time to pose the bodies as if the old couple were simply enjoying time together in the tub.

There wasn't a drop of blood to be seen on the old man, although his tongue lolled from between purple, swollen lips. His eyes were bloodshot, bulging as if he'd died only moments before they were about to pop all the way out from their sockets.

Tracy had seen enough CSI to know either the gimp or the dominatrix had strangled the poor guy and had taken their own, sweet time in doing so. Which one of the two had done the deed? Had they forced the dear old lady to watch before they'd caved in her head? Was she going to be next to feel hands tightening around her throat or feel the sickening crunch of her skull smashing in?

Tears welled up to blur Tracy's vision. She truly didn't want to be their next victim.

"Here you are," the dominatrix purred as the gimp reappeared with the glass of water in hand. Mercifully, he'd closed the bathroom door behind him, and Tracy was no longer forced to look into the cold, dead eyes of the old couple, although the cloying stench of death hung heavy in the air even with the bathroom door shut.

The dominatrix cupped the back of Tracy's head with one hand and held the glass to her parched lips with the other; it was an almost tender, caring gesture.

Tracy shook her head.

"It's okay." The dominatrix gave her a reassuring smile. "It's just water."

"No." Tracy forced out the word; she wanted nothing more than to quench her gnawing thirst, but the fear of what her captors may have added to the water held her back.

Still smiling, the dominatrix lifted the glass to her own lips. She took a delicate sip, followed by a mouthful. "See. Nothing to be afraid of at all. It's only water."

Giving in, Tracy took several hearty gulps of the water; some of it spilled from her lips, trickled down her neck, and between her breasts. It tasted so wonderfully refreshing upon her desiccated tongue but carried with it the unmistakable sour tang of fluoride.

Where the hell was she?

How long would it be before Sandra and J'Terrica realized she was missing and not just hooking up? Would they call the cops straightaway? If so, how long before the police saved her—assuming, of course, they had any idea where she was being held?

How could this be happening to her? What had she done to put herself on the radar of these sick people?

The gimp had returned to filming Tracy in uncomfortable close-up. Before moving the camera's inquisitive eye back down toward her feet, he'd knelt down beside her to film the dominatrix allowing her to drink the water. He was so damn close to her ear; Tracy heard the tight rubber encasing his body squeak and his heavy breathing as he struggled to suck air in through the zippered mask. Tracy had never felt quite so naked and exposed in her entire life. With her arms and legs tied up and spread, she had no way to even partially cover her bare breasts and vagina. She drew some comfort from the fact her long-neglected bush would be concealing much of what she had going on down there.

It was, however, cold comfort.

Sure, she'd dated creeps who'd crossed a line with her before; typically, they expected kinky stuff from her—anal, watersports, bondage, foot stuff—and had gotten aggressive when she refused. Tracy had kicked them all to the curb the moment she felt threatened. But *this*, this was crazy and sick and way beyond anything she'd experienced before. As threatened as some of the creeps had made her feel, Tracy had never once felt gut-clenching fear for her life.

At the hands of the dominatrix, this was entirely different; was the gimp filming her before they killed her?

"I think we should get started." The dominatrix took the water away from Tracy. As she made the short walk over to the closest nightstand, Tracy looked at her pointed heels digging into the thick pile of the carpet and the glass that was too far away to even be considered a potential weapon.

The dominatrix adjusted her mask and plucked a TV remote from the nightstand. Pointing it at the flat-screen, she thumbed at the buttons until the TV burst to life with a flash of bright light and babbling voices, which made Tracy jump and strain against the biting ropes once more.

"Oops, I'm *so* sorry." The dominatrix lowered the volume and the voices quietened—evidently the volume level was set for the impaired hearing of the bedroom's recently deceased owners.

Tracy recognized herself immediately. Up there, in 4K HD on the sixty-inch TV in the dead people's bedroom, was a semi-nude Tracy. Beside her, Cole Gianni smiled as if he was experiencing true love for the very first time. It was their fourth and final night together, and they'd been treated to a full spa evening with all the treatments they could have imagined. Tracy and Cole had the exclusive spa completely to themselves—except for the camera crew, sound guy, director, producer, and various minions, of course—and had indulged in sensual couples' massages at the hands of attractive masseuses, a mud bath, sauna, and a bubbling, hot spring Jacuzzi. Since it had been the penultimate night of her week on the show, Tracy had been required to at least keep on her black bikini bottom, although the wardrobe girl had ensured her it would be miniscule to the point of being obscene.

"You looked so beautiful," the dominatrix in the mask told Tracy. "It was such a shame you didn't make it to the fifth night—you'd have been an absolute star making love to Cole."

Tracy forced herself to look at the dominatrix's face, into her eyes. She was a *Gentleman's Choice* fan, albeit a sick, twisted one, which gave her and Tracy a little common ground; perhaps she could use it to connect with her and escape with her life?

"The show people made me play hard to get," Tracy explained, her voice wavering. "You can see how much I loved Cole—we were meant for each other." She nodded toward the screen. There, Cole nuzzled her neck and caressed her bare nipples just below the Jacuzzi's frothing waterline. "Cole is a desirable gentleman." The dominatrix placed the remote back onto the nightstand; it clinked against the water glass. "It's a wonder you managed to keep your hands off him and his off you. I would have enjoyed watching the two of you consummate your love."

"The producer made sure we kept it to heavy petting." Determined to keep the conversation going, Tracy did her best to ignore the gimp as he once again filmed her face from mere inches away; he had one eye glued to the camera's eyepiece and the other squeezed tight shut. "They even had the masseuses give me and Cole a hand job to keep us from screwing each other—although that didn't make it onto the show."

"Of course it didn't." The dominatrix appeared angry by Tracy's revelation. "If the audience had been able to get off watching you and Mr. Gianni getting hand relief, they would have switched off as soon as they'd finished. And that wouldn't make for good advertising revenue, would it? That's all the show is about—making money and squeezing every last dime out of their desperate audience. It makes me fucking *sick*." Tracy's skin crawled at the dominatrix's expletive and sudden rise in temper; that she was angered by an internet show made her seem all the more psychotic. It made Tracy's predicament all too *real* as she stood there by the side of the mattress, peering down through her mask, eyes tracing every inch of her captive's bare skin—every curve, mound, and crease. "You know a lot about the show." Tracy strained to keep things going, to find that connection that could save her.

"It's very popular in our… *circles*." The dark red gash of the dominatrix's mouth split into a wide, toothy grin, and as if she'd orchestrated it, the lingering shot of Tracy and Cole in the spa's hot tub switched to rough, shaky footage of dozens of naked and scantily clad bodies dancing in a club.

Tracy had never attended a swingers' club before, except for the third night on the show with Cole, and that had been so faked it really didn't count. It had been meticulously staged in a closed set and populated with hot, sexy young couples—all of whom had been paid to play with one another and not the host and his date. In direct contrast to that, up on the screen, the nude revelers were all considerably older. Many were white haired with matching pubes and so disgustingly wrinkled they really ought to have been forced to put some clothes on.

"Say hi to Joyce and Derek." The masked dominatrix's voice was unmistakable, even booming out of the huge TV. "Say hi, guys!" The camera zoomed in on the faces of the old couple, which Tracy had just seen hanging over the rim of the clawfoot bathtub.

"Don't let management catch you filming in here," the old woman said with a naughty, conspiratorial giggle.

"It's not that *we* mind," her husband chipped in, grinning, "but some of this lot don't take kindly to being on camera. Me—I *love* to perform!" The shot zoomed back to take in Joyce and Derek in their entire naked glory. Derek was visibly aroused, and his thin dick bobbed about like some scrawny farmyard chicken pecking around for seed.

"Perhaps we should take *our* party someplace else?" The dominatrix's voice oozed suggestion.

"We have a new sex swing Derek installed for our anniversary." Joyce beamed into the camera. "You can help us christen it if you want."

"*Hey*!" A voice out of the shot rang out, and everyone in the swingers' club turned around to confront Joyce, Derek, and their new friends. "You can't film in—"

The screen flicked back to *The Gentleman's Choice*. Tracy was in the middle of a hot, heavy French kiss with Cole, and there was the distinctive rhythmic movement of hands beneath the water. Tracy knew nothing had really been going on, as the creepy producer had strictly forbidden anything too provocative for fear of her and Cole throwing show rules to the wind and mounting one another right then and there in the Jacuzzi.

Tracy remembered the sexual tension between her and Cole fondly and well, and along with it, the deepest regret that she hadn't made it to the final night to consummate the love she just *knew* had grown between them. "Well, it's time to begin *our* show." The dominatrix addressed Tracy. "Are you ready for your big moment, Tracy?"

Tracy shook her head. "Please… no…"

Kneeling down, the dominatrix slipped something out from beneath the mattress, and Tracy heard a faint metallic clank as she laid out a pair of rusted pruning shears and a handsaw on the carpet bedside her.

Terror crawled through Tracy like some insidious disease; her bare skin prickled with goose bumps and the sour stink of fear sweat permeated from her every pore. Unable to contain herself, she let out an ear-piercing scream, a primal, wordless sound that resounded about the bedroom and hurt even her own ears. Tugging at the cruel, biting ropes that held her fast, Tracy bucked and twisted her body in a desperate, fruitless attempt to be free from her nightmare.

In a calm, soothing tone, the dominatrix said to her cameraman, "If you can focus on her pretty feet, I think we'll start there this time."

"*Pleeeese!*" Tracy screamed as the dominatrix in the mask took a firm hold of her left foot and placed the pinkie toe between the age-bitten, ragged jaws of the pruning shears.

Tracy had never before experienced pain like the white-hot agony that shot up from her foot as the shear's rust-dulled blades bit through the flesh and bone of her toe. She screamed out again, and as the dominatrix relinquished her ankle, Tracy kicked out with her wounded foot. She hoped to pull free or connect with her torturer and kick her away, but all she did was spray the woman's naked breasts with blood.

She prayed for rescue or the swift release of death—anything besides the prolonged agony of torture at the hands of the sadistic dominatrix—but had no choice other than to endure the suffering of having each one of her toes snipped away.

Tracy's adrenaline had kicked in shortly after her second toe had been removed under the unblinking scrutiny of the gimp's camera. The pain in each of the severed stumps had dulled to a sickening throb, but the stomach-churning sensation of having her foot coated in the warm stickiness of her own blood made her heave.

"Time to change things up a little." The dominatrix gave Tracy a warped smile. "I don't think these old shears will make it through this, let alone your other joints." For emphasis, she wriggled Tracy's big toe—the only digit remaining on the left foot. Her heavy, untethered breasts wobbled as Tracy squirmed and wept.

"Oh, fuck no… please, no… let me go…" Tracy sobbed through her tears and the thick, bile-laced phlegm that choked the back of her throat. "I'll do anything you want—"

"You're already doing everything *I* want," the dominatrix replied with a glance at the gimp, who had his camera trained steady upon Tracy's mutilated foot. "What more could you possibly do to please us?"

Fighting against the agony clouding her brain, Tracy tried to plead with the dominatrix, to appeal to whatever shred of humanity the dominatrix might still have, but the words spilled from her lips as incoherent babble.

Oblivious, the dominatrix picked up the handsaw from the blood-soaked carpet. Tracy knew no one was about to burst through the door and save her, and there was no way her tormentors were ever going to let her live; she was going to die right there on that mattress.

As it transpired, Tracy barely felt the promised removal of her big toe; the dominatrix's rapid, rhythmic sawing created a bizarre tugging, pulling sensation that jarred Tracy's bones all the way to the knee. When Tracy saw her pink-painted toe tumble free onto the bloodied mattress, consciousness left her.

***

Tracy awoke to the dull, thrumming sensation in her foot, and it took her a moment or two to remember where she was and why she was tied to a smelly, blood-stained mattress in a strange room.

"You were on the show too?" A voice drifted through her mind, and for a second, Tracy thought she'd imagined it, as it sounded nothing like that of the dominatrix; this was soft, hesitant, scared. "*The Gentleman's Choice*—I was a contestant a few months ago."

It took a great deal of effort for Tracy to turn her head to face her new companion. She'd strained so hard when the dominatrix had severed her toes that the tendons in her neck were agonizingly sore. Nonetheless, Tracy took the time to scan the room; the dominatrix and the gimp were nowhere to be seen, and the TV was still playing her episodes of *The Gentleman's Choice*.

"Don't worry, they're not here." Tracy saw the voice belonged to a girl perhaps a few years younger than her own twenty-four. She was naked, handcuffed to the corner post of the bed, and her pale, skinny body was covered with bite marks—the tooth imprints distinctly human. Her head had been shaven smooth—the job done roughly and without much care—and her bare scalp was dotted with streaks of dried blood from a multitude of cuts. She stared blankly up at the TV as if mesmerized by Tracy and Cole. "I think they're having something to eat."

A pained laugh escaped Tracy's throat. It seemed an absurd notion that her tormentors would be taking a break to have a snack before resuming her torture. "How long have you been here?"

The girl took her attention away from the TV. "They brought me in straight after you passed out, I guess—I heard you screaming from the pantry."

"They had you locked in the pantry?"

The girl nodded. "For the three days since they caught me."

Tracy thought that an odd choice of words—as if the girl had been hunted down like some wild animal and not snatched from her couch. "Do you know who they are, or what they want?"

"I think I still love Cole." The girl returned her attention to the TV, where Tracy and Cole were sharing a passionate fireside kiss. "I only made it to the second night, though, so I never got to tell him."

"I'm sorry you missed out." It was a struggle to speak—her throat was dry and tasted of blood where she'd torn it screaming—but Tracy was determined. "I made it to—"

"Night Four," the girl interrupted. "I watched the shows while you were sleeping."

A chill ran along Tracy's spine; just how long had she been out? "They said I was too aloof," the girl continued. "I was voted off because I played a bit too hard to get." She let out a quiet, breathy laugh. "Me too," Tracy told her. "I guess the viewers prefer the easy girls?"

"I wouldn't have minded too much, but I *am* easy," the girl said with a cynical smile. "It was the show people who told me to make Cole work for my affections."

That resonated with Tracy, and her sympathy went out to her new companion. "It was just a dumb show," she said.

"Do you think that's why we're here?" The girl turned to Tracy once more; she saw the pain and desperation in her eyes, a *need* to connect to another human being.

"The show?"

"We're both contestants… *ex*-contestants."

Tracy thought it was a theory just bizarre enough to be true but couldn't bring herself to believe it. "That would be *too* crazy," she said. "What did they do to you?" As the girl glanced down toward Tracy's feet, she realized they were covered with a mound of pillows taken from the bed. Blood had soaked through a couple of them and dried to a dark maroon color.

It took some effort, but through the pain, Tracy managed to kick away the pillows.

Gagging, the girl coughed up thick yellow bile that poured down her front. "*Oh my God*!" she screamed. "Your fucking *toes*!" Hysterical, she yanked at the chains that held her to the bedpost, ignoring the steel cuffs that bit cruelly into her wrists.

"Christobel!" The dominatrix stormed into the bedroom, her ever-present gimp following on with his camera; there was menace in her tone. "That is no way to behave, young lady!"

"Leave her alone!" Tracy yelled as the dominatrix grasped the girl's arms to hold her still.

"Do you know what happens to girls who are difficult?" The dominatrix relinquished her grip as the girl went quiet. She made her way over to Tracy and picked up the handsaw. "Well, you're about to find out—isn't she, Tracy?"

"*No!*" Tracy cried and kicked out as best she could as the dominatrix knelt down beside her, took a firm hold of her shin, and began sawing through her ankle.

Christobel yowled along with Tracy as she watched the saw's blade bite through gristle and bone, and blood poured out from the wound; through her agony, Tracy knew the poor girl was witnessing her own fate and could imagine nothing more terrifying.

The dominatrix carefully placed Tracy's foot on the floor next to the mattress and set to work on her knee. All the while, she kept hold of the shin to prevent Tracy kicking her with the leg she'd just freed. The pain was nothing like Tracy had ever imagined; it set every nerve alight and filled her entire body. Through it, she was aware of the relentless stream of blood pumping from her wounds; it made her head feel stupidly light, her mind disconnected, and Christobel's panicked screams sounded as if they were a thousand miles away.

The dominatrix in the feathered mask switched legs after removing the lower half of Tracy's left leg, and by the time she set to removing the right leg at the knee, Tracy felt she was dying; she knew her tormentors would be disappointed she'd not lasted longer.

Chapter Four

"That really was some badass shit you did with the horse yesterday," Skippy was saying between overlarge bites of breakfast bagel as he and Cole made their way into the cramped office. "And totally unscripted, too."

"How could we have scripted in a snake, Skippy?" Cole grumbled; it grated on his nerves when Skippy tried too hard to speak American—what was wrong with using that dumbass Michael Caine accent of his?

"If I'd known the effect that sort of thing had on the chicks, I'd have definitely written one in—even if we had to use a plastic prop snake. I've never seen a contestant get so hot and horny after a horse ride." He took another obscenely large bite, skillfully avoiding a cream cheese disaster down the front of his pristine white button-down shirt. Skippy then maneuvered his bulk into the office and sat himself down in the extra-wide wheeled chair behind the desk.

Cole contemplated his partner as he struggled to sit down; it had shocked him to see how much Skippy had let himself go over the years. When they'd met, Skippy had been the stocky guy with a wicked Cockney accent all the Americans simply *adored*. But as the show took off shortly after season two and money started rolling in, Skippy had seemed determined to eat himself to death.

"I thought you were going to go easy on those?" Cole nodded at what remained of the bagel. "What happened to fruit for breakfast?"

Skippy pulled a face. "I told you before, it's all monkey food," he said through his mouthful of bagel and cheese. "And those shakes you recommended tasted like piss."

"I care too much about you to sit back and watch you kill yourself like this." Skippy was the only person he could let his guard down with, the one true friend who knew him for who he really was, and Cole was determined not to lose him.

"It's just one bloody bagel, mate." Skippy laughed at him. "You can keep the schmaltzy, Care Bear stuff to yourself. You have an image to keep up, remember? Our subscribers pay to see Cole the sex god, not some mushy bleeding heart."

It crossed Cole's mind to point out he was not in front of the cameras but decided against stating the obvious. Skippy's clumsy attempt at rudeness was nothing more than deflection. He knew Cole cared enough to say something, but in true British fashion, he didn't know how to deal with affection awfully well.

He decided he'd let the subject drop and tackle his friend when his mood was lighter.

The tiny office was utilitarian at best. It contained a cheap, laminated desk, two chairs, and a water cooler that had never been refilled in all the years they'd leased the place. The room itself was situated behind the studio space they rented for some of the show's indoor scenes. Skippy had struck a good deal with the studio owners back in the show's early days: through the production company they'd formed at the inception of *The Gentleman's Choice*, they paid a low monthly retainer for the bedroom set they had permanently dressed to resemble an eligible bachelor's boudoir. If they ever required more space—such as, for example, the swingers club the set dressers were busy making ready for the Fourth Night scenes to be shot later that evening—they'd top up their payments to cover its use. As it was, Cole was tired and in no mood for any of Skippy's bullshit.

As soon as the cameras quit rolling the night before, he'd left his date to sleep at the sumptuous log cabin all by herself and driven all the way down to Houston from Fairfield Lake.

Maybe Mai Ling had given the old cowboy a call to scratch the itch Cole had left her with after he'd gone— who knew what the contestants got up to after shooting wrapped for the night? Either way, it wasn't really Cole's business as long as she wasn't dumb enough to do the guy bareback and bring some unpleasant STD to the show.

Although, Cole *did* see it as his business. He'd grown to like Mai Ling, *really* like her, and he longed for the chance to show he did give a damn about what she got up to when they were apart as he would in a real relationship. And therein lay the crux of Cole's problem. In all the years he'd been making the *The Gentleman's Choice*, he'd never had a single relationship outside of it, and that was something he craved more with each passing week. And that in turn drove his desire to get himself away from the show and finally be himself.

After they'd showered off the dust and horse stink from their ride, Cole and Mai Ling had spent a couple hours in a steamy but entirely sexless fireside clinch, which had left him with the worst case of blue balls he'd experienced since his teen years. The Asian chick had definitely been eager to go all the way with Cole, as most contestants were by the third night. But the show's protocol dictated they stop short of "full sexual intercourse," as Skippy had it worded in the contract he'd had the lawyers draw up.

And who said romance was dead?

"Mai Ling is proving to be an awesome contestant." Cole figured he'd best shift the conversation; awkward silences watching his business partner eat were not high on his fun list. He sat himself down on the only other chair in the office; it was an unwritten rule between he and Skippy that the producer got to sit in the position of power behind the desk with Cole opposite him even though he was the star of the show. "The audience absolutely loves her—I've seen the figures."

"Who the fuck *doesn't* love a hot Asian chick?" Skippy sprayed bagel crumbs across his desk as he spoke. "Especially one who isn't shy at shedding her clothes on camera."

It was another one of Skippy's quaint Britishisims— the fact the producer of one of the highest-ranked internet smut shows in the US was too embarrassed to say "get naked" never failed to amuse Cole.

"I'm really hoping she makes it through to Night Five—I reckon she'll put on a fucking *lively* performance." Skippy pushed the remainder of the bagel into his mouth and chewed noisily at it.

"I figured you might be looking forward to that," Cole said with a sigh. They'd worked together for over six years on *The Gentleman's Choice*, and there were no secrets between them—after all, the producer did get to see his protégé seduce a different woman on screen every week— although Skippy's lascivious attitude toward the show's women did get wearing at times.

As for Cole, despite how the show portrayed him, he had nothing but respect for all of the contestants. He saw it as his job to make sure they not only had a wonderful time on their dates, but they exited the show with their dignity intact. The fact he had admired women of every shape, size, age, and color since his early days in Cochabamba had helped Cole embrace the variety of contestants Skippy put before him—and diversity was certainly the producer's favorite word.

"The votes are pretty much fifty-fifty right now, but I reckon tonight's episode will sway them in Mai Ling's favor." Skippy broke through his friend's reverie.

"Of course," Cole replied. "That's why you decided to make it an orgy night."

"The great unwashed viewing public go bloody crazy for orgies." Skippy brushed the multitude of crumbs from his desk planner onto the floor—it would give their cheap, undocumented Mexican cleaner something to do. "There's just something about a whole load of naked people doing the dirty together that brings out the primal lust in people."

"*You* included, Skippy, my old buddy." There was little humor in Cole's reply; the guy's increasingly inappropriate behavior was something else the two needed to address sometime very soon.

Missing the menacing cue, Skippy nodded with enthusiasm. "Orgy night is always one of my favorites, you know that, Cole. Orgies are always good value for money— there's always so much to *look* at, and I've never been above sloppy seconds... or thirds for that matter. I do enjoy women in heat like that, Cole, because they really don't care who takes 'em once they're turned on—it's your basic trickle-down dynamics."

And take part in, Cole kept the thought to himself. He was well aware of his partner's penchant for insinuating himself into parts of the show that appealed to his transgressions, albeit behind the scenes. The very nature of *The Gentleman's Choice* meant there was an endless stream of nubile young women, all excited for their chance at fame and fortune—the *Desperates*, as Skippy liked to call them. The majority were fully prepared to do *anything* to achieve their objective of getting in front of the camera, including giving it up for the show's producer no matter how obese and unattractive the man turned out to be.

Unfortunately, those were not the wannabes who were cause for Cole's concern; it was the *leftovers*, those contestants ousted from the show after the first couple of nights. For each wannabe contestant who gave in to Skippy's coercion on the promise of a coveted place on the show, there were a dozen or so others who turned down his request for a simple blow job. Skippy's failure rate was embarrassingly high for a man in his position, which only served to fuel the jealousy toward Cole he'd become terrible at hiding. It turned out fellatio was something Skippy barely considered to be sex at all, and he'd often cite Bill Clinton in his argument to justify his actions to Cole, but every single one of those girls was just a lawsuit waiting to happen.

It was a good thing they'd forked out for good entertainment attorneys to draw up the show's contract, complete with a brutally thorough nondisclosure clause, which meant the show practically owned the women's souls. Cole had known of Skippy for a year or so before they'd gotten together with their idea for *The Gentleman's Choice*, and while he didn't really consider him a best friend, the guy was certainly the closest Cole had to one. Skippy had been Mason Webman back then, which he'd always maintained was the perfect surname for their internet streaming joint venture. In times of uncharacteristic sentimentality, he'd even go as far as to say it was a message from God, or some kind of divine providence, and he and Cole had always been *meant* to produce the show.

For Cole, it ran deeper than a mere business arrangement; Skippy was his friend and confidante, the one person he'd been able to rely upon in all his time in the country. Skippy was the only one who knew just how shy and awkward he was when not playing a character and understood it was why Cole was driven to be an actor—he *needed* something more extroverted to hide behind. Skippy had been the one to create the Cole persona their viewers saw every week, and it was no secret between the two that he'd projected a huge amount of his own charismatic personality into the character. There were times Cole felt himself lost within the Skippy-esque role as if he were little more than a puppet Skippy had dancing at the end of his strings.

Something about Skippy's extrovert, lover-of-life-and-ladies Cole was highly addictive and had provided Cole with a confidence that had spilled out into his life away from the show. Although he was sure he'd never be quite so smooth as Skippy could be when he set his mind to it. The guy was so damn manipulative at times, Cole would swear he was using subtle neurolinguistic programming or maybe even hypnosis to get his way.

But whatever it was they had between them, Cole and Skippy had created something proven to be far more lucrative than the beer-and-women money Skippy was interested in back at the beginning or the endless parade of fresh meat to sate his increasingly odd appetites.

"You wanted to talk?" Cole cut to the chase. If he didn't, he knew Skippy would waffle around, procrastinate, and say nothing 'til time ran out on them. They did have a show to prepare for, and it usually spelled disaster if they left the crew to their own devices for too long.

"Yeah." Skippy rubbed at his multitude of wobbling chins, which rasped with two days' worth of stubble. "About the *Hustler* deal…"

Cole exhaled loudly and fought to contain his ire. Skippy was hellbent on filibustering the crap out of the subject until Cole gave up and avoided it altogether—it was how he so often got his own way. "It's too good an offer to not even consider it," he said.

"We went through all of this when *Playboy* offered to put the show on their network, Cole, and look how that turned out." Skippy looked his partner straight in the eye, a sign of defiance.

"Their offer is *still* on the table—it's you who chooses to ignore it, my old friend." Cole emphasized the old *friend* part in an attempt to appeal to Skippy's human nature in the vain hope of getting a sensible business conversation out of him for once.

The approach from the Playboy Channel had come just as *The Gentleman's Choice* had stepped away from its cult following and was gaining good traction across the internet as *the* must-watch "adult entertainment" show; back then, good ol' Heff had still been alive and banging nubile, gold-digging bunnies a quarter his age.

"We'd lose all creative control, you know that," Skippy protested. "Unless we can be guaranteed total control by any network, my stance will remain a firm *no*."

"If we were to come in under *Playboy* or *Hustler*, the show would gain a much wider audience," Cole told him. "And respectability."

That had Skippy laughing. "*Respectability*? It's a bloody *porn* show, Cole. You fuck hot girls on camera for a paying audience—it's as *respectable* as that. We've always only ever been one click away from the live sex cam business."

Cole didn't laugh along. Skippy's crappy attitude toward moving the show and their production company forward had become a bone of contention between them over the past couple years. The early *Playboy* offer had hung over their relationship like some big, smutty dick of Damocles, even though it carried with it the lure of one hell of a fat payday for them both.

Of course, Cole knew Skippy's real reason for stymieing that deal, along with the more recent Hustler offer, was his fear of losing more than just creative control. He knew—they both did—either network would want to bring in their own production team, which would mean the deal was meant as more of a payoff for Skippy. And, although the money would set him up for whatever future grubby little projects he had in mind, it would be scant compensation for the access to an endless parade of willing young women *The Gentleman's Choice* had always offered him and an end to his living vicariously through the Cole character he'd created and so meticulously shaped. The Cole the show's subscribers saw was very much an extension of Skippy and was the producer's fantasy as much as their viewership's.

Cole was confident he'd be okay, for a good while at least, as he was the face of the show. Neither network would dare remove him from the show at least for as long as his good looks held out.

"You know how much we'd get watered down on a network," Skippy continued with his well-worn argument. "While ever we remain internet-only, we can broadcast whatever we want, uncensored. Water down what we're doing, and the show dies on its fucking arse."

"We're talking adult channels here, Skippy, not fucking ABC," Cole countered. "You've seen what they get away with on *Swingers* nowadays. They show group sex, kinky games, oral, *and* penetration—times have moved on in the past three years. A show like ours would be a huge hit on a cable TV channel."

"I'm sure it would be, Cole." Skippy leaned forward in his seat, which creaked and groaned at the very effort of containing him. "I can see *The Gentleman's Choice* being the number-one viewed show in cheap hotels up and down the country. But, without me—*us*—in the driving seat, it'll be nothing more than a pale imitation."

"I'm sure we can negotiate creative control with these people—we *own* the copyright to the format, remember?" Cole gave Skippy what was meant to be a reassuring smile.

"That's still not stopped other people copying us." Skippy scowled; Cole had hit upon yet another bone of contention with the man. "There are lightweight versions of our show all over Pornhub and Xhamster—you've seen them."

"That's all they are," Cole replied. "Crappy, cheap copies, no better than the shitty movie parodies the porn studios insist on churning out because they think they're being clever and creative. If anything, the bad plagiarism drives viewers our way. You saw how our subscriptions increased when *A Gent's Selection* came out."

Nodding, Skippy had no option but to concede that one. "You're getting away from my point here," he growled.

"Look, Mason." Cole always used the producer's given name when things got serious between them. Skippy had played the dominant partner over their years together, and Cole found it increasingly difficult to make himself heard, but call the guy *Mason* and Cole knew he had his undivided attention. "We both know your real reason for ignoring all the money on the table—and it's nothing to do with creative control. With the money you'll make selling to *Hustler*, don't you think you'll have pussy coming out of your fucking ears?"

"Not everything is about pussy." Skippy's voice rose an octave; Cole had *definitely* touched the raw nerve.

"Then what *is* it about, Skippy? Why do you insist on standing in the way of making something really big out of our show?"

The fat man leaned back in his creaking chair and steepled his fingers beneath his nose. "All those years I spent on the *Amish Orgy* series back in England, I could only dream of having something anywhere near as successful as what we have built together, Cole." There was a wistful lilt to his voice that Cole knew was purely intended to manipulate. "*The Gentleman's Choice* is something truly special—can't you *feel* that in your heart?"

Truth be told, Cole had little patience for Skippy when he waxed lyrical about the grubby little porn show they'd just happened to make into an internet success. Even in its sixth year, it hadn't provided them with the millionaire jetset lifestyle they'd promised themselves; by the time they'd taken out studio rent, production costs and living expenses, there was nowhere near enough left over from viewer subscriptions for buying Ferraris and helicopters. And, while selling out to one of the adult networks wouldn't quite bring about that level of riches, it would certainly make one hell of a difference to Cole's life; perhaps he would be able to take a shot at Hollywood again?

"I just want you to give it some serious thought," Cole said with a glance at his fake Cartier wristwatch; time was beating him once more. "There's nothing for me to think about, Cole, you know that." Skippy dismissed him. "We sell out and the show goes down the fucking toilet and along with it, six years of bloody hard work. I can't believe you're prepared to throw that all away."

Standing up from his seat, Cole narrowed his eyes at the producer. "This won't... *can't* go on forever, Mason—

even you have to know that. I want to be more than just a body and a dick. I want to be respectable, do something important with my life."

"Like conquer Hollywood again?" Skippy goaded.

"And why shouldn't I? I've done it before, and I can sure as hell do it again, Skip."

"After what happened to you? You're deluding yourself, mate."

Cole took in a deep breath; there was no arguing with Skippy when he was in the right mood to go straight for the jugular like that. Besides, there was always the chance he might just be right. "We've done well to last as long as we have, Skippy. Our luck is going to run out sooner or later."

"I believe we all make our own luck, Cole. You know me well enough by now," Skippy said as Cole made his way out of the office.

Ignoring Skippy's aggravating platitudes, Cole left and closed the door behind him. The guy really was going to have to see past his own creepy libido someday soon, and hopefully before the show ceased to be such a hot property. The adult entertainment industry was even more fickle than its mainstream counterpart—this week's darling could so very easily become next week's has-been.

And Cole Gianni was under no illusion he was the has-been in that particular scenario.

Chapter Five

"If I could just speak with your husband for five minutes, Mrs. Hickersley." Charlotte Michaels struggled to make herself heard above the Hickersleys' dog, a huge, gray pit bull that growled and snapped as it tried to force its broad snout through the narrow gap in the door.

"We're sick of you people harassing us for your sick stories," Barbara Hickersley said, her voice level restrained.

"I promise you I'm not a reporter, Mrs. Hickersley." Charlotte pulled out her ID badge and held it up for the woman to read. The dog jumped and snapped, and Charlotte felt flecks of its spittle on the back of her hand. "We don't want to talk to any money-grabbing private investigators either, so please just go away and leave us alone."

Charlotte couldn't begin to imagine what the poor woman was going through; to lose a child was tragic enough, but to lose a daughter in such a brutal, public way must have been unbearable. Even so, Charlotte was at the Hickersleys' impressive home to help—as well as line her own pockets, of course.

As Barbara began to ease the door shut, unable to slam it in Charlotte's face because of the dog, Tom Hickersley appeared in the expansive vestibule behind her—his ruggedly handsome face looked drawn, darkened by days' worth of stubble.

The PI had one last chance.

"Please… just a few minutes of your time, Mr. Hickersley. Just listen to what I have to say about Tracy's murder and then I'll go."

Tears welled in Barbara's tired eyes. "If you don't leave us alone, Miss Michaels, we'll call the police."

"No, you won't," Charlotte replied with conviction. "Mr. Hickersley has made it quite clear what he thinks of the police and how badly they're handling Tracy's murder." Charlotte took no pleasure in seeing how Barbara flinched at the word; she had no desire to inflict further suffering on Tracy's poor parents but had to get through to them somehow. "There are similarities between what happened to Tracy and what happened to a friend of mine a couple years ago." Charlotte pulled a crumpled photograph from the back pocket of her jeans and held it up to the door. "The police aren't even looking in the right direction."

"Bed." The suddenness of Tom Hickersley's voice made his wife jump a little. In an instant, the dog fell silent and calmly padded away from the door.

"Mr. Hickersley—"

"Five minutes." Tom pulled open the door and gently ushered Barbara away. He stepped aside, one arm outstretched toward Charlotte by means of an invitation.

Nervously, Charlotte made a quick scan for the dog and was relieved to see it sat in its bed and was eyeing her with nothing more than curiosity. "Thank you," Charlotte said as she stepped inside and Tom closed the door behind her.

"You're not the first investigator who's tried to take advantage of our… *situation*, Miss Michaels." Tom led Charlotte into a small library room just off the entrance hall; Barbara followed on, scrutinizing their visitor with suspicion. Charlotte sat herself down in one of the high-backed armchairs; it was red velvet, antique, and not at all comfortable.

"Five minutes, Miss Michaels." Tom took the chair opposite, his wife standing behind him.

"Please, call me Charlie." Charlotte smiled; she had the man's attention—even in such terrible circumstances, being an eye-catching, statuesque brunette had its advantages.

"No, I'm not going to do that." Tom fixed her with cold, unfeeling eyes.

"This is a very difficult time for us." Barbara spoke before Charlotte had the chance. "Knowing what that wicked man did to my poor baby's body after he killed her will be stuck in our minds forever. Why must they announce such terrible things to the entire world? Our only comfort is that Tracy didn't suffer."

Charlotte checked herself; now was not the time to contradict Mrs. Hickersley. She'd seen the coroner's report, along with the photographs of Tracy's body, and there had been no doubt the girl had been tortured to death. But, if Tracy's mother found even a grain of comfort in believing the horrific wounds on her daughter's body had been inflicted postmortem, then Charlotte wasn't about to burst her bubble. People like Tracy's murderer liked their victims alive for as long as possible, and loved to take their time; they also tended to escalate and wouldn't stop killing until they got sloppy and caught, or the cops got lucky and stopped them.

Charlotte's eyes met Tom's, and she read the pain in his face. He knew.

"Who is the woman in the picture?" Tom broke the awkward silence. "Her name is… *was* Omawumi." Fiddling with the photograph, Charlotte straightened it out on her knee and studied the beautiful, smiling ebony face there. "She was a friend of mine—came to America with her mom and sisters to escape the oppression in Nigeria and wound up…"

"Dead?" Barbara whispered the word as if it physically hurt her to say it.

Nodding, Charlotte put the photograph away and looked forlorn. Of course, she'd stretched the truth, insomuch that Omawumi had never been a friend; in fact, Charlotte only knew the girl through the police and coroner's reports—she was nothing more to her than a cold case Charlotte had forgotten about until she'd seen the online reporting of Tracy Hickersley's brutal killing.

"There are similarities between what happened to Omawumi and Tracy," Charlotte offered.

"Similarities?" Tom scratched at the salt-and-pepper stubble on his chin.

"I've studied both reports and there are too many to ignore," Charlotte replied. "I can detail them if that would help—"

"That won't be necessary, Miss Michaels." Tom cut her off; he looked up at Barbara, who seemed ready to burst into tears.

"I understand Tracy was estranged from you." Confident she'd established a connection, Charlotte cut to the chase.

"There was a falling out, yes," Tom said.

Charlotte read something in his expression that told her the man was hiding something. Sure, all families had their secrets, but she reckoned there was more to the falling out with Tracy than her appearing on *The Gentleman's Choice*.

"She *insisted* on going on that awful internet show," Barbara added. "We begged her not to, but you know how stubborn young people are these days."

Charlotte gave the woman a sage nod and wondered just how old Barbara thought she was; at twenty-nine, Charlotte still considered herself among the *young people*.

"I'm sure we'd have reconciled, though." Tom looked wistful. "Once Tracy came to her senses and apologized for bringing such shame onto our family."

"Omawumi was on *The Gentleman's Choice*, too." Charlotte's words hung in the air. "She was a contestant a few years ago—she applied in the hopes of using the prize money to help her family. I did everything I could to find who killed her, even after her mother's money ran out. The case just went cold after a year or so."

"So, you failed?" Barbara said. "What makes you think things will be different now?"

"Because he's killed again and with practically the same MO as with Omawumi—right down to the specific injuries inflicted on the body; the details of many of them were never released to the media. I'm trained to see patterns and follow them, Mrs. Hickersley, and I'm seeing far too many parallels for Tracy to be a coincidence or a copycat."

"You are confident the same person killed my daughter?" Tom asked. "I'd call it a confident hunch… a definite possibility I'd like to look into," Charlotte told him. The cops had failed to make the connection most likely because the murders took place in different states, and Charlotte was not about to make it for them. Not when there was money to be made. "And I suppose you want us to pay you to follow your hunch?" Tom was right on the nose.

"I knew it!" Barbara snapped. "Get out of my house!" Angry, she pointed at the door.

Tom got to his feet. "Let's at least hear her out, darling—if she thinks she can find whoever took our little girl, then we'd be crazy to turn her away. I want justice for Tracy as much as you do." Charlotte remained sitting and looked on as Tom pacified his distraught wife; it tugged at her heartstrings to see such misery in ostensibly good people—it was a part of the job Charlotte knew she'd never quite get hardened to.

Tom urged Barbara to sit down in the chair he'd just vacated. "Okay," he addressed Charlotte. "I'll pay you whatever you need."

"Tom!" Barbara shot him a cutting glance.

"I know what I'm doing, my darling," Tom reassured his wife. "Leave this to the police, and they'll get nowhere—we should give Miss Michaels a chance to do what needs to be done."

Barbara said nothing, but the look in her eyes told Charlotte her welcome had worn out.

"Thank you, Mr. Hickersley," Charlotte said as she got to her feet and made for the door. "I can have my invoice to you later this morning." Tom escorted Charlotte to the front door, hands thrust deep into his pockets. "If you do find the bastard who did… *that* to my daughter, I'll fucking double it."

Charlotte left the Hickersleys to their wrecked lives and distress; she figured it really ought to bother her that she hustled people for money when they were at their most vulnerable—but it didn't. Instead, she was already planning her next move; now she had the money behind her, she would take the necessary steps to flush out Tracy's killer, even if it meant putting herself in the firing line.

She had a couple fake identities on standby—in Charlotte's line of work, it always paid to be able to be someone else in an instant—and one in particular that would fit the bill perfectly. Even though it meant dying her naturally light brunette hair and wearing colored contacts, Charlotte Michaels was going to transform herself into the entirely fabricated Vanessa Young.

Chapter Six

One hour to showtime and the club set was nowhere near ready, although the set dressers had done an amazing job of transforming the studio into an uncanny semblance of the orgy room at Houston's most exclusive swingers' club.

Cole walked alongside Skippy through the expansive room, which was bedecked with fat, overstuffed maroon leather couches and matching beanbags, plush, red satin curtains, and fake stone pillars. There was a twelve-person hot tub in one corner of the studio and a vast bed at its center; they'd pushed four California kings together and dressed it with luxurious, white Egyptian cotton, 1800 thread-count sheets, which they'd had especially made for the show. On Skippy's insistence, it was always nothing but the very best for *The Gentleman's Choice*—no matter how much of a dent it put in the budget.

"Where the fuck are the velvet cushions?" Skippy barked at the nearest set dresser, a tall, skinny trans guy who insisted everyone address him as the androgynous "Kit" or "they." Skippy had no time for such bullshit. "I asked you a fucking question."

The guy winced at the sound of Skippy's voice; Cole saw it was more than a little put on. "I'll look into it," Kit replied with a shrug and a scowl as he played on his supposed offense. "They're probably still in storage."

Cole looked on with growing amusement as Skippy's cheeks reddened and his jowls wobbled with rage. "They're no bloody good in fucking *storage*, are they?" he ranted. "Listen to me, you arsehole; you've got two minutes to get those fucking cushions on set, or you can just piss off!" Skippy's native cockney accent always strengthened in direct proportion to his fury, which never failed to entertain his partner. "You need to calm yourself down there, buddy," Cole soothed as they both watched Kit scurry away like Skippy had kicked him in the ass. "You're going to blow a gasket if you don't keep your blood pressure down."

"My blood pressure is perfectly *fine*," Skippy growled as the color left his cheeks as quickly as it had appeared. "It's dickheads like him who are the fucking problem."

"Seriously?" Cole scowled at the producer; the guy really had to get with the PC program.

As Skippy chuckled along at his own joke, his anger dissipated, and along with it, some of the tension between the two. "And if you're going to start lecturing me on how selling out the show will alleviate my stress levels, don't waste your fucking time, Cole. I have many other ways of dealing with my stress, and they're all more pleasurable than counting to ten and meditating, thank you very much."

His eyes twitched across to one of his assistants, a sweet young thing in a thigh-skimming miniskirt displaying endless, shapely bare legs; Cole reckoned the girl couldn't have been much older than nineteen. If she was plying the producer with sexual favors, it was only to further her career. But, while Skippy's penchant for the younger girls and his frustration at the near-constant rejection by the show's contestants worried Cole, he was happy to detect some humor to his partner's tone; perhaps the guy's hard-no stance at selling out was starting to crumble a little around the edges?

Cole allowed the brief silence to do the talking for him. He was doing his damndest to shift the dynamic between them and get Skippy to see reason, and to make the producer regard him as less of the pretty boy star of the show and more of the business partner he actually was. Sometimes, Skippy couldn't see through the persona he'd created for Cole.

Skippy had been the dominant one from the get-go, even though the show concept had actually been Cole's. Because he'd brought to the table a wealth of producing, directing, and distributing experience from his days of peddling British porn, Skippy had automatically taken control while Cole had looked on in awe and focused on wooing the show's contestants. Six years on, and Cole felt it was about time something had to give. "Can we check the lighting?" Skippy yelled over Cole's head at the pretty young assistant. She visibly jumped at the command and gave Skippy a forced smile as she thumbed the button on the side of her black walkie-talkie and mumbled into it.

On the chick's command, the lights in the studio dimmed. The room's ambience had been carefully planned to provide dimmed, discreet lighting—but not too discreet to prevent the show's viewers from witnessing the action as it unfolded. Foils had been added to the studio lighting dotted around the room's periphery—which would be entirely invisible during the broadcast, of course—to cast sensual red and purple hues about the place. Cole considered the whole thing to be terribly cliché, but also, he understood the viewing audience liked their smut served with a huge dollop of cliché. For the show's paying patrons, the familiar—even the *over* familiar—evoked just the right mood for their full enjoyment of the proceedings. The demographic analysis Skippy paid large amounts of money for showed the majority of *The Gentleman's Choice* audience—eighty percent of whom were women—watched the show while masturbating alone or with a partner, cuddled up in bed as a precursor to sex, or actually fucking, and they expected the perfect mood to be set for them.

No shit, Sherlock.

"Looking good, Skip," Cole said.

"It'll do, I suppose." Skippy was rarely happy with the sets and locations prior to filming but would always gush as to how awesome things had been after the fact. It was as if he didn't dare praise their staff ahead of time in case it invoked bad luck or something.

"I'd best go get myself ready." Cole checked his watch; the limousine would be along to pick him up any minute, and he hadn't even showered yet.

"I thought you *were* ready." Skippy scanned Cole up and down; as usual, he looked perfectly handsome and immaculately dressed in his tight-fit 501s and crisp, pale cerulean button-down.

"I'm wearing the tux tonight, remember?"

Skippy's eyes searched the ceiling. "Ah yes, we're wheeling out the James Bond thing again."

"I'm still not entirely sure how it fits in with… *this*." Cole swept an arm out to take in the giant bed and its alluring surroundings, all ready for sex. "But I'm sure our audience will get the general idea."

Skippy sighed. "Even if they don't get it, they'll be more than happy when the action starts—who the fuck doesn't love a good orgy?"

"Who, indeed?"

"That reminds me, where in God's name are our… *people*?" Skippy made an exaggerated point of looking around the set with a hand over his eyes like some sea captain of old.

The people in question were the orgy-goers who would populate the scene to provide an authentic background to Cole and Mai Ling's date. Some were genuine, exhibitionist swingers who had been recruited from one of the more upmarket swinging websites—they were always up for some free group sex. At Skippy's insistence, ornate masquerade ball masks were to be worn, which would guarantee anonymity for all, and hooked in even the shyest among the swingers. They had also brought in paid actors and actresses—Skippy's euphemism for prostitutes—who would do precisely as directed. All of the participants— paid and otherwise—were chosen for how they looked naked, although Skippy had been careful to not have them all *too* perfect. Experience had taught that, for an orgy scene to appear authentic and ultra-realistic, it was necessary to have at least a few imperfections on show— on the girls, smaller, uneven breasts, tattoos, even slight tummies and cute C-section scars were admissible; as for the men, they certainly didn't all have to be six-one and built like The Rock, and Skippy was happy to entertain a whole range of types.

Skippy really did have the whole deception off to a fine art—the deluded audience at home wouldn't know the difference between the studio setup and a real-life swinging orgy.

They'd approached the biggest, most exclusive swinger's clubs in Houston and Dallas—nothing could ever be as authentic as the real thing, after all. Back in the show's early days, Skippy had been convinced the clubs—held at some of the largest, grandest mansions Texas had to offer—would have bitten his hand off to be featured in a fast-growing internet show like *The Gentleman's Choice*. But they had been turned down flat—the house owners didn't want *that* kind of publicity, apparently. And, since filming was strictly banned as part of every swinger's club etiquette, Skippy and Cole had little choice but to re-create the houses in the studio and emulate the best of the best without getting sued for outright plagiarism. On the plus side, it allowed the show optimal camera and lighting placement, plus the opportunity to maintain total control over every single participant. Cole saw that very much as a win-win, even though he knew it still rankled Skippy to have been turned down by *a bloody perv' house*. Cole and Skippy went their separate ways, Skippy on a mission to round up the background players for the evening's meticulously stage-managed orgy, and Cole to slip into his tuxedo and get himself into character for his fourth date with the deliciously hot Mai Ling.

Chapter Seven

"Hi," Cole said, clambering into the black stretch Hummer that awaited him out front of the studio.

"Good evening, Cole," Mai Ling replied with a coy smile; she'd been ensconced in the limo for some time, while Cole made himself even more presentable. However, she didn't seem too annoyed at having been kept waiting.

"I'm so sorry I'm running a little late—I always struggle with these." Cole tugged gently at his black bow tie, which he'd actually had to get the wardrobe girl to tie for him; it was something he'd never quite gotten the hang of. He settled down in the car's luxury leather seat and poured himself a glass of champagne from the open bottle in the car's minibar. It was alcohol-free, of course, as Cole couldn't afford to have anything affect his performance. Although there was to be no sex with Mai Ling, as per the show's strict rules, that wasn't to say they wouldn't be expected to play with the other orgy goers; the audience at home would expect nothing less than a sterling performance.

Mai Ling smiled at Cole again, her eyes glinting in the limo's sparkly interior. She and Cole had not seen each other since the previous night's session of heavy petting in the lakeside cabin, and it was obvious she was delighted to once more be in his presence. The single camera—manned by a middle-aged, balding guy named Jeff—picked up every nuance of the girl's desire while, at the same time, taking gratuitous shots of her braless cleavage down the front of the plunging black minidress that clung to her every curve like a second skin.

They'd use film they'd shot months ago of Cole arriving at the posh hotel to pick up his date. Skippy insisted they keep the stock footage refreshed at least every six months or so—it was far more cost-effective in terms of both money and time to not have to film the round trip to collect the contestant every single night.

After so many years of *The Gentleman's Choice*, Cole knew the routine by heart: On the prerecord that ran before the live show, they'd show Cole getting into the vehicle before the shot dissolved seamlessly to him sitting in pensive anticipation at the thought of his date—they used that footage time and again, and if any of the show's viewers noticed, nobody cared enough to complain. The limo would then be shown driving through either Houston or Dallas, depending upon the week's location, to be greeted at the hotel by the smartly dressed doorman.

They'd then cut to Cole and his date inside the car as it ostensibly drove them to the location of their date. In reality, it was a quick circuit around the block and then straight back to the studio. Skippy had master-minded some guerrilla footage of a few of the huge swingers' houses and of the limousine pulling up at the end of their long, sweeping driveways. When cut with footage of Cole and his date of the week pretending to climb from the vehicle, and an outside shot of the car's door opening, it looked, for all intents and purposes, as if they were alighting to join in the sexual shenanigans within the exclusive club.

The scene would cut just as Cole emerged to him and his date walking into—what the audience had been hoodwinked into believing was—the swinging mansion with its sumptuously sensual atmosphere and semi-naked, cavorting revelers.

It was nothing more than simple smoke and mirrors, of course, the likes of which the movie world had been creating since its infancy. The hedonistic proceedings would be streamed live from inside the studio set, in which Skippy had recreated the orgy room of one of the great houses down to the finest detail. It wasn't that the show's subscribers actually gave much of a damn about *where* the sex scenes were shot. So long as they got their dose of bare flesh and hot sex, they'd be more than satisfied. But it mattered to Skippy and Cole—they had agreed upon the importance of setting up the scenarios from the very beginning, and Cole truly believed it was what set *The Gentleman's Choice* apart from all the others in the industry that simply jumped straight into the sex acts with none of the buildup.

"I hope you're looking forward to tonight." Cole slid along the seat to be close to his date. He draped an arm about her bare shoulders and planted a long, lingering kiss on her full, glossy lips.

"Very much so," Mail Ling replied, breaking the kiss. "I have never been to an orgy before."

"You're gonna have so much fun." Cole remembered the lines Skippy had written for him perfectly—the producer tried his best to keep the dialogue fresh, but there were really only so many words one could say about such things without getting too crude. "I only wish we were allowed to play with each other." Placing a hand gently on the girl's knee, Cole slid it a little way up her silky-smooth thigh. Yes, he had to say that as a reminder to the show's audience to not expect him to be seducing Mai Ling at the orgy, but he was surprised to discover he genuinely meant it. Cole had grown fond of the cute Asian girl over the course of her time on the show and harbored hopes of them continuing the relationship he felt had formed once her stint was over—preferably after some wonderful Fifth Night sex.

"You'll get to see me having fun with others, though," Mai Ling delivered her line with slightly less conviction; was that a hint of hesitation there? "Won't that turn you on, Cole?" Pressing her lips against his, she slipped her tongue into his mouth to seek out his.

Cole felt the old, familiar twinge in his groin as things stirred prematurely into action. Removing his hand from his date's warm, smooth leg and pulling away from the smooch, he willed himself to wilt. It was going to be a long, exciting night, and it certainly wouldn't behoove him to peak too early in the game. Skippy would never allow him to hear the end of it if he did.

The limo came to the end of its brief trip around the block. The chauffeur, who came as part of the rental package, climbed out and opened the door. There was a camera outside to greet Cole and Mai Ling.

"Looks like it's showtime," Cole said with a smile as he took Mai Ling's hand to help her get out of the car without flashing her freshly epilated crotch to the camera; it certainly wouldn't do to give the audience a full-on look at the goodies before the action even got started.

Mai Ling smiled directly into the camera as she'd been instructed; three nights on the show and the gal was acting like a pro. Cole gave her tiny hand a squeeze and hoped once again this was to be the beginning of something special.

As Cole escorted Mai Ling into the less than salubrious, utilitarian building that housed the studio, the show was starting up with the usual prerecorded preamble. Skippy liked to play it over the Tannoy as a means of setting the mood, although Cole didn't like hearing the voice of the persona he was forced to adopt for the show before embarking on a sexual adventure; it would often have the opposite effect and dampen his ardor.

"Hi, I'm Cole Gianni, and I'm searching for the love of my life." Cole's voice came from the speakers; he sounded like some over-smooth, sexually confident lothario, and it never failed to make him cringe. "I have everything I could ever want," the intro played on. Cole was painfully familiar with the piece—they'd played it at the beginning of every show since the beginning, although Skippy had done reshoots over the years to keep it as fresh as the limo stock footage. There would be the green screen projection of a huge house with its sparkling blue pool, the yacht, and the collection of obscenely expensive sports cars, none of which were owned by Cole or his producer— smoke and mirrors once again.

Cole's voice regaled himself and Mai Ling as they waited patiently by the narrow steel door that would open to reveal the hedonistic delights of the orgy beyond. "The problem I have with being so fabulously wealthy is, I can never be sure if a girl loves me for *me* or just my money." That comment always struck Cole as awfully entitled and whiney, but Skippy reckoned the poor little rich boy with trust issues act somehow resonated with their female audience. Just how many multimillionaires tuned in night after night to watch Cole getting off with a succession of women, albeit hot ones?

"I truly hope I'll find love this week," Cole's prerecord was really milking the act for all it was worth. "I believe Mai Ling and I have a very special connection and that she likes me for *me*, and not my many offshore bank accounts." They had shot that part at the beginning of the first day, right after Skippy and the casting director had chosen that week's contestant, and before Cole had so much as laid eyes on the sexy Asian girl. The script was pretty much the same for every contestant, save the name, although Skippy did his best to ad-lib a little where he could to avoid sounding too stale.

"Our dates so far have been so wonderful, and I just know tonight's is going to be off the charts," Cole heard himself say. "I'm going to enjoy watching my beautiful date having lots of sexy fun. It will definitely add sparkle to our final night together—when we will get to make love for the very first time…" Cole had all but gagged upon delivering the *watch my beautiful date* line. Skippy wheeled it out every time an orgy night was planned for the show, and it was just so damned corny. Cole vowed to insist again he be allowed a hand in writing the scripts to save the show from Skippy's stilted dialogue; the contestants all deserved so much better. Holding tight onto Mai Ling's hand, Cole noticed it was ever so slightly damp and that her breathing had quickened—the sweet, twin mounds of her breasts rose and fell beneath the flimsy material of her dress, her nipples stiff with arousal.

Turning her head slightly to look into Cole's eyes, Mai Ling offered a warm, seductive smile and squeezed his fingers hard. "I'm *really* looking forward to this, Cole," she told him, unscripted, and with no camera to play to. "Let's have some fun in there."

A heartbeat later, the steel door swung open as if by magic. Cole's voiceover had stopped—mercifully for him—and as he guided Mai Ling over the threshold with a gentlemanly hand at the small of her back, he was welcomed by the pair of cameras that would follow every move he and his date would make throughout the course of their adventure; they were carefully angled to capture the rapt look on his and Mai Ling's face, while not giving away the stark gray corridor beyond. *Give Skippy his due*, Cole thought; he had choreographed every single detail to maintain the illusion for their audience.

Chapter Eight

"**W**ow." Mai Ling appeared to be genuinely impressed at the sight that greeted her beyond the steel door.

"It really is something, isn't it?" Cole led her into the seductively lit room and they both looked around at the semi and fully naked couples, threesomes, foursomes, and moresomes taking pleasure from one another upon the couches, bed, and in the hot tub for the delectation of the viewers. Everyone in the room was masked with the exception of Cole and Mai Ling—it simply wouldn't do to hide the faces of the two people everyone at home had tuned in to see. There were cameras practically everywhere, of course, all unmanned and remotely controlled, apart from the two following the stars of the show.

"Welcome," a soft, sultry voice purred close to Cole's ear. He'd been so entranced by the acrobatic frolicking of two tanned, muscular young men and one incredibly flexible black girl, he'd not seen the young couple approaching. "I'm Danielle, and this is my partner, Aaron." Danielle thrust a flute of champagne—the genuine article this time—into Cole's hand, and the broad-shouldered Aaron did likewise to Mai Ling.

That Danielle and Aaron were entirely nude didn't faze Cole one iota. He'd seen it all before and, no matter that Skippy had selected the most beautiful pair in the room as their first point of contact, he felt wholly unmoved. Cole had gotten more aroused at the simple, innocent touch of Mai Ling's thigh during their fake limousine ride.

"Thank you," Mai Ling said, and as she sipped at her drink, her eyes roamed first over Aaron's body and then Danielle's.

Aaron was classically handsome, at least as far as Cole could tell beneath his white leather face mask—there was a strong jaw line there and cheekbones he guessed were of Greek origin. The guy was of stocky build, no more than five-nine, five-ten at the most, and sported a golden, all-over tan; it was impossible to discern whether that was natural or from a spray booth. His entire body had been shaved—or waxed, something Cole had never been tempted to try, on account of his aversion to excruciating pain—of every single hair, and a long, thick, circumcised cock rested heavy against his thigh.

As for Danielle, she made for the perfect pairing with Aaron—although Cole knew Skippy was paying the two for their time, and they were not actually a couple. Nonetheless, Danielle was obviously stunning behind the simple black lace mask that covered her face from the line of her shoulder-length, platinum blonde hair to just below her button nose. Her full, plump lips were painted a shocking, glossy scarlet, and her smile was dazzling. Danielle's body, in contrast to Aaron's, was tall and slender, her breasts full, natural, and heavy; they jiggled like shimmering liquid with her every move. She did share a complete lack of body hair with Aaron, though, and Cole's gaze followed Mai Ling's down the creamy-skinned smoothness of Danielle's stomach, over the deep indentation of her navel, and onto the pronounced bump of the hairless mound between her trim thighs.

Cole began to feel uncomfortable in his briefs as Danielle's presence had the desired effect. As a distraction, he took a swig of his champagne and was surprised to discover Skippy had actually sprung for the good stuff for once. Typically, it was some five-dollar-a-bottle cheap shit with a plastic cork from Kroger, but Cole's well-trained palette was telling him this was most likely Veuve Clicquot Yellow Label—Skippy's personal favorite. Okay, it wasn't quite Dom Perignon, but it sure made for a pleasant and welcome surprise.

"We were just about to get into the hot tub," Aaron said to Mai Ling; the line was scripted, and he'd done well to remember not to say *Jacuzzi*—using brand names on the show had gotten *The Gentleman's Choice* sued on more than one occasion in the past. Skippy and Cole had learned the hard way; most reputable companies didn't take too kindly to having their hard-earned brands bandied about on pornographic web shows.

"Would you two like to join us?" Danielle added to make it totally clear for the viewing audience *both* of the show's stars were being invited. Then, without waiting for Cole's obvious reply, Danielle pulled open his black tuxedo jacket and began to unbutton his shirt.

"You can leave your dress over there," Aaron told Mai Ling. He pointed to a neat row of a dozen or so ornate brass coat hooks on the wall opposite the tub. "It'll be totally safe, I promise." He flashed a too-wide smile that made Cole wince; the amateur may as well have added *because we're in a studio set* at the end of his stupidly improvised line!

The two couples having sex in the hot tub climbed out as Cole, Mai Ling, Danielle, and Aaron climbed in; it was critical there were no distractions from the main attraction, and the background players kept their place as set decoration unless required to step up; Skippy would have made sure of that in his preshow briefing, once he'd rounded up the extras. Cole eyed the women of both couples, admiring the shiny-wet curves of their naked butts as they made their way out of the Jacuzzi and across to the stack of white, fluffy towels that had been thoughtfully laid out. He mused that there really was no way to get out of a hot tub with one's dignity intact, especially when nude.

"I see you're already enjoying yourself," Danielle purred for the benefit of the camera. Her hand slid beneath the frothing water, and she made exaggerated motions with her arm as she took Cole in hand.

Cole let out a sigh and eased himself back against the side of the tub. Although the touch of the beautiful woman's fingers felt electric, it was the high-speed jet squirting water into his lower back that elicited Cole's reaction; the sweet relief of a hot water jet in just the right spot of his lumbar region was a rare treat indeed.

As Danielle massaged Cole under the water, her voluptuous breasts pressed hard into his side, Mai Ling was finding her own entertainment at the hands of the impossibly toned Aaron. Clearly, Skippy had fully instructed the pair as to their respective roles for the evening, which was to seduce the show's star and his sexy young date, so the viewing audience could imagine themselves in their place. Mai Ling, for her part, was throwing herself into the scenario with aplomb. She was locked in a deep French kiss with Aaron, who had her on his lap in the deepest part of the hot tub. Cole's imagination ran riot as to what might be going on beneath the concealing bubbles, and he really wasn't liking the way it made him feel.

And there it was.

Cole struggled to believe it, but he'd actually experienced a pang of jealousy. Of course, he knew the rules of the show: he and Mai Ling were forbidden to have sex until the final night, and during orgy night, they could play—all the way to full sex—with any of the other participants, just not one another. Naturally, it meant Mai Ling's hot tub dalliance with Aaron was perfectly within the show's boundaries, as was Cole's with the delightfully busty Danielle; in fact, both activities were fully expected by their viewers. Hence, Cole found it hard to accept the unfamiliar emotions coursing through his mind; was it possible he'd actually *fallen* for the Asian girl?

"I think your date is having fun over there," Danielle stage-whispered loud enough for the camera's sensitive microphone to pick up. "She's so freakin' hot—I think I may just *have* to play with her myself a little later. You and Aaron can watch us pleasure each other on the bed..."

Cole wasn't convinced.

There was something in Danielle's eyes as she delivered her scripted lines that gave away the fact she wasn't in the slightest part attracted to Mai Ling. Maybe the girl wasn't the body type she went for, perhaps she just didn't like Asian chicks, or maybe she was as straight as a die. Despite the adult industry's insistence *all* women would turn lesbian at the drop of a hat, Cole had encountered many performers for whom the thought of being with another woman wasn't all that much of a turn-on no matter how enthusiastic they appeared on screen. In many ways, it put Cole and Danielle in the same boat: both were stuck playing a role neither were comfortable in for the sake of earning a living.

Nonetheless, Danielle was playing her allocated part of liberated seductress, and playing it well. With her right hand firmly wrapped around Cole's dick, she reached out across the Jacuzzi to fondle Mai Ling's breasts, which bobbed about on the water's surface as she kissed and groped with Aaron.

Cole smiled at the startled look on his date's face as Danielle's immaculately manicured fingernails teased her nipples. Cole imagined Skippy in his little production booth congratulating himself on just how good the show was, enthused at how it was just the kind of hot foursome scene he'd upload to *Pornhub* and the like to snag those all-important subscriptions.

But as Mai Ling settled into the pleasure of her ménage à trois, rolling her half-closed eyes and biting softly down on her lower lip as she played her part to perfection for the cameras, Cole fought hard to shake the sharp pangs of jealousy and the gloomy, all-enveloping feeling of being left out—even though Danielle was making such an expert job of stroking him under the water.

"Want to make an Oreo?" It was an evening of seductive voices and the tantalizing waft of warm breath against his ear. Cole spun around in the tub to see the owner of the voice, which was so deep it was almost masculine. Danielle's hand slid from Cole as his body moved and she sidled up to Mai Ling's side to sandwich her between herself and Aaron. Danielle's freed hand took its place on Mai Ling's shoulder as she moved in to replace Aaron's passionate kiss with her own.

"An *Oreo*?" Cole asked with a wry smile. Of course, he'd heard the phrase many times before, but it always paid to play the sexually naive rich boy—surveys had shown their audience demographic just *loved* to watch the show's star and his dates being taught something entirely new, even if a particular scene had been featured in previous seasons.

Either their typical viewers had exceptionally short memories or they just enjoyed seeing what was familiar to them.

"With me and my friend." The voice's owner was a statuesque, ebony-skinned goddess of a woman. She wore a neon-yellow string bikini that only just covered what it was supposed to and, as she crouched down by the side of the Jacuzzi, her long, slender toes flexing to keep her balanced, Cole had an unobscured view of her deep, dark cleavage. "You want me to join you and your friend?" Cole knew to repeat the line—just in case the viewers didn't quite catch the gist the first time.

Even if they had, it helped build sexual tension and gave the cameraman time to adjust his shot to take in the black lady's friend.

"I'm Ebony, by the way," the lady lied. She held out a hand for Cole to shake. "And that's my friend, Chanese." With a toss of her head, which had her butt-length braids whipping about her shoulders like a whip's tails, she diverted Cole's attention from her breasts over toward the orgy bed, which had been cleared of all cavorters bar one.

There, lazing by the bed's edge with her head propped up on one arm and a hand snuggled suggestively between her legs, was Chanese. She'd been posed there in the optimum position for the camera to take in her strikingly voluptuous body and smooth-shaven head. Her dark skin was a perfect match for Ebony's, as was the bikini that struggled to contain her breasts and disappeared between the magnificent twin orbs of her ass cheeks.

For the benefit of the cameras, Cole took a long, lustful stare at the sexy black chick on the bed, and to the best of his acting ability, his expression portrayed a man imagining a whole host of lascivious scenarios with the two ebony beauties. Normally, Cole would be beside himself with excitement and mentally thanking Skippy for scripting the sensual scenario, but his mind swam with thoughts of Mai Ling with Aaron and Danielle. His gut churned with the anticipation of what the night undoubtedly had in store for her.

Ebony tugged on Cole's hand to encourage him from the hot tub. Taking the cue, Cole clambered out and allowed her to lead him to the bed. In the interests of maintaining the shot, he eschewed the towels—he'd dry off sooner or later, and besides, the lady viewers loved seeing his glistening, naked body. Next to Cole, the cameraman pointed his lens without shame at Ebony's jiggling buttocks, which, for Cole, were just a tad too skinny for his tastes—he preferred a woman to look better fed, like her friend, Chanese. Nonetheless, he couldn't help but admire the long, sensual curve of Ebony's naked back and the sway of the heavy braids against her flawless dark skin.

Chanese welcomed Cole to the vast expanse of the orgy bed with open arms and a deep, wet kiss that had her tongue invading his mouth like some lithe, squirming creature eager for a mate. Meeting the girl's tongue with his, Cole climbed onto the bed and lay down beside her. Ebony took her place at his other side, and thus the "Oreo" was complete; it was an immensely popular fantasy, especially among the show's more mature male demographic, and it was the job of *The Gentleman's Choice* to cater for all such fantasies.

It just wasn't one of Cole's.

The inadequately small, neon bikinis soon came off as Ebony and Chanese explored Cole with fingers, lips, and tongues; they gave each other attention too, of course, complete with dirty, suggestive looks into the camera as they sucked, licked, and pawed at one another's gloriously naked bodies with highly vocal enthusiasm.

Then Mai Ling and her two new friends joined Cole and his upon the bed. Like Cole, Mai Ling was not offered the opportunity to dry off from the Jacuzzi, and her pale, naked body shimmered beneath the dimmed red lights that hung from the studio beams above.

Cole exchanged only the briefest of glances with Mai Ling, as he was being kept busy by his playmates—they were determined to not leave one square inch of his body unexplored—and he wondered if she could see the longing in his eyes. Mai Ling smiled at him and looked about to say something, but Danielle silenced her with a passionate kiss.

Then Mai Ling was gone, her slender body obscured by Danielle and Aaron as they went about their carefully choreographed seduction; it wasn't too much longer before Cole heard the sweet, breathy moans of his date's pleasure, which sounded too convincing to be merely for the benefit of the cameras.

More couples appeared on the bed, along with a select few single women—all masked, all naked. Each one had been chosen personally by Skippy, fully briefed on when they were to approach the bed and what they were to do once they got there. Some couples simply had sex with each other, while others invited couples or one of the singles to join them. Off to Cole's right, a young pair of Latino descent maneuvered themselves into a soixante-neuf with the nubile young lady straddling her partner's face; Cole could easily discern the real couples from those Skippy had paid for, and the Latinos were definitely in the latter category. There was just something about the mechanical nature of their coupling that didn't quite ring true to him— most likely it was the way the guy approached his girl as if she was someone new to him; there wasn't a trace of the familiarity one would expect from seasoned lovers.

Adjacent to that couple, a pair of young men set about enjoying a plump, flat-chested gal who encouraged them both with a stream of foul sexual language; next to her, a skinny bronzed girl with fascinating crisscross tan lines lay with her face buried in the silky black sheets and her rump high in the air.

And so, the sex went on in its myriad forms as, all around Cole, Skippy's orchestrated orgy played out for the cameras and the voyeuristic delight of the show's viewers. As always, the producer ensured there would be something for everyone upon that bed; he considered the activities of the extras to be "set dressing" for the main event, which was the pleasures of Cole and whichever date got picked to experience the show's Orgy Night.

Of course, Skippy was so intent on ensuring every orgy featured on the show was just perfect, he'd insist on running what he liked to call *un*dress rehearsals. Cole had questioned him about the practice on many occasions on the grounds of both cost and appropriateness, since he knew of no other adult content producers who *ever* rehearsed. But, once it became clear rehearsal time was more about Skippy sating his own perversions than getting everything right on the night, Cole had backed off, even though it rested uneasily with him knowing Skippy would join in with the cast, touch, and fuck, all under the pretext of *directing*.

It was of endless wonder to Cole they had not been sued, although there had been more than one vocal complaint about the creepy, far too *handsy* producer.

Aaron was fucking Mai Ling. Chanese moved around to straddle Cole, which left him with an unobscured view of his date with her dainty bare feet up on Aaron's shoulders as he was buried deep inside her. Danielle lay by Mai Ling's side; one hand caressed the girl's breasts, the other she fondled between her legs, while Aaron did his job with mechanical efficiency. As Cole watched, and for his benefit, Danielle leaned in to kiss Mai Ling full on the mouth, muffling her noisy groans as she neared climax. Ebony lowered herself down onto Cole's face and suckled on her friend's bouncing breasts; she alternated between each nipple as Chanese rode Cole hard to an angry orgasm, which she skillfully affected in sync with Mai Ling's.

As Mai Ling came with a loud, guttural moan, she reached out to grab Cole's hand. It did nothing to assuage the gnawing sensation in his gut—he could barely stand to look at his date let alone enjoy the feel of her fingers in his.

Chapter Nine

"Cole, the subscribers have voted her through to Night Five," Skippy protested.

"I'm sorry, Skippy, but I really need you to do this for me," Cole said; the producer's claustrophobic office was doing little to even out his mood. "I would really appreciate you taking her off the show."

"Is this because she fucked that guy with the big dick?" There was a sarcastic, teasing tone to the producer's voice. "You do realize that's exactly what she was *supposed* to do?"

Cole ground his teeth. Skippy's attitude also wasn't helping his mood any. Jealous and insecure, he'd insisted he and Mai Ling leave the orgy almost the minute they'd both finished what they were there to get done. They'd left their respective playmates back on the bed to carry on fornicating with the extras. "Yeah, but not like *that*." Cole felt sadness and regret at the thought of not seeing Mai Ling again, but he just couldn't shift the mental image of her with Aaron, and it made him sick to his stomach. "I thought she put on a good show," Skippy replied. "I honestly thought she'd be a bit too uptight when it came to exhibitionism—I went out on a limb putting on an orgy with that one."

"I really wish you hadn't bothered," Cole replied.

"You're actually pissed off because she enjoyed herself in there." A smirk spread across Skippy's sweaty, wobbling face. "That's right, isn't it, Cole? You've gone all fucking sweet on Mai Ling."

"You don't understand what it's like." After so long working together, Cole knew Skippy could read him like a book, although it really didn't take a genius to figure out what was eating at him. Yes, he'd grown fond of Mai Ling during the course of the show, which was something that had only happened a handful of times in a half-dozen years. And yes, it had upset him to watch her enjoying Aaron as much as she had—*nobody* could fake ecstasy as well as that, especially some amateur the casting department had picked out in the interest of keeping *The Gentleman's Choice* diverse. "I just don't see her making a good Fifth Night, that's all."

"We have to consider the voting," Skippy countered. "She cleared 81 percent to remain on the show for tomorrow night. If she puts in as good a performance then as she did at the orgy, she's going to walk away with the prize money."

Cole knew Skippy was trying to bait him, and he fought hard not to rise to it; his head wasn't in the right place for arguing with the man. "Come on, Skip—it's not like it would be the first time we've... *manipulated* the voting figures."

Shaking his head, Skippy leaned back in his chair and interlaced his fingers to support the back of his neck. "Yeah, and I thought I'd made it clear we couldn't do it too often, didn't I? You know we're only ever one audit away from being shut down."

As much as it grieved him, Cole knew the producer was right. Because *The Gentleman's Choice* subscribers paid to vote via *Choice Tokens*, which they bought with real money, the show was liable to independent audits at any time. Sometimes, all it took was a complaint, other times, nothing at all, and Skippy would be legally obliged to hand over all the voting figures for some faceless bean counters to pore over. It had happened on a bunch of Brit TV reality and Saturday night peak viewing shows, and when the discrepancies were uncovered, the fines and negative publicity had been devastating. Cole was aware such an eventuality would likely be the death of *The Gentleman's Choice*, as paying internet subscribers didn't take kindly to being ripped off—and they could all too easily take their masturbation money elsewhere.

"I'm asking you to do this one for me." Cole's attempt to appeal to Skippy's sense of fair play was met with a smirk. "This will *definitely* be the last time I ask you to do this." Cole found that ironic, since every other time they'd fudged the voting figures had been solely for Skippy's benefit. Either they hadn't been able to afford for that week's contestant to win the prize money—the only thing worse than fiddling the figures was not paying out; wronged contestants were all too quick to air their grievances on social media—or Skippy had tried one of his clumsy moves, and it was best for all concerned that a contestant be distanced from the show as quickly as possible.

"I really don't think we should," Skippy replied following a brief silence. "Mai Ling is incredibly popular. They all love the Asian chicks out there!"

Cole stood up quickly; his chair scraped loudly on the floor and almost toppled backward. "If you want a God-awful Night Five, Skippy, *this* is the right way to go about it. I'm guessing your reluctance to can Mai Ling has more to do with you wanting to fuck her than having the show audited."

If Cole had hit the homerun with his accusation, Skippy gave nothing away; Cole had always thought the guy would make an impressive poker player should he ever find the patience to bother learning the game.

"You disappoint me, Cole." Skippy was quick to turn passive-aggressive when he knew he was losing; it gave Cole some satisfaction that whatever his partner was about to say before giving in to his request to bin Mai Ling, it was little more than hollow protest. "If I agree to ignore the voting figures and pull the chick off the show, you're going to have to pull something *really* special out of the hat for the next contestant."

Cole sighed. He'd anticipated that one coming; there was *always* a condition with Skippy, and Cole knew he'd pay for getting his way later. It had been a while since they'd had some hardcore BDSM on *The Gentleman's Choice*. Cole definitely didn't share his producer's love of watching people in pain and had vetoed it off the voting list most of the times Skippy had snuck it back on. Cole figured *Fifty Shades* crap would be very much back in the frame for the next contestant, perhaps with him playing the sub and being on the receiving end of some uncomfortable stuff. "Don't I always?" Cole let out a loud sigh. It had been a trying night, he was riddled with disappointment at how things had transpired with Mai Ling, and his body ached almost as much as his heart. All in all, it had not been one of the best nights for Cole Gianni.

Skippy peered across the grubby top of his desk. "Not always," he said. "If we'd not had other stuff going on tonight, the whole scene would have been ruined, thanks to your little diva fit."

"I did *not* have a diva fit." Cole's retort came out a tad too shrill to be entirely convincing; he was well aware of how he'd reacted to Mai Ling's actions. "I saw the scene out and then left—just like you wrote in your script."

"It was written all over your bloody face, Cole," Skippy told him. "And the cameras definitely picked it up—you looked like a guy pissed off his date was getting fucked by a bigger knob than his. We can only hope there are people out there who get their jollies on that sort of bullshit."

"You know there are—it's why you love your orgy nights so much."

"Fair point," Skippy conceded. "Then at least tonight wasn't a complete loss."

Tired of looking at his partner's smug expression, Cole made to leave. "So, you'll tell Mai Ling she's off the show?"

Skippy sighed and leaned forward to rest his elbows on the desk; he had the appearance of a fake prophet about to impart some profound nugget of wisdom to brainwashed followers. "Yeah, *I'll* can the poor girl for you," he said with an exaggerated wink. "Tell her to come in."

Yanking open the office door with a weary sigh, Cole replied, "Tell her yourself, Skippy."

Just looking at Mai Ling in the little black dress she'd worn to attend the staged orgy had Skippy's balls aching. So much so, he'd had to lean against the edge of his desk rather than sit down. And even though he'd emptied them a couple of times watching over the proceedings from the secluded darkness of his production booth, Skippy's dick was good to go for a record third time that night.

"I'm sorry, but you have not been voted through to the final night," Skippy told Mai Ling while peeping up the hem of her tiny dress; she hadn't worn panties to avoid the dreaded VPL through the skintight fabric, and he was hoping to catch a glimpse of her.

"Seriously?" Mai Ling narrowed her eyes with suspicion, and for a second or two, Skippy imagined she'd seen straight through his ruse. "I really needed that prize money."

"You'll get all your out-of-pocket expenses reimbursed." Skippy offered the disappointed girl a smile. Sometimes he wished he'd not been so hard and fast with the all-or-nothing rules; he'd shamelessly plagiarized elements of *Who Wants to be A Millionaire* for the show, including the rotating nature of the contestants—one in, one out—but had stopped short of the graded prize money. It had been a simple matter of economics back in the early days of *The Gentleman's Choice*, but it had stuck because he didn't want to mess with their winning formula.

"That's not a hundred thousand dollars, is it?"

"I'm so sorry, but our subscribers can be a fickle lot." Skippy shifted his wide ass against the desk; he could feel its sharp edge digging a deep crease in the fat. "We never can tell which way they're going to vote. If it is any consolation, I voted for you to stay."

"It isn't." Mai Ling looked to be close to tears, which had Skippy hardening even more. "I did everything right tonight—I put on one hell of a performance with that guy."

"Indeed, you did." Skippy stood straight and hoped the bulge in his pants would catch the girl's attention and make his intentions clear; he really couldn't remember the last time he'd wanted to bang one of Cole's leftovers so much. "You were an absolute pleasure to watch—I saw how much you were enjoying yourself on that bed. Actually, the orgy is still going on in the studio. Perhaps you would like to take advantage?"

"Excuse me?" Mai Ling shuffled uncomfortably in her seat.

"We don't stop the action when the filming is over." Skippy gave Mai Ling what he considered to be his seductive voice. He took a step toward her. "We keep things going for the swingers—it's kind of a perk of the job for them, and it means we don't have to pay them too much. Most of the paid extras have gone home—no fucking off the clock for them." Skippy overexplained, all too aware he was babbling. He just couldn't help himself—the Chinese girl was having one hell of an effect on him. "You want me to go back in there?" Mai Ling laughed. "With *you*?" Skippy loved how the girl's eyes danced when she laughed, but even so, her scornful words cut him deep. "Why not?" He heard himself say. "Maybe we could work out a way to… *enhance* your expense claim?"

Mai Ling jumped to her feet, those dark, dancing eyes ablaze. "You have got to be fucking *kidding* me?"

"I-I meant—"

"I know what you *meant*, you fat fuck," Mai Ling spat. "You think because I got thrown off your stupid little show, I'm desperate enough to fuck you for money? You really are something else."

Skippy was taken aback by the girl's pure ferocity. Normally, the show's rejects jumped at the chance to make a little money on top of their expenses, especially when offered the chance of more work in the adult film industry—Skippy still knew a few people around the studios who would pay top dollar for fresh meat who could deliver the goods on camera—and Mai Ling had proven herself admirably. "I can put you in touch with some people…" Skippy knew he was sounding desperate, but just couldn't help himself.

"Fuck you, loser." Mai Ling sidestepped Skippy's bulk and made for the door.

"Don't go." Skippy grabbed Mai Ling's bare arm so tight his chubby fingers bit deep into the soft flesh of her bicep. "Please…"

"Get your hand off me, or I'll scream this whole fucking place down and tell the cops you raped me." Mai Ling struggled to be free of Skippy's grip; her face reddened with the effort; her breasts trembled beneath the flimsy material of the dress. "I fucking *mean* it, asshole."

Skippy held firm, not ready to let the girl go just yet— there had to be something in his armory he could use to get her to bend to his will.

"I said, *let me go*!" Mai Ling delivered a hard, stinging slap to Skippy's cheek; the sharp, fleshy sound it made was more of a surprise to him than the pain.

Startled, Skippy relinquished his hold on Mai Ling's arm and took a step backward. His hand went to the tingling cheek. Skippy felt the anger rise up inside of him, and his vision clouded red.

"You fucking, prick-teasing Chinese skank!" Spittle flew from his chubby lips as he screamed at Mai Ling. "You fucking *whore*!"

All the bravado drained from the Asian girl's face and, in that moment, she appeared scared and vulnerable, which brought some comfort to Skippy's wounded ego. "Let me go, please."

And then Mai Ling was gone—scooting around Skippy to run out of the office and through the adjacent fire door.

"Fucking… *dirty bloody cow*!" Skippy just couldn't help himself, and as his go-to childhood insult echoed along the empty hallway and his dick shriveled with the rejection, he felt the rage burning deep inside.

Chapter Ten

He watched as Mai Ling had the cab driver drop her off outside one of the pretentiously trendy Montrose bars; she'd taken a Yellow Taxi directly from the studio, which he thought odd, as most people used Uber or Lyft. Although it was close to midnight, the bar was busy, filled with people

Mai Ling's age and the thrum of voices and contemporary background music. Listening from the shadows outside, he found it a refreshing change from the country and western and 80s hair rock most of Houston's bars seemed to play.

She placed her purse on the bar and ordered an ice-cold Shiner Bock and Whiskey chaser from the handsome young barman who *insisted* upon leaning over the bar top and kissing the back of her hand like some chivalrous English knight.

Undoubtedly, the barman liked what he saw—a cute Chinese girl all by herself in a tight, skimpy dress—and figured if he flashed a smile or two and flexed his impressive pecs, she'd feel honored to sleep with him. He saw the familiar look on Mai Ling's face that showed she was considering responding to the barman's obvious charm. At least she wouldn't have to fuck him in a studio set in front of a film crew.

He wondered if Mai Ling felt cheap, bearing in mind she'd just participated in an orgy broadcast across the internet. He'd watched, engrossed, as she frolicked with the good-looking couple for the cameras.

Mai Ling glugged down half her beer and knocked back her whiskey shot in one go; she then waved over the permanently smiling barman and ordered the same again.

He watched as the barman shook his head and picked up Mai Ling's empty shot glass. Mai Ling's smile left her pretty young lips. The bar was about to close, and he figured the Chinese girl wouldn't want to go back to the hotel room to be on her own—he could tell she needed to be in the company of regular people, *real* people.

Smiling, the barman glanced at his watch and said something to Mai Ling that brought the smile back; if he was directing her to one of the nearby clubs that stayed open 'til two, it would mean she wouldn't be jumping straight into a cab.

And that meant opportunity.

Mai Ling downed the remainder of her beer in one and slammed the bottle down on the counter.

From his place in the shadows, he saw heads turning in Mai Ling's direction as she slid from the bar stool and made her way toward the door, and he could see she enjoyed the attention.

The streets were mostly quiet; the occasional car or taxi zipped by, and small groups of people clustered around the myriad of food trucks in the parking lots on either side of the road. The bistro restaurants were long closed, and the bars had yet to turn out, so he had to be discreet following her—it wouldn't do to arouse her suspicions so early on.

So, he stuck to the shadows and doorways a good way behind her, but close enough to hear the friendly female voice on Mai Ling's GPS. Naturally, he couldn't discern what directions the voice was giving, but when Mai Ling turned off the main drag and onto a smaller street, he had a good idea where she might be going. Fishing out his cell phone, he tapped out a quick text.

The street was narrow and not well lit; doorways to small stores and houses were directly upon the sidewalk, creating more shadowed areas in which he could skulk, and that had Mai Ling quickening her step.

Stopping to peer at her phone's small screen, her face illuminated in the gloom, he thought Mai Ling appeared annoyed at her GPS for having brought her that way, and, when the recorded voice fell silent, Mai Ling heard the sound of his footsteps behind her. Holding her purse close to her body, she gripped her cell phone tightly and began walking again.

"Pardon me?" he said from behind her. Startled, her shoulders twitched. "*Miss*?"

Without slowing her step, Mai Ling glanced over her shoulder and saw him behind her; he was fifteen, maybe twenty feet away. He knew he blended in with the shadows well enough for his face to be obscured, and his squat form was made shapeless by a long, ankle-length coat.

Ignoring him, Mai Ling walked as quickly as she could without actually running; she'd be trying to get to where there were people quickly. "I need help, miss," he called out to her and closed the gap between them. "Please…"

"Leave me alone!" Mai Ling lifted up her phone as in indication she would have no hesitation in using it; although they both knew if she called 911, he'd be off into the night long before any cops arrived to help. He followed

Mai Ling as she rounded a corner and saw the car parked ahead, its lights still on. A little way beyond that, a red neon sign lit up the sidewalk with *Club Rio*.

Chancing another peek behind, Mai Ling saw him behind her—almost within grabbing distance. She began to run.

"Wait! Miss!" He was a tad out of breath with the exertion. "I need—"

Panicking, running, Mai Ling turned her head to look at him; she ran headlong into the woman coming the other way on the sidewalk.

"He's chasing me—" Mai Ling blurted out as, without saying a word, the woman grabbed Mai Ling's arms and pulled her toward her soft body.

Mai Ling tried to scream, but he was upon her, his large, clammy hand pressed against her mouth from behind.

With his free hand, he slipped the black burlap bag over Mai Ling's head and looked on as the woman stuck the girl's neck with the hypodermic needle. In an instant, Mai Ling's body went limp, and her cell phone and purse hit the sidewalk as her legs folded beneath her. She would have fallen to the ground, too, had the woman's strong arms not supported her.

Chapter Eleven

"Do you know why I've stopped you, ma'am?" The voice outside the car was muffled and frustratingly close.

"Was I speeding, Officer?" Another voice—female—came from within the vehicle; it sounded vaguely familiar.

It was unbearably hot in the trunk of the car, especially so in the humid Texas night. Every single labored breath Mai Ling struggled to take scorched the back of her throat and stung her mouth with the sour reek of gasoline fumes; it was so nauseating she wished she still had the dark bag over her face to filter out at least a little of the terrible stink. Desperate, she tried to scream for help and kick at the inside of the trunk lid until the cop realized she was trapped in there, but Mai Ling's body simply refused to cooperate.

"I noticed your taillight is out."

"I honestly had no idea, Officer. It was definitely working when we checked it before we left home, wasn't it, darling?"

Mai Ling felt a pang of hope; surely the cop would see through the woman's ridiculous claim—people just didn't check their taillights—and he'd get suspicious.

"I'm gonna cut you a break this time, ma'am." The cop's southern Texas drawl made him sound warm, *safe*. "Just be sure to get it fixed first thing in the morning."

"Thank you, Officer." The woman sounded relieved, and it was obviously at more than just avoiding getting a ticket. "We'll get it into the shop the minute it opens tomorrow."

"You have yourselves a blessed evening, folks."

"Goodnight, Officer," the woman said.

Mai Ling listened helplessly to the sound of the cop's heavy boots as they walked by the rear of the car. If only she could muster the willpower to override the paralyzing drug to make some kind of noise that would attract the officer's attention—then there would be an end to the waking nightmare in which she was trapped.

But no, Mai Ling's body lay limp and useless in the darkness of the trunk, her only movement the rhythmic rise and fall of her chest.

The car's engine gunned, and a blast of warm, sour heat once more assaulted Mai Ling's nostrils as it pulled away from the roadside to continue its bumpy journey off into the night.

Mai Ling had lost track of just how long she'd been in the trunk. For the first part of her journey, she had been unconscious, and since they had taken away her cell phone, there was no way of gauging time or how far she'd been driven. All Mai Ling remembered was an abrupt darkness as the rough cloth bag had been put over her head, and the sharp jab of the hypodermic needle in the lefthand side of her neck; the entry point still throbbed with hot pain like the sting of some deadly insect.

Panic gripped her; what did these people want from her? She had no money to speak of—her family was comfortable white collar, hardly wealthy, which led Mai Ling to the unthinkable conclusion she'd been taken to be used for sexual gratification, possibly even to be trafficked like some valuable commodity, or murdered and her body disposed of.

Mai Ling had read Houston was one of the country's biggest centers for human trafficking—young women disappeared there all the time, and many others were brought in from all over the world to work in the seedy massage parlors and underground brothels. Was that to be her fate, to spend what remained of her life in a drugged stupor servicing an endless parade of dirty old men paying to use her body for their own sick gratification? The thought terrified Mai Ling, and she regretted her drunken decision to put in her application to appear on the stupid, seedy little web show—her very public performance had most likely made her a target.

In which case, whatever was to become of her was all of her own doing.

* * *

The car finally came to a stop. The bright, fresh light of a warm Texas dawn seeped in through the hair-thin gaps around the trunk's lid.

"*Help*!" Mai Ling found her voice at last; the drugs had worn off enough to enable her to form words, even though her throat was bone-dry and sore from the stale, stinking heat in the trunk. "Is there anybody out there? *Please, help me…*"

Silence.

Mai Ling shuffled a little against the hard metal beneath her. She winced at the sore spots the spare tire beneath the threadbare carpet had created on her back as she'd been bumped along for God only knew how many miles of Texas road. Of course, she was making the blind assumption she was still in Texas, as it was entirely possible she'd been driven across the state line to Louisiana—it really wasn't all that far from Houston.

She heard voices, at first distant but drawing closer. The woman's, Mai Ling remembered from the night before as the cold, confident voice that had so efficiently appeased the traffic cop, but the man's was new to her—it was thin, wheezy. It sounded as if its owner had been overexerting himself, and there was an odd twang to it she couldn't quite place.

"Don't just leave her in there!" There was anger and frustration in the woman's voice. "How long do you think she's going to last in this heat?"

Heavy, shuffling footsteps approached the car. "If you'd told me to get her, I'd have gotten her," the man's voice grumbled.

"I'd have thought you'd have figured out she couldn't stay in the fucking car all morning!" The woman sounded a little farther away, her voice muted as if she was going indoors. "You're not *that* stupid."

Although the woman sounded cruel and controlling, she obviously wanted Mai Ling alive. The man was slow, possibly even retarded, which meant the chance of a careless slipup that might give Mai Ling the opportunity for escape. And, while those thoughts provided a grain of hope, Mai Ling was too terrified to even guess at what plans her captors had for her. Bracing herself for the trunk opening, Mai Ling listened to the rasping, metallic grate of old keys in the lock and the low, indiscernible grunting of expletives from the man fumbling with the awkward mechanism. For a second or two, Mai Ling thought he'd given up and feared she'd die a slow, miserable death trapped in there.

"Put your mask on, Buddy, for Christ's sake!" The woman's screeching, angry rebuke had Mai Ling lose control of her bladder. She felt the wet, spreading warmth of her own pee soak through her panties.

As the man opened up the lid, harsh, dazzling light flooded the trunk, and Mai Ling couldn't help but screw up her eyes against the sharp pain it brought with it. Nonetheless, she lashed out with her foot at where she guessed the man opening the lid would be and felt her shoe sink into soft flesh, along with the satisfying crackle of the bone beneath it.

The man let out a loud grunt and, as she forced open her eyes to clamber out of the trunk, Mai Ling saw him stagger backward, clutching her dislodged shoe to his broad chest.

"You fucking *bitch*!" he snarled and dropped Mai Ling's shoe in the dirt. The man's words were muffled through the black leather gimp mask that covered his entire head. Save for the tiny eyeholes and zippered mouth, it made for an outlandish contrast against the regular clothes he wore: pit-stained gray T-shirt, faded jeans, and battered cowboy boots.

Mai Ling's head felt impossibly light, and it swirled as she scrambled out of the trunk. Her legs wobbled with the aftereffects of the drug and being in the cramped space for so long, and she stumbled, falling hard onto the dusty ground at the rear of the car.

The man had already caught his breath and was reaching for Mai Ling by the time she'd hauled herself to her feet using the rim of the trunk for support; he was so close, she could smell the bitter mix of sweat and latex emanating off of him.

In her panic, Mai Ling kicked hard at his balls. Her bare foot connected with the grimy, sagging denim between his legs; the gimp stopped dead in his tracks with an expression of pained surprise in his piggy eyes. But, much to Mai Ling's surprise, he didn't drop to his knees, nor did he grab at his wounded genitals. Instead, anger blazed in those eyes, and he came at her with both fists balled.

Mai Ling ran.

At first, she aimed for the huge ranch house that dominated her line of sight at the end of the dirt driveway, drawn toward the obvious sanctuary it offered. But her racing brain reminded her: hadn't she heard the woman's voice coming from that direction, sounding like it was heading indoors? Mai Ling's instinct told her the woman was more dangerous than the overweight man in the black leather mask lumbering after her—the woman was someone to be truly feared.

Mai Ling's abrupt change of direction mid step confused the man, and in the split second it took him to realize the misdirection, she was racing toward the small row of trees that lay a little beyond the side of the house; the thick cover of the saplings promised safety and freedom, and Mai Ling dared to believe she could possibly escape with her life.

Although it was early morning, the sun low upon the horizon, the hard dirt was hot and gritty and dug into the soft sole of Mai Ling's bare foot as she ran; the fine gravel ground between her toes, her other foot still protected by its plain, black flat shoe.

With the trees mere strides away, Mai Ling ventured a backward glance at the man; she'd created a comfortable gap and thanked her lucky stars he and the woman had relied on drugging her and hadn't tied her up in the trunk. However, the man wasn't about to give up; he clumped along behind her, arms outstretched, his wheezing breath so loud Mai Ling could hear him from yards away.

Mai Ling continued to sprint until she crashed through the tree line; the clinging scrub grabbed at her ankles and knees. A tall shape appeared in front of her, as if from nowhere: It was the woman, clad in shiny black leather, breasts bare, her face obscured by a black, feathered mask.

Before she could stop herself, prevented from swerving to either side by the densely packed trees, Mai Ling ploughed straight into the woman. The woman's hands were strong; her fingers dug deep into Mai Ling's arms, holding her tight. Struggling against the woman's grasp, desperately trying to get a grip on the slippery latex covering her flanks, Mai Ling screamed in her masked face and brought a knee up into her crotch; the hard pubic bone sent a jarring pain through her leg and the grip on Mai Ling's arms loosened just enough for her to pull one free.

Mai Ling punched out at the woman with a fist aimed squarely at her vulnerable breasts; she took satisfaction at the agonized groan as her knuckles sank deep into the soft tissue.

As the woman instinctively let go of her arm to cradle her breast, Mai Ling lashed out with her foot at her unguarded belly; still holding her breast, gasping for breath, the woman staggered back into the trees, her legs giving way as she fell.

It was the chance Mai Ling had been hoping for!

As Mai Ling sidestepped the woman, there came the sound of some- thing heavy crashing through the trees and she felt the all-too familiar sting in her neck.

Chapter Twelve

"Well, your claim checks out." Jayne Torrez eyed the potential new contestant with suspicion and tapped her cheap Parker pen against her too-straight teeth. "Although, these things can never be a hundred percent accurate… and there's surgery nowadays, of course."

Cole cringed at Jayne's blunt accusation; none of the show's contestants deserved to be spoken to in such an awful manner. He wanted to step in, admonish Jayne for being so rude, but instead, he looked on as the young girl, Sarah, sat stock-still in the interview seat and returned Jayne's icy stare.

Jayne had been on *The Gentleman's Choice* team since season three and was practically part of the furniture. Cole had no idea where Skippy had found the woman, and she was far from the producer's usual type. Jayne was a mousey woman Cole guessed to be late twenties/early thirties; she was average height, had straight brunette hair she rarely put any effort into, was just a little too squidgy around the middle and hips, and her boobs lay low and flat against her chest despite being contained within a bra. She had the definite air of a woman who may once have been quite stunning but had let herself go over the years. Cole often wondered what had happened in her life to make her give up so young. Still, Jayne was ruthlessly efficient at her job, and Skippy wasn't likely to sexually harass her out of it.

"I can assure you, I *am* definitely a virgin," Sarah said with a firmness Cole found refreshing.

"You're *twenty-two*." For emphasis, Jayne ran her finger down the paperwork fastened to her clipboard; she tapped her teeth with the pen as she did so.

"It is possible to go through high school and college and keep your virginity intact, you know." Cole saw the corners of Sarah's mouth turn upward—just a hint—as if her statement of fact was a direct jab at Jayne's respectability.

"Are you from a religious family?" Cole interjected. "Catholic, perhaps?"

Shaking her head, Sarah replied, "My parents are not particularly religious, so no. I just wanted to save myself for the right man."

"And *he's* it?" Jayne nodded at Cole and cracked a wide smile. "Hey!" Cole feigned offense with a smile. "I'm literally right in the room, here."

That broke the tension Jayne's accusation had created. Sarah visibly relaxed in her chair and her guard came down. "Look, I've held out for this long—I think I've earned the right to decide how I lose my virginity. Don't you?"

"I think it will be a neat angle for the show," Cole added. He gave Sarah another admiring once-over. She looked incredible in her skinny cut jeans and tank top; he especially loved the way the spaghetti straps dug just a little into her freckled shoulders. Sarah wore spike-heeled pumps that showed off her pedicured toes and the sensual curve of her ankle and, that she was a natural redhead pretty much sealed the deal for Cole. "That's just what Skippy said," Jayne replied with a huff; she wasn't one for being ganged up on, even by the show's creators. "Which was why we ordered the hymen test along with all the usual STD stuff." She prodded a finger at her paperwork and her eyes met Cole's.

"You make it all sound *so* romantic." Cole tipped Sarah a wink. He was already looking forward to getting to know Sarah; she had just the right level of chutzpah he enjoyed in a partner. Virgins were not a type of contestant the show typically attracted, although they'd had some play the part over the years; Cole knew the paying audience would just lap it up. "Look, there are girls selling their virginity to the highest bidder all over the internet," Sarah told Cole and Jayne with a wry smile. "Maybe I've realized Mr. Right isn't coming along, and I'd like to monetize what

I've got while I have the chance."

"While you have the chance?" Jayne was an expert at wheedling out the minutiae from potential contestants; she swore it made them more relatable on the show when personal, often embarrassingly intimate details were divulged.

"Sooner or later, I'll be giving it up." Sarah toyed with a stray strand of her short red hair. "It's not like I'm going to remain chaste for my entire life, is it?"

"That's pretty much a given should you get on the show." Cole knew he really shouldn't make that assumption on the girl's behalf—there was never any guarantee a contestant would make it all the way to Night Five, even a true virgin.

Unless Skippy fiddled the voting figures again, of course. "Exactly," Sarah addressed Cole directly. That appeared to annoy

Jayne, who increased the infernal tapping of the pen on her teeth. "So, I figured I may as well get paid for giving up my virginity. That way I can pay off my student loan and set myself up in business—give myself the good start in life my economics and philosophy degree sure as hell isn't going to provide."

"What kind of business are you thinking of starting?" Jayne wrestled Sarah's attention back from Cole. She positioned her pen on her clipboard just so in readiness to jot down the girl's reply.

"I'll most likely capitalize on the fame I get from being on *The Gentleman's Choice*," Sarah explained. "After all, having a sex tape out there didn't do Kim Kardashian any harm, did it? I can set myself up on *OnlyFans* and sell pictures and videos, maybe even use some of the prize money to set up an exclusive webcam business on the side."

"Impressive," Cole chipped in. For a twenty-two-year-old virgin, Sarah sure had her head screwed on right—the girl was one smart cookie, which he truly admired. Then again, she was just the right amount of pragmatic he would have expected from someone willing to sell her virginity on a live streamed web show. "You seem to have your future mapped out."

"Doesn't everyone?" Sarah's question was genuine.

Cole couldn't help but chuckle at that one—perhaps the girl was sweetly naive after all. He figured most of the show's contestants looked no further beyond pocketing the hundred-grand check and getting drunk, let alone using any of the money to better themselves. But the girls came and went, a constant stream of faces and willing bodies, each one usually as forgettable as the last—there was no way on earth they could be expected to keep up with what any of them did after the show, although Cole would often wonder.

"It's difficult to tell," Jayne threw in. "We don't keep tabs on any of our contestants."

"So, there's no aftercare or counseling?" Sarah appeared surprised; just what she was expecting from *The Gentleman's Choice*, Cole couldn't be sure. If she kept it up, she might just talk herself out of being a contestant and rob the show of one hell of a crowd puller.

"We take good care of all the young ladies who appear on the show." Inwardly, Cole winced at his trite reply. "They are thoroughly vetted and profiled as part of the selection process, plus we get a psych evaluation done ahead of filming." He hoped Sarah wouldn't ask exactly *who* did the evaluations, as Jayne didn't have any formal qualifications of which he was aware; she was incredibly insightful, though, and in Cole's opinion, far more value for money than some two-hundred-dollar-an-hour shrink. "You will also receive coaching prior to the show—providing you make it through the remainder of the selection process, of course." Jayne scribbled down a note.

"Coaching?" Sarah asked Cole. Smart—she plainly knew she was a shoo-in as far as he was concerned, and he could see her confidence had increased exponentially.

"We allocate every contestant with a persona for the show." Jayne took the reins. "Of course, I do my best to keep that as close to your actual personality as possible—but sometimes it pays to enhance certain things to keep the audience engaged."

More scribbled notes.

"And what would you *enhance* about me?"

Cole was even more impressed by the girl. It was not often he got to see an auditionee turn the tables on Jayne like that. Usually they'd sit there, frightened, and simper through the answers they'd preprepared for the interview. If contestants were selected based on personality alone, *The Gentleman's Choice* would be Cole going on dates all by himself. As it was, Jayne was most adept at picking out those who were vacuous and malleable enough to adopt whatever persona she handed to them, and if they had a banging body and supermodel looks, all the better.

As for Sarah, she was the rarity of the bunch: smarts, looks, body, and a genuine virgin on top of all that—just spending that hour with her had helped Cole on his way to getting over Mai Ling's disappointing departure from the show.

"I think I'd cast you as a swooning pushover who is desperate for Cole to initiate her into the world of sex," Jayne said without a hint of irony. "Is that how you see me?" Sarah's jaw dropped. "As some desperate little girl plagued by her own virginity, who needs the sexual affirmation only Cole Gianni can provide?"

Cole recoiled. Was that really how people saw him?

"Not particularly," Jayne said. "But it's how our *audience* will want to see you—it's your basic innocent-turned-harlot Harlequin novel fantasy, and we sell fantasies on *The Gentleman's Choice*, Sarah—have you not watched the show?"

Cole couldn't be sure if Jayne was impressed by Sarah's diatribe or if the wannabe had genuinely rattled her cage; either way, their exchange made for compelling viewing.

"I saw a few episodes to acquaint myself with the format." Sarah quit twiddling with her hair and looked Jayne directly in the face. "I'll be happy to go along with whatever you think is best, Jayne. I wouldn't have agreed to your invasive testing if I wasn't."

It saddened Cole to think there had been a time a girl's declaration of her own virginity would have been more than enough. But, in the modern, much more cynical age, medical intervention was evidently required, and it really was unpleasantly thorough.

What a sorry state of affairs.

"That's what we like to hear, Sarah," Jayne patronized. "I think you'll be a good fit for the show. What about you, Cole?"

"What?" Cole's mind had been elsewhere, and Jayne's question had caught him by surprise. He'd been planning Sarah's dates and making a mental note of which scenes he ought to recommend to Skippy; he thought a three-way night might suit the girl well.

"I asked what you thought of Sarah for the next show." Jayne did nothing to hide her impatience; she was back to tapping her teeth with the goddamn pen again.

"O-Oh," Cole sputtered. "I think you'll do just fine, Sarah—I can see us getting along famously." He offered the girl a warm smile, which she quickly returned.

With Sarah's participation *in the bag*, as Skippy would have put it, Cole made his excuses and left Jayne to finish off the interview. Since Cole made it his business to sit in on as much of the selection process as time allowed, he knew the drill by heart: Jayne would finish up grilling Sarah for more personal information, which she would then filter out for use either when Sarah was introduced on the show or for her to reveal over the course of the five nights. Then, she'd be packed off for a final brief interview with Skippy.

Cole was delighted Sarah was his next match, and he didn't want *all* the surprises to be spoiled.

"It's been good to get to know you a little, Sarah," Cole said as he made his way from the interview room. "I'm looking forward to having you on the show."

"Likewise, Cole," Sarah replied. "We really are going to get along famously."

"So, Sarah," Jayne interjected. "Just how *close* have you come to losing your virginity?"

Cole pulled open the door to the studio and wandered across to where one of Jayne's assistants was busy conducting the preliminary screening for six new girls vying for a place on the show.

The show always did the prelim auditions in batches of six—it was a typical Skippy dictate that had no rhyme nor reason behind it; he wanted a half-dozen girls at a time, and that's all there was to it. They held the auditions on a weekly basis, which guaranteed a constant rotation of hot young things just itching to get their pretty faces—and everything that went along with them—on the show.

The general idea was to make sure they looked as hot as they did in the photographs and self-shot video clips they'd sent in with their applications. It surprised Cole how many young women were skilled with Photoshop but didn't realize how quickly their deception would be uncovered once they got to the studio. Skippy also ran the auditions as an exercise in making sure the young ladies had more than two brain cells to rub together and to find out how comfortable they were in various stages of undress in front of the camera, which, in this case, was manned by a cameraman Cole recognized from the orgy the night before. Cole nodded his acknowledgement as he sauntered by and was met with a distracted grunt.

The girls had all dressed to impress, and, with it being Texas, each one had turned up wearing a midriff-bearing crop top; tight, butt-revealing cut-off shorts; and cowboy boots. For Cole, nothing said *Texas Gal* more than Daisy Dukes and cowboy boots.

Cole immediately recognized two of the girls. They had already been "pre-vetted" by Skippy—one was a petite Vietnamese, the other a slightly plump mixed race—which had invariably meant an exchange of sexual favors for the promise of an audition. Skippy had never even attempted to make it a secret he used the show to coerce gullible young women into giving him the sex he seemed to constantly crave. Cole would often bump into the producer's conquests on their way into and out of his office. And, if the girls just didn't happen to have what it took to make it through Jayne's rigorous selection process, Skippy was happy in the knowledge there was no one for them to complain to.

Two of the young girls were already stripped down to bras and panties and were entwined in a passionate kiss in front of the camera. Out of shot, a pretty blonde with long, tanned legs and high, overflowing breasts was telling the assistant all about the porn movies she'd made with her ex-boyfriend to sell online. Cole pondered if it might be a neat idea to hook that one up with Sarah—they could have a chance of making something lucrative out of her idea. She also went on to list the other reality shows she'd been on, which included *Survivor*, *Love Island*, and *The Bachelor*; she'd also auditioned for *Big Brother* and won a few prizes on *The Price Is Right*—the girl was a serial contestant; the industry was filled with them. Cole committed the girl to memory and promised himself he'd be sure to mention her to Jayne—he reckoned he could have a lot of fun with a livewire like her.

Sarah's prelim had been so long ago, Cole hadn't recognized her when she came in for the final interview; callbacks were sometimes months after the initial screenings. She hadn't stood out among her giddy, giggling compatriots on the day, but there was something about the redhead Cole found alluring. *Maybe*, he thought, *it's because she's clearly smart and has aspirations to exploit the hell out of her time on the show to improve her lot in life.*

And that was something Cole truly admired.

As for Cole's aspirations—they had withered on the vine a long time ago and had certainly never been to perform as in-house stud for some seedy web show.

It had been ten years and change since Cole Gianni had arrived in America with the intention of becoming a huge Hollywood star—the next Pitt, Clooney, Bale, DiCaprio—Cole really didn't care which niche they slotted him into because he knew he had the movie star looks and acting talent that would put him on a trajectory toward stardom.

After only a few weeks of bussing tables and handing out his resume to every studio, agent, and manager in Tinseltown, Cole had landed a bunch of small parts—mostly commercials and extra's work in daytime soaps he'd never heard of before. Then, through a friend of a director on one of the soaps, Cole had been invited to audition for a small part in an independent action movie—they had Eric Roberts attached to the project, and it actually made a modest return on its miniscule budget.

The director of that movie had introduced Cole to the producer attached to one of the smaller studios in Hollywood, who had done his damndest to get Cole into bed with wild promises of bigtime movie roles alongside Jennifer Lawrence, Chris Pratt, Johnny Depp, Matthew McConaughey, and other A-listers. But, way back then, Cole reckoned he was too good to have to fuck his way to the top, even if it did offer a shortcut.

Considering the direction in which Cole's career had actually gone, the irony of that stance wasn't entirely lost on him.

Sadly, Cole's promising future as an actor had gone south the way of so many others in the business—at the hands of a beautiful woman.

Her name was Janina De Leon and, at the tender age of eighteen, she was hailed as the next Penélope Cruz or

Salma Hayek. She was also the most stunning girl Cole had ever met.

Cole had been introduced to Janina at the action movie's wrap party; plans were being made to bring her in for the sequel, and she was to work alongside the rising star that was Cole Gianni. The sequel was never made, as things turned out, but it marked the beginning of the tumultuous relationship between Cole and the fiery Latino beauty as, for the first time in his young life, Cole knew he had fallen hook, line, and sinker in love.

What he wasn't to know, what he had no way of learning until it was much too late, was Janina was selfishly piggybacking on his rising star, while at the same time spreading her legs on practically every casting couch in Los Angeles.

As with most matters of infidelity, Cole was very much the last one to find out, and when he did, Janina made no attempt to even begin to lie her way out of it.

"You know how this game goes," she'd told him with a grin far too cynical for her age. "If we're gonna make it big, we have to use what we've got."

"Including *me*?" Cole's heart had broken at the precise moment she'd refused to deny any of the rumors.

"I've got *this*." She'd wiggled her tits at Cole and cupped her crotch in one hand—Janina could be one mean drunk when she put her mind to it—and she'd laughed in his face. "You've got whatever it is you've got, and between the two of us, Janina De Leon is gonna be a huge star!" The cheating to further her career, Cole could understand; using his status to promote herself, he could admire that... almost. But to laugh in his face like he was some poor dumb schmuck unaware he was married to the town whore had been more than Cole could stand.

So, in a momentary lapse, he'd slapped her.

That one, solitary action—which he'd regretted even before the red imprint of his hand appeared on Janina's smooth, olive-skinned cheek— finished Cole's burgeoning career as surely as if he'd committed murder. It being LA, she'd lawyered up within hours, and before Cole knew what was happening, he was paraded into court like some wife-beating thug. All the while, movie contracts and lucrative sponsorship deals evaporated around him like dew on a Texas summer's morning. For her part, the ever-toxic Janina played the poor, brutalized victim to perfection. Give the gal her due—she really was one hell of an actress.

When it was all over, Cole had sought solace in booze and cocaine, and eventually—inevitably—drifted into the porn industry. At least there, nobody cared too much that he'd been labeled a woman-hater; as long as he looked pretty and his dick worked when it was supposed to, he was all good. They didn't even bother changing his name, as Cole's level of notoriety helped boost downloads of their cheesy skin flicks.

There's no such thing as bad publicity, or so the saying went.

While Cole struggled along back at the very bottom of the Hollywood pool, Janina used the highly publicized court case as a springboard into the town's A-list. She snagged work with Rodriguez, Tarantino, even JJ Abrams, and went on to become the big name she'd always told Cole she was going to be. She married some billionaire hedge-fund manager twice her age and never failed to look stunning on his arm at all the right functions; she was fucking around on him, of course, and the world knew it— but the old boy didn't give a shit because he had *the* Janina De Leon in his bed on the nights she wasn't in somebody else's.

All through the lies and humiliation, Cole still loved Janina with all his heart, and knew a part of him always would.

Cole had been at his lowest ebb when Mason "Skippy" Webman had blustered into his life. Between them, they'd concocted their adult version of all the god-awful reality shows that plagued the networks with faked titillation and empty-headed, plastic young people.

Although Cole often rued the day he'd allowed Skippy to manipulate him into doing *The Gentleman's Choice*, he reckoned he ought to be more grateful. Had it not been for the porn producer and the show, Cole had an inkling he'd have drunk himself to death or wound up living in the vast network of drainage tunnels beneath the city. He'd visited the tunnels as research for a role that had subsequently been pulled out from under him but had found the sprawling underground communities dwelling there as fascinating as they were tragic.

The Gentleman's Choice had saved Cole from all of that, but it had since grown to become the albatross around his neck; the longer he remained seducing hopeful young contestants week after week, the lesser his chances of returning to Hollywood to rebuild his mainstream career. The town was notoriously forgiving, especially for the bad boys everyone loved to hate, and Cole was confident he could easily find a new niche, even if it was playing villains instead of the love interest.

Chapter Thirteen

"… **a**nd this week's lucky contestant is Sarah. Sarah hails from Wisconsin but says her heart will always belong to San Antonio. Sexy Sarah is twenty-two, a college graduate with majors in philosophy and social history, whose interests include photography, animals, travel, good food, and lively conversation. Believe it or not, Sarah is a genuine, verified virgin with sweet, old-fashioned values. She's has been saving herself for Mr. Right and is confident Cole will prove to be just the perfect match as they get to know each other over their next five nights together on… *The Gentleman's Choice*."

Cole listened, cringing inwardly to his own voice as the show's prerecorded introduction played on the tech girl's slim silver laptop; the unmistakable timbre and his fake accent filled the restaurant. Once again, Skippy's words in his mouth had succeeded in making Cole feel awkward, even though he thought he actually sounded good with the audio cleaned up.

Just what was Skippy thinking by the term *verified virgin*? Cole doubted the producer could have made Sarah's condition sound any more clinical if he'd tried, but he was nonetheless obliged to read exactly what was in the script no matter how dumb he thought it to be. Cole cursed Skippy again for insisting they play the cheesy intro bit at the show's beginning on set before the cameras began rolling—not that the producer would be listening to it in his production booth back at the studio; Cole knew Skippy never had more than a perfunctory interest in the show's First Night, as it was all far too innocent for his liking. At best, he'd have one eye on the show just in case of any technical difficulties and the other on *Pornhub* seeking *inspiration for future shows*—as Skippy was wont to justify his penchant for pornography.

"And… cue Cole!" Jayne's voice snapped him out of his woolgathering, and in a heartbeat, Cole was back in the room and on point.

"I can't believe you've never had Indian food before," Cole said to Sarah with a friendly smile. "I think you're really going to love it."

Sarah leaned forward in her chair to dip a fragment of spicy poppadom into the sweet pickle dish that sat in the center of the small, cozy table; Cole caught a tantalizing hint of cleavage as she did so and was pleased that, for once, the wardrobe girls hadn't dressed up a contestant to look like a cheap street walker. It was all part of maintaining Sarah's chaste, unsullied-by-men persona, of course. Even for an adult-themed show, it paid to emphasize the point the girl was a virgin and dress her accordingly. For their first night's date, Sarah wore a classically simple little black dress that sat just above the knee and was tastefully scooped at the front to give a hint of what was to come. The dress was tight, of course, to accentuate Sarah's naturally curvy body and long, bare legs and, instead of the vertiginous stripper shoes Cole's dates were typically made to wear, was accompanied by preppy, patent leather Mary Janes with modest heels. "I'm entirely in your experienced hands, Cole; I'm a complete novice at this. My family are surprisingly conservative when it comes to food; spaghetti was considered exotic when I was growing up."

Cole was impressed: Sarah delivered her stilted, scripted line without a trace of irony, and even managed a light, realistic laugh at the end.

Skippy's far less than subtle hint at Sarah's virginity had come across as clumsy at best to him, although he doubted anyone watching would have picked up on that. Then, to hammer home the point for the show's viewers who might not be so quick at picking up nuances, Sarah was obliged to deliver her next line; "I'm a complete novice at a few other things, too—you will be my very first time, Cole."

Taking his cue, Cole reached across the table and took Sarah's hand in his; her skin felt cool and dry. If the girl was nervous, she sure as hell wasn't showing any signs of it.

"I promise I'll be gentle with you, Sarah." He smiled at her to show he was delivering a well-worn cliché, and he just knew the show's less than discerning audience would be lapping it all up. "I want you to know you'll always be able to trust me."

It was a sweet, cozy scene—even considering the fact the entire setup was bogus and Sarah and Cole were joined on their date by the camerawoman, tech/sound girl, and Jayne Torrez, who sat on the sidelines like some overprotective mother hen ready to advise on suitable topics should the conversation lull. It wasn't often Jayne was on set for anything other than the show's Fifth Night, and Cole found her presence oddly unsettling; perhaps she thought Sarah would struggle with her lines or would require additional coaching from the sidelines to appear a tad less wooden. Or, maybe Jayne had Sarah pegged as a potential troublemaker who might be apt to go off script and would require reining in.

The show had taken over a function room at the rear of one of Houston's famous downtown Indian eateries and populated it with fake diners. It was an establishment they'd used many times in the past, and the management seemed to enjoy the notoriety their association with *The Gentleman's Choice* brought with it; there was no doubting business had thrived because of it, more so after Skippy caved into the Patels' suggestion to shoot a Fifth Night orgy in the back room.

For the purposes of the show, they'd picked out a bunch of good-looking young couples with which to "decorate the set," as Skippy referred to it. The couples, all local, were more than delighted to get a top-quality free meal and fifty bucks between them for their time. They were aspiring actors recruited from the Houston independent movie scene and were all desperate to get their gorgeous young faces on screen and a line on their resume, even if it was as an extra for a porn dating show.

Cole understood it made a great deal of sense to shoot in a controlled environment. It went a long way toward reducing the element of the unknown that would invariably come along with any group of people. Back in the early days of the show, before they'd learned any better and had any kind of budget to pay for set dressing, they'd had arguments break out between couples, a drunk guy throw up in the background of an Italian dinner, and even one woman who went into very loud labor midway through the supposedly romantic meal; that really had put a damper on the whole scene for Cole and his date.

As per Skippy's expert direction, the camera had panned in on Cole and Sarah after giving the audience a look at their fellow hot young diners, as if it was catching them at the beginning of their date. The producer maintained nobody wanted to hear the boring preamble of them ordering food and drinks, which was something he and Cole agreed upon; he was all for allowing the viewers to fill in that particular blank for themselves. The tech girl, there to ensure everything ran smoothly via her array of laptops and expensive sound equipment, had strategically messed up the pristine plates of poppadom and pickles in order to give the appearance that Cole and Sarah's date was well underway. Sarah hadn't actually eaten any, as she claimed to be on a strict diet to get herself back down to the 108 pounds she'd been when she left high school at the behest of her girlfriend. She'd also declared, somewhat too loudly, that spicy Indian food would only serve to irritate her IBS, and nobody in the restaurant would want that.

"So," Cole retrieved his hand from Sarah's so he could eat; it was time to make with the romantic chit-chat before the entrees arrived. "Tell me all about *you*, Sarah."

"Oh, I'm really not all *that* interesting," Sarah replied with a flirtatious laugh and coy flick of the head.

"I wouldn't say that—you have a philosophy degree," Cole countered. "I find that really fascinating." He'd read through Jayne's comprehensive notes on Sarah and was well aware his date's qualifications were actually in the physical sciences; Jayne had considered that to be just a little too nerdy and potentially off-putting for their audience demographic, so she made the change to Sarah's script accordingly. Cole's line was, of course, little more than a catalyst to get the two talking, although not about philosophy, a subject in which neither of them had much knowledge.

"I can promise you, it really is not all that interesting." With all the skill of a seasoned actress, Sarah steered Cole away from the subject. "I much prefer animals—horses are my all-time favorite."

"Ahh… mine too." Cole smiled through his scripted, obvious line. "I've had a great love of all things equestrian for my entire life."

"I know. I saw you on last week's show—you handle horses exceptionally well, Cole."

Cole was genuinely flattered. "I grew up around horses—my family always had them when I was a child, and I learned to ride almost before I could walk." Dark memories of his family crept into Cole's mind.

He pushed them aside.

"You were so lucky to grow up with all that." Sarah smiled. "Like most little girls, all I ever wanted as a kid was my very own pony."

"I get that. What little girl doesn't desire her own horse? Or little boy, for that matter." Cole nibbled on a sliver of poppadom and watched with intent as Sarah fiddled absently with the neckline of her dress. She was subconsciously drawing attention to her breasts as she did so, and Cole's experience told him there was definitely some chemistry brewing between him and the beautiful redheaded girl.

"Where was it?" Sarah made eye contact, and for a moment, it was as if the camera wasn't scrutinizing her every word.

"Where was what?"

"Where you grew up?" Sarah replied.

"It was Europe." Cole felt the slightest twinge of panic. The girl had gone off script—often it happened when a contestant forgot what Skippy had penned for them to say, even though he always did his best to keep things nice and simple, but Sarah was straying into dangerous territory as far as Cole was concerned.

"Yeah, I understand that much, but what *part* of Europe?" Sarah pressed.

Studying his date's face, Cole considered the fact that perhaps she knew more about him than she was supposed to; was it possible she had links to the past he'd gone to so much trouble to bury and was about to reveal his darkest secrets live to thousands of people on the internet?

In his peripheral vision, Cole could see Jayne, who was visibly agitated at Sarah's deviation. With one hand, she crumpled up the flimsy script, and with the other she waved over her head to catch the attention of the wait staff. All the while, she stared across at Sarah as if a simple, glaring look could get the girl back on script; if this was something Jayne had predicted Sarah might have done, her presence really wasn't helping.

"Oh, it is a tiny country in the very eastern corner of Europe," Cole lied and desperately wracked his brain for a way to switch the conversation. "It's one of the obscure -*stans* no one in America has ever even heard of." Cole gave Sarah a light, dismissive laugh, which he hoped would put a stop to her questions.

It did not.

"Actually, *I* may have heard of it… I traveled through a lot of Eastern Europe in my summer vacation after high school—it was just me and a couple of school friends. We had an awesome time around all of those creepy old castles and tiny villages—it was like visiting a real-life Count Dracula movie." Sarah smiled fondly at her own memories. "So, which of the -*stans* did Cole Gianni grow up in? If I was to guess, with that surname, I'd say it was unlikely to be Uzbekistan or Kazakhstan."

As Cole struggled to concoct an answer on the fly that wouldn't expose him as a complete and utter fraud, the wait staff materialized as if out of nowhere; they brought with them the sumptuous entrees that had been ordered for

Cole and Sarah before the cameras began rolling. Cole glanced across at Jayne and gave her a wordless *thank you* for being on the ball enough to orchestrate the obvious distraction. The array of aromatic food became the main topic of conversation, and Cole took the opportunity to steer things away from Eastern Europe and distant countries he'd never as much as set foot in, let alone could even begin to call home. "This is the vegetable korma for the lady," the waiter explained as he carefully placed a steaming bowl of pale brown curry in front of Sarah; it was a stipulation by the Patels that the food get a mention on the show. "I hope it's okay with you, Sarah, but I ordered that for you because it's less spicy than the lamb roghan ghosht, and certainly nowhere near as hot as the vindaloo." Cole nodded to his own steaming dish. "Feel free to try some of mine; you might just like it. I'd recommend dipping your Peshwari naan in to taste—the sweetness of the bread makes for a delicious contrast with the spices."

Sarah appeared suitably impressed at Cole's culinary knowledge and looked at him as if he were, indeed, an experienced man of the world. "You weren't kidding when you said you'd guide me through anything new," she said with the hint of salacious tone.

Cole hid his sigh at Skippy's line well. At least Sarah was back on track, the conversation suitably trite, and the all-too-obvious double-entendre was back in play.

"I can assure you, Sarah—I never kid around when it comes to food… or *love*, for that matter." Cole heard himself saying it and all but cringed as the words tumbled from his lips.

Sarah reached out for Cole's hand, gave it a fond squeeze, and gazed into his eyes just as Jayne had instructed. "Thank you, Cole. You know, I honestly believe we are going to be very good together—I'm already feeling a wonderful connection between us."

Cole allowed himself to relax; the date was under control, and he was happy to put Sarah's off-script moment down to her nerves and forgetting her lines. He could concentrate on the superlative food and seducing the beautiful girl just as he had so many before her.

Chapter Fourteen

"Hey! She says she can already feel a connection between them!" John Beechwood called across to Amy.

"On the first night?" Amy replied. She stood facing the long mirror above the twin his-n-hers sinks with one short, slim leg perched up on the countertop as she deftly inserted her diaphragm. "I hope she knows what she's doing saying that so early on—you know how Cole doesn't like the clingy ones."

"Yeah, right. But Sarah's a special one, remember?"

"Maybe he'll make a special allowance for a virgin?"

John tore his attention away from the sixty-five-inch 4K flat-screen TV fixed to the wall opposite the bed and studied his girlfriend through the door she'd left wide open. Fresh from the shower, Amy was towel-dried and completely nude, her copper-red hair still dripping wet and plastered to her scalp. She'd trimmed her pubes neat and short, just how John liked them, and had slathered her body head to toe in some weird lotion she always brought along for her alternate weekend visits—it gave Amy an exotic scent of coconut and jasmine oil, which John thought made his girl all the more sexy.

John longed for the times when she'd insist on keeping the bathroom door shut. Amy would say it was necessary in order to maintain an *air of mystique* between them. And, more often than not, she would emerge from the bathroom dressed up for him in alluring lingerie or sexy role-play outfits—every one of them guaranteed to fire up John's passions.

But after over two years together, Amy and John had lapsed into being comfortable around one another, and John couldn't help but think the lack of secrets between them was perhaps what had caused the recent lull in their sex life.

He'd meant to explain to Amy again how desperately he ached for the nights where she donned sexy, exotic, slutty outfits; unwrapping the gift was the best part of foreplay. Suzanne Johnson, the long-lost love of John's younger years, had never once gotten into their bed naked. She'd worn everything for him, from silky lace to shiny latex, and the sex had been dynamite.

Like so many men in so many couples, John didn't dare say anything to Amy. Although, drunk, he'd mentioned it the one time before, and Amy had gotten all offended— she'd accused him of being a misogynist who was objectifying her and only wanted to *make love to the outfits*, or some other bullshit she'd read about in *Cosmopolitan*. John was well aware that, at forty-five and a humble claims adjuster for an Orlando insurance company, he was punching way above his weight class with Amy Woodburn, a petite firecracker ten years his junior. He really didn't want to run the risk of upsetting the woman whose opening gambit when they'd first met was she'd fuck absolutely anywhere—*even outside*.

It wasn't as if sex with Amy was entirely boring, even if it was without all the trimmings John craved. She was a more than willing accomplice between the sheets and at first, had been more than happy to try absolutely anything he asked of her. Since they'd begun watching *The Gentleman's Choice* together, things had been looking up a little in that respect, but John wished he'd not been quite so reticent in introducing her to the show in the first place.

On his alternate Saturday nights with Amy, John thanked the gods for Cole Gianni and his parade of eager lovelies for the inspiration they provided.

"I wonder if she'll bleed when they finally get down to it," John wondered out loud, his attention once more on the flat-screen that lit up the bed.

"I'd doubt it," Amy replied. Diaphragm duly inserted and all ready for action, she rinsed her hands off beneath the faucet and dabbed them dry on a beige hand towel before padding over to John's bed. "Even if Sarah's genuinely for real, she's most likely used tampons—and didn't she say she loved horses?"

"So, you *were* listening?" John teased. "I thought you said the first-night dates were always boring."

Amy smiled and climbed onto the bed; the sweet scent of her moisturized body tantalized John's senses as she sprawled out nude on the bedspread, her breasts pointing at the ceiling fan. "Just because I find the lack of action dull, it doesn't mean I don't take an interest in the contestants," she told him. "The more relatable they are, the more they turn me on when they get to do stuff with Cole."

"Do *stuff*?" John laughed; Amy's euphemisms for sex had always amused him, especially since she was a big fan of dirty talk once he got her in the right mood.

"Yeah, *stuff.*" Amy rolled onto her front and propped her chin up with both hands. Kicking her sexy size five feet up behind her, Amy presented John with a coquettish, Lolita-style pose that couldn't possibly fail to catch his attention.

"You want to do *stuff* with me?" John eyed Amy's bare butt, which he'd always considered perfect.

"Do *you*?"

"I always want to do stuff with you." Leaning forward, John kissed Amy. Immediately, he felt the soft touch of her warm tongue across his lips, and as he responded in kind, he buried his hand in the dampness of her hair to pull her closer.

Amy pulled away.

"What's wrong, baby?" John was puzzled. He knew sex was very much in the cards; otherwise, why the hell would Amy have just gone to all the trouble with the birth control? "Did I do something wrong?"

"Not at all," Amy purred. "I just thought, perhaps we could play a little."

John sat himself back against the stack of pillows he'd carefully arranged for an evening of TV viewing; on the screen, Cole and Sarah went about their innocent dinner date as Sarah told him—and the viewers at home—all about herself and her aspirations for the future. John didn't think she looked much like a businesswoman no matter how smart she sounded.

"There's no need to look quite so terrified, John," Amy said. "Unless you're only in for a quick, five-minute missionary and then sleep?"

John shook his head. Had Amy finally picked up on his signals and was willing to do something about spicing things up? "Did you have something in mind?"

Twisting her head, Amy eyed the TV, where Cole regaled Sarah with tales of his childhood in some obscure corner of Europe he appeared to be a little evasive about. "Do you remember the episode we watched a couple months back?"

"You're gonna have to be a bit more specific." John tipped Amy a wink—they watched the show together from their respective homes almost every night when they were apart and tuned in every bedtime when Amy visited.

Amy flipped herself around and play slapped John's thigh; she left a small, red handprint there. "I was getting to that part!" The coyness in Amy's voice hinted to John she was a tad shy at suggesting they act out something from *The Gentleman's Choice*—they'd fantasized about so many of the sexy scenarios they'd watched together but hadn't gotten around to acting upon those fantasies.

"The one where Cole was the cat burglar." Amy returned her attention to the TV as if she was too shy to look at her lover.

John found it weirdly exciting to see Amy being so bashful—she couldn't even look him in the face to make her sexy suggestion. Perhaps she had also been too nervous to propose they try anything out of the ordinary in bed? "The erotic asphyxiation episode?"

Amy nodded. "That whole episode was *so* hot—didn't you think so?" They'd watched the show from their respective beds, as it had been midweek. Listening to Amy masturbating as Cole role-played the part of a sadistic burglar had been so intense, and Amy's orgasm so long and loud, John had thought she'd faked it. "Okay… so, which part do you want us to do?"

"*All* of it."

"You mean—?"

"Yup," Amy replied with a salacious smile; she turned back around to face him, wanton lust in her eyes. "I want the whole nine yards, John. I want you to do all of it."

It wasn't that John had an issue with play strangling Amy—they'd touched upon that fantasy way back in their early days, although they'd never done anything too heavy on account of her not wanting her twelve-year-old daughter to see bruises around her neck when she returned home. If Amy wanted to emulate what they'd seen on the show, it would appear that was no longer a problem.

"*All* of it?" John repeated. "You *really* want me to strangle you?"

Amy furrowed her brow. "No. I want a mysterious, sexy burglar to break in and wake me up with his strong, murderous hands around my neck…"

The familiar stirrings of arousal kicked in. John felt his dick stiffen beneath the bed sheets. "Yeah, I can do that. You want to get into bed now?"

Amy huffed. "No, John. I said I want us to do *all* of it—just like they did on the show."

"You mean, you want me dressed up like a stupid ninja?"

"You have black pants and shirt—and I bought you a ski mask off Amazon." Amy bit down on her lower lip; it was her tell that she was getting horny. "I laid them all out in the garage for you while you were showering."

John was taken aback. After over a year of having lapsed into the boring, safe realm of vanilla sex, Amy was taking the initiative and showing her adventurous side again—and he had *The Gentleman's Choice* to thank for it. "I guess I could…"

"So, what are you waiting for?" Amy slapped John's thigh again— hard—for emphasis. "You wouldn't want me to lose interest in the idea while you hem and haw over it, would you?"

John shook his head no. "Are *you* going to wear something for me?" If ever there was a right moment to raise the subject, it had definitely come. For a fleeting moment, John thought he'd blown it. A glimmer of frustration crossed Amy's round, pretty face. "Are you seriously bringing *this* up right now, John?"

"I'm sorry… I didn't mean…"

"I'm sure you didn't." Amy replied curtly. "What I mean is, how the hell would a sadistic cat burglar know *what* I was wearing until he broke in?"

Relieved, John scrambled out of bed before he did something to spoil the mood—what did it really matter if Amy was naked or not for their little game? After all, she'd just invited him to strangle her to the point of unconsciousness while they fucked, which was kind of a big deal.

Without another word, John made his way from the bedroom and left Amy to watch Cole eat fancy food and make small talk with the delectable Sarah.

It was hot and humid in the garage, and although he wore only boxer briefs, John felt immediately uncomfortable; it would be best to get himself dressed up quickly before he began sweating too much.

As promised, Amy had laid out John's pants, shirt, and a brand-new ski mask—an expensive one with neat, white embroidery around the eye and mouth holes—upon the hood of the car. She'd thrown in a pair of black leather gloves to complete the illusion.

John also noticed Amy had put together a small canvas bag of tools and rope—his burglar's housebreaking kit; she really had thought of everything. The only thing Amy had missed out from John's fantasy ensemble was footwear; but then again, Cole Gianni had been barefoot when he'd acted out the scene on the show.

Making his way back to the bedroom, John felt a little foolish when he caught a glimpse of himself in the hallway mirror; he looked more like a plump shadow than a sleek ninja. Even so, his heart quickened when, gently, he eased open the bedroom door and saw Amy snuggled beneath the sheets pretending to be asleep.

Slowly, moving silently on bare feet, John crept into the room. Amy had switched off the TV, and all was quiet; the only light was the flickering glow from a solitary candle on the dresser.

Standing by the side of the bed, John contemplated Amy's small, still body, and the way the comforter rose and fell with each breath—she was playing at being asleep so convincingly, he began to wonder if she'd nodded off waiting for him to return from the garage.

The thought spurred John on all the more—that Amy might genuinely be asleep and, in her first moments of wakefulness, think her attacker was for real made him throb with anticipation.

Placing the little bag of tools down by the side of the bed, John pulled the covers off Amy's body. He was thrilled to see she had put on a sheer, pink shortie nightie and miniscule matching panties; the flimsy material left her legs wonderfully naked and accentuated her body to perfection.

John leaned over the bed and clamped a hand over Amy's mouth. Her eyes opened.

"Not one fucking word, bitch," he snarled inches from Amy's face. "If you know what's good for you, you're gonna do exactly what I tell you—do you understand?"

Frozen in place, eyes wide, Amy nodded beneath John's hand. Her breath was warm and moist against his palm, her breasts quivered beneath the see-through material of her nightie; their rosebud nipples were already stiff with arousal.

"I'm gonna take my hand away now." John adopted his best menacing voice—impersonations weren't really his thing, but he recalled how well Cole had played the intimidating attacker and did his best to emulate that. "Make one fucking sound, and I'll fucking end you."

Was that genuine fear in Amy's eyes, or was she a better actress than John had given her credit for?

John took his hand away from Amy's mouth and grabbed hold of her bare shoulder. Flipping her over onto her stomach, he grabbed her wrists—Amy wasn't the only one who'd memorized the show's cat burglar episode.

Clambering up onto the bed, John straddled Amy's body with his powerful legs either side of her hips. He clasped both of her slender wrists in one hand and reached down to fish out the rough hemp rope Amy had secreted in the tool bag. He then bound her hands together behind her back, pulling the rope so tight Amy grunted out loud in pain.

"I told you, no noise, *bitch*!" John lifted up Amy's inadequate nightie, pulled her panties to one side, and delivered a hard, resounding slap to her ass. Amy squirmed and bucked a little as her cheek turned red, but she remained silent as instructed.

Satisfied there was no way Amy was going to wriggle out of the knots he'd tied, John rolled her back over. He remained straddling her hips—the heat of her body and the view of her breasts and hardened nipples served to further arouse him.

"You're enjoying this, aren't you, you dirty girl?" John growled and pawed at Amy's body, enjoying the feel of her pliant flesh through the thin leather of his gloves.

"You… you're the cat burglar who was on the local news?" Amy ignored John's command she keep quiet—all part of playing the game.

John leered down at Amy, his eyes crawling over her body like he was some voyeuristic pervert seeing her exposed for the very first time. "Yeah—one and the same— but right now, all I'm gonna take is you, *bitch*."

"Please no… don't hurt me."

John slapped Amy so hard across the face her head snapped to the side. "Shut the fuck up, *whore*! You know you want this."

"*Please*!" Amy was acting her part well; John was immersed in the scenario and *believed* she was terrified of him—that she couldn't see his face had a dehumanizing effect, which reduced him to nothing more than a dangerous stranger who could very well hurt her—and that was all part of their game.

John slapped her again, exacerbating the red handprint on her cheek created by his previous strike. "What the fuck did I tell you, *slut*?" He snarled in a menacing voice. "I'm going to take whatever the fuck I want to take, and there's nothing you can do to stop me. I'm gonna start with these…" John shuffled himself a little ways down Amy's hips, hiked up the flimsy nightie all the way to her pierced belly button, and hooked his fingers under the thin waistband of the tiny panties. With a grunt, John then gave them a good, hard yank—just like he'd seen on the movies—and was surprised when they didn't simply tear away in his hand.

Amy gasped as the unyielding elastic bit deep into the soft, sensitive flesh of her hips. But, true to character, she didn't utter a single word.

John winced as he saw the angry red welt appear on Amy's pale skin; he fought hard to stop himself saying sorry—to have done so would have ruined the illusion and likely put an end to their game. Instead, he maneuvered himself off Amy's body and yanked the panties down her legs in one rough motion; he took a moment or two to savor her exposed sex before positioning himself between her spread legs.

"Please, sir, no…" Amy begged.

"*Shut up, bitch,*" John snapped and forced the panties into Amy's open mouth; judging by the soft moan she made, she appeared to like that—John made a mental note for the future. Lowering himself close to hear ear, his body pressed against hers, John whispered as he undid his belt and unzipped his pants, "You're *mine* now, *whore.*"

And then John was inside her; the singular motion so swift and decisive it elicited a gasp from Amy he'd never heard before; an intense, sensual combination of pleasure and surprise.

It was strange for John to not have the touch of Amy's soft hands and busy fingers on his body as he screwed her—they remained tied together behind her back, which gave her an air of vulnerability he found intoxicating. What he and Amy were doing was more about control than lovemaking, and that was essential for the next part of their game.

On the show, Cole had whipped the belt from his pants in one deft action, which John and Amy had speculated at the time was most likely the result of several takes to perfect. As it was, it took John some tugging and wiggling to release his leather belt from the tight loops around his waist—he had to support himself with one hand on Amy's chest while he did so, which constricted her breathing a little and brought a flush of red to her already glowing cheeks.

Amy spit out the panties, bucked her hips to meet her lover's thrusts, and grunted, "Go on, you bastard, fucking choke me if you dare." She'd remembered the lines from the show word-perfect.

John experienced only a second or two of hesitation before he wrapped the belt around Amy's neck and secured it through the buckle. He remembered from the show all he needed to do was pull on the end and the leather would tighten around Amy's throat to cut off blood flow to her brain and air to her lungs. It should have concerned him that neither of them had done any kind of breath-control play before, and they should have begun with just his hands around her throat. But in the throes of passion and the desire to re-create the show's hot, sexy scene, it was nothing more than a fleeting thought; John pushed it to the back of his mind.

Pulling hard on the belt, John fucked Amy; each thrust harder than the last, each tug on the leather restricted her breathing a little more. Amy's chest heaved and moans of pleasure wheezed from her gaping mouth; John noted the flush of red had spread down Amy's straining neck, across her breasts, and all the way down to the taut abs of her belly as she writhed and squirmed beneath him.

"John… *please…*" Amy whispered.

"That is not my name, *dirty whore!*" John yelled in Amy's face and yanked harder still on the belt.

Amy let out an odd gurgling sound, mouth opening and closing wordlessly, and her eyes bulged out of their sockets as she thrashed her head side to side.

John was close to release; the pressure building up in his balls was to the point of painful, and he was no longer in control of either his climax or the leather belt wrapped around Amy's throat.

On the verge of John's orgasm, Amy's knee slipped beneath his and she brought it up swiftly into his balls— the pain, both agonizing and exquisite, brought John to his inevitable climax in an instant, and every muscle in his body tensed as he came deep inside Amy. Unable to help himself, John let out a long, low groan of pleasure and wrenched on the belt as his arm spasmed.

Beneath him, Amy lifted up her head from the pillow. Clear strings of spittle dribbled from the corners of her mouth, and she let out a strained, gurgling sound; her eyes implored him to *please stop* and then John remembered they hadn't agreed on a safe word or signal, which was pretty much the first rule of BDSM.

In the split second of pure panic sweeping through John, the belt jerked in his hand and there came the faintest *snapping* sound from Amy's throat.

In a heartbeat, Amy's chest quit heaving, her eyes rolled upward in their sockets, her head flopped back down onto the pillow, and her body fell limp.

Chapter Fifteen

"If you could lean away from the microphone a bit more, please," Skippy asked him with a loud, theatrical sigh. "I'd have thought you'd have got the hang of all this by now, Cole."

Cole ignored the dig but shuffled back in his seat a few inches and leaned away from the mic, which was hidden behind a black pop filter bigger than his face. Skippy had consistently vetoed his idea of bringing in a professional voice-over artist to do the show's recaps and announcements, and Cole had never felt entirely comfortable in the producer's cramped booth—it made him feel claustrophobic, *trapped*.

"Okay, once more from the top." Skippy made a finger gun and pointed it at Cole to give him the cue.

Cole counted three beats in his head and then spoke in his best announcer's voice, "After the romantic Indian dinner on their first date, Cole and Sarah hit it off right away and went on to enjoy a skinny-dipping adventure together on their second date."

He paused as footage played on the monitors of him and the beautiful, redheaded Sarah dashing naked into the sea at McFaddin nude beach on the Bolivar Peninsula, few dozen miles away from Galveston. They'd cleared a small stretch of sand to avoid capturing any of the actual nudists on film. Skippy had decided they would be overweight, wrinkly, old people.

Instead, they'd populated the section of beach with a bunch of paid naked extras. Cole had been surprised at how readily Sarah had shed her clothes; the girl had one hell of a sweet body and wasn't shy about showing it off. "For their third date, Cole treated Sarah to a couples' massage, followed by a relaxing afternoon together, making the most of all the amenities at the exclusive spa." Cole could never figure why Skippy insisted he record the announcements in the third person. Even though he put on a fake voice, Cole was convinced their viewers would know it was him—surely the show's demographic wasn't *that* stupid?

Cole watched in contemplative silence as he and Sarah were massaged together. Their massage tables stood side by side, and the masseuses—a tall, hot-looking guy for Sarah and a slim, Swedish blonde for himself— moved in perfectly choreographed synchrony as they went about their work. Then Cole and Sarah had spent a cozy few hours in the spa's sauna and hot mud rooms after filming had stopped; they'd talked nonstop, and Cole had listened with growing interest as Sarah told him all over again about her aspirations for the future and the businesses she wanted to start up. She was one smart cookie and had the type of intelligence Cole had always been attracted to. Even though he knew from Sarah's interview she had a cold, mercenary streak, Cole couldn't help but be drawn in by the sexy redheaded girl, and he'd begun to imagine a relationship beyond the show.

The spa footage gave way to the purple painted walls of a dungeon. Cole, clad in leather straps and nothing else, was strapped facedown onto a St. Andrew's cross while Sarah, resplendent in a red latex catsuit, matching hood that left her face exposed and hair pulled out through a hole near the top in a high, dominatrix-style ponytail, and six-inch spiked heels lashed his bare backside with a cat o'nine tails.

"But did Sarah wow *The Gentleman's Choice* viewers enough to make it through to the fifth and final night? Will she be back to consummate her relationship with Cole and have the chance to win one hundred thousand dollars and a luxury vacation?" Cole paused there—Skippy just *loved* his dramatic pauses; he'd slip in an advertisement to further build the anticipation.

"Okay, Cole, bring it in, mate." Skippy flapped his hand in Cole's direction.

"And… you, the viewers, *have* voted Sarah through to night five of *The Gentleman's Choice*! Her sexy adventure with Cole will be revealed live on the show!"

"And… it's a wrap!"

"No retakes?" Cole asked.

"No retakes," Skippy told him. "We've got this down to a fine art, mate. You're good to go prepare for tonight."

Cole took the hint and stood up, grateful for the relief being back on his feet offered his sore ass. "Which way did the vote go for the date? I hope it's a good one, Skip."

"You know better than to ask me that, my dear friend." Skippy smiled and exaggerated his accent. "We have to keep some element of surprise—so your reaction is genuine and all that."

"Can you at least give me a hint as to what to expect?"

"Look, Cole." Skippy struggled to his feet. "I know you like this girl…"

"It's not that," Cole protested, even though it was—Skippy could read him like a damn book.

"I know exactly *what* it is—how many times is it now you've fallen for one of the contestants?"

Cole had no idea as to the precise number, but saw no harm in bonding with those contestants who touched him emotionally; wasn't that the expected subtext to the show anyway?

"All will be revealed when Sarah opens the golden envelope on tonight's show—I'm sure you can wait until then to see what Fifth Night delights we have in store for the two of you." Skippy raised an eyebrow; his eyes twitched toward the door. It really was time for Cole to leave.

"Okay, as long as it's not another orgy, Skip." Cole turned to leave. Skippy let out another long, protracted sigh. "Give me some bloody credit, will you, Cole? I'm hardly going to put out another orgy less than a week after the last one—especially after the fucking farce you made out of that one."

It did cross Cole's mind to rise to Skippy's bait, but then common sense prevailed; it wouldn't do him any good to reignite an argument he'd already had with the producer so soon before showtime—whatever the show's paying subscribers had voted on for his night's activity with Sarah, which would inevitably leave her no longer a *verified* virgin, Cole had to mentally prepare. Contrary to Skippy's belief, there was a soupcon more to *The Gentleman's Choice* than seduction and screwing.

Sitting beside Cole on the bed in lacy black lingerie with scarlet trim, Sarah looked beyond beautiful. She wore sheer silk stockings held up by a delicate garter belt that matched the ensemble and sat high up on her waist; she looked every inch the sex siren, something akin to a '50s pin-up girl. By means of complimenting Sarah's style, the wardrobe department had dressed Cole in black jeans and a crisp white button-down shirt; unquestionably, he looked every part the suave, sexy seducer.

"I'm so excited to see what's in the envelope," Cole prompted Sarah with a nod toward the shiny gold envelope she had clutched in her hands.

"Whatever it is, Cole, I just *know* it's going to be magical," Sarah recited her line as she fiddled to open the envelope.

Cole looked on with interest as Sarah's trembling fingers slid beneath the gold flap and she tore the envelope open. From within, she retrieved a plain white card upon which was printed the sexual adventure awaiting them for Sarah's fifth and final night of the show.

A lascivious smile parted Sarah's lips as she read the card aloud. "Cole and Sarah, for your fifth and final date night, and to celebrate Sarah's very first time making love, you will be joined by Katie Simons for an erotic threesome."

Cole placed a hand on Sarah's stockinged leg and smiled directly into the camera. "I honestly couldn't have thought of a more sensual way for you to lose your virginity, Sarah. I'd like to say a big thank you to all of our subscribers for voting for us to have a threesome—and with such a legend, too. You're going to be in good hands tonight, Sarah."

"Hey, guys." Katie's voice drifted over from somewhere off-camera.

Cole and Sarah greeted the porn star with smiles and warm hellos as she made her way into the shot with a hand out ready to shake. She'd been on the show a year or so ago, and Cole was delighted to see she still had her trademark short, black, spiky hair, and she'd added to the array of colorful tattoos that adorned her slim, surgically enhanced body—which she showed off to maximum effect in tight denim shorts, a white, midriff-baring tube top that did little to contain her 38DD breasts, and five-inch platform sandals with thin teal straps snaking all the way up to her knees.

"You must be Sarah." Katie approached the bed, her perfect, pear-shaped ass to the camera, a goodly amount of butt cheek bulging out beneath her shorts' inadequate amount of denim. "It's *so* lovely to meet you." She shook Sarah's hand and bent over to deliver a somewhat chaste kiss to each of the girl's cheeks.

"Hey, Katie, good to see you again." Cole took his cue as Katie settled herself down between him and Sarah; he was treated to an innocent kiss to both cheeks, French-style.

"I am *so* looking forward to getting to know you two," Katie purred as she gave Sarah's beautiful, lingerie-clad body an unabashed, lingering up and down for the benefit of the cameras. "You look really hot tonight, Sarah." Leaning in to kiss Sarah full on the lips, her hand reached up to cup the redhead's breast.

As Katie and Sarah shared a deep, passionate kiss, Cole once again turned to the camera. "Don't forget, if you'd like to see Sarah win *The Gentleman's Choice* grand prize of one hundred thousand dollars and a luxury vacation to a romantic location of her choosing, you can vote at any time during the show. In the meantime, I'm going to join Sarah and Katie to have some sexy fun." He gave another inward cringe at Skippy's tacky lines.

Cole assisted Katie in undressing Sarah, and Sarah's reciprocation, until both women were entirely naked. Then, they helped Cole out of his clothes—all beneath the watchful eyes of Skippy, Jayne, and the crew.

While most men harbored wild fantasies of being a porn star, Cole knew firsthand how difficult it was to perform in a studio setting—the presence of scrutinizing strangers and prying cameras made it a million miles removed from the intimacy of making love in the privacy of one's own bedroom.

But being able to hide behind a fake persona certainly made the difference for Cole. That he could be the dashing, sexually liberated, extraordinarily confident Cole Gianni for the show's viewers offered him the distance he needed in order to perform night after night.

The strategy worked well until a contestant wriggled her way behind the façade and into Cole's affections, which had happened more frequently in recent years; maybe he wasn't as up to the job as he used to be?

Katie and Sarah, having become intimately acquainted with one another's bodies with lips, fingers, and tongues, set about seducing Cole in perfect sync. Under Katie's expert guidance, Sarah made all the right moves, taking her cues from the porn star as if she, too, was a seasoned performer. She was actually so convincing, Cole wondered just how much of a virgin his Fifth Night date really was.

Cole lay back on the bed and immersed himself in the unique pleasure only the attention of two enthusiastic, beautiful young ladies could deliver. Closing his eyes, he focused his mind on the soft, urgent kisses Sarah and Katie planted over his shoulders, chest, and upon his belly as they made their way with some haste downward to their ultimate target, their moans and sighs of ecstasy duly exaggerated for the benefit of the cameras and paying subscribers.

As Katie and Sarah pleasured Cole, he looked on and made the encouraging noises his audience would expect; at the same time, he did his best to ignore the cameras, crew, and Jayne, who was glued to the script and keeping track of the time. As irritating as the woman could be, there was no doubt it was she who made Fifth Night successful with her meticulous attention to detail; it was on her insistence they film the final night with a three-minute time-lag in order to catch any mistakes and get the camera angles just right.

After a few minutes, Skippy interrupted the action to direct Sarah and Katie into the ubiquitous soixante-neuf position, which they adopted with ease, and set about pleasuring each other with noisy enthusiasm. Cole always felt like the proverbial spare part at that particular juncture in any threesome but understood its importance to the repertoire; he also knew the cameras wouldn't be spending any time on him, so he propped his back up against the headboard, enjoyed the live lesbian show, and looked forward to the next part of the proceedings.

Eventually, the time came for Cole to seal the deal with Sarah. It was the moment the audience had been eagerly anticipating throughout the previous four nights, and Cole had been really looking forward to making love to Sarah for her very public first time.

"Do you remember your line, Sarah?" Jayne chirped up; she'd silently appeared at Skippy's shoulder.

Sarah sat up on the bed and nodded; her bare breasts jiggled. "Oh, Cole, I'm so pleased you're my first." She delivered the line back to Jayne dry and deadpan, which made it sound quite ridiculous; what young girl dreamed of her first sexual experience being surrounded by cameras and watched by countless strangers?

"Perfect," Jayne said without a hint she'd caught Sarah's deliberate facetiousness.

Skippy checked his watch. "Places, please. It's showtime."

Cole scooted down on the bed to lie by Sarah's side, his face inches from hers, their bodies close. Katie seated herself by Sarah's butt and caressed the gentle curve of her back.

"*Action!*"

Leaning toward her on the pillow, Cole kissed Sarah and tasted Katie on her soft, welcoming lips. In a heartbeat, Sarah's tongue slipped past Cole's lips and probed inside his mouth as she pressed her naked body into his.

With one smooth, well-practiced motion, and without breaking the kiss, Cole rolled Sarah onto her back. Parting her legs with his, he positioned himself between her thighs and readied himself for the big moment.

"Oh, Cole, I'm so pleased you're my first." Sarah pulled away from their kiss just long enough to deliver her line; this time, her words were breathless with passion, believable. Sarah arched her back to allow Cole to slip inside her and gripped his buttocks with both hands.

"*Cut!*"

"Are you kidding me?" Cole rolled off Sarah to face Skippy. "We've got to get the cameras in just the right positions for p… the big moment, Cole. I want one camera close up on Sarah's face—and one… *there*. But not too bloody gynecological—this is supposed to be sensual, not *instructional*." Skippy pointed at Sarah's denuded mound; she had long since given up attempting to hide herself.

It took Skippy a minute or so to be happy the cameras were in optimum position and the light hit perfectly on all the appropriate parts of Sarah's exposed body. Only then did he return to his spot.

Cole repositioned himself on top of Sarah and patiently awaited Skippy's instruction, even though the heat of Sarah's body beneath him, the touch of her hands on his butt, and the scent of Katie on her breath almost proved too much for him to control his animal instincts; Cole was lucky he had so many years of experience of soulless sex under his belt.

"Action!" Skippy's voice filled the studio.

Sarah dug her fingernails hard into Cole's buttocks and pushed down hard on them as she lifted her hips to position him just so. "Fuck me, Cole." Her voice was low, hoarse with pure lust.

And with that, the deed was done.

Chapter Sixteen

"We really ought to have more virgins on the show!" Skippy enthused, his eyes bright with excitement. "Tonight's votes were off the bloody charts, Cole!"

Cole shuffled his feet on the coarse office carpet; it had been a little over an hour since the show had wrapped, and for once, he was in no mood for Skippy's debriefing session—it was the early hours of Saturday morning, and he just wanted to go home. He also found himself already missing Sarah and had been disappointed not to have found her in Skippy's office.

"We've made a small fortune on votes, my friend—and that's not counting the boost in subscriptions she's brought in," Skippy continued; he was never one to pick up on Cole's cues. "Your young, virginal Sarah has earned every fucking penny of her hundred grand."

"You've paid her already?"

"Hit the button on the money transfer twenty minutes ago. It should be in her bank account by now. I also gave her the information on the vacation—figured it best to get all that over and done with at the same time as the money."

Cole was surprised: typically, Skippy would make the show's winning contestants wait a week or two for their hard-earned prizes. What had Sarah done to persuade the guy to part with his cash and free vacation so soon?

There it was again—that faint twinge of jealousy.

"You did good, Cole, my old friend." Skippy produced a half-empty bottle of Jack Daniels from his desk drawer and wiggled it at Cole.

"Thank you, no. I'm ready for home."

"Of course you are, you old dog, you." Skippy laughed. "You put on one hell of a performance with your young virgin. It is a shame she didn't bleed a little, though—it would have been a great end to the show to catch a spot or two of blood on the bed sheets, don't you think? Maybe next time we should add a bit of fake blood if there is none forthcoming…"

Cole declined to reply; at times, his business partner's derogatory attitude toward women went beyond offensive. That he objectified Sarah as something even less than the usual naked bodies they had on the show to be fucked and filmed was just awful—she was *Sarah*, and over their five nights together, Cole had discovered she had far more depth than simply *being a virgin*. So, instead of laughing uncomfortably along to Skippy's odious comments, Cole remained silent.

"You know, I'm really surprised she didn't hang out with me in here to say goodbye to you." Skippy poured himself a large drink in a plastic cup and downed half in one gulp. "I thought you two had something really special going on there."

"Did Sarah leave already?" Cole felt an unexpected surge of panic rising up in his chest; the thought of not seeing Sarah again truly *hurt*.

"Just before you got here—you just missed the gal by minutes." A glimmer in the producer's eye told Cole there had been a good reason Sarah had not been in the office when he arrived—there was little doubt she'd been subjected to the old, tried-and-trusted Skippy moves. The question remaining in Cole's mind, though, was had she succumbed on the promise of receiving her prize money before she left the studio?

It was a question Cole couldn't bring himself to ask, as he really had no desire to hear Skippy's answer. "I'm going to go now—we can pick this up tomorrow."

"You sure you won't have a drink? Maybe I could call a couple of the girls I know…?" Skippy seemed reluctant to let Cole leave.

"We can do that tomorrow, too." Cole reached for the door handle. "If you hurry, you might still catch your little virgin," Skippy said with a wink; he really could read Cole like a book. "Although, I guess we can't call her that anymore—not after what you did with her tonight." Cole left Skippy to his obnoxious, childish little comments and Jack; he really couldn't stomach either one. There'd come a time, Cole promised himself, he'd confront Skippy about his antiquated attitudes, maybe even get him to mend his bigoted ways, but the wee hours of the day after an exhausting show was definitely not that time.

And besides, he did want to catch up with Sarah before she left; he had to let her know he would love to take the relationship they'd built together on the show further.

Heart racing like some love-struck fool, Cole dashed along the studio's deserted hallways—most of the technical people had gone home, although Cole figured Jayne would likely be still lurking around somewhere in the building; the woman always seemed to have something to do late at night.

To Cole's relief, he came upon Sarah at the front entrance. She was saying her last goodbyes to Katie, who had somehow managed to avoid the bedraggled post-sex look both Cole and Sarah had following the shoot. No doubt about it, the porn star was a total pro.

As Cole made his way through the doors and out into the tepid Texas night air, Katie had her arms about Sarah's neck and was kissing her goodbye; it looked to Cole to be a little more than a friendly farewell peck, and for a moment or two, he once again felt like that spare part back on the bed.

"Oh, hi, Cole." Katie broke the smooch to greet him.

"Hi, Katie." Cole was convinced she looked guilty.

"Hi, Cole." Sarah had no hint of guilt or awkwardness about her at all. She smiled at him.

"I thought you'd be long gone by now," Cole aimed his comment at Katie—it was her cue to leave.

"I was just on my way. Bye again, Sarah. I had fun." Katie slipped an arm about Sarah's waist and pulled her in for another long, lingering kiss. Cole was no fool; that kiss was very much intended for his benefit,

Katie's way of toying with him, and it didn't elicit a jealous pang like the one he'd broken up a few moments before.

Having made her point, Katie let Sarah go and strutted away to her gold Lexus SUV, which was parked across the parking lot; she'd been smart enough to leave it beneath one of the tall lights.

"Can I give you a ride somewhere?" Cole broke the silence between him and Sarah.

Sarah shook her head. "My Uber will be here in a few minutes. Thank you, though." The smile was cursory, Sarah's tone flat.

Cole fished his keys from his pocket and jangled them at Sarah for emphasis. "I'd be more than happy to save you the cost."

"I honestly thought you'd drive a Porsche or something." Sarah eyed the Mustang key fob in Cole's hand with a wry smile. "What with you being a big internet star and all."

Cole gave her a sheepish grin. "I'm not really a millionaire, you know. That's just a character, all part of the show—I thought you understood that." Pointing the fob out into the darkness of the parking lot, Cole hit the button and the lights flashed on a black GT a few spaces along from where they stood. "I do love Mustangs, though, and it is a convertible. You sure I can't tempt you?"

Sarah checked her cell phone; the little map lit up her beautiful face. "My Uber is literally around the corner," she told him.

"Maybe another time, then?" Cole was not about to give up. Sarah was clearly as tired as he was, and no doubt just wanted to get back to the posh hotel the show had her booked into for one more night.

"I'm flying back to Iowa tomorrow afternoon, Cole."

"Then we should meet up for breakfast." Cole seized the opportunity—it was the perfect segue. "We still have to discuss the vacation."

"The vacation?" Sarah narrowed her eyes; it made her look mean. "The one you just won… on the show?"

"What is there to discuss about it?" With a look of growing impatience, Sarah checked her phone once more.

"Well, for a start, there's where we want to go—the budget will stretch to Jamaica, Puerto Rico, Cuba…"

"Oh, I was planning to take one of my girlfriends," Sarah was quite matter of fact on the subject. "Jasmine has always wanted to holiday on the British Virgin Islands… kind of ironic, given the circumstances, don't you think?"

The innocently coy smile Cole had fallen in love with spread across Sarah's face.

"But I thought we—"

"You thought the naive, virgin Sarah would just *jump* at the chance to go on a romantic vacation with *the* Cole Gianni—the man who deflowered her live on the internet?"

Cole's heart sank; how was it possible for Sarah to be so cynical? And how was it possible he'd read her so wrong? "All the winners' vacations are with me," Cole explained quietly. "It's kind of a show tradition—and it's a great way to get to know each other better and on our own terms."

"I don't recall reading anywhere in the contract I signed that I have to take the vacation with you."

"It's not in the contract, but—"

"Then I shall be taking Jasmine."

Cole was crestfallen. He took hold of Sarah's hand, her fingers warm and fragile in his. "Sarah, I thought we had a connection. I would really love to get to know you away from the cameras and studio sets. I think you feel the same way too."

Sarah snatched her hand away. "Actually, I don't, Cole. I'm not even sure I like you all that much, if I'm being totally honest. How I've acted around you these past five days… it was all part of the show. I thought *you* understood that."

The Uber—a silver Nissan Rogue with a *Baby on Board* sticker in the rear window—pulled up in front of the studio. Sarah pulled open the door. "Goodbye, Cole, and good luck with whoever you get on next week's show."

Cole watched with an ache in his heart as the Rogue drove away; how on earth had he not seen Sarah for the worst kind of money-grabber *The Gentleman's Choice* had the tendency to attract? She'd just given up her virginity live online for a cash prize, one-week vacation, and a fleeting shot at fame. The more he thought about how she'd played his emotions on the show, the more Cole's sadness turned to anger; it took all the fortitude he could muster not to head straight back up to Skippy's office and take him up on that offer of Jack Daniels and hookers.

Chapter Seventeen

"I just can't do this anymore, Skippy. I'm done." Cole slumped down in his chair and ran a trembling hand through his hair.

Skippy contemplated his partner across the desk; it wasn't the first time Cole had run through the whole, pitiful *woe is me* act; it happened on an almost cyclical basis, every six weeks or so, and Skippy had seen it coming from Cole's very first night on the show with Sarah. She'd been a special one for sure, and not just for the virginity she'd so cynically exploited, and Cole had fallen hard for her—harder even than he had for the Asian chick. But Skippy had the redhead figured out from the start and had looked on, impressed, as she played the game perfectly and won over not only Cole's heart, but the hearts—and credit cards—of the show's audience.

And that was *really* what mattered to Skippy when it came down to it; the money they'd made on the final night's voting alone had far surpassed anything they'd made on any one of the contestants in well over a year. Subscriptions had shot up 8 percent overnight as word spread around the internet about the hot redheaded virgin on *The Gentleman's Choice*. So, when the flame-headed beauty had demanded her prize money and vacation vouchers right then and there, after the show, Skippy had been more than happy to comply. The truth was, her cold-blooded mercenary streak had reminded him so much of himself, Skippy had been more than a little intimidated—so much so, he'd not even considered putting the moves on her until long after she'd strutted out of his office like some queen fucking bee who owned the place.

"You'll be okay, mate." Skippy was growing tired of constantly having to placate his partner—the man had gotten worse with the lovelorn act in recent months, and Skippy guessed it was only a matter of time before it began affecting his performance on the show, and thus, the very show itself. Skippy was also aware it would be fueling Cole's drive to sell out to one of the cable channels who were still waving fat checkbooks in their faces.

Cole let out a long, mournful sigh to let Skippy know his heart was breaking. "I really thought Sarah and me had a good thing going, Skip." He shuffled upright in his chair and scratched the bridge of his nose. "I *know* Sarah genuinely liked me, and I felt we could have made a lot more of what we had together."

"You said the exact same thing about Me Lin, or whatever her damn name was, and Juanita before her, and Carol a couple months ago... you get the general idea, Cole. Sarah was only ever in it for the money. They all are. You're just getting a bit softer with the contestants, that's all." It was tough love, but Skippy reckoned Cole needed to hear it.

"Maybe I am, but doesn't that tell you something?"

Skippy fiddled with a couple of pens on his desk and chose to say nothing. He knew damn well what was coming.

"We need to seriously consider the *Hustler* proposal, Skippy. Or even the *Playboy* offer if that's still on the table."

Skippy met Cole's eyes—he couldn't believe the sap was actually trying to stare him down. "We've been through this how many times now?" he grumbled. "The show is going strength-to-strength—we'd have to be a special level of dumbfuck to let it go now. Cole, can you really, honestly, see yourself sitting on the sidelines and watching one of the big boys make millions out of our baby? After all the years of blood, sweat, and tears, to just hand it over and walk away on the brink of going really big would crucify you."

"And what if this is as big as it's ever going to get? These things never last forever," Cole told him. "And what if we wait too long to bail out? We'd just go down with a show on the decline. But, if we sell now, we get to ride it out and grow fat on somebody else's dime."

Skippy fought back the urge to leap from his chair and shake Cole 'til the man saw sense. If anything was likely to force him to sell out, it would be the thought of not having to go through Cole's pathetic pity parties and nagging any longer.

"Cole," he said. "We do that and you'll be nothing more than an employee. Just another faceless number on the channel's bloody payroll. Is that what you really want?"

"Maybe it is, Skip, or maybe I just need to get the fuck out of this business altogether—before it's too late."

Skippy had no desire to waste yet more of his precious time listening to Cole's fanciful dreams of how he was going to walk away from more than six years in the adult entertainment industry to become the next overnight

Hollywood sensation, yet he didn't have the heart to piss on the guy's bonfire while his ego was still smarting over Sarah. "Look, I'll take you down to meet Vanessa," he deflected. "She's the sexy young lady you'll be having dinner with this very evening." Standing up, and with a theatrical flourish of the hand, Skippy urged Cole to get up off his ass and quit feeling quite so sorry for himself. There were millions of priapic young men who'd give their eye teeth to swap places with Cole Gianni. And there'd be other Sarahs, other Asian chicks, and maybe one of them might just be *the one* and Cole would ride off into some romantic sunset or some bullshit? Skippy seriously doubted that particular scenario, but he was okay with encouraging the show's moneymaker to think it was always a possibility.

"I think you're really going to like Vanessa." With a hand in the small of Cole's back, Skippy all but pushed him out of the office. "She's still in briefing with Jayne. I'll introduce you, give you a chance to get to know the contestant *before* the show for a change."

There was the slightest hint of hesitation to Cole's step. It was as if he was being led to the gallows and not into the company of a beautiful young woman who he might be fucking in five days' time. Skippy led him along the hallway and toward the stairs, nonetheless.

Chapter Eighteen

V anessa Young sat patient and quiet while Jayne probed her for personal information. She'd met Jayne Torrez during the first round of interviews for *The Gentleman's Choice* and surmised the woman was something akin to the show's human resource manager and general mother hen; it seemed to Vanessa she enjoyed prying into the contestants' private lives, especially the sexual aspects, as much as she liked to play the big shot around the studio.

"I've planned for you to play the part of the hopelessly romantic, idealistic young woman who is looking for love…" Jayne tapped a cheap Bic pen against her front teeth, which Vanessa found irritating. "You'll fall instantly in love with Cole on the first date… no… at first *sight*. Who doesn't enjoy seeing love at first sight?" She scribbled a few lines of notes down on the pad attached to her purple clipboard and nodded her approval.

Vanessa counted to three in her mind before giving her reply. "Do you really think that's the best use of my personality type?" The question was rhetorical; Vanessa knew she held all the cards, as she had everything else the show required. Also, she had an altogether different role in mind, one more befitting of the false personal information and string of outright lies she'd fed Jayne from the moment she'd applied to be on the show.

"As a matter of fact, I do." Despite Vanessa's soft approach, Jayne's defenses were up; it was evident she was not accustomed to having her decisions questioned, especially by a mere contestant.

"I'm thinking I'd be put to far better use as the hard nut to crack—the girl who can be a challenge to Cole's doubtless seduction techniques and charms." Vanessa offered Jayne a disarming smile to let her know she was there to help, not undermine any obvious authority. "I'm sure your viewers would love to see Cole having to work hard to get a taste of this…" Vanessa indicated her body with a sweep of one hand. She was tall at five-ten, wore a tight white minidress that showed off long, toned legs, perfectly proportioned breasts, and narrow waist; she had a natural California tan, which was only a shade lighter than her eyes, and which gave her flawless skin a honeyed, caramel tone. It complemented her long, raven-black hair that frizzed out and cascaded about her shoulders in beautiful, iridescent glory.

Visually, Vanessa was an absolute bronzed goddess, and she exuded the undeniable confidence that went with such outstanding beauty. That she was also incredibly smart and shrewd beyond her twenty-nine years meant she would have little problem imposing her will over Jayne.

It was only a matter of when and how.

Fixing Jayne with her radiant smile, Vanessa continued, "It'll be more like real life—a man having to make an effort to capture a lady's heart, don't you think? And who doesn't love a challenge?"

"I'm not sure Cole will go for it." Already Jayne was deferring the decision. Vanessa didn't think the woman would crumble quite so soon. "Well, why don't we ask him?" Vanessa glanced across the studio; Cole and his producer were on their way over. Jayne followed her gaze, and her shoulders slumped visibly as the two drew closer.

"Ask me what?" Skippy blurted out with a laugh. He made a show of stepping aside to put Cole center stage, which Vanessa interpreted as a demonstration of dominance. "Vanessa, meet Cole. Cole... Vanessa."

"I'm very pleased to meet you, Cole." Vanessa got to her feet, gripped Cole firmly by his shoulders, and planted a kiss on both his cheeks, continental style.

"And you too, Vanessa." Cole blatantly checked her out, eyes lingering on her legs.

She'd taken Cole by surprise by being so forward, which Vanessa considered to be a good start in disarming the guy. She knew she looked good, and now Cole knew she had more to her character than the show's usual sappy bimbo types.

"I know this is not normally how we do stuff around here," Skippy explained, his British accent most pronounced. "You two meeting before the show, I mean. But, hey, we gotta switch things up every now and then, don't we, Jayne?"

Refusing to stand, Jayne nodded at Skippy from her seat and tap- tapped at her teeth with the pen.

"Speaking of switching things up." Vanessa seized the producer's inadvertent cue. "Jayne and I were discussing the concept of having me play a hard-to-get character... we figured we'd make Cole put in a little work through the dates. It's been a long time since the show had a contestant the audience can love to hate." She flashed her bright smile at Skippy and gave him a second to take in her proposal.

Jayne finally got to her feet—she had her territory to defend. "I've scripted Vanessa as the hopeless romantic," she told Skippy. "The stats show our primary demographic—couples aged twenty-five to forty-five—gravitate more toward a belief in all things romantic."

"But women do prefer to see a man fight for love—and sex, of course. Portray me as your bad guy instead of objectifying me as some old cliché, and your subscribers will go crazy."

Jayne stepped forward. "I really don't think—"

"I love it," Skippy declared.

"Yeah, I can see that working," Cole agreed without taking his eyes off Vanessa.

Jayne opened her mouth to say something, but nothing came out. "If we're gonna mix things up, we may as well go the whole hog."

Skippy turned to Jayne. "You okay with that?"

"I guess so." Unmistakably, Jayne was not okay with that. She shot Vanessa a withering look. "I suppose I can dig out one of the old scripts and tweak it as necessary."

Skippy clapped his hands together, which Vanessa thought to be an oddly effeminate gesture. "It's going to be a very good week, Vanessa. I'm so pleased we chose you; we really are in desperate need of a breath of fresh air on the show."

Vanessa followed Jayne's lead and sat herself back down once Skippy and Cole excused themselves and went on their way. She expected a frosty reception from Jayne, having just undermined her authority. But it appeared the woman was more resilient than that, and she picked up how she'd left off, tapping at her teeth with the pen, business as usual.

"Of course, at the beginning of tonight's show, it is very important you remember to pretend not to have met Cole before—our viewers love to see that very first, surprised reaction." As she spoke, Jayne drew a long, heavy line through her notes before tearing the page from her pad and scrunching it up. "Now, where were we?"

Vanessa only half-listened to Jayne as they ran through the remainder of the briefing and the dos and don'ts of her first night on the show: do reveal a little about herself, don't dominate the conversation, do flirt and show how attractive she found Cole, don't be overtly sexual, and do hang on to every word Cole said as if he were the most fascinating man on the planet. Just how Jayne expected any of that to dovetail in with playing hard to get, Vanessa wasn't too sure. But she was confident she'd figure it out as she went along—after all, she had gotten so far on falsehoods and playing a part.

"I guess that's about it, then," Jayne concluded with a final tap at her teeth. "Do you have any questions, Vanessa?" Blunt, to the point.

"There's none that spring to mind, Jayne." Vanessa paused for a beat or two to give the impression she was actually putting some thought into it and taking the whole thing as seriously as was expected of her. "But if I do think of anything, I'll be sure to hit you up—if that's okay?"

Jayne stood up. "That's what I'm here for." She tucked her clipboard and pad under her arm and slotted the Bic into the back pocket of her loose-fitting jeans.

"Would it be all right if I took a little look around?" Vanessa got to her feet; her willowy frame towered over Jayne. "I'd like to get myself better acquainted with the studio and crew, and I've always wanted to take a peek behind the scenes at a movie studio."

Jayne scanned Vanessa up and down, as if sizing up a rival. Her nose crinkled and she began to walk away. "Go right ahead—knock yourself out."

Vanessa watched Jayne go; the conversation with Cole and Skippy had undeniably pissed the woman off, and Vanessa wondered if that would have any bearing on how long she was likely to remain on the show. But it had been unavoidable, as Vanessa was there to do a job, and it was imperative she play the hard-to-get part and not the sappy little romantic Jayne had in mind for her. The most important thing was both Cole and Skippy liked her and absolutely loved the idea of Vanessa ostensibly providing a much-needed challenge for Cole's tried-and-trusted methods of seduction, even if it served as a harsh reminder to Jayne Torrez she didn't actually run the show.

Left to her own devices, Vanessa wandered around the studio and observed the crew going about their business, which appeared to involve a lot of standing around waiting for other crew members to do their jobs. She peeked in at the sets she recognized from researching old episodes of the show, and eavesdropped on conversations—very discreetly, of course.

Meeting Cole Gianni had been a welcome surprise and had started her off on the right footing; Vanessa had not expected to see the man himself until she was announced as the next *Gentleman's Choice* contestant live on that night's show. She was also pleasantly surprised to find Cole was actually much nicer in real life than the overconfident lothario he portrayed on the show; he had a sweet, modest disposition that contradicted his public persona, and it was clear he played second fiddle to the producer.

It was also clear to Vanessa, even from their brief meeting, Skippy was insanely jealous of Cole; she knew both he and Cole owned 50 percent of the show each, but Skippy obviously felt the need to present himself as the controlling partner—most likely because of his obvious physical inferiority and lack of finesse around women. From the way he insisted on walking a step ahead of Cole, to commandeering the conversation and undermining a subordinate to her face, to openly leering at the contestants, Skippy had reinforced Vanessa's suspicions; as a private investigator, she was fully experienced at reading people— not that Skippy Webman had been difficult to see through, of course.

And that's what made the producer an almost textbook case in Vanessa's mind. Someone so visibly uncomfortable around the opposite sex made Mason "Skippy" Webman the prime suspect for Tracy's murder. Not that the Brit producer was the only suspect, not by a long shot. Vanessa had drawn up a short list before she'd even set foot in the studio—she was known for being as ruthlessly meticulous in her research as she was for her willingness to do whatever it took to get the job done. With the latter in mind, however, Vanessa didn't expect to get to the fifth night of the show; she considered that highly unlikely given the statistics associated with characters similar to the one she'd insisted upon playing and how she planned to act around Cole. Her objective was plain and simple: to get the information she needed for her client by night three—four at the latest—and be gone from the show before crunch time. But it would have been remiss of Vanessa to have not contemplated what might happen if, by some weird twist of fate, she hadn't uncovered what she was there for and the show's viewers voted for her to remain on the show all the way through to the end. The question remained: would she see it through to Night Five's ultimate conclusion with Cole? Sure, Vanessa had very few morals when it came to getting her work done, and on previous cases, she had screwed both men and women in the line of duty but never in such a publicly intrusive way. And, while the idea of such exhibitionism didn't entirely repulse Vanessa—Tom Hickersley was paying her more than enough money to happily consider prostituting herself—Vanessa hoped she wouldn't make it far enough to have to put her lack of moral fortitude to the ultimate test.

She noted there was no shortage of sexy young women in the studio—there appeared to be a constant rotation of sweet, nubile wannabes vying for a place on the show—which made it all the easier for Vanessa to blend into the background; she smiled and nodded pleasant hellos as she went about her business of putting actual people to faces and the detailed backgrounds of those she'd thoroughly checked out in the obvious places on the internet: *Facebook*, *Instagram*, *Twitter*, *Pornhub*, *Xhamster*, and the plethora of dating and more blatant hookup sites. It never ceased to amaze Vanessa what information people were happy to make public—and what parts of that could be so readily bought and sold. And it wasn't just via the murky corners of the dark/deep web, as most people were recklessly brazen in broadcasting their activities to anyone at all who cared to take a look.

Combined with the ex-employees Vanessa had pried information from, the wealth of internet information she found for practically everyone she investigated made her job that much easier. She often wondered how the hell PIs used to cope in the days before the World Wide Web.

Vanessa had applied the same thorough research when it had come down to getting herself onto the show; naturally, she'd studied past episodes to establish the most popular types of girls they seemed to prefer. *The Gentleman's Choice*, like so many, had a distinct and ultimately predictable pattern when it came to the nature of its contestants, which had been easy for Vanessa to ascertain once she got hold of the viewing statistics. Again, the information hadn't been very challenging to acquire and had cost her far less in bribes than she had budgeted for; she'd very quickly honed in on the key person at the online company Skippy paid to gather and analyze the show's viewing stats—it was an internet porn show, after all, not a political campaign. Consequently, security was hardly watertight.

Armed with the knowledge of exactly what they were looking for, for her first interview, Vanessa had changed her name and dyed her naturally light brunette hair inky black. She'd also worn something much classier than the typical denim shorts and cowboy boots—a dark-blue skirt suit with a thigh-skimming skirt and white, low-cut camisole had given her a "sexy business woman" air, while still showing sufficient skin to bolster the attention she'd earned with her carefully written application and full-body photographs. She'd paid particular attention to her shoes that day, too, and had worn tall-heeled, open-toed black pumps. Her intel had pointed to someone at the studio having a serious foot fetish—and, having finally met the guy, Vanessa had pinned that on Skippy; he'd been making surreptitious glances at her exposed, perfectly manicured toes throughout the entirety of their short meeting.

As for the rest of the process, Vanessa had relied upon the neurolinguistic programming techniques she'd shelled out a small fortune to learn several years back; her very first employer, a grizzled old PI who mentored her early career right up to the point at which he investigated the wrong member of the Sinaloa Cartel and wound up with his head on a stick in Mexico City, had advised her it would be a worthwhile investment and give her a definite edge over the myriad of hack investigators who clogged up the profession.

Vanessa's well-practiced NLP had worked perfectly on Jayne Torrez during the first round of the selection process. The show's HR woman had been unbelievably susceptible to even the most basic of Vanessa's methods, and Jayne had sailed through to the second round with ease. Naturally, Jayne was also a suspect, but only in the way in which everyone associated with the show had to be until Vanessa eliminated them.

Vanessa had not ruled out Cole Gianni, although, having met the man in person, she couldn't see him having the disposition to torture and kill young women. He was hiding something behind his fake smile and phony accent, that much was a given, but Vanessa very much doubted it was a secret double life as a sadistic killer. Even so, she would keep a close eye on the show's star because she'd learned the hard way it didn't pay to act purely on first impressions; there was always a possibility Cole might just take his perceived entitlement to the contestants a step too far if the wrong one said no and the mood struck him.

Higher on Vanessa's list was the head technical gal, Shazza, who was an ardent feminist and confirmed lesbian; according to her social media posts, she had an obvious axe to grind with the male-centric *The Gentleman's Choice*. She'd claimed, on more than one occasion, she planned to bring the show down from the inside one day. And then there was Pete, who was employed as second camera even though his experience far surpassed that of Eric, the show's most senior camera operator. During her research, Vanessa had dug up a bunch of arrests for petty theft, indecent exposure, and voyeurism from Pete's native California; while they didn't amount to much by themselves, given the context of Tracy Hickersley's death, it was always possible they were a precursor to more violent sexual crimes, and the guy could be escalating.

Vanessa spotted both Shazza and Pete doing their respective thing around the studio; their interactions with the other staff, crew, and the contestants appeared to be normal to Vanessa, although that far from excluded them as suspects. Just how many times did friends and neighbors declare a serial killer to be *just a regular guy* when the truth came out?

It was disappointing Joe Scranton was nowhere to be seen; Vanessa had expected to see the old man around the studio, as she was aware he enjoyed hanging around the potential new contestants as they put themselves on display to attract attention and win a coveted spot as one of Cole's dates. Scranton, the biggest financial backer of the show from way back in its infancy, came from old Houston oil money and apparently loved to swan about the studio and sets with a clipboard in one hand and his dick in the other.

Unsurprisingly, Vanessa took the latter rumor to be an exaggeration put out by disgruntled employees. Although, given the nature of the show and those associated with much of the porn industry, there was every chance the hearsay was actually true. Either way, Joe Scranton was a known sex pest who enjoyed the liberty his money and status afforded and could often be seen wandering about backstage and in the girls' dressing rooms to get his cheap, grubby thrills. It was reported behavior that put him high on Vanessa's list of suspects. In her experience, rich men like Scranton often considered themselves above the law and had the tendency to view people as highly disposable commodities.

"Miss Young?" A voice from behind startled Vanessa. A quick glance around told her she hadn't wandered into a part of the studio that appeared to be off limits, which came as a relief; the last thing she needed to do was draw attention to herself by getting caught nosing around.

"Oh, hi," Vanessa addressed the young woman who'd crept up on her in near-silent white K-Swiss sneakers. "It's Olivia, isn't it?"

The girl, Skippy's PA if Vanessa recalled correctly from her part in the first round of selection, seemed delighted to have been remembered. "Yes, ma'am," she replied with a wide, toothy smile. "We need you in wardrobe and makeup—your first date with Cole starts soon."

Checking her watch, Vanessa frowned. It was a good three hours to showtime—how much preparation did they think she needed to be presentable for dinner with Cole? "Thank you, Olivia," Vanessa said. "I think I got myself a little lost—this whole studio is like a rabbit warren."

"You get used to it." Olivia's smile faded. "I can show you the way to wardrobe; they're waiting for you."

Vanessa walked alongside the girl, who she guessed wasn't much older than nineteen, twenty at the outside, and found she had to quicken her step to keep up as they made their way along a narrow hallway.

"How long have you worked for Mr. Webman?" Vanessa asked.

Olivia pulled a face. "A couple months now—although most days it does seem like a hell of a lot longer."

"You don't enjoy working here?"

"It's a job." Olivia grunted. "I guess it could be worse, though—I could be one of the contestants. No offense."

"None taken." Vanessa laughed; the girl definitely had the looks and top-heavy figure to be a shoo-in on *The Gentleman's Choice*. "What makes you say that?"

Olivia stopped by the door to the wardrobe department, which was a somewhat grandiose title for what was really just one room with an array of racks filled with minidresses and lingerie; Vanessa dreaded to think what manner of inappropriately slutty outfits Jayne picked out for her, given their earlier clash.

"My job is barely minimum wage and is a complete waste of my chemistry degree. I know I only got it because Skippy wants to fuck me. But it's okay experience, and I don't have to get naked and screw on camera for a bunch of pathetic people to get off to."

"Touché, Olivia." Vanessa was truly impressed. Olivia was a bright one and cynical way beyond her years—that much was for sure.

She'd also just talked her way onto Vanessa's growing list of suspects.

Chapter Nineteen

They'd waited 'til the early morning to strip Mai Ling naked and hose her down in the muddy backyard, having left her locked in a small, empty room for days with only the smell of her own body and stale pee for company; Mai Ling had marked the time by the toilet breaks they'd allowed her, which had been just two per day—a total of eight since they'd forced her into the tiny room. The dominatrix had given Mai Ling an inadequate amount of water and a single slice of bread on each brief trip to the restroom, for which she was meant to be grateful.

As they sprayed her naked body with the long, snaking hose, the dominatrix, clad in her bustless leather outfit and feather mask, had chastised Mai Ling for urinating in her jeans and making a run for the trees. All the while, the silent gimp aimed the strong, cold stream of water directly between Mai Ling's legs; she guessed that was meant to be retribution for kicking him hard in the balls during her vain attempt to escape.

Without taking the time to dry her off, the two had strapped Mai Ling into a red leather BDSM harness that forced her to kneel in the center of the tiled kitchen floor with her wrists restrained behind her back and strapped to her ankles. They had kept her totally nude and vulnerable, of course, and Mai Ling couldn't help but notice the lust in the eyes of the dominatrix as she circled with a glinting razor blade in her hand.

"Please…" Mai Ling sobbed. "Please, don't…"

"Don't *what*?" the dominatrix mocked her.

"Let me go." Mai Ling struggled to make eye contact with the woman as she stalked around her helpless body. "I'll do anything you want me to do. *Anything*."

"That's very much a given, Mai Ling," the dominatrix purred. "You're hardly in any position to refuse us what we want, are you?"

Mai Ling tried to reply, but the words refused to form, her throat clogged with tears and thick, slimy phlegm. In her mind she tried desperately to place the woman's voice—there was that vague familiarity, but it was concealed beneath the too-obvious phony accent. That the dominatrix and her gimp bothered to disguise their voices gave Mai Ling a grain of hope—it could mean they intended to let her go once they'd taken their pleasure from her. Then again, it could also mean they were both playing a part, and the odd accents were simply part of their twisted fantasy.

It was a thought Mai Ling couldn't bear to entertain.

"You don't have to do everything he says, you know." Mai Ling found her voice; although the woman was playing the part of the dom, Mai Ling guessed it could have had little bearing on who the actual dominant one in the relationship was. The gimp could just as easily *chosen* his part and allowed his partner to play hers. "You can let me go before he comes back." She eyed the silver blade the dominatrix held so carefully between forefinger and thumb and tried not to think about what the woman might have in mind for its use.

"You don't know what it's like, Mai Ling," the dom hissed. "Some of us have no choice but to do as we're told. And some of us are victims of an unfortunate fate. Perhaps if you hadn't been such a slut at the orgy, you wouldn't be here right now."

"Is that what this is all about?" Mai Ling's heart pounded hard against her ribs; the cool hardness of the tiles hurt her knees. "Are you punishing me for being on that stupid show?"

The dominatrix stopped abruptly in front of Mai Ling and stared down at her, eyes blazing behind her mask, bare breasts heaving with each angry breath. "It is *not* a stupid show!" she snapped. "*You* are the stupid one for being such a whore with those people—it was obvious to anyone Cole was unhappy sharing you, but you were too busy *fornicating* with that awful couple to notice."

Mai Ling flinched as the dominatrix pointed at her with the razor blade, its keen edge only inches from her cheek. "I was only doing what they told me to do," Mai Ling protested; perhaps if she could abdicate responsibility for what had upset her captor, she could garner some empathy? "It was nothing more than playing a part—I had no choice but to do as I was told."

"Then maybe you *do* know what it's like." The dominatrix smiled at Mai Ling; her glossy, scarlet lips opened up like a fresh, bloody wound. The kitchen door opened, and the gimp came in. He carried a straight razor in one latex-clad hand and a TV remote in the other; his eyes studied the floor tiles as he walked toward Mai Ling.

"*No…*" Mai Ling gasped as her eyes fixed upon the shiny blade that had emerged from the white, pearlescent handle.

As the dominatrix stepped aside, the gimp flicked on the TV above the countertop, and a jerky home movie appeared on the flat-screen. Although the image was a tad grainy and the sound turned down low, Mai Ming instantly recognized her kidnappers; they were in what appeared to be some seedy swingers' club. In the background were naked couples fucking in plain view of everyone.

"We are going to play a game," the dominatrix announced. "We shall begin with a quiz."

"I don't want to play anything with you." Mai Ling couldn't help the tears rolling from her eyes, nor the pitiful cry that caught in her throat.

"Like I said, Mai Ling"—the dreadful overfamiliarity with which the dominatrix used her name filled Mai Ling with a dread she'd never felt before in her life—"sometimes we don't always have a choice in what we do."

The gimp shuffled to a spot someplace behind Mai Ling; his breathing was heavy, labored within the tight confines of the leather mask. And, although she could no longer see the cruel silver blade he held in his hand, it terrified Mai Ling to no longer have the man in her line of sight. "Your first question…" The dominatrix stepped forward. Once more, she stood directly in front of Mai Ling. "What kind of snake frightened your horse?"

"Excuse me?"

The dominatrix looked over Mai Ling's head at the gimp, and then back again. "*Answer the fucking question!*"

Mai Ling twisted her head to the side as the dom thrust the razor blade at her face. She slowed up at the last second, and Mai Ling felt the cold, thin steel resting lightly against her cheek. She was desperate to move away from the thing but didn't for fear of it slicing deep into the soft skin of her face.

"What kind of snake—"

"I don't know!" Mai Ling blurted out the truth; she hadn't seen the snake because she'd been too busy doing her damndest to stay on her rearing horse. "I *honestly* don't know."

Through her tears, Mai Ling caught the dominatrix's barely perceptible nod and the faintest flicker of a smile on those dreadful lips.

There came the sound of sudden movement from behind Mai Ling and the creaking rustle of leather; along with it came the cold caress of steel down along the left-hand side of her naked back. Mai Ling yelped and flinched with surprise; at first, she felt no pain, only the hot, wet trickle of blood making its way down the indent at the small of her back and between her buttocks.

"Second question," the dominatrix declared as the long, deep cut along Mai Ling's back ignited in sharp, searing pain. There could be no denying the pure, unadulterated relish in the woman's voice: it was a singsong tone that filled Mai Ling with dread and had her praying for a quick release.

"Please, no." Mai Ling's voice sounded so weak, pathetic in the vast kitchen, and she felt truly ashamed of herself for feeding the dominatrix's sadistic pleasures.

"Mai Ling… what country does Cole Gianni come from?"

Was the dominatrix deliberately trying to sound like a prime-time game show host? The tone made her all the more sinister to her victim. "See, it's a nice, easy one—I'm not a *complete* monster." The smile she gave Mai Ling suggested otherwise.

Fighting back the tears and trying her best to ignore the agony radiating from the wound in her back into every corner of her body and the warm, sticky blood pooling between her bare toes, Mai Ling managed to force out a few words. "It's some small town in Bolivia," she replied. "I can't remember the name, but it was *definitely* somewhere in Bolivia."

"*Wrong!*" The dominatrix's sudden flash of anger terrified Mai Ling; she flinched and leaned back, desperate to be even a few inches away from the woman's evil wrath. She would have likely toppled over had it not been for the gimp's powerful hands appearing from behind to grab her shoulders.

At first, Mai Ling thought the gimp had cut her again with the straight razor, and she flinched at his touch. But all she felt were his hot, moist palms on her bare skin and preternaturally strong fingers digging into her flesh. With a grunt and a rough jolt, the gimp pushed Mai Ling forward and held her still.

"He's from *Eastern Europe*, you stupid, ignorant little girl!" The dominatrix bent over to shout in Mai Ling's face, flecks of spittle flying every which way. "*Everybody* knows that! Even people who haven't seen the show know that— and *you've been on it*!" As she toyed with the razor blade between her fingers, the glinting virgin steel caught the light; it twinkled in Mai Ling's eyes. "Did you not pay any attention to that poor man at all? Were you too preoccupied with who you were going to fuck in front of him to appreciate how he opened up to you? Or do you just like being hurt, Mai Ling?" She stepped toward Mai Ling, so close her spike-heeled shoes pressed against the girl's trembling knees.

Mai Ling shook her head and tears welled up in her eyes; she felt so hopeless, scared, vulnerable. Of course, she knew the official line regarding Cole's origins, but she also recalled him slipping up and revealing where he was actually from—it had been a sweet off-camera moment between the two of them. Thus, Mai Ling had assumed the dom's question to be a trick one, and that she, too, knew the real answer. Well, even if the awful woman did know the truth, she was frighteningly pissed at Mai Ling's reply.

"You know the rules by now, Mai Ling." The dominatrix brandished the razor blade inches from Mai Ling's eyes.

"*Please!*" Mai Ling cried, although she knew begging for mercy would do her no good at all; her captors had no concept of compassion; they had made that much painfully clear.

Held tightly in place by the gimp behind her, Mai Ling was powerless to move or resist. All she could do to block out the nightmare was clamp her eyes tight shut as the dom placed the keen edge of the small blade onto the hard ridge of her clavicle. There, she pressed down hard enough for the razor to cut deep into the sweat-slicked skin and grate on the bone beneath.

Mai Ling took in a sharp gasp of breath at the terrible sensation of cold steel invading her flesh. She wriggled her torso, trying her best to pull away from the gimp's grasp, but he was deceptively strong for such a little man, and she was held fast.

"*No—please…*"

Smiling, spurred on by Mai Ling's sobbing, the dominatrix drew the razor blade downward over her victim's body, tracing over the gentle mound of Mai Ling's heaving breast and directly through the center of her pink, puckered nipple.

Mai Ling let out a piercing, bloodcurdling scream as the cruel blade bisected the sensitive flesh. The pain was like nothing she'd experienced before, even eclipsing the agony of her cut back. It lit up her entire body, had her mind swirling gray and nebulous, and made her wish more than anything she would die right then and have it all over and done with.

Eyes still shut tight against the torture, Mai Ling felt the blade slip out of her flesh as the dominatrix reached the lower curve of her breast, a hair's breadth away from digging into the ribs there. A rivulet of warm blood flowed freely from the vertical slice the dom had made. It poured down Mai Ling's belly, filling her navel, over her thighs, and onto the tiled floor. In her mind's eye, Mai Ling pictured herself drenched in a blanket of thick, congealing scarlet, her once-beautiful body ruined.

"That's what you get for being so *fucking* stupid, you… stupid girl!" The dominatrix grabbed at Mai Ling's face, squeezing it hard. Her long, pitiless fingers held the girl's chin and cheeks even tighter than the gimp held her shoulders. "Look at me, stupid girl!"

Mai Ling felt the warm, wet heat of the woman's command in her face and the spray of fresh spit spackling her tear-dampened skin. And, as much as she wanted to stay within the relative sanctuary of the darkness her screwed-up eyes afforded, she knew she had no choice but to comply.

To refuse to do so would inevitably incur the evil woman's wrath and bring about yet more pain.

Sobbing, Mai Ling forced open her eyes. She was met by the dominatrix's malevolent eyes, which remained behind that God-awful mask of hers; their faces were little more than an inch or two apart, and Mai Ling smelled her captor's hot, sweet breath as it invaded her nostrils.

Beyond the dominatrix, the TV on the kitchen wall played the orgy scenes from *The Gentleman's Choice*, and Mai Ling saw her naked self there, immersed in the three-way fucking with Danielle and Aaron; what had once been a pleasant memory of a unique experience became associated in her mind with pain and terror.

"I hope you do better with your third question." The dominatrix squeezed Mai Ling's face harder still and pulled down on the girl's chin so their eyes were dead level—there was no escaping her awful, penetrating gaze. "Otherwise, things are going to get a hell of a lot worse than *this*."

The dominatrix forced Mai Ling's head downward 'til her chin rested on the top of her bloodied sternum; Mai Ling choked back the acid taste that bubbled up from the nausea in her stomach to the back of her throat at what she saw. Her meticulously sliced, ruined breast dripped with thick, dark blood, and with every quivering breath she took, more pulsed out of the deep, red line that ran down its full curve. The blood snaked down her heaving belly; it was hot and sticky and crawled between her thighs like unwelcome fingers. Wave upon wave of agony washed over Mai Ling's body, both front and back, and yet she had no means of escaping any of it, no hope at all.

"Next question… what is Cole Gianni's shoe size?" The dominatrix spoke softly with a tone that belied the sinister nature of the seemingly innocuous question.

Mai Ling's head whirled with blind panic. How the hell was she supposed to know the answer to that? In her time both on and off camera with Cole, his shoe size had never been discussed; who asks a guy the size of his feet on their first dates together? What was she supposed to do to answer the dom's question? Guess?

It then occurred to Mai Ling that, unlike the previous two questions, she was not *meant* to know the answer.

"I'm waiting, Mai Ling." The dominatrix stood up straight and stepped away, while the gimp retained his tight hold on her shoulders—it was clear the two didn't want their victim moving too much. "Either you know the answer, or you *don't*. Which is it?"

The realization of her fate brought Mai Ling some comfort, and for the first time since she'd been kidnapped, she felt a little in control—just a little. She looked up at the dominatrix, at the garish scenes from her own brief spell on *The Gentleman's Choice* and the gratuitous amounts of bare flesh on show—much of it was hers—and just wanted it to all end, for the unbearable pain to be over.

"Why don't you just kill me, *bitch*?" She forced herself to quit blubbering and presented the dominatrix with her defiant face; she snarled the final word, which was one she never used, and looked the woman square in the eyes. "Instead of playing your stupid, sick games?"

The dominatrix laughed at Mai Ling—she *actually* laughed. "I think our contestant is missing the entire point of our game show," she said to the gimp. "I guess, much like she *completely* missed the point of *The Gentleman's Choice*."

Reaching over Mai Ling's head, the dom retrieved the gimp's straight razor from the countertop beside him.

"Now, Mai Ling…" The dominatrix crouched down next to Mai Ling and with one hand, she parted the girl's blood-slicked thighs just enough to reveal the soft, sensitive flesh that lay between. Speaking slowly, deliberately, her voice oozing malice, the dom asked, "Do you know Cole Gianni's shoe size, or do you *not* know Cole Gianni's shoe size?"

Despite her best efforts to remain defiant, to goad the woman into killing her, the tears returned to Mai Ling's eyes, and she began to sob uncontrollably. "I don't know," she wailed. "*I don't fucking know*!" Weeping, begging, Mai Ling could do nothing more than brace herself as the dominatrix traced the gimp's straight razor up the inside of her thigh until the coolness of the blade bit into her most intimate place.

Chapter Twenty

I nevitably, Vanessa had made it through to Night Two of *The Gentleman's Choice*. It was pretty much a given, since she'd done her homework and pulled out all the stops in order to pander to the show's audience; according to Skippy, they'd apparently voted in droves to see her burgeoning relationship with Cole move on to the next step toward the ever-looming fifth night.

Vanessa was delighted with her own thoroughness in preparing for her role on the show; she'd really gone over and above the call of duty in the Hickersley case by researching past episodes of the show, the personalities of winners and losers—which she now knew were more often than not faked—and the audience demographics. Vanessa was more than confident she had enough in her armory to see her through to that final night, whether she decided to go through with its expected conclusion or otherwise.

And, for as much as Vanessa tried to convince herself it was all about seeking justice for Tracy and enjoying the self-satisfaction that came with connecting the dots to the Omawumi case, she knew in her heart she was pushing way beyond her comfort zone the avarice Tom Hickersley's cold, hard cash afforded her.

After all, that's really what had driven Charlotte "Charlie" Michaels into the PI business in the first place.

"I'm really looking forward to this," Cole whispered to Vanessa as they were led along the narrow hallway between studio sets by one of the young production assistants. She was a thick-set young woman who took her job way too seriously and was so obviously emulating Jayne Torrez; she'd even clutched her plastic clipboard to her chest the entire walk from the dressing rooms. "I don't know about you, but I really could use a good massage right about now."

Vanessa turned her head to smile at Cole. She thought the guy looked kind of cute, especially clad in the oversized white, fluffy robe that matched hers, and there was something about his sweet naiveté that made getting a couples' massage with Cole Gianni on their second date seem like the most natural thing in the world to Vanessa—albeit in front of the cameras and watched by countless strangers.

"Yeah, it's been quite the week so far—I could use some stress relief," she said, hoping the double entendre hit home. Her research had shown it unquestionably paid off to keep Cole interested off camera as well as on. "And this is only Day Two." Cole returned the warmth. "I hope you're having a good time, Vanessa."

Naturally, Vanessa was well versed in the less-than-subtle workings of the male ego to recognize Cole's clumsy fish fishing for compliments. "Well, I'd be lying if I said it wasn't all taking some getting used to—with the cameras and everything," she confessed. "But I'm really enjoying spending time with you, Cole—you make all this kinda fun."

Another warm smile, and Cole's fragile ego was duly stroked and eased back into place.

"Here you go, you two." Clipboard still pressed to her chest, the production assistant stopped dead in her tracks and pushed open a numberless, nondescript door that sat two-thirds of the way down the hallway. "You can both get yourselves ready and wait in here; the masseuses will be along in just a few minutes."

Vanessa noticed the production assistant was watching her as she made her way through the doorway. She saw harsh judgment written all over the girl's face; whether it was because of some inherent feminist agenda or simple jealousy because she wasn't the one taking part on the show, Vanessa couldn't be entirely sure. The door was closed and the assistant gone before she could make any further assessment.

"Well, this is *really* nice." Cole peered around the cozy room Vanessa was sure he'd seen a thousand times before. "You know, I feel more relaxed already."

"Me too," Vanessa replied. She couldn't help but be impressed with the pleasant massage room the show's set dressers had put together deep in the bowels of the studio.

They'd gone all out to make the room resemble a professional massage parlor in some exclusive mountain spring spa—the kind of place Vanessa often planned to treat herself to following the successful conclusion of a particularly trying case but never quite got around to booking. The dressers had obviously been meticulous in their research; the room carried none of the grubby fakery Vanessa associated with the chain massage parlors slotted into seemingly every strip mall in America; it simply oozed luxury. And, of course, it was absolutely nothing at all like the seedy, back street rub-and-tug shops Vanessa had spent far too much time frequenting during her early PI days, back when locating trafficked young women was the bread-and-butter of her new business.

The massage room was dominated by twin burgundy massage tables. It was subtly lit by a dusky, orange-red glow from concealed lighting, which was accentuated by the warm, dancing yellow from the dozen or so candles dotted around the place on tiny, purpose-built shelves. Upon each one of the shelves sat a tiny vase containing a single, pink lotus flower. Soft, subliminal music wafted out from hidden speakers; Vanessa identified it as something definitely new age played on overbearing panpipes—it was a tad stereotypical *massage music* for her tastes, but it certainly set the scene with the musty, cloying, smoky smell that hung heavy in the warm air.

"Isn't this heavenly?" Cole enthused over a smoldering stick of incense, the source of the smoky aroma; it sat at a forty-five-degree angle in a black porcelain holder designed to catch the falling ash.

"It reminds me of my carefree days as a student." Vanessa wandered across the room and took a sniff at the thick, white smoke spiraling up from the end of the stick. It unquestionably carried the distinct whiff of marijuana with it, along with the more subtle bouquets of ginger, rosewood, and an undertone of eucalyptus.

"You liked to smoke too?" Cole appeared excited by the revelation. "Do you still…" Stopping himself short, lifting a hand to his mouth to mime drawing on a fat roach, Cole's eyes glanced up at the miniscule camera in the corner over the door—it was one of four strategically placed around the room Vanessa had spotted the moment she'd stepped inside. She was certain there'd be more dotted about she wasn't meant to see—there always was.

As disconcerting as it was having her every move scrutinized that way, Vanessa had quickly learned to ignore the ever-present cameras as well as to watch every word that left her mouth. She simply couldn't afford any sort of careless slipup so early on in the game. Saying the wrong thing at the wrong time would run the risk of her either alienating the discerning audience and getting voted off or giving herself away as a fraud with an ulterior motive. And, with the hope Tracy's killer was most likely watching the show—either on a screen somewhere or closer to home among the production itself—Vanessa couldn't be too careful at all. "I guess it's time we get naked, then." The innocence in Cole's tone meant his words didn't come across as lascivious, and Vanessa was grateful for that. The last thing she wanted was to be trapped in such a small room with a pervert interested only in watching her undress, no matter how handsome she might find said pervert to be.

They'd shot the preamble to the date scene earlier on that afternoon, which meant Vanessa had spent most of her day wearing the fluffy, ankle-length bathrobe with nothing beneath it. The robe was thick enough to cover most of Vanessa's body and offer as much comfort as she could have wanted, but she'd still felt more than a little exposed as she'd been ushered between sets and her dressing room; it was as if the absence of proper day clothes held the danger of opening up her duplicity to discovery. "I shall let you go first, ma'am," Cole said in a pretty passable English accent. He made an exaggerated show of turning his back to Vanessa and fixing his eyes straight ahead, upon one of the flickering candles. "That is most chivalrous of you, sir." Vanessa couldn't help but chuckle—she knew her date was playing to the cameras, but it was a nice touch, nonetheless.

Shrugging off her robe, Vanessa pushed all thoughts of the cameras to the back of her mind. The show's subscribers were going to see all of her at some point or another throughout the course of the week, so she figured it was as good a time as any to reveal her body in all its naked glory. Besides, there was something sweetly chaste about the couples' massage scenario that made the gratuitous excuse for nudity seem okay. Naked, Vanessa slipped beneath the small, thin towel that had been neatly folded and placed in the center of the massage table. She lay face down, and the towel just about covered her buttocks, leaving her back and legs completely bare for the delectation of the viewing public. The soft vinyl of the table was refreshingly cool against her skin; gooseflesh prickled her arms and legs at its touch.

"My eyes are averted, good sir—your modesty is quite safe." Vanessa played along with the tone Cole had set, even having an awful stab at the Brit accent; it was actually quite fun. "I promise you I shan't peek." She twisted her head so she faced the door and had no chance to catch even an accidental glimpse of Cole. She listened as he disrobed and made himself comfortable upon his table, and she imagined him attempting to cover himself with a small pink towel of equal skimpiness to hers. It did strike Vanessa as a little contrived, though, seeing as though countless people across the World Wide Web had *not* averted their eyes and were no doubt already in the early stages of excitement having just watched her and Cole getting naked.

"All done," Cole said with an exaggerated stage whisper. "You can look now, Vanessa."

She half expected to turn around on her massage table to see Cole in all his naked glory, his famous erection pointing in at her like some long, fat, accusing finger. But no, true to the show's title, and opposite to its premise, Cole was facedown with his bare ass covered the best he could manage with the tiny towel. And for that, Vanessa was grateful.

The door opened, light flooded in from the humming, flickering strips out in the hallway, and in walked two tall, white-clad figures; they were followed by a cameraman so short as to make the masseuses appear Amazonian.

"Hi, Cole and Vanessa, I'm Olga, and this is my twin sister, Ana. We are from Sweden," one of the white-clad figures breezed in an obviously—badly—faked Scandinavian accent.

Vanessa suppressed a cynical sigh and almost rolled her eyes: tall, sexy Scandinavian masseuses, and twins to boot—of course they were. Skippy Webman really wasn't above rolling out the clichés to pander to his less than discerning audience.

"I shall be massaging you, Vanessa, and Ana will be taking good care of Cole," Olga continued as the two positioned themselves adjacent to each of the tables and pulled out a bottle of massage oil from the front pocket of their tight, crisp, obscenely short masseuse uniforms that clung to their every curve and showed off endless smooth, tanned legs.

"I'm very pleased to meet you, Olga." Vanessa twisted her neck to greet her masseuse 'til it crackled; maybe she was even more in need of a massage than she realized—that only ever happened when she was severely stressed out. Vanessa had somewhat limited experience of couples' massages; she'd once dated a guy who would book them into a local joint ostensibly to bond and enjoy some relaxation together, only to confess after a half dozen sessions or so it was actually to feed his fantasy of watching his girlfriend being touched by another woman. Naturally, Vanessa had ended the fledgling relationship there and then. She'd been rightly annoyed at the asshole's underhandedness. Had he just been honest with her about his inclination from the start, she had a bunch of girlfriends and female acquaintances she could have called on at a moment's notice. Any one of them would have been more than delighted to help her fulfill the guy's fantasy without the need for pretense and the outrageous expense of a *Massage City* membership.

"So, let us get started here. Are you ready, Ana?" Olga's deep, husky timbre and appalling accent filled the room.

"Yes, I am ready to massage Cole, Sister."

Ana's reply to Olga had Vanessa cringing; even given the lowest denominator of the show's demographic, it really wasn't necessary to hammer home the twin angle with such relentless unsubtlety—they really should spring for a decent scriptwriter.

Silently, the diminutive cameraman scooted around the tables, poking his lens in turn at Vanessa and Cole before he turned its attention to the fake Swedes as they went about their work.

Vanessa hadn't been entirely sure what she was supposed to expect from the evening's activity, as none of the shows she'd watched in preparation for her appearance had actually featured a couples' massage. That had been down to the luck of the draw rather than sloppy research, of course, as there was no way she could have gone through the entire *The Gentleman's Choice* back catalog. Nonetheless, it came as no surprise whatsoever when, only a few minutes into administering an expert massage, both Ana and Olga stripped off their tiny uniform dresses and stepped out of their flat shoes. For the benefit of the camera, they both stood still, tall, naked, and totally epilated next to the massage tables.

"For your special night together, you and your lover are to receive a Nuru massage for couples," Olga said, more for the benefit of the cameras than her clients. As she spoke, behind her, Ana poured oil between her own breasts and smiled seductively as it ran through her ample cleavage and down her taut belly. "And that means Ana and I will be massaging your whole bodies with ours."

Vanessa was surprised to feel the warm air caress her bare butt as the deliciously nude Olga whipped away the towel; she lay there entirely naked and feeling even more exposed than she had beneath the miniscule towel, which had at least provided a soupcon of psychological cover. Vanessa heard the sharp *click* of a bottle top and then came the slippery warmth of the thick, aromatic massage oil dribbling along her back and over and between the twin mounds of her buttocks. Looking across at Cole, Vanessa saw he was receiving the exact same treatment from Ana, whose heavy breasts swung and quivered as she clambered up onto the table to straddle his lower back with her toned thighs.

As Olga followed her sister's lead—there was no doubting they were bona fide twins, as even their breasts were identical—Vanessa did her level best to relax and forget she was about to be massaged by a ridiculously hot blonde woman for the benefit of complete strangers, who would be getting off on watching her oiled up and rubbed down. She also pushed the fact that the whole scenario had her more than a little turned on—and had kicked her erotic brain into gear, to the back of her mind; it wasn't something she'd planned for, and she needed to keep her mind on the job. As Olga went about her work with strong, busy hands and firm, slippery body, Vanessa fought the unwanted arousal by turning her mind to Tom Hickersley, Tracy's father.

She'd caught something in the man's eyes the afternoon she'd called by the Hickersley house. It was a fleeting look that lurked at the back of her mind long after the lucrative deal to unearth Tracy's killer was struck, and she was well on her way home.

Although she couldn't be 100 percent certain, Vanessa had a hunch there was a lot more to Tom and Tracy's falling out than a father's disappointment with his daughter's choice to cheapen herself on some unpleasant little internet show for the whole world to see. Vanessa's hunch had been further exacerbated by how Tracy's mother had preferred to remain in the background, other than to let loose her open hostility, and appeared *resentful* someone was at her home for Tracy's benefit.

And then there were the family photographs around the few parts of the house Charlie Michaels, PI, had been permitted to see. Or more to the point, the lack thereof. There'd been a handful of Tracy, of course. Tom was in each one, a broad grin on his face and an arm around the beautiful daughter of whom he was so obviously proud. There had been maybe two, no more than three, of Tracy and her mother, and in those, they stood *almost* shoulder to shoulder, never touching. The half-inch gap between them yawned like the embodiment of an unspoken chasm in their mother-daughter relationship.

Could Tom Hickersley's motivation for throwing such a large amount of cash at a random PI have been deep-rooted in guilt? She'd just happened to hit the right buttons with a thumbnail-sketch comparison between Tracy's death and that of another *Gentleman's Choice* contestant, and he'd cut her a check on the spot. The thought had stuck with Vanessa, and she wouldn't rest until she asked him and got to the truth.

Was it possible the man had taken his father-daughter relationship a step too far? Had Tracy been destined to step into her mother's shoes one day? Barbara Hickersley definitely had the air of a wife only hanging around for the money, and with her marriage as dead as her daughter, she was likely little more than an expensive alimony suit away from running off with the pool boy or some such. If Tom

Hickersley engaging an expensive PI in the miniscule hope of uncovering his daughter's murderer was nothing more than to assuage his own conscience at having betrayed her trust, then what did that make the PI he'd commissioned?

Complicit somehow?

It made her a hell of a lot of money, that's what.

Chastising herself for overthinking, which was something she had a tendency to do when things were going well, she was *waiting for the other shoe to drop,* as her eternally pessimistic mother used to call it. Vanessa allowed herself to switch focus to the exotic caress of Olga's full, slick breasts; maybe the distraction of a little arousal wouldn't be such a bad thing after all. The full weight of Olga's breasts slid all the way down from Vanessa's nape to the tops of her thighs, soft skin gliding over soft skin, the hardness of the masseuse's nipples adding to the sensuality of the full-body massage.

"Okay, it's time to turn over, Vanessa," Olga declared. So saying, she slid her statuesque frame from the table and stood by Vanessa's head, hands on hips.

"Are you sure?" Vanessa moaned and tried her best not to stare directly at the faux-Swede's denuded pudendum that stood mere inches from her face—it really was difficult not to. "I was *really* enjoying that."

"Absolutely positive, Vanessa," Olga purred. "And believe me, if you enjoyed that, you're going to totally *love* what's coming next." The masseuse's faux accent slipped a tad as she was clearly focused upon sounding sexy, and Vanessa thought she caught a twang of New York City—Queens, the Bronx perhaps?

Out the corner of her eye, Vanessa noted Cole had no hesitation whatsoever in flipping his oil-slicked body over on the table, nor about presenting Ana with his semi-tumescent dick; it looked to be every inch as magnificent as Vanessa remembered seeing it on the archived shows she'd pored over, if not more so for being in the flesh.

There was no stalling the inevitable; taking a deep breath, Vanessa turned herself over on the table and braced herself as the stunning Olga repositioned herself on top of her. The masseuse wriggled herself into place, her legs either side of Vanessa's butt and that smooth, hard mound resting upon the shallow dip of her belly.

"Is this all okay for you, Vanessa?" Cole asked. There was a distinct, breathy tremor in the guy's voice as Ana went to work on his chest with her oily breasts; he let out a barely perceptible moan when she dipped low to massage his belly and she brushed against his penis with a nipple. "I hope you're finding this massage as hot as I am." The line came out hackneyed and forced—it was quite obviously prewritten.

"Yeah, this is unbelievably hot, Cole," Vanessa heard herself saying, her voice labored as Olga's breasts pressed hard against hers. It wasn't quite the line Skippy had prepared for her, but she'd never had even the slightest intention of delivering the line he'd given her: *it's making me so wet having my body massaged by a hot lesbian.* Being on the porn show for a case was one thing; leaving what little remained of her dignity at the door was entirely another.

There was no escaping the fact Olga was unbelievably hot, so much so, she awakened desires deep within Vanessa that she'd considered to be long buried in her formative, exploratory years. The sensual caress of the masseuse's silky soft skin on her body, the warmth of her peppermint breath, the raw wantonness in her eyes—all tore Vanessa's mind away from thoughts of Tracy Hickersley, her probably highly inappropriate father, and the terrible wounds she'd shared with the poor Nigerian girl. Who the fuck got their kicks out of severing young women's fingers and slicing up their bodies to a point beyond recognition, while they screamed so loud for mercy their throats tore on the inside?

Vanessa closed her eyes against the gruesome thoughts, forgot about the cameras, and embraced the myriad of sweet sensations coursing through her body. Starting again at Vanessa's neck, Olga slid her firm, slick body all the way downward. She paused to massage Vanessa's breasts with firm, circular strokes of her own and then, continuing, she gently nudged Vanessa's thighs apart. As Olga's nipple slipped into just the right spot, Vanessa finally let herself go and let out a long, low moan of pleasure.

Chapter Twenty-One

"Have you seen this total *bullshit*?" Skippy gave out a dramatic huff and turned the sound on the flatscreen down low.

"Of course I have," Cole replied to the producer's obviously rhetorical question; Skippy knew damn well he'd always made it his business to know what was going on beyond the closeted confines of *The Gentleman's Choice*, especially when there was a chance of something adversely affecting everything they'd painstakingly built up over the years.

Cole had barely set foot on the studio lot before Skippy demanded his presence in the office—the big guy loved nothing more than to have an audience to rage to whenever something ground his gears. Cole had been nicely relaxed up to that point; his skin was still pleasantly smooth and just a touch oily from the night before, his muscles pleasantly loosened up from the expert massage Ana had given him—it turned out she and her twin sister were genuine masseuses. Ana had definitely known what she was doing to ease Cole's tension, and, if the noises Vanessa was making were anything to go by, Olga had done a tremendous job.

He'd also spent some nice off-camera time in the green room with Vanessa after their massages. They'd talked, laughed a little, and grown a touch closer just like any regular couple getting to know one another; Cole had adapted over his years on the show to treat the cameras and fake scenarios as the norm—it was that which kept him from going crazy. It had been a good night, all in all; Cole had gotten to see the beautiful Vanessa completely naked in the massage room and had found out a little more about her, although she did appear to be more guarded than most contestants after Night Two. Nonetheless, he'd actually enjoyed her company without the specter of expected sex hanging over the two of them. "It's kinda tragic, when you think about it," Cole said to Skippy, knowing damn well it would be like waving a red rag in front of a bull. "Damn fucking right it's *tragic!*" Predictably, Skippy took the bait and spat out his words. Fuming, he threw the TV remote down on his desk so hard the battery compartment flew open, and the twin double-A batteries rolled onto the floor. Ignoring them, Skippy leaned back in his creaking chair. Cole thought he'd never seen his business partner looking more like he needed a drink than he did right then, and really wouldn't have blamed him for reaching for the bottle he kept out of sight in his bottom drawer. But, mercifully, ten o'clock in the morning was still a tad too early to hit the sauce, even for a pissed-off Skippy Webman.

"The poor guy killed his wife, Skippy." Cole's attempt to appeal to the man's latent compassion was met with an upturned lip and an animal noise that sounded like a growl.

"Yeah, and the asshole's blaming *us* for it!" Skippy pointed accusingly at the TV. There, a sad-faced John

Beechwood was being hurried from the courthouse by an attorney in a two-thousand-dollar pantsuit, and one expensively manicured hand held up to shield her client from the sea of surrounding cameras.

Cole sat in silence and watched the drama play out with piqued interest as the scrolling feed at the bottom of the screen explained Mr. Beechwood had been granted a hundred-thousand-dollar bail at his arraignment—pending psychiatric evaluation. He'd entered a plea of not guilty on the grounds he and his girlfriend had been engaged in an entirely consensual BDSM sex game, which had gone tragically wrong when he'd accidentally strangled the life out of her. To Cole's cynical mind, it was either a horrific misadventure or the perfect way to dispose of an unwanted lover.

"It's the classic *Fifty Shades* defense." Cole broke the quiet between him and Skippy—if there was one thing he couldn't stand more than Skippy's rants, it was the man's red-faced, petulant silences. "There's been a whole raft of them since the books first came out—even more since those God-awful soft-core movies—and most of the defendants have been poor saps like Beechwood and his gal trying to add a little spice to their bedroom."

Cole contemplated the photograph of Amy Woodburn that flashed up on the TV; she wasn't unattractive, in a plain Jane kind of way, although she did appear to be carrying a little too much weight for Cole's liking. "Exactly," Skippy fumed. "There's all that BDSM and torture porn out there, and that prick's blaming *The Gentleman's Choice* for murdering his fucking girlfriend!"

"He's saying it was an accident, Skip, that's kinda the whole point of his defense." Cole flapped a hand in the direction of the TV for emphasis. Beechwood had been bundled into an awaiting car, and the TV station's cameraman had dutifully followed its progress down along the street until it took a right on the red light at the end.

"Accident my bloody ass," Skippy growled, his mood not lifting any with the departure of Mr. Beechwood. "And since when were we ever responsible for what Joe fuckin' Public does in his bedroom—and to whom?"

Cole smiled; even in his most irrational tempers, Skippy's Britishness demanded correct grammar. "What is it you always say, my old friend? There's no such thing as bad publicity?"

Despite himself, Skippy cracked a wry smile at that one. "Sure—this kind of crap always seems to boost our subscription figures. It gives us top quality, prime-time coverage, all thanks to ham-fisted idiots like that who want to get away with murder and use the likes of us as their scapegoat. There's no way on God's green earth we could ever afford that level of exposure, even if we were allowed to advertise anywhere near the networks."

"But…?"

"You know the *but* as well as I do, Cole." Skippy pulled a sour face as if he had an unexpected bad taste in his mouth. He pointed a chubby finger at the TV once again as if somehow all the pain happening in his world was its fault. "*This* kind of publicity never fails to bring out all the puritanical do-gooders who believe anything at all to do with sex is nothing less than the Devil's work. Beechwood and his ilk give those loonies a platform to wave their illiterate, Bible-spouting placards and protest outside every adult movie studio they can find."

Obviously, it wasn't the first time someone had blamed *The Gentleman's Choice* for an unfortunate boudoir mishap—although Beechwood's girlfriend was the first actual death attributed to the show—and there had even been the odd lawsuit or two. Not one of those had managed to stick, as their highly efficient lawyer, Reuben Goldblatt, had batted each and every one away with brutal efficiency.

"You honestly think the guy *meant* to kill his girl?" Cole studied the screen in the corner; WFTV was milking every last grubby detail of the case for all it was worth. They were rerunning the footage they'd shot less than an hour earlier of John Beechwood making his way into court while his attorney snapped *no comment* at the barrage of questions from the awaiting press.

"Are you fucking kidding me?" Skippy laughed. Finally, his mood was lightening—perhaps the day wasn't going to be too dreadful after all, and Cole wouldn't have to spend the majority of it avoiding his producer. "Just look at that arsehole—if that's not guilt written all over his stupid, lower-middle-class face, I dare you to tell me what it is."

At times, Skippy's observations of his fellow man could be brutal—astoundingly insightful, but brutal, nonetheless. There was a certain haunted look to John Beechwood's sallow features—there really was no denying that. But, then again, the man was facing a murder rap for killing his girlfriend in the throes of passion—who the hell wouldn't look haunted? "There's every chance he's innocent," Cole countered. He'd always been an advocate for innocent until proven guilty, and for giving good people the benefit of the doubt. He thought John Beechwood looked like good people, just the wrong man performing erotic asphyxiation to the wrong woman. "He just got carried away copying what he saw on our show, that's all. It happens, and don't forget Reuben advised us to put a disclaimer out at the end of all our BDSM episodes— *to cover our sick little asses*, I think he put it."

"Nah," Skippy dismissed Cole's argument with a snort. "Beechwood wanted rid of his chick and saw the perfect opportunity. They'd been together a year or two past their relationship's expiry date, and he didn't know how to break it off without her getting all emotional and things getting messy."

"So, he killed her?"

"So, he killed her."

"And what makes you think their relationship was past due, Skip?" Cole played Devil's advocate.

"That's easy—why else would John Beechwood and his middle-aged, homely girlfriend be playing sick sex games instead of *making love*?" Skippy replied as he yanked open the bottom drawer of his desk and pulled out the half bottle of bourbon he kept there.

Chapter Twenty-Two

anessa contemplated Cole as he eased back on one of the overstuffed leather couches. There were three in the green room, all of them made of chestnut brown leather that appeared fashionably distressed but was, in actual fact, just terribly old and cracked beyond repair.

She and Cole were taking a little time out before shooting the preamble to the evening's show, and she definitely welcomed the opportunity to spend as much time as she could with its star away from the cameras. So far, Vanessa had managed to accumulate a list of possible suspects from among the crew and miscellaneous hangers-on but had gotten nowhere close to eliminating any of them, let alone homing in on anyone who had obviously murderous intents. If only her job could ever be that easy. "We told Skippy after the first BDSM-related accident attributed to the show to add warnings to all relevant episodes," Cole lamented. "And here we are again."

"We?"

"Me and the company lawyer." Cole drained the last of his Diet Coke and crumpled the can with one hand; it was an unexpected, overtly macho act, and it took Vanessa by surprise—in the almost three days she'd known Cole Gianni, he hadn't shown any such traits at all. "Reuben Goldblatt has been with *The Gentleman's Choice* since the beginning. We pay the man a goddamn fortune, and Skippy insists on ignoring his advice—what's the point in that?" Cole let out a long, weary sigh and tossed the squashed soda can at the freshly emptied trash can in the corner of the room.

"Great shot." Vanessa smiled as the can sailed home. "So, you think the whole court case is going to affect the show?" Not that she was the least bit concerned about the show's reputation getting damaged by John Beechwood laying blame squarely at its door for killing his girlfriend—accidentally or otherwise. The show would survive the scandal and finger-pointing just as it had survived the other court cases and lawsuits that had popped up over the years. What did worry her, however, was the effect such a blare of publicity might have on the killer she was hunting. If he—or she, Vanessa had yet to rule out that unpleasant possibility—laid low to avoid the spotlight, then Vanessa's time on the show could well amount to nothing. With her overall objective being to draw out the killer, anything that might have him going to ground would be a more than significant setback.

Vanessa was, however, pleased *The Gentleman's Choice* didn't keep contestants from happenings in the outside world. It was very much the norm on the likes of *Love Island*, *The Bachelor*, and *Big Brother*, although the contestants typical to such shows were hardly likely to be avid followers of current events anyway. Whether it was deliberate on the part of Skippy, or he was just sloppy, Vanessa was more than happy to take every opportunity to keep up with the news; it was an old habit of hers and certainly a good trait to nurture in her line of work.

"Look, I really shouldn't be telling you any of this." Cole shuffled closer to Vanessa 'til their knees touched. It wasn't sexual in nature or any kind of subliminal come-on; to Vanessa, the gesture felt more conspiratorial—as if Cole was about to spill the world's biggest secrets. "We've had a couple of the major adult networks sniffing around the show, and the Beechwood thing has apparently upped their interest—it's sick, I know, but it is what it is."

"That sounds promising. Which networks?" Vanessa prompted, genuinely interested.

"I really shouldn't tell you that, but *Hustler* and *Playboy* are at the top of the pile. They want to take the show mainstream on their cable channels." Cole reached over to the low table in front of the couch for another can of Coke; it was his third of the day.

"You don't sound too excited by the prospect, Cole. I would've thought something like that could work out well for you, financially speaking."

Shaking his head, Cole popped the tab on his can and flinched as it fizzed a little into his face. "Skippy won't have any of it. He's too caught up in keeping the show just the way it is—he's convinced we'll make the big league all by ourselves. This Beechwood case has brought the big boys out of the woodwork again—Skippy's tried his best to keep it from me so I keep my head in the show, but I know that slippery bastard too well."

"And you don't think the show will hit the big time under its own steam?" Studying Cole's face carefully, Vanessa read the man's reply before he opened his mouth.

"Well, we haven't managed it so far," Cole said. There was sadness in his eyes, a look of resignation. "And, to tell you the truth, if I'm *really* honest, I believe *The Gentleman's Choice* plateaued a year ago, maybe even eighteen months."

Vanessa detected a distinct undertone of bitter regret in Cole's voice, which was almost—but not quite—masked by his obvious frustration at his business partner's reticence to move on. Cole was fighting hard to hide it, but he clearly felt the need to talk to her about it—to just talk with *someone*. The guy was very unhappy, and Vanessa got the distinct impression he wanted out. But did he want out enough to kill?

"Won't Skippy even talk with the network people?" Vanessa probed. It was second nature to keep her suspects talking; sooner or later they'd let loose that one golden nugget that always gave them away.

"Oh, he talks to them all right," Cole laughed. "We have another meeting this afternoon, as it happens."

"That's promising—at least he's prepared to hear what they have to say."

Cole chugged at his drink and then let out a quiet, discreetly silent burp behind his hand. "You'd think so, wouldn't you? But we'll go to the meeting and good ol' Skip will nod and smile and say all the right things and then come up with a million reasons why we shouldn't sell out in the car ride home. Every goddamn time. It's just one big, fat ego trip for Skippy Webman—all he wants is the affirmation of their offers to buy us out. The more they offer, the more deluded he becomes that *The Gentleman's Choice* is gonna become the next big thing, and he digs his heels in even deeper."

"So why do you put yourself through it, Cole?" Vanessa rested a hand on Cole's knee in a gesture of solidarity, of empathy.

"Because I can be a hopeless optimist at times." Cole sighed. "And, because you never know… one day the idiot might just let network money seduce him, and he'll sign on the dotted line before he changes his goddamn mind."

"What will you do if that happens, Cole?"

Cole shrugged and looked at Vanessa as if he hadn't really considered that option. She wasn't so easily fooled, though, and reckoned Cole thought of little else. She once more wondered if he was desperate enough to want to discredit the show to kill it off and murder past contestants to do so.

Either that or he harbored such a deep-rooted hatred of his creation he would kill to vent against it?

"I sometimes wonder what I've created here, Vanessa." Cole returned his half-finished can to the small table and stared wistfully at it. "When me and Skip came up with the show's concept, it seemed like the best idea *ever*. It was simple, engaging, sexy, and above all, it was *original*. Do you know how hard it is to come up with original, marketable ideas in this industry?

Of course, Vanessa did not.

"It was only ever supposed to be a stepping-stone for the two of us, our key to bigger, better things," Cole continued, eyes fixed on the Coke can. "Our plan was to be in mainstream movies by now—Hollywood, no less— either that or we'd be the next Larry Flints and living it up on a sun-kissed tropical island someplace."

"I guess this was never part of the big dream, then?" Vanessa looked around the green room that, while cozy enough, was hardly the salubrious trappings of runaway success.

"What gave the game away?" Cole tore his attention away from the soda can and managed a smile.

Vanessa squeezed Cole's knee in support. "Oh, call it a hunch—"

"*Can you fucking believe this shit!*" Skippy's angry, booming voice entered the room a second or two before his bulky frame burst through the door.

Startled, Vanessa and Cole jumped apart on the couch as if they'd been caught in a position somewhat more compromising than just having a tender heart-to-heart.

"What the hell, Skip?" Cole got to his feet as the producer stormed across the green room. His sweating face was an alarming shade of red, his breath puffed and panted from his lungs like an asthmatic's. Skippy Webman looked, for all the world, like he'd just run a half marathon.

"*This!*" Skippy waved his cell phone above his head. "This is all we bloody well need right now!"

Vanessa remained seated; whatever the big guy's beef, it didn't directly concern her, nor did she wish to appear *too* inquisitive. A loud, muffled voice blasted out from Skippy's phone; the screen was lit up with what appeared to be a young woman's face—no doubt she was the source of the producer's anger.

"Calm down, Skip, you're gonna give yourself a heart attack." Cole lifted up his hands in an attempt to placate his partner, all to no avail.

"*This* is going to give me the bloody heart attack!" Skippy snapped back. He tossed his phone onto the low table, evidently not caring whether he broke the thing's screen or not.

Vanessa peered around Cole the best she could as he stared down at Skippy's cell; on the screen, a pretty, young Hispanic woman was talking directly into the camera—it looked like she was directly addressing Cole and Skippy.

"*I found out eight weeks after I left the show, and I have definitely not slept with anyone since that last night with Cole Gianni—I'm prepared to take a lie-detector test to prove that.*"

"What is she saying, Skip?" Cole's entire forehead furrowed; his eyes narrowed to thin slits; Vanessa watched recognition creep across his face as he studied the girl on Skippy's cell.

"*I am now six months' pregnant with Cole's baby, and nobody from* The Gentleman's Choice *will return any of my calls. I really don't know what I'm supposed to do now.*"

"She's saying you knocked her up, Cole, my friend." Skippy slumped down onto the couch opposite Vanessa, his huge frame sinking into the leather.

"That's impossible—you know that, Skip." There was an air of desperation in Cole's voice.

"Yeah." Skippy made a scissor gesture with the fingers of his left hand. "But the general public at large don't know that. Also, vasectomies have been known to fail from time to time, you know—I guess we insist on a DNA test." He rubbed a damp, meaty hand down his sweaty face; he'd calmed down some, but the redness remained. "This is all we fucking need on the back of that arsehole Beechwood."

Vanessa considered putting the suggestion out there the pregnant girl had popped up *because* of the John Beechwood case, and they shouldn't be too surprised if a few more appeared as the trial drew closer. But she reminded herself it wasn't her fight, and definitely none of her concern, so she opted to keep quiet.

"Did she call?" Cole asked quietly. "What?"

Cole pointed accusingly at the cell phone and spoke slowly, if somewhat loud. "Did that girl call you with any of this?"

Skippy threw open his arms. "How the hell should I know? I've got whatsername fielding all incomings now— I sure as hell haven't spoken to anyone claiming you put them in the family way." Vanessa picked up on the iota of glee in the big man's words and made a mental note—it was hardly the tone of a true friend, let alone someone who could be trusted. "I guess we have something else to discuss with Reuben when we get back from the *Hustler* meeting, then." Cole plucked his Coke from the table and sat himself back down next to Vanessa.

"Yeah," Skippy grumped. "Like we don't pay bloody Goldblatt enough of our hard-earned already." Heaving his bulk up off the couch, the producer snatched his phone up from the table and stormed out of the green room.

Vanessa watched Skippy go and flinched a little when he slammed the door so hard behind himself, the plaster around the frame broke out into a spiderweb of minute cracks. She studied Cole from the corner of her eye and thought he looked very much like a man with the weight of the world upon his shoulders.

Chapter Twenty-Three

The guy in the gray flannel suit introduced himself as Jeff Flaxton, vice president of acquisitions, and shook Cole's hand with firm, dry confidence. His associate, a trim, tallish, middle-aged lady in a pale-pink skirt suit did likewise with Skippy before the four switched over like a pair of first-time couples at a swinger's party.

"Stephanie Reactor," the woman said to Cole, "but everybody calls me Steph."

"It's a pleasure to meet you, Steph," Cole shook her hand and marveled at how strong her slender, soft, over moisturized fingers felt in his. It crossed his mind to offer commiserations of some sort in the light of Larry Flynt's recent demise but thought better of it. He reckoned it was highly likely the two executives hadn't even met the guy let alone known him well enough to be emotionally affected by his death.

It was all very much business as usual for the *Hustler* executives. The four sat down practically in unison.

"Thank you for agreeing to meet with us this afternoon." It was Flaxton who kicked off the meeting.

"Thank you for coming all this way to see us." Skippy turned on his customary disarming charm and eyed the box of complimentary chocolates that sat temptingly on the glass-topped coffee table.

"It's absolutely our pleasure," Steph chipped in with a friendly, white-toothed smile.

Cole got the impression Steph just felt the need to have something to say, to keep herself relevant to the conversation, like she considered herself little more than set decoration. Even so, Cole very much doubted the woman had derived much pleasure from flying halfway across the country from LA to spend a couple hours in a plush suite at the Sheraton North Houston to make an offer to a pair of porn-mongers who'd turned her company down a handful of times already. Cole guessed she and her associate would be hopping straight back on the charter jet the minute the meeting was over; they wouldn't even have the time to sample Houston's many delights.

"*The Gentleman's Choice* has been getting a lot of good publicity of late. I'm sure you're more than aware of that fact." Flaxton addressed Skippy directly. "Which is why we decided now was the right time to reach out to you and your… associate."

Cole raised an eyebrow at the guy; as used as he was to being treated as little more than a company asset, it didn't mean he had to be happy with it. He was equal partner with Skippy Redman—fifty-fifty. The show had been his baby from the very beginning, and yet he was being made to feel as if he was little more than window dressing. In that much, he felt empathy for Stephanie Reactor as she sat quietly in Flaxton's shadow.

"Well, it's *always* wonderful to meet with you guys," Skippy enthused. "We are very much looking forward to hearing what you have to say—especially in the light of, shall we say, *recent events*?"

"The John Beechwood case has your little show trending on Twitter this week," Flaxton said. "And just about every other social media platform. Our people have been watching its progress on TikTok with interest. I have to say, it does seem to be doing tremendously well on a platform designed primarily for preteen girls."

"I'd hardly call us a *little show*." Skippy took the exec's bait. "Our subscriber base is the highest it's been and growing by the day. Compared with other independent subscription-based content providers, *The Gentleman's Choice* is way ahead of the pack—especially when you compare us with similar single-content companies."

"I hear you, Skippy—is it okay for me to call you Skippy?" Flaxton patronized, and Cole wanted to slap the smirk off the man's face. "But just imagine how much more your creation could be if you expanded into multilevel platforms, embraced new, fresh content, and pulled lesser-known shows under *The Gentleman's Choice* umbrella. You could even create spin-off shows to capitalize on the interest."

Already bored with the guy's marketing speak, Cole stared absently out of the hotel suite's expansive window; witnessing firsthand Jeff Flaxton's unabashed delight at the PR furor stirred up by Amy Woodburn's terrible death made him sick to the stomach, disgusted at the monster he'd helped create.

The Sheraton was so close to George Bush International, Cole could practically smell the jet fuel as an endless stream of 747s climbed silently into the sky. The hotel's soundproofing was certainly most impressive.

"With the more recent accusations of unplanned pregnancy coming from Lola Garcia, *The Gentleman's*

Choice is gaining even more in popularity," Steph threw in.

Steph's voice brought Cole's attention to the meeting, as did the mention of the supposedly pregnant girl's name. Lola's face popped up in his mind, along with fond thoughts of her warm, well-rounded body and silk-smooth ebony skin. As he recalled, she'd been one of the quieter contestants, and Cole remembered making conversation with the girl had been especially difficult; it wasn't that she wasn't smart, she just struggled to articulate. Still, the show's subscribers had utterly fallen in love with her, and she'd been voted through to the final night by a landslide. At the time, Skippy had been beside himself with excitement at the huge amount of vote money she'd brought in, and Cole remembered well the impromptu, booze-soaked all-night party he'd thrown at the studio after they'd wrapped.

Had it not been for that ridiculous volume of votes, there'd have been no Night Five, no sex, and most likely no accusations of Cole having gotten Lola pregnant. As it was, thousands upon thousands of viewers had borne witness to the supposed impregnation, so there'd be no wriggling out of it by Cole simply denying having fucked her.

"It seems the planets have well and truly aligned for *The Gentleman's Choice*." Flaxton plucked out a soft-center dark chocolate and nudged the box an inch or two across the table toward Skippy. "Your show is in real danger of emerging from the gloomy shadows of pornography and out into the bright lights of the mainstream… all it requires is a little push from a big name."

"And you're that big name, of course?" Skippy helped himself to a couple of chocolates.

"Naturally. *Hustler* has the presence and financial wherewithal to make *Choice* a global phenomenon." Flaxton then turned his attention to Cole. "And what does the star of the show have to say, Mr. Gianni?" Cole looked Flaxton square in the eye. For a start, he didn't take kindly to the show's name being abbreviated by some arrogant prick from La La Land, and second, he took exception to the guy treating him like some dumb bimbo—*himbo* as they were known in the trade. Swallowing all that down like the consummate professional he was, Cole gave a courteous reply. "I definitely like the idea of expanding the concept and having the opportunity to incorporate and develop more shows with different formats. But… all of this is little more than conjecture without knowing the remuneration you have in mind, Mr. Flaxton."

"Straight to the point! I really do like this guy!" Flaxton seemed taken aback by Cole's forthright stance, his enthusiasm a transparent cover-up. Of course, it was by no means Cole and Skippy's first rodeo with adult industry bigwigs, so they both knew all too well how the pitch meetings went.

"Look, we've all been here before." Flaxton read Cole's mind. He leaned forward in his chair, hands clasped, elbows resting on his thighs. "Not me and Steph—but I'm sure you get the picture."

Cole and Skippy nodded in synchrony: yes, they got the picture all right.

"So, let's cut to the chase here." Flaxton gave a sideways glance at his colleague. Steph took that as her cue to grab a dark tan attaché case from behind her chair and open it up on top of the table. The click-click of the case's locks filled the silent anticipation in the hotel suite as Flaxton, Skippy, and Cole watched Steph pull out a fat contract with all the theatrical flourish of a magician's assistant pulling a rabbit from a top hat.

"There's fifteen mil on the table right now." Flaxton broke the silence as Steph returned the attaché case to its hiding place.

"Plus, residuals and executive producer credits," Steph filled in; the two were turning out to be quite the double act. She leafed absently through the contract as she spoke, pausing here and there as if she was reading it for the first time. "All of which adds up to a substantial future income for the both of you." Looking up from the paperwork, Steph gave a fleeting look at both Skippy and Cole in turn, making sure to make eye contact with both.

"Now, that is a most generous amount of money." Skippy looked over at Cole. "What say you, partner?"

Cole imagined he caught a faint glimmer of excitement in the producer's eyes at the offer, albeit hidden by the faux coolness he portrayed to Flaxton and Steph. Could it be possible Skippy Webman was *genuinely* interested in taking the money and handing over control of the show? Was fifteen million dollars his price for giving up the endless parade of young women and his opportunity to persuade them to succumb to his lascivious desires? It was by far the biggest amount any interested party had ever thrown at them, and it certainly represented a hell of a lot more than the fresh start Cole had been dreaming about for so long.

"I say we will definitely consider it." Following Skippy's lead, Cole played it cool, although he knew for certain everyone in the room knew just how excited he was; it would be written all over his face. He really would have made a truly crappy poker player.

"You'd be fools not to, if you don't mind my saying so." Flaxton chanced a little overfamiliarity; he got away with it because he held all the aces… fifteen million of them to be precise. "You want my advice, guys? Pitch in with us before *The Gentleman's Choice* is copied by every man and his goddamn dog. I've taken a look at your copyrights and, while they're pretty watertight, they'll only ever be as good as the vast amount of money you have to throw at your lawyers to enforce them. The industry is far less likely to take you on with our weight behind you—one look at the *Hustler* name and they'll be shitting their pants!"

"We will have to pass it through our attorney," Skippy told Flaxton, quite matter of fact.

"Of course, of course—where would any of us be without those vultures, eh?" Laughing, Flaxton stood up and smoothed his jacket and pants with one hand; the meeting was evidently over and done with. "The offer is good for seventy-two hours. I sincerely hope we hear from you before then."

"Oh, you'll definitely be hearing from us." Skippy struggled to his feet and held out a hand to Flaxton for the shaking. "I'd like to say we can all consider this a done deal, Jeff, but Reuben Goldblatt will kick my bloody arse if I even *think* about doing something like this without him looking at the contract first. I'm sure everything is in order, though."

"There are no nasty surprises lurking in there, if that's what you're saying," Steph said with a soupcon of humor. "I'm sure your Mr. Goldblatt will be more than delighted with what our attorneys have put together."

"Of course, he will." Cole got to his feet and held out a hand. He smiled his most seductive smile at Steph Reactor. "It's been brief, but definitely a pleasure." The old Gianni charm brought an unmistakable flush to the woman's cheeks.

"Thank you very much for this opportunity, Jeff," Skippy enthused as he pumped Flaxton's hand with enthusiasm. "I *promise* I'll get back to you the second our attorney has had his eyes on that." He nodded down to the fat contract on the table and then looked across at Cole. "Once it's rubber stamped, we'll absolutely, positively be getting back to you." Cole shook Jeff's hand and, professional courtesies out of the way, he led the way to the suite's door. It had been one of the quickest meetings he'd had to endure in the name of stroking Skippy's mountainous ego—the guy just loved to be courted and practically got off negotiating big-figure money offers he had no intention of ever accepting.

But things felt different to Cole: Skippy had made no attempt to up the offer, most likely because it was almost double the last one they'd entertained, and hearing *fifteen million* had stunned the man into silence. As he walked out into the air-conditioned hallway of the Sheraton, Cole allowed himself to feel more than a little optimistic—every man has his price, as they say, and he thought it quite possible the power couple from

Hustler had just found Skippy Redman's.

Chapter Twenty-Four

It took Skippy until they were back at the studio before he burst Cole's bubble. The producer had sat in total silence the entire drive from the airport hotel, a rare event for Skippy, which typically meant he was mulling things over, which made for a welcome change from his more usual shoot-from-the-hip-and-be-damned approach.

"They must think we're bloody desperate!" Skippy spat the instant he and Cole were in his office.

"What?" Cole was genuinely taken aback by the producer's venom. Unless he'd dreamt it all, they had just been offered fifteen million dollars by one of the biggest names in the adult entertainment industry; where was even a sniff of desperation in that? "Please don't tell me you're not interested, Skip?"

Skippy perched his wide ass on the corner of the desk. "Of course, I'm interested, Cole—it's a shit-ton of money. I'm only human, after all."

Cole ignored his partner's attempt at a conciliatory smile. "So why do I get the impression you're about to tell *Hustler* to stick their offer where the sun don't shine?"

"Because it's their *first* offer—have you learned nothing about negotiation, Cole?" Skippy grinned. "Just think how much more cash we could get if we hold out— you know *The Gentleman's Choice* is hot property right now, all thanks to John bloody Beechwood and his strangled girlfriend."

The uncomfortable surge of nausea surged through Cole's belly again; the show was supposed to be about romance, about seeking that ever-elusive, lifelong connection with someone special, and playing a part to inspire everyone watching to not only hand over their credit card details, but to add a little spark to their own lackluster sex lives. Skippy had turned the whole thing into nothing more than a cynical exploitation of the sad, lonely, and desperate on both sides of the cameras.

"It's more money than we ever dreamed of, Skippy," Cole protested, desperate to get the man to see some sense. "How the fuck can you turn it down on the off chance of something better coming along?"

"I guess because I dream bigger than you, Cole." Skippy sounded smug. "There's a lot more where that fifteen million came from—if not from *Hustler*, then from one of the other big boys."

"You intend to shop this around?"

"Why the hell shouldn't we?" Skippy sounded defiant; he'd obviously been thinking through the potential numbers in his earlier silence. "Surely we owe it to ourselves to get the very best deal we can?"

Whatever happened to quit while you're ahead? Cole wondered. "When we started the show, it was only ever going to be until we made enough to go mainstream before we got typecast as porn-makers. If we'd had an offer like this on the table back in the day, we'd have snatched their goddamn hands off."

"We'd never have had an offer like this back then, Cole. It was before we built up our fan base and a solid bedrock of subscriber dollars. And it was before we got more free publicity than we could have ever hoped for. On the back of John Beechwood, I reckon we could double the *Hustler* offer without even breaking a sweat. And then there's Lola…"

Cole rubbed at his chin with both hands; he was badly in need of a shave. "And what if something happens to devalue the show, Skip? What happens if one day it's worth nothing and we rue the day we turned down fifteen million?"

"Some asshole strangled his girlfriend because of us, we have some hot chick saying you got her pregnant, and we have *Hustler* practically kicking our doors down to stuff money in our G-strings. What the hell has to happen to bring down *The Gentleman's Choice*? I'd say we're virtually untouchable right now, matey."

"Nobody is untouchable, Skippy." Cole eyed his partner and tried to imagine in what dark, dismal corner of Skippy's world fifteen million dollars wasn't going to be enough. Had their goals drifted *that* far apart, he wondered, and whatever happened to the Skippy Webman he knew who was content with making enough dough to act flashy and trying his luck with any of the show's crew and contestants unlucky enough to catch his eye?

There came a cursory knock on the door, and Jayne Torrez walked in clutching her ever-present clipboard.

"Sorry to disturb, Skippy, but I thought Cole would like to see tonight's revised script—I made a few tweaks here and there, but it's essentially the same as you wrote it."

"Thank you, Jayne." Cole took the thin script from Jayne and attempted to hide his annoyance at her barging in with only a perfunctory knock, presumably because the door was not fully closed. It also bothered him to think she may have been lurking outside in the hallway for some time. If so, just how much of his conversation with Skippy had she heard? "You're welcome." Jayne shot Cole a thin smile. "I'll be heading home in a half hour. I'll do my damndest to be back for the shoot. You can reach me on my cell if you need me."

Jayne said the same thing every time, and she always made it back for the shoot. Cole couldn't quite figure out if it was because she felt the need to be wanted, or it was her passive-aggressive way of letting them know she'd organized everything with her typical efficiency and they'd definitely *not* be needing her. Either way, Cole found the woman more irritating than usual and wanted her gone from the office; he wasn't finished with Skippy just yet. "Is there anything else, Jayne?" Cole said as sweetly as he could manage through gritted teeth.

"Nope. That's everything, Cole." Jayne took Cole's unsubtle hint with umbrage and made her way back toward the door.

"If you could close it behind you, please," Cole instructed as she left, and then he turned his attention back to Skippy.

Chapter Twenty-Five

In the days that followed the dominatrix's sadistic quiz, Mai Ling learned if she lay perfectly still in the darkness of the closet, she could keep the worst of the pain from her wounds at bay. The dom and her gimp hadn't tormented her since the night they'd set about her naked body with such cruel intent and left her back, breasts, buttocks, and vagina lacerated and bleeding profusely.

The gimp had checked in on her from time to time; he fed her a morsel or two of food—bread and weak soup mostly—bathed her and stitched and dressed her wounds. Everything he did was under the watchful eye of his dominatrix. She stood silently, dressed in her leather corset and heels, watching from the closet doorway with hands on hips and her scarlet lips pursed. It seemed to Mai Ling the dominatrix disapproved of the gimp showing any grain of compassion toward her but understood the importance of keeping their captive alive; his ministrations were merely a means to an end.

Through her pain and mental anguish, Mai Ling knew she shouldn't even begin to consider the forced kindness a sign her captors were ever planning to let her go—not after having witnessed firsthand the pleasure they'd derived from inflicting such terrible pain upon her.

No, Mai Ling knew they were only keeping her alive to exact more sick pleasures from her ruined body.

As the days dragged by for her in an agony-filled haze, Mai Ling noted there would be long periods of silence in the house: no TV, no voices, no footsteps. Mai Ling heard doors open and close in what she guessed to be mornings and evenings, and from that deduced either the dom or the gimp was leaving the house—perhaps even both of them. Not that it gave her any chance of making a break for freedom; they had her trussed up like a Sunday roast with expertly tied nylon ropes that bit deep into her soft flesh. It did make her wonder, though, if her captors had regular daytime jobs they went out to. In her imagination, Mai Ling pictured the two of them in normal, everyday work clothes going about their days like nothing untoward was happening in their private lives. It was a terrifying thought: her torturers walking freely about in the world, quite possibly seeking out their next victim, while she faced certain death at their hands.

Wherever it was they went, whatever they did, they were back in the house. Mai Ling heard them talking, and before long, there came the ominous *click-clack-click* of the dom's stiletto heels on the wooden floor, growing ever louder and closer.

The harsh white glare from the room beyond the closet stung Mai Ling's light-starved eyes. Twisting her body what little she could manage, she tried her best to turn away from the light that made her eyes water even through tight-shut lids and the gimp who waddled into the closet with his typical passive purpose.

"Bring her to the kitchen." The dominatrix barked the order with a little more venom than Mai Ling considered usual. "And don't let her procrastinate this time." Storming from the room, the dominatrix made her way through the house, no doubt to await her victim.

Mai Ling cried out when the gimp loosened the ropes—he left her hands strapped tight behind her back—and hauled her to her feet. Mai Ling's body had cramped up since they'd last allowed her to stand. Her legs felt weak from so long lying on the hard floor, and every one of the wounds on her body screamed out in agonized protest.

"*Please...* it hurts," Mai Ling sobbed at the emotionless gimp; his beady eyes glared at her through his mask as he manhandled her by the upper arms toward the closet door.

A dizzying rush of panic overcame Mai Ling; her heart pounded wild and hard against her rib cage, and catching a breath against its beat became an impossible task. Desperate to remain within the dark confines of the closet, Mai Ling struggled against the gimp's grip—her prison seemed infinitely preferable to the unspeakable horrors she knew awaited her in the kitchen.

"Come," the gimp grunted and dug his fingers hard into Mai Ling's biceps.

"*Owww!*" Mai Ling wailed as she was yanked roughly into the light of the bedroom beyond the closet. There, she saw the distinct pattern of her own bare feet had made on the hardwood after her previous trip to the kitchen, each one perfectly outlined in dried blood.

"You're only making this harder on yourself, you stupid girl." The gimp pulled Mai Ling so hard toward the bedroom door, the victim almost lost her footing. She felt the stitches the gimp had inserted into the wounds between her legs tear; a thin trickle of fresh blood snaked down along the inside of her thigh and added to the dark-red trail on the floor.

Duly maneuvered into the kitchen, the gimp forced Mai Ling to kneel at the dominatrix's feet, the floor's cold tiles hard and unrelenting against her bruised, naked skin. Looking up at the cruel woman, all ready to plead for her life, to beg for her to please put a stop to the pain and mental torture, Mai Ling saw her tormentor wasn't regarding her in the least. The dom's attention was fixed firmly upon the TV screen, which was tuned to *The Gentleman's Choice* and showed Cole and his most recent blonde on their third date; they were eating sushi from the naked body of a pretty Japanese girl laid out before them on a low table.

"Just look at that." The dominatrix's snarl had the gimp flinch a tad. "This piece of shit show should be going down the toilet where it belongs! But it's more popular than ever! What the fuck is it going to take to put a stop to this fiasco?" She poked angrily at the remote with a scarlet-painted talon to change channels, and the screen filled with a grainy, poorly lit movie of what appeared to be the inside of a seedy, rent-by-the-hour motel room.

Mai Ling's attention switched from the distracted dom to her gimp, then to the TV; there, the two of them had two people tied up on the motel's queen-sized bed. The couple was considerably older, judging by the copious amounts of wrinkles and liver spots upon their nude, wrinkly bodies. They appeared to be less than comfortable at being tied up, ball-gagged, and completely at the mercy of the masked, PVC-clad couple they'd no doubt picked up at some nearby swinger's party.

"*Quit your complaining!*" The dominatrix's voice boomed out from the TV. The fake accent was different from the one Mai Ling was familiar with, but unmistakably hers. She delivered a resounding slap across the old man's face and his head snapped to one side. *"You wanted this, so just shut the fuck up and enjoy it."*

Mai Ling looked up from her place by the dominatrix's spiked heels; she was so close, her nostrils filled with the sweet-sour tang of the woman's latex outfit, and her bare skin prickled at the proximity to her tormentor's body heat. As she watched the dom straddle the old man, press her thighs to either side of his face, and lower herself down to restrict his breathing, Mai Ling's mind lurched toward thoughts of escape. Could she scramble to her feet and flee while the dominatrix and her gimp were distracted by reliving past glories? How far would she get, naked, badly wounded, hands strapped tight behind her back? All it would take was the kitchen door being closed and she'd be utterly stymied. Then she'd be forced to face the wrath of the dominatrix and endure yet more pain—possibly even worse.

So what?

Didn't she want her ordeal to be over one way or another?

That flash of clarity yanked Mai Ling from her grim resignation.

Survival instinct kicked in and she knew she had to at least *try*.

Ignoring the sharp, gnawing pain that sparked between her legs with every movement, Mai Ling forced herself to stand up; the brief walk from the closet had loosened her muscles just enough to maintain balance without the aid of her hands, and in moments she was upright.

If the dominatrix and the gimp had noticed Mai Ling getting up off her knees, they didn't show it; both remained glued to their own perverted exploits up on the screen. There, the gimp had the older woman flipped over onto her stomach and was thrashing her scrawny buttocks with the buckle end of a thick leather belt. The woman screamed against her gag and thrashed around on the bed as thick red welts and vicious, bloody cuts appeared in her thin, exposed flesh. Beside her, the old man's legs kicked out as he was denied breath by the dom's crotch, each kick growing weaker by the second.

It was only when Mai Ling sprinted for the door, her feet slippery with sweat and blood and struggling to find purchase against the slick tiles, that the dominatrix seemed to notice, her attention wrenched away from the TV.

"Don't just stand there, stop her!" she snapped at the gimp. Startled into action, he ambled across the kitchen after Mai Ling.

The door was tantalizingly close—it was even slightly ajar. Mai Ling saw the warm darkness of the evening outside, and it looked like heaven. She had little idea what she would do if—when—she made it. Other than *run*, of course.

Mai Ling thrust out her right foot, aiming to pull open the door with her toes, and her left foot betrayed her. Losing traction on the slick tiles, it slid from under her and flew out to the side.

Mai Ling felt and heard her hip joint pop from its socket, and she crashed to the ground in a blinding flash of fresh agony; the gimp's rudimentary stitches along the long cuts on her back and breasts tore free, the wind punched so hard from her lungs that the accompanying scream wheezed out silently.

"I'm so bored with you now." The dominatrix strode over to where Mai Ling lay weeping in a crumpled heap. Seemingly from nowhere, she produced an Italian style switchblade, its polished, red onyx handle a perfect complement to her scarlet lips. Mai Ling lifted up her head; the dom's weary words were far more chilling to hear than the sight of the knife.

This was certainly it. This was the end.

A press of the button on the ornate handle and the long, pointed blade shot out from the knife's end; the sharp *snap* echoed deep within Mai Ling's soul, and she realized, despite the pain, she'd never coveted life more than she did at that moment. She tried in vain to move away from the woman towering above her, but Mai Ling's leg had been rendered useless by the fall and she had no means of getting to her feet.

"You do it." The dominatrix reached over Mai Ling's prone body to hand the knife over to the gimp.

"No," Mai Ling managed to say as the gimp dutifully took hold of the knife in one hand and, bending over, grabbed a handful of her hair with the other. Pulling her head up and back, he exposed Mai Ling's blood-streaked throat, and all she could see were the dom's eyes staring with utter contempt at her—and those awful lips.

Without a second thought, the gimp ran the switchblade across Mai Ling's neck like he'd done the same to countless others before her. The cold steel sliced with ease through her skin and windpipe, blood poured down her breasts, and a rush of warm air bubbled out through the slit. When the gimp let go of Mai Ling's hair, she slumped to the floor fighting for breath as blood began to fill her lungs; her legs kicked out involuntarily as she squirmed in the growing pool of her own blood—she wasn't even afforded the false comfort of holding her hands to her wounded throat to attempt to prevent the bleeding.

"For God's sakes!" Mai Ling heard the dominatrix spit. "Can't you do *anything* right?"

The dominatrix snatched the bloodied knife from the gimp's hand and knelt down beside Mai Ling; her shoes filled the girl's vision. Grabbing a fistful of hair, she yanked her victim's head back with a grunt. The wound on Mai Ling's neck opened up, which increased the flow of blood from her throat and had Mai Ling staring once more into those dark, soulless eyes. "You should know how to do this properly by now." The dominatrix snarled at her gimp and stabbed the knife into Mai Ling's neck, the blade aimed behind the girl's windpipe.

Mai Ling's body fell slack as if life had already left it; in an instant, her mind turned blank, nothing more than a dull, gray nothingness—no family memories, no happy place, not even an overriding feeling of dread or agony or impending darkness.

The dominatrix drew the knife forward, its blade slicing through tendons, arteries, and Mai Ling's windpipe; a bright arterial spray spattered the dom's legs, latex corset, and bare breasts, and reached all the way up to splash the kitchen ceiling. The dominatrix let go of her victim's hair, and Mai Ling's head hit the tiles with a sickening wet crunch.

As the last of her life drained away with her blood, Mai Ling saw her killer stand up and step over her with indifference, like she was a turd on the sidewalk. She heard the woman growl at the gimp, "Get rid of *this*." The fake persona slipped, momentarily forgotten, and in her final moments, Mai Ling realized where she'd heard that awful, cruel voice before.

Chapter Twenty-Six

It was still dark when Cole pulled into the studio parking lot. Dawn was still a good half hour away and the ride in hadn't been entirely unpleasant, although it never ceased to amaze Cole just how many vehicles there were out driving on Houston's roads at such an ungodly hour of the morning.

He'd been awake half the night with an upset stomach and, as sleep had eluded him since the small hours, Cole decided to make his way into the studio to get a head start on the script before Skippy made his usual ham of the whole thing. The sushi he'd consumed during the previous night's date with Vanessa had not sat well with Cole at all, and he'd suffered frequent dashes to the restroom despite only wanting to sink into a series of restful REMs.

He'd enjoyed the *nyotaimori* meal immensely, though, as it had been far too long since he'd gotten to eat sushi from the body of a naked Japanese girl. All he could hope for was Vanessa had fared better and their Night Four date would not be compromised; upset stomachs were never conducive to a romantic or sexy atmosphere. All in all, once the errant food was out of his system, Cole had begun to feel a whole lot better, albeit a tad queasy in the pit of his belly. He reckoned it was worth it to produce a particularly stand-out episode of *The Gentleman's Choice*. Cole locked up his car and made his way across the lot; his was the only vehicle there other than the security guard's little white van. The guard, Norman, had been around almost as long as the studio, and more often than not spent his time napping in his vehicle instead of driving around the lot. Even so, there had never once been a break-in or any form of vandalism—even though there was an entire homeless community in residence beneath the overpass just a couple of blocks away. The worse they ever seemed to get at the studio was dumped trash and the occasional broken grocery store cart.

Which was why Cole thought nothing of the small pile of trash he spotted by the studio's back door; mostly hidden by shadows, partially in the doorway, it was indiscernible from a distance, but Cole reckoned it was either discarded garbage or one of the homeless folks sleeping off their night's hit of cheap crystal meth.

"What the fuck?" Cole groaned as he neared the door; an unearthly stink greeted him on the tepid morning air, a cloying, putrid smell of excrement and rotted meat. Cole had been in close proximity to Houston's displaced folk before, but the reek currently assaulting him was far and above that of unwashed, soiled bodies—it was a combination of odors that transported him right back to his formative years, a stench that was undeniably death.

At first, it was difficult to make out the small, fragile shape that lay slumped in the doorway; it had been partially covered by dark-stained clothes and an old, tattered piece of blue tarp. A single foot poked out from one corner;

petite, dainty, its pink-painted toenails were split, the varnish chipped and smeared with what Cole surmised could only be blood. "Are you okay there?" It really was all he could think of to say.

Stomach churning, growling its complaint, Cole held a hand over his mouth to stave of at least some of the awful reek and leaned over the shape in the vain hope of finding some sign of life. He fished out his cell phone and hit the flashlight app, although he really had little desire to see what his nose was telling him lay beneath the tarp.

"Miss?" Gingerly, Cole pulled at the tarp with his foot, the scraping sound loud, grating in the still air. Where the hell was Norman when he was needed? If ever there was a time Cole needed some moral support, it was right then. "Are you—"

The words died on Cole's lips as the tarp rustled and shifted and fell away to reveal a blood-smeared, lifeless face with still, staring eyes. The young girl's head was tilted back, her throat cut open with such savagery, Cole made out the pink-white nubs of her vertebrae amid the exposed raw meat of her neck; he thought it looked like a second, gaping mouth, a hellish, toothless maw.

Cole's stomach roiled and lurched as he rested his light upon the dead girl's face, and he finally recognized her sweet, delicate features.

"Mai Ling?" Bile burned the back of Cole's throat, and he turned away from the stagnant eyes of the girl he'd had removed from the show because of her overenthusiastic performance at the staged orgy. He couldn't grasp how— *why*—someone would do such a terrible thing to such a sweet young person with a life stretching before her.

"Everything all right over there, Mr. Gianni?" The security guard's voice drifted across the lot, along with the rhythmic clump of his heavy work boots.

It was all Cole could do to wave a hand over his head in acknowledgement before his legs buckled beneath him; he dropped to his knees and threw up the last remnants of the previous night's sushi onto the blacktop.

Chapter Twenty-Seven

"You still look like shit," Skippy said to Cole. "Need another hit of bourbon?"

"I'm good, thanks." Cole looked up at the producer from the couch. It had been a couple hours since he'd found Mai Ling's body in the studio doorway and his guts still were still turning somersaults. The last thing he needed was to exacerbate his nausea with yet more alcohol.

"The cops are gonna want to talk to us, of course," Skippy told him. "They're doing their CSI thing out by the back door and out in the lot. They said they'll come up and take our statements after they finish up—I just hope they don't interfere with today's show. At least we have an off-site shoot tonight, which means we can get away from here—assuming the cops let us leave the scene of the crime, that is."

"And why wouldn't they?" Cole studied his producer and couldn't quite shake the feeling the guy was actually enjoying the whole thing; he certainly didn't seem terribly moved that one of their recent contestants had been butchered and left on the doorstep.

"Because they're bloody cops, that's why." Skippy turned his nose up. "If they don't have an instant prime suspect, they'll hound innocent folks like us 'til they can make one. I hope you have a bloody good alibi, Cole, that's all I can say."

Cole ignored Skippy's too-loud laugh at his own joke; he *really* was relishing the attention. "You know damn well I was live on the show getting food poisoning from cheap sushi, Skippy, and there are literally *thousands* of witnesses." Literally, the first question the detectives had asked Cole earlier that morning was where he'd been between ten and twelve the night before, which was their estimated time of death for Mai Ling. As for Skippy, Cole assumed he'd spent that time in his little producer's booth making sure all camera angles were present and correct. Having said that, Skippy had been uncharacteristically quiet throughout the show—although, had he left the studio, there would have been a plethora of crew and hangers-on to see him leave.

Cole checked himself.

What the hell was he thinking?

That his old friend Skippy Webman was capable of slitting young girls' throats to boost the show's ratings and sale value? Sure, he appeared to be more concerned about any potential disruptions to the shooting schedule than Mai Ling's death, but that made Skippy a shitty person, not a killer. It shocked Cole to his core to realize he'd even fleetingly considered Skippy a suspect, whether it be for some sick publicity stunt or because the hot Chinese girl had turned down his inevitable advances after he threw her off the show. The guy had spent the night producing and directing the Third Night date's shoot, and Cole figured he knew him well enough to know he didn't have the wherewithal to orchestrate an outside hit, no matter what the reason.

Even so, no matter how fleeting, Cole had *thought* it, and he was disgusted with himself.

"You think it has something to do with Beechwood?" Cole ventured. "Who knows?" Skippy declared with a loud sniff. "That kind of publicity brings out all the bloody loonies, you know that much. Just look at little Miss Pregnant—it sure as hell didn't take her long to come crawling out of the woodwork once Beechwood had his sorry ass dragged into court. I hear she's bringing out a sex tape later this week—exclusive to Pornhub, by all accounts, plus some big-money tell-all about the show. And that's without any paternity suit she decides to throw your way. It's all gonna make her bloody rich at our expense, even if you're not the father of her bastard. Maybe she's not such a dumb bimbo after all."

"How can she do a tell-all?" Cole's hackles were up; the threat of the paternity suit somehow seemed to be the least of his worries. "Goldblatt says our nondisclosures are watertight."

"Tighter than a duck's arse, my old friend—and they're bloody watertight." Skippy smirked. "But, if whatever punitive costs we stick her with are trumped by what she stands to make for spilling the beans, it's going to be well worth the girl's while to tell everything she knows to anyone who'll pay her."

Cole didn't recall Lola coming across as dumb on the show, and the thought of her releasing some sordid sex tape to cash in repulsed him. Was the glut of clips for *The Gentleman's Choice* doing the rounds on every internet porn site not enough? Nonetheless, if the girl *was* in the family way—either because of him or some other poor, unfortunate soul—Cole kind of admired her for making the most of her fifteen minutes of fame. She'd make her money, support her kid making crappy porn, graduate to *OnlyFans*, and fade back into the obscurity from which Skippy Redman and *The Gentleman's Choice* had plucked her.

"And it doesn't bother you at all she'll be spewing all of our show's secrets?" Cole asked. "All the behind-the-scenes stuff we go to such great pains to keep a lid on?"

"Bother me?" Skippy laughed. "Why on earth would it bother me? On top of Beechwood, and now a nice, juicy murder, your pregnant gal is only ever going to add to the PR—our show is going to be bigger than ever! I *knew* it was a good idea to hold off on the *Hustler* offer—just think how much moolah they'll be willing to throw at us after all this!"

Again, the all-too familiar niggle at the back of Cole's conscience had him wondering if, just if, Skippy had something to do with Mai Ling. "And speaking of Beechwood, I saw on the news this morning he'd made bail," Skippy continued. "Caught the newsfeed on my phone while you were busy hurling in the toilets. It was only a hundred grand, oddly enough, because the judge decided he wasn't a flight risk or a serial killer in the making. The girlfriend's family is not pleased, as you can imagine."

"That can't be a good thing," Cole said. "It means the court believes his story that it was an accident caused by copying what they saw on our show."

"And that's not a good thing because…?" Skippy baited.

"Because it makes us *liable*, Skip." Cole couldn't believe the producer was being so naive. "We didn't put a disclaimer or warning out with the show and some poor sap strangles his lover to death. Do you have any idea the magnitude of lawsuits that could be coming our way?"

Skippy shrugged, which Cole knew was his go-to expression for any difficult question he didn't want to face. "If we hold out until *Hustler* or one of the other big boys comes up with a golden offer, and we sell at the right time, any lawsuits will become their problem. Goldblatt will see to that—you know how good that wily old bastard can be."

While it was encouraging for Cole to hear Skippy talk positively in terms of selling out, the man's strategy hung on circumstances far beyond their control, which had Cole thinking it was little more than big talk stimulated by the more than generous *Hustler* offer. "How long do you expect to hold out, Skip? We miss the timing on this, and we could end up with nothing."

"Do you think I haven't thought about that?" Skippy cracked a broad smile. "You need to trust me, Cole. I'm the business brains of the outfit, and I know what I'm doing here."

Cole didn't return the smile. The last time he'd heard that speech from Skippy, he'd wound up as the star of a sleazy internet porn show.

***

"They upped the offer!" Skippy stomped into the green room all full of pomp and self-importance.

Cole and Vanessa looked up from the script they were sharing to do the read-through. "*Hustler*?" Cole asked.

"Of course, *Hustler*." Skippy sat himself down on the couch next to Vanessa. He first eyed up her long, bare legs that emerged from tight, faded denim shorts, and then turned his attention to her chest. "How are you this afternoon, Vanessa?" he spoke directly to the tight, green Baby Yoda T-shirt. "I hope last night's dinner didn't have the same effect on you as it did on poor Cole."

"It did not, I'm happy to report—so, I'm all good, thank you. I'm really looking forward to the date tonight." Vanessa's answer was fittingly diplomatic. "I can't remember the last time I went to a strip club to ogle beautiful women."

Cole smirked at Skippy's reaction to Vanessa's revelation; it was clear he sure as hell hadn't expected such a forthright reply. "Could you give me and Skippy ten, please, Vanessa?" Cole didn't want to have a business discussion in front of a contestant—no matter how watertight Reuben Goldblatt considered the NDA she'd signed to be. And, despite the fact he thought he might be developing feelings for the woman, even though he'd vowed never to put himself through that emotional grinder again. Vanessa had proven to be a big hit with the show's viewers in spite of her ice maiden act—or was it *because* of that? Perhaps the subscribers loved to see Cole challenged by a beautiful woman who didn't simply fall at his feet on the first date?

"So… what's the new offer?" Cole asked once Vanessa was gone, the door closed firmly behind her.

"Twenty-two." Skippy whispered the number as if it held some reverence for him.

Cole whistled through his teeth. "That's one big number, Skip," he said. "What made them increase it? Did you shop around already?"

"There's nothing like a murder to pique interest in something," Skippy said, and actually winked at him. "Especially when it's a former contestant, *and* there's an obvious direct link back to the show."

"How did *Hustler* know about Mai Ling?" In his heart, Cole figured he knew the answer before the question was out of his mouth. "The cops haven't released anything yet. Don't tell me you—"

"Called Jeff Flaxton with our news?" Skippy beamed like the cat that got the cream. "Damn right I did, mate. Got the poor bugger out of bed, too—I totally forgot they're two hours behind Houston."

"You told Flaxton about Mai Ling?"

"Well, I didn't exactly name names, but yeah, I told him we'd had a murder and once it gets out, the focus on *The Gentleman's Choice* is gonna totally eclipse Beechwood and your pregnant chick."

As much as it grated on him to hear Lola Garcia described as *his*, Cole decided to let it go. Skippy was becoming too much of a loose cannon, and it worried Cole how easily the whole thing could get out of hand if the producer went unchecked. Of course, the promise of big money was as alluring to him as it was to Skippy, but at what cost to his self-respect? Skippy was already touting a dead girl as collateral in a business deal. Where would it end?

A knock on the door sounded—rapid, insistent.

"What?" Skippy barked, clearly annoyed at the rude interruption to his self-aggrandizement.

Cole looked over as the green room door eased open and, timidly, Skippy's young assistant poked her head in.

"There's a cop here wants to talk to you both." As the girl delivered her poor diction, a plump, middle-aged Hispanic guy in a cheap blue suit slipped past her and made his way across the room, arm outstretched.

"Detective Hurtado," the cop introduced himself. "This won't take more than a minute, gentlemen—I think I got most of what I needed from you both this morning, and your alibis check out."

"I hope it won't take long," Skippy grumped as he got to his feet. "We're already behind on today's shoot as it is."

"Yeah, about that." The cop rubbed at his weak jaw line with one hand. Looking at the guy, Cole reckoned if he hadn't had the foresight to grow a beard, he'd likely have no discernible chin at all—it hardly inspired confidence in law enforcement. "You might want to consider postponing your show for the next few days until all this dies down—it's gonna be big news once the press get hold of it."

"Do you have any idea what that would cost us in lost revenue?" Skippy retorted.

"No, Mr. Webman, I do not," Hurtado admitted. "But, until we can be sure this is not a direct attack on you or the studio, it might be the best for the safety of everyone concerned. I'm sure your… clientele won't mind, given the circumstances."

Cole watched from the couch as Skippy's cheeks reddened; if there was one thing his partner hated, it was some arsehole layman telling him how to run his business.

"Our subscribers will mind all the more *because* of the circumstances." Skippy folded his arms across his broad chest, his belly bulging out below them. "I know it might sound mercenary, Detective, but there's nothing quite like a murder to get folks excited."

Cole exhaled loudly. Mercenary was hardly the word, and if Skippy carried on extolling the virtues of having a mutilated corpse left on the doorstep, he'd talk himself right back onto the top of Hurtado's list of suspects.

"Are you telling us we have to stop shooting?" Cole stood up from the couch and positioned himself an inch or two closer to the cop than his producer. He knew it was up to him to act the voice of reason and save Skippy Webman from talking himself into almost certain disaster.

"No, sir," Hurtado replied. He looked to be relieved Cole had jumped in; Skippy was obviously grinding his gears more than a little. "Although, I would *advise* you to consider it—in light of what's happened."

"Well, tonight's shoot is off-site, if that makes any difference," Cole told the cop.

"Off-site?"

"We like to mix things up every now and then and film a date or two on location."

"Plus, it would have cost us a king's ransom to recreate a high-end strip club *and* ship in enough strippers to make it look good," Skippy threw in.

"So… we will be taking the show downtown tonight," Cole said. "We're even staying the night at one of the big luxury hotels in the city center—kind of a special treat."

"And which hotel would that be, Mr. Gianni?" Hurtado appeared to relax a little upon hearing Cole's information.

"We haven't decided yet," Skippy replied on Cole's behalf. "We never do—just in case any lunatics find out and…"

"Kill somebody?" Hurtado said without the slightest hint of irony. "If I were you, Mr. Webman, I'd keep the hotel location on a strictly need-to-know basis. Miss Ling's murder may just be a one-off, but we can't rule out the possibility someone out there has a serious grudge against you, your show, and its contestants."

"You think we may be in danger?" For the first time since looking into Mai Ling's cold, dead eyes, Cole contemplated his own safety—what if he was destined to end up under a blue tarp somewhere?

"We can't afford to rule out anything at this stage." Hurtado glanced at the clock on the wall above the couch and fished through an inside pocket of his cheap jacket. "If you can please keep me informed of your whereabouts— including the hotel you choose tonight—I would appreciate it." He handed over a crumpled, cream-colored card.

Skippy plucked the card from the cop's fingers and gave it a cursory glance; Cole knew damn well he wouldn't keep it and he had absolutely no intention whatsoever of keeping the cop informed of his whereabouts.

"Is that all, Detective?" Skippy tossed the card onto the couch. "For now," Hurtado told him. "I do need to speak to Vanessa Young, though—just a formality, considering she's your current contestant."

"I hope you're not planning to scare her off." Skippy was quick to get defensive.

"Not at all, Mr. Webman. I just need to have a quick chat with her, somewhere private, if that's okay with you."

"I guess so," Skippy grumped. "Can you go find her, Cole? God only knows where she's wandered off to."

In any other situation, Cole would have taken offense at Skippy treating him like one of his teenaged interns and called him out for it. But the truth was, he was more than happy to be out of the green room and away from the cop, Skippy's nauseating greed, and the overwhelming feeling of dread Mai Ling's horrific death had brought with it. So, without complaint or even a perfunctory goodbye to Detective Hurtado, Cole made his way out into the hallway and set about locating Vanessa.

Chapter Twenty-Eight

Vanessa studied the cop as he spoke to her; she'd learned over many years of dealing with law enforcement it was often best to let them say their piece before offering anything in return and then only give up the bare minimum.

"We looked you up and know who and what you are, Miss Michaels—or do you prefer Charlotte? Or Charlie?"

"I'd prefer Vanessa Young, Detective Hurtado," Vanessa said quietly with a nervous glance about the room. Cole had kindly ushered her and the cop into an old equipment room in one of the farthest corners of the studio. It was filled with antiquated cameras, editing hardware, Apple Mac computers decades old, and dusty furniture that hadn't seen action in a long time. But even with everything in the room dead and decaying, Vanessa was still on edge— if even the slightest hint of her true purpose on the show got back to Cole or Skippy, then her time would be done and the gig well and truly up.

Which is why it rankled to hear her real name spoken out loud by the indiscreet cop.

"Of course you do." Hurtado gave Vanessa a look she'd seen a thousand times before in the course of her work: the patronizing stare a cop reserved for someone they deem to be playing detective. "You really have gone to a lot of trouble to hide your true identity. I'm impressed—you private dicks don't usually go into so much detail."

"I'm known for my thoroughness." Oddly, Vanessa felt the need to defend herself.

"And paid handsomely for it too, so I understand." Hurtado's macho façade slipped a tad, and Vanessa saw what looked a lot like jealousy lurking behind it. "How much is Tom Hickersley paying you for this?"

Again, Vanessa recoiled at the sound of the name; the damn cop really had done his homework. "I'm not at liberty to discuss that, Detective," she said. "Client confidentiality—you know how it goes."

The cop tugged hard on his earlobe and huffed. "It's no big deal, Miss Michaels—I have it written down somewhere."

"So, you know who I am and why I'm here?" Vanessa ignored the cop's deliberate slip-up on her name; she knew his type all too well—he'd quickly tire of the childish little power game once he realized he wasn't going to get a rise out of her.

"Of course." Hurtado pulled an old office chair out from beneath one of the discarded desks; the blue fabric covering its seat and arms was all but worn away, revealing the grubby yellow foam beneath. The chair's quartet of rusted wheels squeaked loudly as it moved, and one refused to move altogether. As Hurtado sat down, a cloud of dust puffed out from beneath his ass.

"Did you say anything to Mr. Webman about me?" Vanessa decided against grabbing a chair for herself—they all looked decidedly nasty, and she wanted to maintain what psychological advantage she could by standing over the cop.

"I really don't think we'd be having this conversation here if I had, Miss Young, do you?"

"You're a cop—you could have easily instructed him to say nothing until you've finished questioning me."

Hurtado laughed. "Yeah, I guess I could have done that. But I didn't, so there's no need for the paranoia, Vanessa—you're much more valuable to us on the show than off it."

"Us?" Vanessa was surprised at how quickly the detective had gotten round to using her pseudonym, even going so far as to make with the familiarity of her first name; he definitely wanted something.

"The police department." Hurtado huffed at Vanessa as if she'd just asked the world's dumbest blonde question. Leaning forward in his chair, the cop continued, "Mr. Webman has refused to shut down filming, even though we've advised him it would be a good idea."

"So, why don't you take the choice away from him?" Vanessa knew how cops worked—it would be a cakewalk to seal off the entire studio. Hurtado definitely had some hidden agenda.

"We could..." The cop paused a beat or two, most likely for effect, Vanessa thought. "But, when we discovered your secret and realized we had somebody on the inside, it became in our best interest to keep the cameras rolling as they say."

"*Somebody on the inside*? You expect me to work with you?" Vanessa had to admire the cop's chutzpah if nothing else.

"I'd prefer to think of it as you working *for* us." Hurtado gave Vanessa a wry, lopsided smirk. "And we can start by you telling me everything you know about Tracy Hickersley so far."

"And if I don't?"

"If you refuse to cooperate, then I'll be more than happy to have another conversation with Mr. Webman, and then you can see how much longer you'll last on *The Gentleman's Choice*."

Vanessa felt like she really needed to sit down but fought the urge.

The cop had shown her he had the upper hand as his opening gambit—so much for her maintaining the psychological advantage.

"Look, Vanessa," Hurtado fished around in the inside pocket of his jacket; the thick polyester fabric rustled as he did so. "You're in a unique position to help us with this case—and that's without me going into how you managed to put Tracy Hickersley and Omawumi Musa together long before we did."

"You think their murders are linked?"

"We do now." The cop held out his cell phone, its screen facing Vanessa. There, she saw Tracy's body laid out on the stainless-steel mortician's table, her belly opened up and hollowed out, her guts in a white plastic container off to the side. "And there are definite similarities to the young woman found outside the studio this morning—we believe it's the same MO. Did you know her?"

"She was on the show a week or so ago—we never met." Vanessa couldn't tear her eyes away from the cop's cell as he flicked through image after image of first Tracy, then Omawumi. She'd seen a handful of autopsy photographs in the records she'd managed to get her hands on, but Hurtado appeared to have the full set on his phone.

"Both victims had wounds we believe were caused by a straight razor, and there are quite specific cut patterns in and around the genitalia." Hurtado expanded an image of Omawumi's buttocks, her smooth, chocolate skin sliced open to reveal the red flesh beneath; it was obvious the cuts went all the way around to the front. "The kind they used in the Wild West for shaving."

Vanessa once again ignored the cop's patronizing tone; just how dumb did he think she was? "And the girl this morning?"

Hurtado nodded and flicked through to a handful of pictures he'd taken of the corpse Cole had discovered in the studio doorway. Although she was partially covered with clothing that appeared to have been randomly tossed onto her body, Vanessa saw the long, deep cuts running down her breasts, and one exposed nipple sliced perfectly in two.

"Oh, dear God." Vanessa fought against the nausea and lightheadedness the photographs conjured; she really did wish she'd had the foresight to sit down on one of the crappy old chairs. Holding on to the edge of a dust-coated table, Vanessa steadied herself and took in a few much-needed deep breaths.

"We think it's the same perp, obviously." Hurtado slipped his phone back into his pocket; it had done its job. "Especially with all three victims being connected to the show."

Vanessa nodded along with the cop's conclusion. She'd made the correlation a long time ago, back when there'd only been two sliced-up corpses.

"We figure the killer is someone with a grudge against the show— maybe someone they fired, or perhaps a contestant who didn't get as far as she'd have liked with Mr. Personality." Hurtado smiled at his own joke. "Although, we haven't ruled out a contestant's family member with a warped sense of justice."

"Could it be some sick moral crusader out to make a point?" Vanessa added her other theory to the mix and her mind jumped to Tracy Hickersley's father; with the growing list she had going on, she was prepared to consider any one of them as a prime suspect—even Tom Hickersley. After all, his precious little girl had degraded herself in his eyes by taking part in the sordid little sex show, and she figured it might just be easier for him to deal with that if she was dead. Rich guy like him often saw their family as possessions, especially those who carried more than a fatherly interest in an attractive daughter. Yeah, the more Vanessa pondered Tom Hickersley and their weird meeting, the more she was convinced something untoward had been going on there.

It also held a possible explanation as to why he might go on to kill more—either he saw Tracy in each of his victims, or he'd discovered a liking for murder—but not why he'd commissioned Vanessa to investigate his daughter's death. Perhaps it was a means of assuaging his conscience or deflecting his wife's suspicion?

"It could be practically anyone with any motive at this stage." Hurtado sounded frustrated. "But there's the definite link to *The Gentleman's Choice*, which is where you come in."

"You want me to be bait?" Vanessa had guessed as much already, but it felt good to confront the cop with the obvious.

"I'd prefer to call it working from the inside, but yeah, that's just about the long and short of it." Hurtado held up his hands to make air quotes, which Vanessa thought made him look ridiculous. "You've managed to worm your way into the inner sanctum, which gives you access to everyone behind the scenes—and I'm sure there's plenty of gossip you can pick up on. Everybody likes to tell stories about company oddballs of the past."

"There are plenty of those in the present." Vanessa ventured a half-hearted smile. "The hard part is filtering out those who aren't capable of slicing up pretty young girls."

"Welcome to my world." The detective stood up and brushed the dust from the seat of his crumpled pants. "And speaking of oddballs, what do you make of Mr. Gianni?"

"He's nice enough once you get to know him—he's nowhere near the ageing Romeo he is on the show. Is he one of your suspects?" The notion didn't come as much of a surprise to Vanessa; she'd not quite eliminated the guy herself.

"Of course, he is," Hurtado said. "His past exploits have him sitting high on my list, that's for sure."

"And they would be?"

"Gianni's real name is Antonio Duran—you don't know he's wanted back in Bolivia for murdering his stepfather in cold blood? Judging from the reports the Bolivians sent over, it looked like some family trouble that had been simmering for years. Don't tell me you didn't know he's from Bolivia? Some shithole town called Cochabamba, apparently. His family is old money, and it's kinda murky as to where it all came from. We may consider having him extradited once we catch up with whoever killed our three girls."

The cop's revelation stunned Vanessa; the cop had evidently done a lot more homework on Cole Gianni's background than she'd been able to—Interpol had never really been one of her go-to information sources. While she'd deduced Cole was definitely hiding a secret or two about his origins—she'd not once bought into any of the Eastern European crap—Vanessa was astounded to hear he'd actually killed someone, no matter the circumstances.

It certainly bumped Cole Gianni up a notch or two on her list of suspects.

"So… you might want to watch yourself around him," Hurtado warned. "Especially out of sight of the cameras—there's no telling what someone like him might be capable of."

"You're talking like you've found the man guilty already," Vanessa said.

"Until we find out otherwise, he may well be."

"Which is where your bait comes in?"

"Precisely." Stuffing his hands deep into his pockets, Hurtado hawked loudly to clear his throat. "I have no doubt you can take good care of yourself, Vanessa, and now that you know almost as much as I do, you're well-equipped to dig around and see what else turns up. I would like you to check in with me at least twice a day—more if necessary."

Vanessa was relieved the cop hadn't insisted she wear a wire, although, given the nature of the show and the various states of undress involved, it wouldn't have remained concealed for long. "I can try my best, but no promises," she offered by means of compromise. "Things get pretty intense around here, and there's absolutely no privacy." She took another look around the dingy room, still half expecting to see the telltale red LED of a poorly hidden camera.

"I do understand, Miss Young." Hurtado took a step toward the door like he suddenly had someplace far more urgent to be. "Once a day, minimum, so we know you're keeping out of trouble."

"I said I will *try*, Detective." Vanessa failed to mask her annoyance at the cop's insistence; he appeared to think he owned her.

"Thank you." Hurtado had his hand on the doorknob. "I have to ask… if you make it all the way through to Night Five on the show, you think you're gonna do the deed with Mr. Gianni—given the fact you're only here because you're working a case?"

Ignoring the cop's intrusive question, Vanessa followed him out of the equipment room. The truth was she really didn't know which way her Night Five date on *The*

Gentleman's Choice would go—she hadn't made that decision.

Chapter Twenty-Nine

Given the continued police activity back at the studio and that the Night Four date was to be filmed in some upscale, downtown strip club, Vanessa had suggested she go to her hotel to relax for the rest of the day. And, while Skippy had been none too ecstatic about her suggestion, Cole agreed it was a good idea under the circumstances; having the parking lot cordoned off and a bunch of uniformed cops milling about was hardly conducive to a sensual atmosphere.

The hotel room was nicely furnished, spacious, and boasted a huge picture window that let in plenty of natural Houston sunlight; the AC ran almost full blast to counter the heat that brought along with it. There was a pair of expansive California king beds and, in the cavernous bathroom, a six-man Jacuzzi tub. Throw in a well-stocked, entirely free mini bar and, all in all, the show had pulled out all the stops to make sure Vanessa was comfortable during her stay. She knew she wouldn't be returning there after that night's date, though, as there was a penthouse suite in the offing for her and Cole—perhaps Skippy was hoping there'd be some after-hours action ahead of the eagerly anticipated Night Five finale.

Inevitably, Vanessa didn't spend too much of her time relaxing— having spent a good half hour soaking in the tub, she flopped out on the bed in her pink hotel robe and fired up her laptop.

There was little to be found on the internet about Antonio Duran, although Vanessa was able to unearth snippets about the Duran family: they had lived in Cochabamba for five generations, owned a hell of a lot of land around the town, and were renowned race horse breeders—the latter, it was rumored, was little more than a respectable front for the family's less legal activities, the most notable of which was purported to be cocaine exporting.

Frustrated by the lack of information to back up Detective Hurtado's claim Cole—*Antonio*—was wanted for murder back in Bolivia, and the shortage of any kind of detail on him or the purported death of the stepfather, Vanessa activated her computer's proxy, clicked on her Onion app, and delved deep into the murky corners of the Dark Web.

"Well, hello, Antonio Duran," Vanessa greeted the familiar face that popped up on her screen after a good twenty minutes or so of searching. Cole looked younger in the photograph, of course, and he sported a full black beard, but there was no mistaking those roguish good looks and sparkling eyes. The photo had been taken outside a long stable block, which sat adjacent to a paddock so verdant, at first the grass appeared to be fake. Young Cole stood next to a handsome tan-brown gelding almost as tall as he was. One hand rested upon its rippling muscular withers, the other on his hip; Antonio Duran looked every inch the dashing hero of a Brontë novel.

Scrolling down, Vanessa learned Antonio's mother was Rosalita—and that she was still very much alive—his stepfather was Roberto, and Antonio was an only child. What had become of his biological father was shrouded in mystery, even in the darkest recesses of the Dark Web; all Vanessa unearthed was scant talk of a *tragic accident*, after which Roberto had inserted himself into the family to take over as patriarch when Cole was just fourteen. It would seem that even in Bolivia, money could buy silence and cover up unpleasant things.

A little further down the web page, Vanessa came upon a video clip. It appeared to have been filmed in a teenager's bedroom in the house of a poor family: the walls were bare except for a crucifix above the bed, the furniture old and worn.

Clicking on the tiny play button in the center of the video, Vanessa was greeted by a young man who appeared in the shot from the left-hand side like he'd been waiting on some silent cue; the lighting was terrible, and the kid's voice drifted in and out as if his camera was running low on juice.

"Hi, I'm Jorge Estenssoro, and I live in Cochabamba." The young man's English was pretty good, his accent not so thick as to be impenetrable. "Antonio Duran is my best friend, and I want to tell his story so people will understand what he did and will not think bad things about him. "We have been friends since we were children—Antonio's family is very rich, but he has never looked down on me or his other friends who have no money. We are friends, and that's all there is to that. Antonio was very happy when I first knew him when he lived with only his mother. His father died in an accident before Antonio was even born, so he never knew him to miss him. He would often tell me he was envious I had my father around—even when the bastard walked out on Momma, me, and my four sisters. Antonio would tell me that at least I had thirteen years to look back on—all he ever had was his mother, until Roberto married Mrs. Duran when Antonio was fourteen."

A grainy wedding photograph flashed up on Vanessa's screen: a plump bride and her dashing young groom, and a lanky, awkward-looking teenaged Cole; Vanessa was having a hard time thinking of him as Antonio. Cole stood six inches or so from his mother's side. It wasn't a vast distance, but it spoke volumes to Vanessa: Cole/Antonio was already being pushed out of his mother's life by her handsome new husband, and the look of sad resignation on his young face was simply heartbreaking.

Then, Jorge reappeared. He stared straight into the camera, which gave Vanessa the illusion he was looking directly into her eyes. "Antonio's Momma insisted he call Roberto 'Papa,' and Antonio refused. He'd call him Rob, or Stepfather, and I think that only made things worse between them. Roberto had never really liked Antonio, although he pretended to so Mrs. Duran would say yes to marrying him. Once they were married, his true colors came out and Antonio told me how his stepfather hated that he was a constant reminder of Mrs. Duran's life before they'd met. That's when Antonio began spending more time out on the streets with me and our friends—he'd often say he just didn't want to go home.

"Roberto hated Antonio's love of reading—he called him a sissy and would throw out his books. This one time, he snatched Antonio's favorite poetry book from his hands and tossed it in the garbage, and when he caught Antonio digging it out of the trash can, he backhanded him so hard his jaw was swollen for a week. He made Antonio tell his momma he'd hurt himself falling from one of the horses. Riding was the only thing my friend could do that his stepfather didn't call him names over. I guess that's why he got to be so good with horses, although he always dreamed of being a big Hollywood action movie star."

A photograph of Cole sitting atop a magnificent chestnut mare popped up, and Vanessa thought he looked proud, happy—most likely because of the temporary respite from his stepfather's berating that horse riding afforded him.

"It was about a year after that picture was taken that Antonio found Roberto's gun. He'd been snooping around his momma's room for money, liquor, porn—anything really because he was bored. He found the gun in an old shoebox at the back of the closet—a silver six-shot revolver, just like the ones in the John Wayne movies. He wasn't gonna steal it or anything—his stepfather would know who'd taken it if he did, and he was putting it back when Roberto walked in and caught him red-handed. Antonio told me later he deserved to be in trouble for snooping, but Roberto was blind, stinking drunk, and his Momma was out visiting with friends, so things just got worse."

Vanessa studied Jorge's sweet face and saw the pain he carried for his friend; it was good Cole had someone so loyal in his life, someone he could turn to in times of trouble. It was, however, sad that Jorge was helpless to prevent Cole's abuse at the hands of his stepfather.

"The bastard threatened Antonio with the gun, told him it would be all too easy for it to *accidentally* go off and that would be that. He had my best friend kneel down and he held that pistol to his head for a long time as he thought about pulling the trigger. Antonio didn't tell me he'd peed himself, but when he ran to my house later that night, my momma had to wash his pants. Roberto told Antonio his mother hated him, that he was a drain on her money, and she wanted him gone—and then he beat the crap out of him when he tried to get away. Antonio stayed at my house for a few days until the bruises went down and his busted lip healed some. His sick bastard stepfather told Mrs. Duran her boy had gone camping with me."

Vanessa paused the video there, her head spinning. The Cole Gianni she'd gotten to know had given nothing away about such a traumatic childhood; it made her wonder: if he was hiding that so well behind his affable façade, what other deep, dark secrets lay hidden?

Murder, perhaps?

Padding across the room, Vanessa retrieved a couple of miniature vodka bottles from the mini bar, along with a few cubes of ice. She grabbed a cut glass tumbler from the credenza, dropped in the ice, and proceeded to empty the bottles into it. Taking a long, much-needed slug of the fiery liquid, Vanessa flopped back onto the bed and clicked the play button on her laptop.

"After that, Roberto would hit Antonio every time he got the chance, and Antonio was scared to fight back; not because he was frightened of that *el cabrion*, but out of respect for his momma. She had no idea what was going on or that Roberto was spending her money on drink, card games, and cheap hookers—he'd even bring whores into the house when Mrs. Duran was away visiting family or friends. Come to think of it, she was away visiting more and more—maybe Roberto was beating on her too?

"I told Antonio to talk to his momma, to explain what was going on before her husband ruined the family or killed one or both of them. All she said was she was aware Roberto was a troubled man who had his flaws, but she loved him with all her heart and hoped that would be enough to change him."

The sadness in young Jorge's eyes tugged at Vanessa's heartstrings; it was rare to see such compassion in someone so young, especially such a young man. Jorge had evidently been carrying his best friend's pain for a long time.

"The last time I saw Antonio was the night he caught his momma and Roberto having sex. They'd left their bedroom door open, and he couldn't help but see what was going on in there—sometimes Roberto would do that deliberately so Antonio would see what he was doing to his momma. Antonio couldn't call what he saw lovemaking because his stepfather had both hands around Mrs. Duran's throat, strangling her hard while they…

"Antonio said he honestly thought his stepfather was going to kill his momma, so he shouted for him to stop. Roberto and Mrs. Duran jumped up from the bed—Antonio had never seen his momma naked before, but he told me he was more shocked to see her body covered in bruises like those Roberto had inflicted upon him. Roberto got his gun from the closet, pulled on some pants, and set off after Antonio, all the while shouting he was gonna kill him.

"Mrs. Duran tried to stop him, but he broke her nose with his fist and threw her onto the floor. Antonio heard him call her a pitiful bitch and scream in her face that he only ever wanted her money, but she was not even worth that to him anymore.

"That was the last time Antonio was ever in that house. He ran off into the night, all the while expecting to hear the crack of Roberto's gun and feel a bullet in his back—perhaps if the man hadn't been stinking drunk as usual, that may have happened.

"As it was, Roberto somehow cornered Antonio in a back alleyway downtown—only a few blocks away from my house. There's a bunch of abandoned houses there, where we used to hang out before the crackheads took them over; even they moved on after a roof fell in on the middle house and squashed some of them. My friend was on his way to the one place I guess he felt safe."

Vanessa downed the last of her vodka and contemplated topping up her glass; there were only a couple more minutes of Jorge's video to go, so she promised she'd treat herself once she'd gotten through it. The young man's story was compelling, to say the least, but her mind was still struggling to connect any of it with Cole Gianni.

"Roberto took a couple of shots at Antonio, but he was so drunk he missed. Antonio ran off into one of the old houses before his stepfather's luck changed, and Roberto followed him. Antonio swore all he did was try to take the gun, to disarm Roberto and leave him there in that house. But Roberto fought back, and finally, Antonio decided it would be okay to defend himself—after all, he'd just witnessed the man strangle his momma and punch her square in the face. In my friend's mind, all bets were off.

"Antonio did get the gun off Roberto; I'd have shot the mean son of a bitch in the face for what he'd done, but Antonio just tossed the gun and began to walk away. I guess that only made Roberto more pissed, and they both ended up in one of those messy fights where nobody seems to be winning until it's all over—sloppy punches, kicking, biting, ball-grabbing—you get the idea.

"Well, the fight was over for good when Roberto fell out of the upstairs window and his head cracked open on the sidewalk. Antonio told me he'd thrown up at the sight of his stepfather's brains spilling out the back of his skull— not that he wasn't pleased to put an end to the man's violence and save his momma from dying at the bastard's hands.

"Antonio made it to my house, and my momma and me patched him up. We gave him fresh clothes and what little money we had—he refused to stay with us because he didn't want to bring his trouble into our home. Antonio said he'd skip over the border and make his way to

America—said it'd be easy for him to disappear there, at least 'til things died down here enough for him to come back. He also told me he'd work at being a movie star there, too. My friend deserves to have that dream come true.

"That was three years ago now, and it was the last time I saw my best friend."

Another photograph appeared as Jorge's sweet face faded to black; the picture was of him and Antonio, stripped to the waist by some murky-looking pond, grinning as if the world was all theirs for the taking and the future looked bright.

Deep in contemplation, Vanessa stared at her screen; was it possible Cole—*Antonio*—had been so traumatized by killing his stepfather that he was motivated to kill the young women he met on the show, in particular those who played hard to get? A sociopathic mindset was certainly motive, and Cole, without a doubt, had the opportunity since he wasn't in front of the camera 24/7.

But *would* he?

Vanessa made good on her promise and fixed herself another drink; there was plenty of time to be stone cold sober before she was due to be picked up for filming. And besides, the first pair of vodkas had barely even touched the sides.

She did have Tom Hickersley to check in with—it was not a call she was especially looking forward to—but first, she did a little research on Jorge Estenssoro of Cochabamba. It took some digging, as there was no mention of the young man anywhere. Nothing at all, which was weird because *everybody* left some trail on the internet. Eventually, Vanessa found a tiny reference among the obituaries in his town's local newspaper, which had been diligently archived going back to the late seventies. Jorge had apparently been killed in a tragic automobile accident only a few days after he'd posted the video Vanessa had just watched.

Just another unfortunate accident associated with Antonio Duran's family.

Vanessa sipped at her fresh drink; the ice cubes bobbed around, clinking against the sides of the glass. Picking up her phone, she pulled up Tom Hickersley's number and hit dial—she figured she might as well get all the crap out of the way in one go, and she wanted something to distract her from the doubts she was having about Cole after what she'd just seen.

"Hello? Mr. Hickersley?" Vanessa said as her call was picked up. Despite his insistence, she avoided calling the man Tom—it was an unwritten rule of hers with every client, and she especially felt the need to maintain a professional distance from Tracy's father.

"Miss Michaels." Tom Hickersley sounded surprised. "Do you have news for me?"

"Nothing concrete as yet, but I do have a list of possible suspects," she told him. She decided against telling him about Mai Ling—he'd hear about it soon enough on the news, and it really wasn't a conversation she wanted to get into right then.

"Are they involved with *The Gentleman's Choice*?"

"So far, yes." She thought Tom Hickersley's question was an odd one, considering he knew where she was.

"I thought as much." He sighed; it was drawn out, filled with sadness. "I never wanted my little girl to go on that terrible show, but I suppose I only have myself to blame for that."

"You couldn't have stopped her, Mr. Hickersley—the more you said no, the more determined she'd be. We were all that age once, remember." Vanessa placated; if there was one part of her job she truly resented, it was playing psychiatrist-cum-priest and listening to her clients' confessions and regrets. Sadly, it came along with the territory and was wholly unavoidable. "May I ask you a question, Mr. Hickersley?" Vanessa took a deep breath as she awaited the reply.

"Of course."

"Was there any… history with Tracy and you?" Vanessa struggled to get the words out: they felt so damned *intrusive*. "I hate to ask, but it will help me to know everything—"

"It was a moment of weakness…" Tom Hickersley's breath came through Vanessa's phone as unnaturally heavy, each exhale practically a snort. "Tracy was thirteen. She'd spent the day in the pool with her girlfriends; the two-piece swimsuit her mother let her buy was obscene for a child to be wearing, and I'd been drinking…"

The phone fell silent for a moment or two and then, "It went on for several years after that—it became kind of a habit."

Vanessa reeled from the revelation.

She knew it! Sure, there had been no way to be certain short of outright asking, but Hickersley had proven Vanessa's gut feeling about him to be correct: he'd abused his own daughter, equated that to her taking part in *The Gentleman's Choice*, which had likely led to her death, and he was beating himself up about it every waking minute.

Vanessa couldn't think of a more fitting punishment for a father capable of molesting his own flesh and blood; for as happy as she was to take the man's money, she hoped he'd rot in hell for what he'd done. "I'm dying, Miss Michaels," Tom Hickersley told her, matter of fact, as if they were discussing the weather over in Houston. "Stage four bowel cancer—there's nothing more they can do for me."

"I'm very sorry to hear that." The words spilled out automatically. She wasn't sorry in the least, but it was what she was *supposed* to say to the dying man instead of *karma is a bitch, Tom*, which was on the tip of her tongue. Vanessa's next thought, of course, was she hoped he'd live long enough to sign the check for the second half of her payment.

"I've got six months, maybe a little less, and I'd like to see justice done for Tracy. It's the least I can do for her."

Again, Vanessa fought hard to hold her tongue. The man was no more doing it for Tracy than she was: Tom Hickersley was seeking atonement for what he'd done to his teenaged daughter.

"I'm doing everything I can to catch whoever killed your daughter, Mr. Hickersley."

"And you are going above and beyond the call of duty to help me make peace with God. I truly appreciate it, Miss Michaels, and I'll be showing my appreciation in your final payment."

Vanessa wasn't sure what the right thing was to say. That she didn't want a pedophile's guilt money? That he disgusted her, and yes, it was more than likely his abuse of her as a young teen that ultimately pushed Tracy onto the nasty internet porn show? Or should she inform him she no longer wanted to do his dirty work so he could ease his conscience and face death with God's forgiveness?

"Thank you," was all Vanessa could think of to say. "I'll check in with you again sometime tomorrow."

"Take care, Miss Michaels." Tom Hickersley's voice was suddenly labored, weak, as if confessing his sin to Vanessa had drained him.

"Goodbye, Mr. Hickersley." Vanessa hung up the call and tossed her cell phone onto the bed. It felt dirty in her hand, and she had the urge to shower despite the bath she'd just taken. Following in Tracy's footsteps by demeaning herself on *The Gentleman's Choice* in the hope of drawing out the girl's murderer no longer felt like a noble cause. It stuck in Vanessa's craw to be on Tom Hickersley's payroll to help him find some kind of warped peace with God and go to his grave without Tracy blighting his soul. The whole notion made Vanessa sick to her stomach.

She was about to go on the fourth date with Cole, and if that was as well-received by the show's viewers as the previous three, she was facing Night Five and the expectation to have sex with Cole—it was even written into her contract.

Vanessa had expected the show would take a brief hiatus in light of Mai Ling's corpse in the doorway, even if it was only a couple of days. That would have given her more time to work on unearthing the killer or, at the very least, eliminate anyone directly involved with the show's production.

But no, Skippy Webman had played his "the show must go on" card to its fullest, and according to Cole, was more delighted than was decent with the extra publicity the murder would generate, and he intended to capitalize upon that to the fullest.

The question remained in Vanessa's mind, however: how prepared was she to go through with having full sex with Cole Gianni on *The Gentleman's Choice*, especially in light of Tom Hickersley's confession? There was finishing the job for which she was being paid handsomely to think about, of course—there was a hell of a lot of good she could do with Tom Hickersley's guilt money. But, then again, was she prepared to whore herself out for the sake of a dying man's soul?

It was a dichotomy Vanessa knew would churn in her mind until the moment arrived, so she appeased herself by deciding to focus upon getting through the fourth date, and she'd worry about Night Five when—*if*—she got there.

Satisfied as much as she could be, Vanessa knocked back her liquor, threw off her robe, and padded naked to the bathroom to take the shower she so badly needed.

Chapter Thirty

When Mistress was in a foul mood, he couldn't help but be on edge; she had a nasty habit of lashing out at anyone in close proximity to sate her anger, which was never a good thing when combined with her dominatrix persona. And, on more than one occasion, he'd borne the brunt of his mistress's temper; his body still carried the marks.

She'd been quiet for most of their seventy-mile trip north to Huntsville, for which he'd been grateful. Lost in his own thoughts, he'd whiled away the time watching the world zip by on the I-45 and listening to a classic '80s rock station until he'd grown tired of the endless tirade of advertisements, which kind of spoiled the tunes and fond reminisces he was wrapped up in. So, for the last twenty minutes, they'd traveled in silence.

"Why is the show still on the air?" she snarled, her eyes fixed straight on the road ahead, her hands gripping the steering wheel so hard her knuckles whitened. Sitting ramrod straight in the driving seat in her brand-new dominatrix outfit, she'd never looked so fearsome… or beautiful. Her corset was black leather, polished to a reflective shine, her breasts covered by intricate black lace interwoven with strips of red satin ribbon. Her mask, an all-black feathered affair, lay on the backseat of the car next to the long overcoats she'd brought along in case they made a stop along the way. Although Mistress was never one to be too shy—she absolutely *loved* flaunting her body.

As for his own gimp get-up, that couldn't have failed to attract the wrong kind of attention, and he was grateful she'd allowed him to forgo the mask and had brought along his overcoat.

"*Why*?" She raised her voice. He winced.

His mistress's voice cut through him like one of her knives, and in an instant, he felt as though everything was his fault.

"And it's even *more* fucking popular because of what I've done!" She slapped the wheel with the flat of her hand; the sudden movement and sharp noise made him jump in his seat.

"Yes, Mistress." He knew his voice sounded weak, timid, and he hoped it would please her.

He contemplated her as she swung the car off the highway a mile or so after the Walls Unit—the locals' nickname for the imposing red brick Huntsville State Penitentiary that loomed by the side of I-45—and figured if he wasn't so intimidated by her, he'd have made his escape a long time ago. He was forced to admit to himself it went beyond intimidation. He was as hopelessly besotted with her as he had been when they'd first met, and he still truly believed he was punching above his weight and lucky she gave him as much as the time of day.

And they'd both gone too far in what she referred to as their *work* to back out now. They were in the whole mess together; with him as complicit as she was sociopathic, and he knew he'd fry just as sure as she would should they ever get caught.

"Let's see just how popular it is when the star disappears." The outright contempt in her tone belied the smile that curled her scarlet lips and showed a sinister hint of teeth. "It's all going to change for Cole Gianni tonight."

"Yes, Mistress." It was all he could think of to say, given the circumstances. She'd planned for them to make their move that very night, to play out their final act and bag what she considered to be the ultimate prize, to bring their work to its inevitable climax.

He wasn't so sure about snatching the star of *The Gentleman's Choice*; while he was comfortable enough taking the silly little contestants and having fun with them once the show had spat them out, kidnapping the high-profile creator and star of the show was something way out of his comfort zone. Still, it was what his mistress wanted, and his role as subservient was to please her, and it pleased her to make plans for Cole and his dumb date to have a very special Night Five indeed.

One they definitely wouldn't forget.

And that meant they had to make their move that night—either that or wait another week or so; she'd followed the contestant's progress enough to be more than confident she'd make it to the fourth night of the show, although beyond that, nothing was certain. Moot point, though, since Mistress had her own finale planned for Cole and Vanessa.

"We're here," she said as the car bounced down a fence-lined dirt track that appeared to lead to nowhere. "Put your mask on, gimp."

He did as he was told, a tad happier to hear the commanding tone back in her voice; it brought him comfort to know the mistress was in control, and he could begin to convince himself everything was going to turn out all right.

The ranch house appeared as they rounded a tight bend; it reminded him a little of Southfork on *Dallas*. Behind the sprawling, two-story mansion was an impressively large stable block, complete with a horse-training arena. Surrounding that were verdant grass fields dotted with magnificent chestnut and black horses, all groomed and shiny to within an inch of their lives.

Feeling the rubber mask tight against his face brought yet another level of comfort, as did the anticipation of the afternoon ahead. He'd questioned—internally, of course; he'd never dare voice dissent to his mistress—the logistics of indulging when they had such big plans for that night, but he was still very much looking forward to it.

Plus, he had a feeling it was all part of Mistress's plans.

"They gave the staff the weekend off—as instructed." She pulled the car up to the front of the house alongside a gleaming Mercedes, BMW, and a black F150. Reaching to the back of the car, she plucked her mask from the seat and slipped it on using the rearview mirror to position it just so.

He waited for her to get out of the car before following suit—a good sub never, *ever* alighted a vehicle ahead of their mistress, unless instructed to do so in order to open said mistress's door. He followed her at his usual respectful distance as she strode toward the imposing double oak doors of the house, her six-inch patent heels click-clacking with echoing menace upon the smooth blacktop.

The Goedekes were clearly waiting for them, as the heavy doors swung open the moment Mistress rapped on the polished wood.

"Good afternoon, Mistress…" Donald Goedeke gave a little bow and stepped to one side to allow his guests inside the cool entryway to his home.

"De Sade."

"Mistress De Sade," Janet Goedeke said as she held out a hand to shake.

He studied the Goedekes. They were mid- to late-forties, maybe even well-preserved early fifties. Trim, gym honed, tan, and incredibly attractive, they made an incredibly handsome couple. Janet had obviously had some work done, as the skin around her eyes was a touch too taut, and her breasts were unnaturally perky for a lady of her age; naked, they jutted out like twin mountain peaks from her slender chest, and he could make out the faint scars around each nipple where they'd been repositioned.

He looked on as his mistress glanced down with disdain at Janet Goedeke's offered hand as if the woman were something unpleasant she'd stepped in outside. For Janet's part, she soaked up the negative attention, clearly relishing a mistress's disapproval as she lowered her eyes and fiddled absently with the hem of the tight black latex panties that barely covered her ass and pussy.

"Welcome, Mistress De Sade." Don Goedeke ushered her in with a broad sweep of his hand. He had on an array of brown leather straps, fastened together with a line of glinting brass buckles down the center of his chest. His nether regions were completely bare, save for a stainless-steel chastity cage that covered the entirety of his long, fat dick.

"Take me to the playground," the mistress said as she made her way along the hallway.

"Certainly, Mistress," Don Goedeke replied and respectfully scooted ahead to lead the way up the long, sweeping staircase. "It's this way… I think Mistress will be pleased."

The gimp slipped in behind the mistress and Janet, his eyes affixed to the latter's rear end. She had what he'd consider *ample* buttocks, which looked especially delicious covered in thin, stretchy latex. He wondered if she'd had plastic surgery on her ass as well as her tits—either way, she was perfectly proportioned. He liked the confidence her appearance afforded both the Goedekes; she knew she looked good and was only too happy to flaunt it. She'd been completely nude when they'd all first met at the sex club the week before, and her husband evidently delighted in having such a hot-looking trophy wife on his arm.

At the top of the stairs and along a long, luxuriously carpeted hallway was a black, leather-clad door. Arched in the style of the medieval castles, it sported fat, black iron studs and a matching keyhole. Hanging on a spiked hook adjacent to the door's frame was an ornate wrought-iron key easily a hand-span long.

Don Goedeke plucked the key from its hook and slipped it into the lock. With a firm, clanking twist he pushed open the door and stepped aside to allow the mistress and her gimp to enter.

"Welcome, Mistress De Sade," Janet gushed as she made her way inside. "We hope it pleases you."

It took a moment for the gimp's eyes to adjust to the gloom within the large playroom, which put him in mind of Christian Grey's Red Room—only in purple and black. The ceiling and three of the walls were painted dark purple, the accent wall was matte black and adorned by a floor-to-ceiling portrait of the Goedekes dressed in matching black patent leather BDSM outfits. Each one of the dozen or so flickering fake candle lights were purple toned as was the polished wood floor, which made for an incredibly erotic atmosphere. The color scheme was pleasing to the eye, sinister in a sensual way, and the perfect backdrop for the twin silver cages, towering St. Andrew's cross, spanking bench, queening chair, and dazzling array of ropes, whips, floggers, and shackles that adorned the walls like prized trophies.

"Fetch me that," the mistress barked at him, and he jumped into action. She pointed a long, blood-red fingernail at a long bull whip that lay across the spanking bench.

Placing the whip in her hands, its smooth leather felt cool against his skin; apparently unused, he could tell the thing was custom-made and most likely had cost the Goedekes a small fortune.

He watched his mistress with great pride as she walked slowly around Donald and Janet Goedeke, scrutinizing every inch of their exposed bodies. He loved how they withered beneath her gaze, their flesh crawling with anticipation as they eyed the whip their new dominatrix toyed with in her elegant hands, caressing it with slender fingers as if it were a living, breathing thing.

"Tie him down," Mistress ordered.

"Yes, Mistress." Eagerly, he led Donald Goedeke to the St. Andrew's cross and strapped his wrists and ankles to it, his bare back exposed and ready for the whip's sting, face mashed against the rough wood. Goedeke groaned out loud as the last of the straps was secured around his wrist—he was already beyond excited as was evident by his swelling dick straining against its steel confines.

"You." Mistress pointed the whip at Janet. "Bend over there." She nodded toward the spanking bench, which looked for all the world like a sexualized version of the vaulting horses found in school gymnasiums the world over. Only, the Goedekes' was topped with plush purple leather and sported wrist and ankle straps along its sides.

Without waiting for the command, he secured Janet's arms and legs to the bench and peeled down her rubber panties to expose her voluptuous rump.

"Okay…" Mistress purred, slapping the curled whip gently against the palm of her hand and glancing at her watch.

The gimp winced as the first stroke of the whip bit into Janet Goedeke's ass. Janet yelped in pain and surprise and wriggled against the unyielding leather straps that held her naked body tight to the bench. A fat, red welt that spanned across both plump buttocks and dotted with bright pinpricks of blood formed on the tender flesh.

He shuffled closer to observe the woman's wounds, which looked painful indeed. It surprised him that Mistress had taken none of her usual amount of time building up the anticipation with gentle strokes of the whip; often she would spend an hour or so caressing her subs' skin with the harsh leather, until they cried out for the sensual release a resounding flogging would bring.

She was in a hurry to get things done, of course, her mind elsewhere that afternoon—that much he dared to assume. It made for a uniquely charged atmosphere in the Goedekes' dungeon room, which was enhanced wonderfully by Janet's quiet sobbing.

The whip cracked down once more, and another crimson stripe appeared on Mrs. Goedeke's backside. Squealing loudly with pleasure and pain, she pressed her pelvis hard into the wood at the side of the bench as if attempting to move her wounded rump out of the mistress's reach.

Another stroke, another deep welt.

"*Please*, Mistress De Sade!" Janet's voice was filled with pain and raw desire. "No more!"

She was playing the part, of course. He knew from the lascivious tone to her plea she was enjoying the mistress's attention; he'd witnessed it many times before with their other submissives—she was begging for brief respite to relish the sensations spreading from her bleeding buttocks to her vagina and beyond. Often, they'd cry out for a break to avoid reaching an inevitable climax in order to prologue the pleasure.

Mistress ignored her.

The third stroke landed high to create an ugly looking wound across the small of Janet's back, and the fourth bit deep into the first stripe she'd created. Fresh blood welled up in the ragged groove and snaked down the back of Janet's smooth thigh.

"*Please!*"

"Very well." Mistress sighed with what the gimp understood to be genuine impatience. So many times, they had been invited to administer to people who considered themselves hardcore members of the BDSM society, only for them to crumble and collapse sobbing at the first few strokes of the whip or bite of the clamp's jagged jaws.

Janet's husband had no opportunity to brace himself for the mistress's onslaught. His face, pressed hard against the St. Andrews cross, faced his sobbing wife's bloodied bottom, and Mistress had deliberately maneuvered herself into his blind spot.

Again, without the benefit of a gentle warming up, Donald Goedeke's flesh was ill-prepared for the first bite of Mistress's whip.

Nor the second, the third, or fourth.

The gimp was impressed with how well Goedeke took his punishment—far better than his pathetically weak spouse. He bore each strike of the whip with an animal grunt, and his body tensed through the pain, the muscles in his back taut and straining.

After the sixth lash, the mistress lay the whip down on top of one of the steel cages and reached into the left lacy cup of her corset's brassiere. "More, Mistress De Sade!" Donald Goedeke urged, grinding his caged dick against the wooden cross.

Mistress ignored him as she fished out a matching pair of syringes, each filled with a colorless liquid. Placing them between her glistening lips, she pulled the plastic cap off both with her teeth to expose the long, thin steel of the needles.

The gimp watched Donald Goedeke's muscular body twitch when the mistress stabbed one of the hypodermics into the soft, bloodied meat of his left buttock. He let out an odd wheezing, whining sound—one the gimp had not heard before from any of Mistress's playthings—and his body fell slack in no more than a heartbeat or two. Limp, lifeless, Goedeke hung by his wrists upon the St. Andrews Cross, completely at the mercy of the mistress he'd all too willingly invited into his home.

"Donald?" Janet ventured, wriggling against her restraints. "Are you okay?" Although she couldn't see him, she'd sensed something was amiss with her husband, be it the abrupt halt to the resonant sound of the whip's cracks, the lack of noise from Donald, or the sudden change in atmosphere in the dungeon room.

He studied his mistress as she stalked with cruel intent across to Janet, the remaining syringe clasped between her long fingers. She looked so magnificent, terrifying, and so totally in control that it shook him to his core; there were times when he felt he was nothing more than an appendage to his mistress, an accessory that could be as easily discarded as it had been acquired what seemed a lifetime ago.

When Janet saw the mistress approach her and the needle aimed at her neck, she yanked against the wrist straps and kicked her legs the best she could manage against those that bound her bare ankles.

"What the fuck?" The expletive sounded entirely alien coming from the woman's pretty mouth, especially as it was directed toward her dominant. "*What the fuck are you doing?*"

Of course, the mistress said nothing.

"*You bitch*!" Janet snapped as the needle slid into her neck all the way to its hilt, and Mistress pressed down the clear plastic plunger with an immaculately manicured thumb. Janet twisted her head side to side in a vain attempt to be free of the hypodermic, but she, too, quickly succumbed to the drug her assailant had expertly administered. Her body relaxed against the bench with a simultaneous loud release of breath and gas.

"Untie them," Mistress barked at him. "Then bring them outside."

"Yes, Mistress." The gimp hurried over to Donald Goedeke and began

to unfasten his restraints, remembering to start at the ankles.

***

The dominatrix stared down with annoyance at her dust-covered boots. The fine red silt spoiling the patent leather's mirror-shine had been kicked up from the dirt floor of the horse-training arena that sat behind the Goedekes' stables. There were two magnificent chestnut mares in the arena, along with the dominatrix, her gimp, and Donald Goedeke's still unconscious, entirely nude body.

She'd had the gimp remove the old man's cock cage in the interest of stripping him of any form or covering whatsoever; it pleased her to see men naked and entirely at her mercy, and she knew just how vulnerable complete nudity could make a person feel. As for Janet Goedeke, she'd had her gimp tie her to one of the low fences inside the stables, unable to move as she was forced to awaken, and in full view of the arena.

The dom didn't want the wretched woman to miss witnessing the fate she had in mind for her husband.

It pained the dominatrix to have to rush things along, but she had her mind firmly set on that evening's ultimate goal. Unfortunately for the Goedekes, they had become simply a means to an end; they'd been targeted the moment they'd shown off cell phone pictures of their exquisitely equipped dungeon room and expansive ranch slap-bang in the middle of nowhere.

The ranch, the Goedekes' whole setup, was absolutely perfect for the final part of the plans she'd made, plans that had finally come to fruition in her mind as she'd extracted her pleasures from the Chinese girl's pain; her sweet screams still played out in the dom's mind, and brought immense gratification.

"Tight." The dom supervised the gimp as he tied a loop of rough hemp rope to each of Donald Goedeke's bare ankles. The other ends, a touch more than ten feet away, were tethered loosely around the necks of the two mares who were facing opposite corners of the arena.

Bending over, taking great care not to kneel down in the rust-colored dirt, the dominatrix tugged at each one in turn until she was satisfied they were totally secure. She then fished out a small, brown glass vial from her corset's right cup and handed it to her gimp.

"Wake him," she said.

The gimp did as instructed, snapping the vial's narrow neck to release the acrid stink of ammonium carbonate under Donald Goedeke's nose. It was an old-fashioned way to wake people from the drug-induced stupor she put them into, but it pleased the dom to see how abruptly they regained consciousness at just one sniff of smelling salts—nicely awake and fully aware of what was to come next.

It didn't take Goedeke long to realize the dom's intent, which disappointed her a little; she'd hoped to watch the slow dawning of his grim fate appear in his eyes as she followed the rope from his ankles to the horses. "You gotta be fucking kidding me?" Goedeke snapped. "This isn't part of the game, Mis…"

The dominatrix smiled down at the man. His body was coated with a fine covering of the same red dust as her beloved boots. He'd just realized he didn't know her real name and clearly couldn't bring himself to call her Mistress De Sade anymore; to do so would be to stay within the role as her sub and imply his complicity in the situation that had begun as sexy fun but had turned all too quickly into something sinister.

She saw raw terror in Goedeke's eyes, and it brought her immense pleasure. The man knew he was going to die, but there would still remain the thinnest sliver of hope that his predicament was still part of the erotic game, a sexy scenario in which he'd be taken to the very edge by his dominatrix only to be released at the final moment. It was such hope, even in the most seemingly hopeless of situations, the dominatrix used to her full advantage when torturing her subs. It was the self-same principle that had men walking calmly to the electric chair to sit stock-still as they were strapped into place.

The smallest grain of hope for reprieve.

There was to be no such acquittal for Donald Goedeke; the dominatrix had plans for his ranch and the deliciously kitted-out dungeon room he and his good lady wife had no doubt spent a king's ransom on. Plans that included neither of the Goedekes.

The gimp was in position, to the side of the rear end of one of the mares. The dominatrix made her way toward the other horse, which nervously stomped its feet and snorted at the fine clouds of dust its hooves stirred up.

In unison, the dominatrix and the gimp delivered a sharp, resounding slap to the rump of their respective horses. The mares grunted in surprise and set off at a startled gallop toward opposite directions of the arena.

In the fraction of a second it took for the ropes tied tight about his ankles to take up the slack, Goedeke glanced across at his wife's horrified face; the color had drained from it, her mouth hung slack and soundless, her eyes fixed upon her naked husband. The dominatrix wondered what was going through the woman's mind at that point in time: horror at the impending demise of her beloved husband, regret at having invited two complete strangers into their home, or just the overriding terror of knowing she was next?

Donald Goedeke let out a short, loud, satisfying scream as the ropes snapped tight and one of his legs ripped from its socket. An arc of bright, scarlet blood spewed out from the ragged stump as flesh and tendons tore—the sound sharp and grating in the still afternoon air.

The dominatrix felt a tad let down that both of her sub's legs hadn't torn away like she'd seen in the movies and that he'd passed out almost immediately; she'd envisioned a long, drawn-out death for the guy with her standing over him as he bled out and drew his final breath.

But no, Goedeke remained silent as his lifeless body bounced along behind one of the horses all the way to the end of the dirt arena. The other mare trotted aimlessly around the periphery, following the line of the rough-hewn fence as if it knew it had just murdered its owner and was experiencing remorse.

"Should I fetch her now, Mistress?" The gimp nodded his latex-clad head in Janet Goedeke's direction.

The dominatrix shook her head. The disappointment of Donald Goedeke's dismemberment had dampened her appetite somewhat, and she was aware time was ticking by fast. "We're running out of time," she said, although it pained her to say so. "I'll deal with her. Drag Mr. Goedeke over to his wife."

Janet squealed and wriggled like a trapped animal, her bare butt and legs grimy with dirt, and her dust-covered face streaked with dirty tears. Striding with sinister purpose toward her, the dominatrix was entirely unmoved by the woman's pathetic, weak pleas for mercy; she could barely hear what she was saying through the blubbering and squeaky thin voice. "Be quiet, worm." Snarling with disdain, the dominatrix came to a halt towering over her grubby, naked sub, who tried her best to shuffle backward, despite being tethered to the fence post.

"Please…"

At last! Something coherent from the stupid woman!

The dominatrix plucked her favorite knife from the back of her tight leather panties—it was warm and moist from her sweat—and flicked it open.

The silver blade glinted wickedly in the dying Texas sunlight, a flame-colored orange twinkle that reflected in Janet Goedeke's face.

"Please, no…" Janet sobbed even louder as she caught sight of the gimp dragging her husband's body across the training arena. It left a wide trail of glistening red in its wake.

Although it sickened the dominatrix to do so, she plunged the knife deep into Janet's left eye. She'd have much preferred to have taken her own sweet time killing the woman, savoring every single moment of her victim's pain, but she simply didn't have the luxury of time.

The movement was so swift that all Janet could do was blink as the blade sliced through her eyelid, punctured her eyeball, and grated on the bone of her eye socket before jabbing hard into her brain.

"*Oh*," she said.

The dominatrix yanked her knife from Janet's face and watched as she slumped to the ground amid a puff of red dust. Blood mixed with the viscous fluids from inside her eye poured down Janet's face, and it looked as if she was crying.

The gimp laid Donald Goedeke's body next to Janet; the man's lolling head rested on her blood-smeared thigh. "Is she dead, Mistress?" he asked. "Of course," the dominatrix replied as, bending over, she sliced open Janet Goedeke's throat. Glancing over at the horse slowly circling the arena dragging its macabre cargo, she said "Get his leg—we have to leave."

Janet's blood splashed the dom's leg and it felt so good. Hot and sticky, its meaty stink aroused the bloodlust that constantly dwelled just below the dom's icy façade, and her mind focused sharply on the pleasures that were to come later that night.

She'd waited a long time, planned every detail meticulously, and was going to take her pleasure.

Chapter Thirty-One

The stripper, a tall, tan blonde with a killer body, squirmed her nude, ample butt against Cole's crotch. Hands supporting her weight on his thighs, the young girl had her back to him, so he had a perfect view of the angel wings tattoo adorning her smooth, flawless skin. The stripper had him aroused from the moment she'd begun her slow, sensual dance to *Rockstar,* and his erection was feeling cramped and uncomfortable in his pants; he felt the heat of the girl's pussy through the thin material of his dress pants, which only added to the eroticism of the scenario.

Beside him sat Vanessa, her thigh pressed tight against his, the bare skin of her leg glowing in the strip club's UV lights; she wore a small, tight, baby pink dress that rode almost all the way up to reveal the miniscule matching thong she had on. The dress was scooped low at the front to show off more than a goodly amount of Vanessa's cleavage and plunged low enough at the back to expose the top curve of her butt when she sat down. A second stripper, equally as naked as Cole's, straddled Vanessa's other leg, her denuded mound grinding against the exposed skin there. She was of Asian origin—Cole couldn't be sure if she was Korean or Vietnamese—and was delightfully petite with a trim body and small-but-cute breasts. Smiling with lascivious intent, the stripper undulated her body a hairsbreadth away from Vanessa's face, teasing her pouting lips with first one brown, taut nipple and then the other. As Cole looked on, rapt, his attention diverted from the naked girl on his own lap as Vanessa's stripper inched forward and caressed her lips with a stiff nipple. Taking the hint, and with a knowing glance toward the ever-present camera, Vanessa opened her mouth and sucked in the stripper's nipple.

All in all, the date was going incredibly well for Cole.

It made for a pleasant change to be away from the studio, especially after what happened to Mai Ling; the police tape was still up around the rear entrance, the bloodstain on the doorstep, and the atmosphere about the place far too somber for the sexual shenanigans of *The Gentleman's Choice*.

Even Skippy had picked up on the grim ambience, which was rare for someone so inept at reading a room. It had been his idea to shoot that night's episode in one of Houston's premier strip joints, *The Pink Palace*. The club was renowned across the city for having the most beautiful—and willingly accommodating—girls, the plushest decor, and the best damn wings in Texas. It also happened to be one of Skippy's favorite haunts—he was there so often he'd become firm friends with Denzel Pemberton, the manager—and had an expansive backroom for private parties that was just perfect for filming. There had been no need to close the place down, and the regular clientele had no risk of being caught on film—in fact, not one of them knew a shoot was taking place behind the double red velvet-lined doors, and no one questioned the comings and goings of the scantily clad girls and hot young couples.

Pemberton had personally selected a half dozen of his best girls for *The Gentleman's Choice* shoot. At his behest, he'd insisted Skippy sign them up as actresses to get around having them legally considered prostitutes. Nothing was more guaranteed to attract unwanted attention from law enforcement and a closure notice than strippers getting a reputation for offering *extras*. And so, once the chosen few girls had signed on the dotted line, they were escorted into the VIP area away from the club's main area and set to work.

Cole had noted Skippy used fewer extra actors than was usual for a strip club scene—no more than a handful of guys and a few sexy young couples; the viewing public just loved to watch couples enjoying strippers together. Cole reckoned it was Skippy's way of keeping costs down. He shuddered to think what Pemberton was charging them to monopolize the *Pink Palace's* back room on a Saturday night, even if the producer was paying through the nose to keep the overpriced, underwhelming quality champagne flowing.

Skippy was somewhere in the background, lurking in the shadows that blanketed the room's periphery; he'd no doubt pop out from time to time to direct one of the two cameramen or one of the strippers, although he'd be sure to stay out of any shots. As much as the guy loved to command from his producer's booth, there was no way he was going to stay back at the studio and miss out on a live strip show on company expenses—Skippy was a consummate voyeur, and the idea of getting to legitimately fuck the strippers after the shoot had been far too tempting for him to resist.

It did mean Cole was a little more on edge, though, especially as Jayne was managing everything from her laptop in the corner of the VIP room and her assistant running things back at the studio. He was relieved she'd managed to be there, and all he could hope was that things would run smoothly.

"Your girlfriend is really enjoying herself," the tan blonde whispered in Cole's ear, her lips caressing his skin with each word.

Cole could see as much for himself; it was unbelievably hot to see Vanessa with the end of one of the stripper's breasts between her pink-glossed lips and caressing the other with her fingertips. She ran her freehand up and down the sensual curve of the Asian's spine as if counting the ridges there.

With expert ease, the blonde turned herself around on Cole's lap and thrust her own ample breasts in his face. With little other option, Cole suckled on the trim, pink nipple on offer and immersed himself in the sensation of having it pressed against his tongue.

In an instant, the warm pressure of Vanessa's thigh against his was gone, and Cole's eyes snapped open. Peering sideways over the expanse of the blonde stripper's bare flesh, Cole saw the Asian girl leading Vanessa by the hand toward a small stage in the center of the room. The stage, little more than six by six feet, sported a chrome pole that stretched all the way up to the black-painted ceiling.

All eyes turned toward Vanessa as her stripper helped her up onto the podium and showed off a couple of moves on the pole, twirling her lithe, nude body around its silver shaft. Hoisting herself up, she lifted her legs above her head and spread them wide as she spun around for the benefit of her audience.

Then, she stepped away and motioned for Vanessa to follow suit. "This is gonna be *so* hot," the blonde purred as she pulled her nipple

from Cole's mouth; it came away with a barely audible slurp and glistened wetly mere inches from his face as the stripper twisted around to take in the impromptu show.

Cole nodded his approval as Vanessa grabbed hold of the pole and, spinning herself around, she hooked one leg around it to lift herself up. "Has she done this before?" the blonde asked. Her constant narrative

was quickly growing tiresome to Cole; he wanted to focus on Vanessa, not some vacuous stripper. "Your girl dances like a real pro."

The blonde's observation was not wrong. Cole watched in awe as Vanessa spiraled around the chrome pole like she'd been a dancer her entire life. She'd not once mentioned it in any of their conversations during the past four days together, but there was no way she could be improvising quite so expertly.

In the blink of an eye, Vanessa peeled off her tiny pink dress, kicked off her strappy shoes, and climbed the pole wearing only the thong, which was comprised of a thin strip of pink material held together by what Cole thought could only be described as colored dental floss.

Gripping the shiny pole between her toned thighs, Vanessa hoisted herself waist high and leaned backward. Cole gasped when his date's hands left the pole and she straightened her bare back to lie horizontally in midair, her pitch-black hair pointing straight down at the podium below. Vanessa spread out her arms to rapturous applause from the paid extras and strippers alike, all of whom seemed mesmerized by the performance—and, like Cole, somewhat surprised.

"I'll bet you can't wait to get her back to your place," the blonde stripper said, turning back to face Cole.

"Yeah, you could say that." Cole had no patience to explain the nuances of *The Gentleman's Choice* to the girl—it really didn't matter much that she'd obviously never seen it, nor understood the brief Skippy had delivered to all of the strippers and extras before filming had commenced. She was little more than window dressing. Vanessa was the star of the show as far as Cole was concerned, and watching her all but naked and owning the stripper pole had him falling hopelessly in lust.

He hoped the show's audience would vote her through to Night Five, although, based on her sexy dance routine alone, Cole had little doubt they wouldn't. Still, he'd be sure to have a quiet word with Skippy once filming had wrapped to make sure the votes went in Vanessa's favor.

But there'd be plenty of time to worry about that later: Skippy had booked the penthouse suite of *The Revere*, one of the city's most exclusive hotels, which boasted spectacular views across the city from the rooftop ten-person hot tub. Once the Night Four shooting wrapped up, he and Vanessa would be ferried there to spend the night.

Studying Vanessa's trim, toned body and endless legs, Cole hoped he'd get the opportunity to get closer to her away from the prying eyes of the cameras. He'd be damned if he was going to wait 'til their Night Five date to make a move; if he'd read her right, the feeling was reciprocated and maybe she'd be more receptive off camera.

It was certainly worth finding out.

They'd cozy up in the steaming tub, sip quality champagne, enjoy the sights, and reminisce about the four hot dates they'd shared thus far—Cole couldn't see how it could possibly fail.

And if Skippy found out, Cole knew it would be no big deal. As long as the paying viewers were none the wiser that the show's stars had hooked up in private, all would be well with the producer. And Cole figured both he and the delectable Vanessa Young were more than capable of playacting the chaste-but-horny couple for Night Five.

Easing back against the padded couch, Cole took Vanessa in as she pirouetted around the pole, her honey skin glistening with a sensual sheen of sweat from her exertions, and he thought he'd never wanted to fuck someone as much as he did right then and there.

Chapter Thirty-Two

Vanessa was most impressed.

The Revere's top-floor suite was every bit as luxurious as she'd expected—and more. From the 1000 thread-count Egyptian cotton bedsheets to the voluminous white bath towels and bowl of exotic fruits—most of the latter were entirely foreign to her—Vanessa felt well and truly spoiled. The suite itself comprised four expansive rooms: a lounge with three long, plush leather couches and what looked to be a sixty-inch flat-screen, a smaller sitting room, a bathroom big enough to hold a party in, and a bedroom with a California king four-poster and yet another couch. And then, through sliding glass French doors, was the rooftop. Overlooking the bright lights of nighttime Houston, it was a sweet sanctuary, carpeted with long, fake grass that felt like expensive carpet beneath Vanessa's bare feet, and was home to the biggest Jacuzzi she'd seen in her life.

"So… what do you think?" Cole asked her, his voice muffled a tad by the sound of the hot tub's countless pumps and jets, his naked torso glistening wet with steaming water.

"It's all very nice, Cole." Vanessa, ever the mistress of understatement, told him with a smile. She slid across the hot tub to him, the smooth seat beneath the bubbling water pleasantly warm beneath her bare butt—she'd opted to go nude, as she didn't see much point in wearing the tiny string bikini Skippy had presented her with. It didn't cover all that much, and the show's viewers had seen just about all of her body. The frothing tub water hid most of her body from the top of her breasts down, anyway. She was a free spirit, happy enough with her own body to be naked in front of complete strangers and had no qualms whatsoever with stripping off for *The Gentleman's Choice*, even in the line of duty. She was, however, pleased her puritanical parents would not be likely to ever watch the show—that was one whole level of parental disapproval she could do without.

Even for a bohemian like Vanessa, such public nudity took some self-justification; she assuaged her inner voice with thoughts of drawing out the killer targeting the show and finding closure for Tracy Hickersley's father. That, and the monster payday from the Hickersleys, which meant she would be able to take a twelve-month sabbatical should she choose to do so.

"I thought it would be a neat end to our fourth night together." Cole slid across to meet her halfway. "It's kinda romantic, don't you think?" He looked out over the city, where the red and white lights of a myriad of cars shone bright despite it being the middle of the night.

Vanessa nodded and was forced to admit to herself she was feeling some kind of attraction to the guy. Maybe it was the sexy atmosphere the show exuded or that she was still aroused from that night's strip club adventure. She'd taken pole dancing classes years ago and had harbored the fantasy of showing off the skills she'd learned in a bona fide strip joint. Dancing for Cole, the strippers and extras—and the cameras, of course—had turned her on to such a degree she was definitely warming to the idea of going all the way with the show's star on their last night together. That was, if she could stop herself pouncing on him then and there in the hot tub.

Vanessa lay back against the Jacuzzi's side, her head on the cushioned headrest, submerged to her chin in the water, and watched her dyed-black hair fan out around her as the tub's jets caressed every inch of her body. It would have been the ultimate sensual experience, to be sure, *romantic* even, had it not been for the cameraman skulking around the outside of the tub to get the best angles and Skippy and Jayne in the sitting room going through that night's footage from the strip club. Occasionally, their voices would rise as they discussed the next day's adventure and argued over clips to compile for advertising the show on free porn websites.

Cole draped an arm around Vanessa, and she sat up a little to allow it to rest across her bare shoulders. Her breasts bobbed to the surface of the water, the dark pink of her nipples visible just beneath the water's roiling surface. Giving in to the moment, enjoying the sensation of his skin pressing upon hers, Vanessa turned her head toward Cole and kissed him.

Allowing herself to melt into the passionate smooch, Vanessa closed her eyes to block out the camera's prying eye as it closed in to capture the intimate moment. She felt Cole's hand on her breast, his fingers strong and warm as they kneaded the soft flesh and teased her stiffening nipples. Vanessa reached down for Cole's cock and found it to be predictably hard; she wondered if perhaps they should eschew the show's rules and just fuck there in the hot tub, camera be damned? It was likely to happen anyway, so why not a night early?

Cole's tongue met Vanessa's, and she felt herself relax into his arms. His hand slipped between her breasts and made its way down the flat of her stomach, Cole's intentions all too clear. A fleeting thought crossed Vanessa's mind: should she put a stop to things before they went too far?

She knew the moment Cole's fingers reached their goal she would be powerless to resist and the inevitable would happen.

Vanessa sighed into Cole's open mouth as his fingers slipped between her thighs. She wriggled her legs apart to allow easier access and moaned out loud when his fingertips caressed her sweet spot.

"*Hey*!" Skippy's voice thundered out through the French doors. It was followed by a loud crashing noise and sounds of a scuffle.

The moment broken, Cole leapt from the tub, his erection bobbing wildly like some fleshy divining rod.

Reaching for the fluffy hotel robe she'd placed strategically by the side of the tub, Vanessa followed Cole. Her mind had switched in an instant to self-preservation mode; she had no desire to be a sitting duck in the Jacuzzi.

Inside the suite's lounge, a tall, well-built African American man was grappling with a pair of security guards who had followed him in through the door he'd evidently all but broken off its hinges. He was dressed in a busboy's uniform, which appeared to have been stolen from someone two sizes smaller than himself, and his face was puffy and slick with sweat. As he struggled to be free, he fought to reach into the inside of his navy-blue jacket; the guards wrapped their arms tight around his and grappled him to the floor. As he hit the expensive carpet, a small book and pen tumbled from his pocket.

Skippy and Jayne were huddled over by the kitchenette area, scared, but Cole confronted the intruder, wilting dick and all. Vanessa stayed back, deliberately keeping Cole between her and the intruder—if the guy was the murderous psychopath stalking the show's contestants, she had no desire to be in his line of sight.

"What the fuck?" The raw aggression in Cole's voice startled Vanessa; it was a side of the guy she'd yet to experience. She saw his fists were balled and reckoned if the guy hadn't been held in a double arm lock by the two burly security guards, he'd have gone in with fists swinging. "I'm not gonna hurt nobody!" the big guy protested. "Honest to God!"

"So, what the fuck did you break the door down for?" Cole snarled, his shoulders squared, tense. He glanced down at the small book with the gold lettering that lay by the man's side. "A fucking autograph?"

A broad, sheepish smile spread across the intruder's sweating face.

He nodded. "Yeah, Cole, if that's all right, man."

It was a farcical scene for sure, and Vanessa suppressed a smile of her own. In the middle of a murder investigation, some random fan of the show, dressed as the world's least likely busboy, broke into their hotel room—despite the extra security Skippy had arranged—to ask for a goddamn autograph. Only to find himself confronted by the naked, dripping-wet star of the show, along with his semi-tumescent penis and bad mood at having been interrupted in the middle of a romantic tryst.

She almost felt sorry for the man.

"Get that prick out of here," Skippy barked at the security guys. "And I'll be asking your boss how the hell you allowed *this* to happen." He waved a dismissive hand at the guards and the dejected fan and, as they turned to leave, a quartet of armed police officers arrived in the hallway, guns drawn, to take the intruder away.

"I only wanted your autograph, Cole!" the guy screamed as the cops dragged him away.

Vanessa took in a deep breath, her heart pounding hard in her chest. For a split second, she'd thought she had drawn out the killer, and chastised herself for being so ill-prepared. What had she been thinking? How could she have been so stupid as to let her guard down like that? Her entire objective was to uncover Tracy's murderer and there she was, nude and unarmed and playing tonsil hockey in the hot tub.

Pulling the fluffy robe tight around her chest, Vanessa made her way across to the mini bar.

She needed a drink.

Chapter Thirty-Three

For Cole, the mood was far from destroyed by the intruder. Okay, so the moment with Vanessa had been interrupted, but the burst of adrenaline and what his brain had advised him was a life-or-death situation had made him all the more horny. His libido had repaired itself faster than the hotel's maintenance crew had fixed up the broken door; they'd arrived on the scene so fast, Cole wondered if weirdos bust the place's doors in on a regular basis.

Added to that was Cole's undoubted attraction to the stunning girl with the long, black hair, and the fact he was looking forward to sealing the deal with her on their final date night. It was almost too much for him to bear, and his self-control would have flown out the window had the autograph hunter not so rudely interrupted his hot tub romp with Vanessa. Cole was confident his lust was reciprocated—he'd been with enough women to know when they were receptive to his undoubted charms. The only question remained, given they were to spend the night together in the luxe suite, would they be able to resist consummating their burgeoning relationship ahead of the show's finale?

"Hey, Skip, can we talk?" Cole approached the producer as the cameraman exited the suite; filming had wrapped early for the night, all thanks to the autograph collector, and he hadn't been invited to stay at the hotel. Clearly, the show's budget didn't extend to those Skippy considered menial workers. With the cameraman gone, that left Cole, Skippy, Vanessa, and Jayne. Vanessa was back in the hot tub nursing the overpriced, single-shot vodka she'd grabbed from the mini bar, and Jayne was back to poring over the show's footage—did that woman ever take a break?

"What's up, buddy?" Skippy was a tad more than relaxed, having downed several whiskeys and a Bud Light to calm his nerves following the break-in.

Cole cast a wary eye in Vanessa's direction and, satisfied she was out of earshot, he said, "I know it's just a formality at this stage, but I want to be sure Vanessa stays on the show."

"We discussed this, Cole…" Skippy huffed and took a slurp of his umpteenth drink.

"Yeah, but things are going well here." Another look through the open French doors at Vanessa's bare shoulders and long, elegant neck. "I want to be a *hundred percent* sure."

"About that." Skippy had that nervy look in his eyes Cole didn't much care for. "I was going to talk to you tonight before…" He glanced toward the suite's door, as if expecting it to fly open any second. "Jayne and me were talking, and we think it's best if Vanessa *isn't* voted through to tomorrow night."

"You've gotta be kidding me!" Cole fought to contain his anger; he couldn't believe what the producer was telling him, not after what had happened with the last contestant he'd fallen for.

Skippy shook his head and attempted a sad frown that he didn't quite pull off. "We believe it's for the best, Cole." Skippy looked across at Jayne, as if expecting her support, or at least to abdicate some responsibility for the decision.

Oblivious, Jayne remained focused on her laptop.

"How can it be for the best, Skippy?" Cole was aware his voice was rising along with his temper and hoped Vanessa couldn't hear over the hot tub's loud hum. "I have *real* chemistry with Vanessa—people love that stuff!"

"You seem to have a lot of chemistry with a lot of contestants of late, my old friend." Skippy smiled. "I'm doing you a favor here by cutting the girl loose before you fall too deep and get your heart broken… *again*."

"Don't do me any fucking favors, Skip," Cole snapped. "You know I'm into Vanessa and you're going to can her just like that." He snapped his fingers in front of the producer's face for emphasis.

"Apart from that, taking away the raw lust between you two at this point in the show, along with the PR we're getting thanks to the dead contestants, will create a shockwave that will put viewing figures thru the bloody ceiling!" Skippy finished up his drink and put the glass down on the countertop. "Leave 'em with blue balls, that's what I always say!"

"You always say a lot of horseshit, Skip." Cole's raised voice carried, and Vanessa turned her head toward him with a look of concern on her beautiful face. "You're fucking full of it."

The producer shrugged his hefty shoulders. "And besides, it means we can get out of paying out the prize money."

"So that's it?" Cole spat. "The great Skippy Webman being cheap once again! What have you spent our money on *this* time?"

"I haven't spent it on anything, Cole." Skippy seemed genuinely offended. "Although this place didn't come cheap. And don't even ask about the strip club—Saturday nights are their busiest time—"

"Spare me your crap, Skip." Cole took a step back from his friend, afraid he would lose control and plant a fist square on the guy's big, fat nose. "You don't give a shit about what I want—we're supposed to be equal partners in this shitshow."

"And we are, my friend," Skippy placated. "Which is why I have the perfect gal lined up for tomorrow night. You get to start all over with a hot Jamaican who is only four-foot seven—you've always loved a spinner."

Cole ignored the comment; his thoughts were with Vanessa, and the idea of not seeing her again made him sick to his stomach.

Resting a hand on Cole's shoulder, Skippy said, "You have tonight, Cole. You, Vanessa, the tub, and this expensive suite. If I were you, I'd go for it, seal the deal while you've got the chance. You may as well, my old friend."

Shrugging Skippy's hand away, Cole turned and headed out to the rooftop; there, the Jacuzzi and a naked Vanessa beckoned, all steam, aromatic hot water, and the promise of sex. Also, Cole needed time to cool down before he said—or did—something he'd regret. He'd speak to Skip in the morning, when he would be sober and more amenable to suggestion. Cole still harbored some hope of talking him around, although his mind was plotting ahead—working out his next move to seduce Vanessa before the night was over.

"May I?" Cole said to Vanessa as he slipped off his robe.

Vanessa smiled up at him, at the rhetorical question, at his stiffening dick. "Of course," she replied. "I was getting all lonely in this big ol' tub all by myself."

Returning the smile, Cole climbed in beside her, all too aware his intentions were already beginning to show.

Chapter Thirty-Four

A champagne cork popped. Vanessa jumped and her body created tiny waves across the already turbulent surface of the tub.

"You okay, Vanessa?" Cole soothed and pulled her closer to him, the touch of his naked skin calming her jangled nerves.

"Yeah, I'm half expecting the door to break in again."

"Skippy doubled the security outside," Cole reassured. "Not even the Taliban could get through that door now."

That did go some way toward helping, and Vanessa allowed Cole to hold her tight; his strong, masculine arm draped protectively around her shoulders and drew her in so her breasts pressed into the hard muscles of his chest.

"I figured we could all do with a real drink," Jayne announced as she stepped out onto the rooftop with a dripping bottle of champagne and three glasses on a silver tray.

"Good call." Cole grinned. "Will you be joining us?" Playfully, he slapped the water with the palm of his hand to make a big splash.

"I don't think so," Jayne replied with her usual dour tone. "I have work to do before tomorrow."

"I think I'll partake, if that's all right with you chaps," Skippy chipped in as he, too, made his way outside.

Vanessa felt Cole tense beside her. She'd heard his and the producer's raised voices earlier and, although she'd been unable to make out much of what they'd been arguing about, she got the impression the discord had been about her.

"Sure, why not?" Cole bristled. "The more the merrier. You sure you won't come in, Jayne?"

"I'm good—thank you, though." Jayne handed Cole and Vanessa a chilled glass of champagne each, having set the tray down by the tub. "I'll put yours here, Skippy," she added, walking back into the suite, having rested the third champagne glass on the corner of the Jacuzzi by the controls.

"Cheers," Skippy said. "I'm going to go get my swim shorts on—I'm not going in the tub naked. Don't want *my* dick all over the damn internet!" With that, he strode back into the suite.

Vanessa pretended to take a sip of her champagne. She didn't want to offend her hosts, but she was determined to keep a clear head. The vodka she'd downed following the break-in had served its purpose in taking the edge off, but that was as far as she felt comfortable going. She had to keep her wits about her. If the intruder had illustrated one thing loud and clear, it was that the killer stalking the show's contestants could be absolutely *anyone*, even some random, unhinged fan. Her notion that the perpetrator had something to do with the show, and she'd be able to easily pick them out, had evaporated when the cops dragged the autograph hunter away. Along with that, Vanessa doubted her instincts at being able to bring the murderer out in the open so she could secure justice for Tracy and the other girls who'd lost their lives to the madman.

Painfully aware she'd set herself up as bait, and faced with a vast selection of possible killers at large, Vanessa at once felt very alone, vulnerable, and out of her depth.

***

Stripped to the waist, clad only in baggy Union Jack swim shorts, Skippy admired himself in the bathroom mirror. With his gut sucked in and ignoring the man boobs, he reckoned he still looked good for a man of his age despite zero exercise and a penchant for fine foods and booze.

"Nothing a few hours down at the gym won't cure," he declared to himself, slapping the sides of his round belly as he let it all back out again. "What woman could possibly resist such a prime specimen of manhood?" Leaning forward to check he had nothing caught between his teeth, Skippy smiled at his reflection in the wide mirror above the twin sinks. In his mind, he pictured Vanessa, her wonderfully proportioned naked body in the hot tub, those delicious, perky tits of hers jiggling in the turbulent water, and he made his plans.

With Vanessa being thrown off the show after that night—he'd be shocked and mortified, of course—he could see no reason why he shouldn't take a crack at her. Sure, Cole had his eye on the girl, and they'd been cozying up real nice, but experience had taught Skippy if he turned on the old British charm, played the big shot producer card, and plied her with enough expensive champagne, he may well be in with a good chance of slipping between those silky-smooth thighs of hers.

And, if she was less than conducive to that idea, Skippy wasn't above adding a little persuasion of his own—he was double her weight, six inches taller, and a roofie surreptitiously dropped into a drink was a terrific way to level the playing field.

Behind him, the bathroom door opened.

"Somebody in here!" He turned to face the door, pleased he'd pulled on his swim shorts before checking himself out in the mirror and annoyed he'd booked a luxury hotel suite with only the one bathroom. "Did you not hear me?" He snapped as the door opened all the way.

Blinding hot pain shot through Skippy's balls as a foot slammed into his crotch. He let out a strangled, guttural grunt and doubled over, hands clasped to his balls. In his tear-blurred peripheral vision he saw his attacker skirt around him and maneuver toward the toilet.

A low, grating sound teased Skippy's ears as he struggled to straighten himself up, fighting against the nauseating agony gripping his gut. Twisting his head, he saw the top of the lavatory's cistern was gone. Adrenaline flooded Skippy's body as his brain told him what was coming next, and he tried his best to call out for help.

The porcelain lid crashed with force into the top of Skippy's head, and he heard—and *felt*—the bones smash beneath the weight. Still clasping his balls, Skippy lurched forward as his knees buckled beneath him and he hit the cold tiles of the bathroom floor face-first; oblivion closed in around him.

"I think I've had enough of the tub for now," Cole said, putting his empty champagne glass on the side of the Jacuzzi. "A guy can only take so much poaching before his stomach gets queasy."

"Three glasses of Dom Perignon won't have helped, either," Vanessa replied with a sly grin. The guy had been knocking back the booze like it was going out of fashion, while she'd only pretended to sip at hers. And yes, the poor guy did look more than a tad worse for wear.

"You know how it goes." Cole shrugged and began hauling himself out of the water. "I think I'll go lie down in the executive bedroom… you're more than welcome to join me, of course."

Of course, she was.

Vanessa studied her date as he swung first one leg, then the other over the Jacuzzi's side, his handsome dick bouncing on the smooth fiberglass as he did so. She felt a fluttering below her stomach and a tingle between her legs, and in that moment, Vanessa decided she would fuck Cole Gianni that night. Away from the studio and cameras, away from Skippy and Jayne, and away from the scrutinizing eyes of innumerable grubby little people across the World Wide Web. It would be just the two of them, no pretense, no expectations, just pure, raw, unadulterated sex. Vanessa allowed her eyes to linger on Cole's magnificent dick as he stood by the tub, dripping wet with a hand outstretched to help her out, and she told herself it would mean nothing more to her than scratching an itch.

Decision made, Vanessa stood up in the tub, and the cool night air caressed her bare, wet skin. She let out a sigh of pleasure as gooseflesh spread over every inch of her body and her nipples stiffened.

Suddenly, the chivalrous hand was no longer there.

Without warning, Cole wobbled backward a couple steps and then keeled over sideways onto the rooftop without a sound.

"Cole!" Vanessa scrambled out of the tub, almost losing her footing on the slick surface, and crouched down next to Cole, who appeared to be wholly unconscious. "Cole!" Vanessa slapped at his cheeks with the flat of her hand and, upon lifting his eyelids, saw his eyes rolled so far back, only the whites stared out at her.

"Skippy!" Vanessa called out. "Jayne! *Help*!"

Jayne appeared through the double doors and dashed across to where Cole lay so unnervingly still that Vanessa made the quick decision to check for a pulse. It was weak, but thankfully there.

"Oh, thank God, Jayne," Vanessa tried to keep the panic out of her voice. "Call an ambulance—he just collapsed…"

Vanessa spotted the hypodermic in Jayne's hand a split second too late to react. Jayne brought the thing down in a wide arc and plunged it deep into Vanessa's neck.

"You couldn't just drink the fucking champagne, could you?" Jayne sneered as every ounce of strength drained from Vanessa's body and she felt herself falling.

Unable to move, helpless, consciousness fading rapidly, Vanessa watched Jayne walk away, tapping soundlessly on her cell phone. Then, after what felt like an eternity—Vanessa's concept of time had warped, and it was more likely to have been mere seconds—the suite door opened, and Vanessa heard voices.

"You took your time," Jayne said.

"I'm sorry, Mistress." It was a man's voice, softly spoken.

"Did you have problems getting past the security guards dressed like *that*?"

"No, Mistress. I told them I was here for the orgy, and you'd verify as much. They let me through."

"Good." Jayne's voice seemed different, lower, gruffer that usual and as if Vanessa was hearing it through an awful long-distance connection. "I paid them well before you arrived—you used the private penthouse elevator?"

"Yes, Mistress."

Lying there, the rooftop chill against her naked body, Vanessa struggled to focus on the two figures who stepped out through the suite's doors; her vision swirled wildly, and there were three—four—versions of the same thing.

One was unmistakably Jayne, while the other looked to be some otherworldly creature with shiny black skin and a flat, featureless face.

"You can get them both down to the car?" Jayne was saying, her voice ever more distant.

"Yes, Mistress." Was that all the shiny being was capable of saying? And when the weird thing crouched down to scoop her up from the ground, Vanessa felt cold, latex hands on her damp skin and made out the gimp suit the squat, solid man wore, complete with black latex mask that hid all but his eyes.

Chapter Thirty-Five

"I'm not here to find everlasting love," Jayne explained to the fat producer; she tucked a stray strand of dyed-blue hair behind her ear as she spoke and noted the producer seemed attracted to that. "I want my fifteen minutes of fame so I can make some real money." She stopped short of telling the guy she was about to get married to Ronnie Ashford, a burly redneck she'd met at a biker bar a year ago—long before she'd sent in her application for the new internet dating show.

"For fuck's sake, don't say that on camera!" Skippy Redman told her. "*The Gentleman's Choice* is supposed to be about romance and finding *The One*."

"So why did I have to sign a contract with a nudity clause?" Jayne teased. She knew damn well what she was getting herself into: she'd be expected to flaunt herself in skimpy clothes, bikinis and such, for the cameras, strip naked a few times, and likely put out for the show's resident bachelor. And Jayne was perfectly fine with all of that. If it meant a nice, white wedding and a good start to married life with Ronnie, Jayne would be more than happy.

"It's for just in case things… happen." Skippy tipped her a wink. Of course, sexy shit was gonna happen—that was the whole point of the show.

"When do I get the prize money?"

"When… *if* you go all the way to Night Five, you'll get the ten thousand." Skippy shuffled in his chair, and Jayne thought he looked a tad nervous discussing money. She'd read a few reviews about the show, posted online by previous contestants, that accused the organizers of withholding prize money or fixing the votes to ensure they didn't make it through to that all-important fifth night. It was a chance she was prepared to take, though. Jayne had resolved to go all out to impress—and seduce—Cole Gianni and put on such a show they wouldn't dare eliminate her.

And, if they did, she'd still have her hard-won fame to exploit and she'd do her damndest to make sure they regretted screwing her out of what was rightfully hers.

"Welcome to the show." Skippy shook Jayne's hand with vigor, his meaty palm sweaty against hers. "And congratulations."

Fast-forward to the fourth night of the show. Things had gone well for Jayne, and she'd put on the performance of a lifetime on every one of the previous three dates with Cole. They'd included a romantic dinner for two at a rooftop restaurant, a visit to a seedy little strip joint in Montrose, a couple's nuru massage at the hands—and slender body— of an oriental girl who looked far too young to be involved in such work. Nonetheless, Jayne had flaunted her body, fluttered her eyelashes, and been over demonstrative with Cole, which had been difficult at first, as she'd found him to be a pompous, self-aggrandizing prick. Yeah, he was gorgeous, but he knew it and treated her as if she was the luckiest woman on earth to even be in his presence. At times, it had been difficult for her to play along, to pretend she was enraptured by Cole's rugged, swarthy good looks and just couldn't wait to spread her legs for the man.

But, as the days wore on and she got to know the real Cole Gianni off camera, Jayne found herself falling for him in a big way, so much so, by Night Three, she was genuinely contemplating calling off her impending nuptials to Ronnie.

It came as a big surprise to Jayne when, by their fourth date at the swingers' club, she realized she'd fallen head-over-heels in love with Cole Gianni.

Which made what came next the biggest surprise of all. "I'm sorry, Jayne…" The producer didn't seem all that sorry.

"You can't do this!" Jayne protested, struggling to hide her body behind her arms. She'd no longer felt sexy and empowered being naked on the orgy bed; instead, she felt small, exposed, and very much alone.

Skippy hadn't even waited for filming to stop before announcing her failure to go through to the final night. In fact, he'd made sure both cameras gave her their full attention to capture her disappointment for the delectation of their internet audience. She sat alone on the vast bed, which was comprised of three king-sized mattresses pushed together and reeked of sweat, perfume, and sex. Cole had scuttled off the second Skippy approached. Jayne realized he'd already known what was going to happen.

Of course, he did.

They were in it together.

"If it was up to me, you'd be a definite for Night Five."

Skippy's attempt to placate Jayne fell on stony ground, and she felt his piggy eyes crawling across her body as he tried to cop a peek of her breasts.

It made Jayne feel dirty, and she wanted nothing more at that moment than to be in Ronnie's strong, loving arms, for him to be stroking her hair and telling her everything was going to be all right. All thoughts of making the most of the fleeting fame *The Gentleman's Choice* may have offered left Jayne, and she just wanted to pull on her little red dress and go home.

***

"*You fucking bitch*!" Ronnie Ashford screamed in her face, his spittle spraying over her cheeks, his fist full of her hair. "*You slut*!" He punctuated the insult with a hard jab to his fiancée's mouth.

Jayne's head snapped back as far as Ronnie's grip would allow. She cried out as she felt her lips split and she tasted blood. "I'm sorry, baby!" She wailed. "I did it for us!"

Ronnie punched her again.

This time, just below her right eye. Jayne saw stars, and Ronnie's face blurred.

"Every fucker at the warehouse saw you!" Ronnie spat, his face puce with fury. "'Come see this slut we found on the internet, Ronnie,' they said, 'she's fucking a bunch of strangers and she's got awesome tits and pussy!' they said."

"It didn't mean anything, baby, I swear," Jayne blubbed. "I only wanted to make some money. You know, for us…"

"*Bullshit*!" Ronnie sucker-punched Jayne's nose. Hard. The resounding *crack* the splintering cartilage made bounced through her head amid a white flare of pain and the sensation of thick, warm blood pouring into her open mouth. "Do you have any idea how dumb you made me look?" The question was rhetorical, of course—how was she to know that? "I fucking laughed along at the poor dumb whore getting dumped on the porno show—until I realized it was you, Jayne. *My* fucking woman with her tits out and looking pathetic for sick fuckers to jerk off to!"

The next blow came as no surprise to Jayne; she saw it coming and was too stunned to even attempt to avoid it. Her face was pretty much numb by that point, and the pain barely registered. Nonetheless, Jayne groaned as her beloved's rough knuckles smacked into her mouth once more with a wet *crunch* and fragments of broken teeth pricked her tongue.

"I'm sorry, baby," Jayne blurted out, specking her lover's face with blood and saliva. "I did it for us…"

"You did it to get laid and show off what ya got!" Ronnie pulled hard on Jayne's hair. Her head snapped back, and she felt roots tear beneath his grip. "You always were a fucking whore!"

Jayne winced when Ronnie hawked and spat in her face; in some ways, that was much worse than his fist. For the man she loved so unconditionally, the one she'd planned out her life with, to treat her with such disgust hurt far more than any physical blow.

"You fucking bitch!" Ronnie yelled at Jayne again, then let go of her hair and stepped away from her.

Jayne crumpled to the floor, her head alight with pain, blood pouring from her lips and nose, and she thanked God it was all over; she'd seen Ronnie's temper in action in the biker bars—never directed at her until then—and knew what he was capable of.

Except that it wasn't over. Not by a long shot.

Ronnie's boot slammed into Jayne's stomach with enough force to knock all the air from her lungs and leave her doubled up on the floor fighting for breath like some stranded fish. The next kick connected with her thigh, and she felt something *give* inside the muscle there. The next flurry of kicks Ronnie aimed at her back; they flared up raw, screaming agony in her kidneys and along her spine.

As Ronnie Ashford took out his anger and humiliation on the woman he was supposed to have loved no matter what, Jayne slipped in and out of consciousness, no longer able to even maintain the defensive fetal position to protect herself from his unrelenting attack. The all-consuming pain drifted into the background as her mind began to let go, and she had the peculiar sensation of it all happening to someone else, with her as nothing more than a bystander.

When, eventually, the assault on her body ceased and Ronnie bundled her into the passenger side of his truck to drive her to the hospital, Jayne could barely move, both her eyes were swollen shut, and she had no feeling in her legs at all.

Ronnie dumped his fiancée outside the hospital doors—he rolled her out of the passenger door like he was illegally dumping garbage—and honked his horn before driving off. The rear wheel of Ronnie's Ram crunched over Jayne's ankles, a final act of desecration to her broken body. Drifting in and out of darkness, Jayne became aware of people running toward her, voices, screaming, and she knew she was finally safe. And at that moment, through all the pain and heartbreak, Jayne's hate twisted her and burned bright; for Ronnie Ashford, for Cole Gianni, for anyone who dared get in the way of what she intended to do by means of retribution for what had happened to her.

It took a long time for Jayne's body to heal, but eventually it did, although the sickness Ronnie had created in her psyche would only ever grow worse. Her flesh wounds were stitched and faded away, broken bones knitted together, the sensation returned to her legs once the swelling on her spine subsided. She required surgery to patch up the damage to her liver, spleen, and kidneys Ronnie's boot had caused, and the hospital's orthodontist fixed up her teeth so nicely her smile was better than ever. They had to reconstruct her face using old photographs her parents kindly provided, along with screenshots from *The Gentleman's Choice*; all in all, the plastic surgeons did a wonderful job of making Jayne pretty again, although she barely recognized herself when they first held up a mirror for her to admire their work.

Jayne met Buddy Torrez during her second month of recovery; he was one of the orderlies at the hospital who brought her food, cleared up the dirty dishes, and took away her bedpan. He was a sweet, impressionable young man whose short, squat stature was entirely the opposite of the body type she usually went for—the exact antithesis of the likes of Ronnie Ashford.

"I recognized you the moment I saw you… from the show, I mean," Buddy said, presenting her with something cold, congealed, and barely edible for breakfast. "Once the bandages came off, of course."

Jayne had been mortified; the guy had seen her naked and in a whole bunch of embarrassing sexual situations on the internet, which somehow seemed to be far worse than having him cart away her shit and pee in the silver bedpan.

"Well, *I* voted for you to stay," Buddy declared, undoubtedly considering that a compliment. "I think they were wrong to throw you off—maybe they counted the votes wrong?"

"It doesn't really matter now," Jayne told him. "What happened, happened, and I paid the price."

"I heard your boyfriend did… *this* to you."

Jayne caught something in Buddy's eyes. Sadness? Indignation on her behalf? Anger?

"He was pissed I went on the show. It hurt his dumb pride that all his work buddies saw what he was getting at home—even though I did it to raise money for our life together."

"You told him that?" Jayne nodded.

"Then the man is a prick."

She couldn't argue with that, and she was startled to detect the amount of venom in the orderly's words; it fit perfectly with just how malleable she saw him to be—he hung on her every word.

"Ronnie will get what's coming to him," Jayne explained. "He's out on bail for what he did to me, and the cops reckon he'll get six years at least—unless the DA can push it to attempted murder, of course. Even so, it's less than that fucking worm deserves."

And the moment Buddy Torrez nodded his agreement, Jayne knew she had him under her spell.

The authorities scaled down their search for Ronnie Ashford less than six months after he disappeared— sometime during Jayne's second month convalescing in hospital. He had friends in Mexico, so the cops figured he'd skipped bail to avoid facing justice for what he'd done to Jayne. He was somebody else's problem by then, but law enforcement did assure Jayne if he ever showed his face in the state again, they'd arrest him, and he'd go away for a long time.

It was less of an issue for Jayne, however. She'd told her new orderly friend how she was scared to leave the safely of the hospital knowing Ronnie was a free man out there to do as he wanted. She told Buddy she thought Ronnie hadn't finished with her and wouldn't be until she was dead and buried. She also told him how much she and Cole Gianni were in love, and she was considering going to be with him once she was well enough, but there was a way a lowly hospital worker could make his way into her good books—and her affections.

And so, entranced by the flame-haired beauty in his charge—the blue dye was growing out to reveal Jayne's natural color—Buddy Torrez murdered Ronnie Ashford and disposed of his corpse in the hospital's incinerator. Jayne never once asked him for the exact details of her ex-fiancé's death, nor did Buddy ever offer them—even after she accepted his proposal of marriage, their nefarious relationship bloomed, and Jayne began planning her revenge against the man who had so cruelly rejected her.

331

Chapter Thirty-Six

The bright morning light hurt Vanessa's eyes; it streamed through the picture window without the hindrance of the thick maroon velvet curtains that remained pulled to either side of the expansive glass. Through the window spanned an endless sea of grass dotted with trees, white fences, and horses.

As she struggled awake, head thumping like she had the worst hangover ever, Vanessa became aware she was on a large four-poster bed in a bedroom that looked vaguely familiar, and for a moment or so, Vanessa thought she was back at the studio—someone had gone to great pains to arrange the room to resemble *The Gentleman's Choice* boudoir set. They even had a big-screen TV in the corner, its volume turned down, playing something Vanessa's blurry eyes couldn't quite make out.

She tried to shift her body, but it all felt strangely numb from her chin down to the toes she could see but not feel.

And, as her head cleared, Vanessa began to recall snippets of the night before.

They were vague, enshrouded in the thick fog induced by whatever had been injected into her neck—she remembered the sharp prick and sting of cold liquid invading her body before everything blanked out—and she remembered feeling naked and vulnerable, hearing voices, and the coldness of the rooftop against her skin.

Whoever had drugged and taken her to wherever the fuck she was had gone to the trouble of dressing her. She wore a thin cotton, baby pink sundress that rode high on her legs and scooped low to reveal a hell of a lot of braless cleavage.

A low, grunting noise to Vanessa's left startled her. She was not alone.

It took a hell of a lot of effort, but she managed to twist her neck just enough to see Cole lying beside her on the bed. His eyes were closed, his mouth cracked open, and he was snoring gently. Whomever had dressed her had covered Cole's modesty with a pair of tight black boxer briefs—the rest of him was gloriously uncovered, his body taut, tanned, and looking magnificent.

"Cole." The word struggled out of Vanessa's mouth and sounded to her to be little more than a grunt. "*Cole!*" She summoned yet more strength and shifted her body onto its side to face him; more of her body was creeping back to life as the drug deadening it wore off, and she reached out a hand toward Cole with the intention of shaking him awake if necessary.

Vanessa's arm moved so far but, six inches or so away from Cole's rippling abs, it stopped. It was then Vanessa's cloudy brain realized she was tied to the bed, both wrists tethered to the post closest to her.

"Oh shit," Vanessa hissed. "*Cole!*" Her eyes followed the twin ropes that ran from Cole's wrists to the post by his head, and her stomach lurched.

"*No!*" The scream jolted Vanessa, and the surge of adrenaline blew through what remained of the drug fogging her mind and numbing her body.

Turning her body away from Cole, Vanessa squinted against the sunlight to see the TV—the terrified voice had come from it, the sound so clear and loud it had Cole stirring on the bed beside her.

There on the screen were two naked people—a man and a woman—both around middle age, both in good shape. They were hogtied on the bare wooden floor of what looked to be a rustic log cabin—the type the wealthy had as lakeside getaways—lying side by side on their bare bellies, wrists tied together and strapped to their respective ankles.

Standing over the couple was a latex-clad dominatrix and a chubby guy in a leather strap outfit, tight black leather shorts, and a gimp mask. "Please, don't do this!" the man on the floor begged. He had tears running down his cheeks and clear snot bubbling from both nostrils. "I can pay you anything you want… *please!*"

Vanessa watched, unable to turn away from the horror unfolding on the screen as the dominatrix grabbed hold of a fistful of the naked woman's hair, yanked her head back, and plunged a stiletto blade into her exposed throat.

The woman's eyes widened, her body writhed against the restraints, and she coughed a spray of blood onto the rough-hewn floorboards. The dominatrix pulled the knife forward; it slid through the poor woman's throat to open it up like a second mouth. The dominatrix let go of the woman's hair as the man sobbed beside her, his cries heart-wrenching, and the woman slumped face-first into the spreading pool of her own blood.

"Kill him," the dominatrix instructed the gimp, her voice familiar. "Yes, Mistress."

As the gimp took the blood-soaked knife from his mistress, she peeled off the latex and black feather mask obscuring her face, not caring she was caught on camera.

"Jayne?" Cole's voice was groggy as he fought to sit up on the bed beside Vanessa. "What the fuck is she doing?"

Vanessa said nothing as she watched the gimp doing his best to dispatch the naked man. His first stab of the knife sliced through the guy's cheeks, the second dug deep into his shoulder, and all the while he cried out in pain and begged for his life.

"You must do better than this!" the dominatrix snapped at the gimp, and he visibly shrank back at her voice. She held out her hand for the switchblade; the gimp's body slackened, most likely with relief at being spared the task in hand.

"Oh, sweet Jesus," Cole groaned as the dominatrix plunged the knife's honed tip into her victim and ended his life just as she had the woman's; the picture froze at the precise point the guy's neck split open and his mouth went slack. "Is that really Jayne? *Our* Jayne?"

Before Vanessa could reply, the bedroom door swung open.

"Of course, Cole." Jayne Torrez strode into the room, and Vanessa barely recognized her from the dour, over efficient coach she'd gotten to know during her four days on *The Gentleman's Choice*. She wore a black and red latex catsuit that shone bright in the sunlight and clung to her every curve. Her breasts were bared by the suit's cupless design, and she wore her red leather mask on top of her head—she obviously wanted Vanessa and Cole to know exactly who she was. She carried a long black leather riding crop, which she slapped against her rubber-clad thigh as she walked.

Behind Jayne, hovering in the doorway, was the squat, dumpy gimp guy from the home movie. In his hand was the remote for the TV.

"What the fuck are you doing?" Cole tugged at the ropes tethering him to the bed post. "Let us go."

Jayne shook her head and made her way to Cole's side of the bed, ignoring Vanessa completely. "No, Mr. Gianni," she said with a sinister smile.

"It was you all along," Vanessa said. "You killed Tracy Hickersley."

"And the others." Jayne sounded pleased with herself. "And Skippy, I'm afraid to say—no great loss to mankind there."

"You sick bitch," Cole spat.

Jayne brought the riding crop down with an audible *swish* onto Cole's thigh. He yelped with pain and surprise.

"Don't speak to me like that." Jayne lifted the crop again in silent threat. "I'm in charge now, not you… or your stupid little date." She nodded toward Vanessa, who figured it best to keep her mouth shut.

***

Cole refused to believe Jayne had killed Skippy, although having seen what she was capable of on the home video she'd had played, he reckoned it was more than likely. He felt a pang of sadness for his friend, which he pushed to the back of his mind—there'd be time for mourning once he was away from Jayne.

Cole's leg throbbed where she'd whipped it. The pain crept through his body as the drug she'd slipped into the champagne the night before wore off.

"Whatever this is about, Jayne." Cole kept his voice as steady as he could despite his numb tongue. "We can work something out."

Jayne let out a laugh Cole knew was forced; there was something terribly unhinged about the woman who'd been such an important part of the show's crew for years, and it terrified him.

"That ship has sailed, I'm afraid," she said. "Almost six years ago, actually."

"Six years?" Cole wracked his brain to recall something, *anything* that would help make sense of his situation.

"You honestly don't remember me?" Jayne leaned over Cole, invading his space, making him shrink back from her piercing eyes and the sharp smell of latex. "Show him," she barked at the gimp, who pointed the remote at the corner of the room.

The TV came to life once again, and mercifully, the bloodied face of the man Jayne had so casually murdered flickered from the screen to be replaced by Cole's.

It was an old episode of the show; Cole recognized the set as being the upstairs room of one of the swingers' clubs they used for filming back in the days before the budget could stretch to a proper studio. But as much as he tried, Cole couldn't remember the girl sitting naked on the crumpled bed.

"That's me, Cole," Jayne prompted. "I liked to dye my hair blue back then, and I guess the surgery I had to have done has made me look a little different—I had them make the nose a touch smaller and plump up my lips. But look at my eyes, Cole—*just look at them.*"

Keen to placate Jayne in her increasingly agitated state, Cole did as instructed, and yes, he could see the resemblance between Jayne's dark hazel eyes and those of the younger girl on the screen. Granted, the girl there was crying, her eyes watery with tears, but there was no denying they were one and the same.

"I know dumping me was all part of the show," Jayne was saying as her younger self on the TV pulled on a tiny red dress, sobbing. "I can only imagine how much it hurt you to have to let me go before our fifth night together. We never got to be together properly, Cole."

Still struggling to remember who the hell the woman was, other than the show's coach and recruiter, Cole did his best to appear sad. The truth was, he'd dated so many pliable, willing young girls since the show's inception, he didn't see how he could be expected to remember them all.

"I forgive you for breaking my heart, Cole. I still love you."

"So why are you doing… *this*?" Cole pulled on his restraints. "Untie me—*us*—and we can talk about this." Ever the smooth talker, ever the optimist, the proposition didn't sound all that unreasonable to Cole.

"It's all for you, Cole." Jayne stepped back a little from the bed, her eyes taking him all in. "Discrediting the show means you'd be freed from it."

"Freed?"

"If you closed the show down, we'd have been free to be together, Cole." Jayne fiddled with the crop as she spoke. Her eyes twitched to the TV, where her tear-stained face filled the screen.

"It's still not too late, Jayne," Cole played along; the woman's sick, warped logic actually made some sense to him. "We could still be together."

Jayne sighed heavily, her latex suit creaking. "Buddy would not be happy about that."

"Buddy?"

"My husband." Jayne pointed at the gimp with the riding crop. "His love for me is so pure and unconditional—Buddy will do anything for me, Cole."

"You said you still love me." Cole had the feeling he was going around in circles, but knew he had to keep Jayne talking if he was to stand any chance of getting out of the predicament alive.

"And I do," Jayne leaned in again to whisper. "I love the Cole Gianni who cruelly rejected me before we could consummate our love. We're going to preserve that Cole forever, my love."

Cole recoiled as Jayne ran a finger down the full length of his sternum, her skin cold and dry against his. Close up, he saw the craziness in her eyes and knew at that moment all the talking in the world wasn't going to save his bacon. He'd have to hope Jayne and her gimp husband would slip up before putting paid to him and Vanessa and give him the opportunity to escape.

Only, they hadn't slipped up at all so far.

"We shall have our very own *Gentleman's Choice!*" Jayne stood upright and clapped her hands together like some bizarre elementary school teacher rallying her class for P.E. "I've picked out suitable dates for you—which you'll carry out with the same level of enthusiasm as you do on the show—and will decide upon a fitting final night, which will be *final.*"

Cole shuddered at the word. Jayne fully intended to kill him, Vanessa too, and she'd do it with a smile.

"You don't need Vanessa," Cole ventured. "Why not let her go?" Even as the words left his mouth, Cole knew just how stupid they sounded—of course they weren't going to let a key witness go just like that. Even so, pretending he cared about his costar's welfare might just be the misdirection Cole needed.

"Of course we need her." Jayne's tone was stern. "What fun would *The Gentleman's Choice* be without a sexy, willing young lady to make it real? I've seen how she looks at you, Cole, and I'm thinking she'd have happily fucked on your fifth night. I'm sorry I interrupted that for you both—but rest assured, there'll be opportunity to enjoy one another before…"

Jayne smacked the crop against the palm of her hand, a sharp punctuation to finish off her sentence, a sentence Cole didn't need her to complete.

Chapter Thirty-Seven

"Get her in the shot," Jayne instructed, and Buddy, her gimp husband, scuttled around the round pinewood table in the ranch house kitchen to make sure the camera caught Vanessa.

Vanessa tried her best to ignore the camera, along with the gun Buddy had tucked into the waistband of his uncomfortably tight rubber pants. By the shape it made straining against the latex, she could tell it was a Sig Sauer P365—a 9mm with a fifteen plus one magazine capacity. If the guy knew how to handle the thing correctly, it would make escaping somewhat problematic, especially as the dominatrix—Vanessa still had a hard time equating the woman to the Jayne Torrez of the show—had a matching gun in her hand.

Unless she and Cole could overpower them one at a time, of course, which would mean either waiting for one of them to leave the room, or somehow manipulating them into separating. It was the latter that had Vanessa's mind working overtime as she made forced small talk over the steak dinner she and Cole were supposed to be enjoying.

"It's nice here," Cole said, his breath causing the solitary candle at the table's center to flicker. "So quiet and tranquil."

"I'd love to take a horse ride with you, Cole. The horses here are absolutely beautiful." Vanessa reached out across the table to hold Cole's hand. "Tomorrow, perhaps?" It was a long shot, but at least she'd planted the seed. Vanessa spared a quick glance at Jayne, who paced the kitchen like an expectant father, and didn't see a glimmer of a reaction to her suggestion.

"I'd really like that," said Cole, who also chanced a sideways look at Jayne. Vanessa hoped he'd cottoned on to what she was trying to do and would play along. "It would be nice to get out into the sunshine and fresh air—it's been far too long since I rode."

"Dinner's over—you're done eating now," Jayne interrupted. She quit her pacing and stood over Cole and Vanessa. Leaning forward, she blew out the candle.

"I'll untie them, Mistress," Buddy said. He placed his camera carefully upon the polished granite countertop and dropped to his knees beside Vanessa.

She cringed as she felt the gimp's damp, trembling hands fiddling around with the coarse nylon rope that bound her ankles firmly to the table's legs. The guy seemed on edge, nervous, uneasy at what Jayne had gotten him involved in. Maybe, Vanessa thought, the initial reticence he'd shown on the old footage of what looked to have been one of their first killings had never completely dissipated. If so, that might just be something she could play on and get him onside enough to give her and Cole a chance to live.

It was the slimmest of hopes, but hope, nonetheless. "Time for dessert," Jayne announced.

"I thought you said dinner was over," Cole replied, clearly without thinking.

Jayne's hand shot out and she swept it across the top of the table, sending dishes, food, and expensive crystal wineglasses crashing to the floor. "I *said* you were done eating," she growled. "Bend over the table, Cole."

"What?"

Vanessa shrank back in her seat as Jayne pointed the gun directly at Cole's horrified face. Her feet were free from the table, but any intentions she had of getting up out of her seat dissipated at the sight of the Sig.

Buddy retrieved his gun from the waistband of his pants—he struggled a little as the latex held it tight—and he, too, pointed it at Cole. "Do as Mistress says," he said to Cole.

Cole got to his feet and bent over the table, his boxer-clad butt in the air—they'd given him an oversized shirt to wear for dinner, which Vanessa thought was due to some warped sense of propriety. Jayne kept her gun trained on him while Buddy busied himself back beneath the table securing Cole's wrists and ankles to its legs.

Once Cole was secured, facedown and spread-eagled on the rustic kitchen table, Buddy picked up the camera and switched it back on.

"Stand up." Jayne jabbed the gun toward Vanessa, who shrank back from its end.

Dreading to think what may be coming next, Vanessa complied. Her every instinct was telling her to make a grab for the gun, scream, run, *anything*, but she suppressed them; her rational mind knew the only way she had a chance of escaping the crazy couple would be to play along and wait for the right moment.

As Vanessa got to her feet, Jayne walked around the table to Cole's rear end. Then, without ceremony, she hiked up his shirt, pulled down his underpants, and raised her hand over Cole's exposed rump. "Spank your boyfriend," she said to Vanessa.

Before Vanessa could reply, Jayne delivered a swift, hard slap to Cole's buttock. Her bare breasts jiggled, Cole yelped and wriggled, and a red handprint appeared on his smooth skin.

"And if you don't do it hard enough, there will be consequences." Again, she pointed the gun with menace, this time at Cole's knee. "I'll take your lover apart joint by joint if I have to."

Clearly, it irked Jayne to think of Vanessa as Cole's lover, boyfriend, or whatever—perhaps she had been totally truthful when she told Cole she still loved him? It was a weakness Jayne had made the mistake of showing to her captives—one she could exploit and maybe work out a way to get her and Cole out of the mess they were in. Of course, Cole would have to play along, but looking at his helpless form there on the kitchen table, his ass imprinted with the shape of Jayne's hand, Vanessa was confident she could count on him.

"*Now*." Jayne's harsh voice startled Vanessa. Feeling a tad foolish, she raised her right hand over Cole's backside and gave his unmarked buttock a slap.

Cole barely registered the blow.

"You can do better than that, Vanessa," Jayne said.

The mad dominatrix's use of her name—albeit a pseudonym—grated on Vanessa's nerves. She knew enough about NLP and manipulative speech to know it was all part of the power play; the thought that Jayne had been hiding such a persona for so long was creepy to say the least.

Vanessa took in a deep breath and slapped Cole's ass a second time. "*Ouch*!" Cole grunted and pulled at the ropes holding his wrists, and

Vanessa was disappointed to see very little evidence of her slap.

"Oh, for fuck's sakes!" Jayne snapped. "I said *hard*!" And with that, she launched a flurry of blows to Cole's buttocks, and the kitchen filled with the sounds of skin hitting skin and pained cries.

Vanessa fought hard not to shy away from what was happening in front of her. Jayne had tipped into a mad frenzy and was laying into Cole with vicious aplomb. Cole, for his part, wriggled and cried out as blow after blow hit the spot, and Vanessa knew he was hurting: the crimson handprints were bruising in places, ugly purple-blue welts standing out on once-perfect skin.

"Your turn, *Vanessa*." Jayne all but spat the last word. She pointed her gun between Cole's legs, the muzzle aimed directly at his balls, her unspoken intentions all too clear. "And do it right this time."

Having no other choice, Vanessa began to spank Cole. She took no pleasure in hearing him groan and watching his body squirm with each smack of her hand. After a half dozen or so, her palm stung and her fingers felt numb.

"Harder!" Jayne jiggled the gun and grinned a loose, maniacal grin, her teeth too white against those dreadful scarlet lips.

Vanessa changed hands and put all her strength behind each blow, making sure to hit the soft flesh of each buttock in a different place each time; it was the least she could to in order to alleviate some of Cole's discomfort.

"*Enough!*" Jayne declared after what seemed to be an age. Vanessa stepped back from Cole as if to admire her handiwork.

Cole's wounded ass was all shades of red, purple, and black, and Vanessa took no delight in seeing the well-defined outlines of her own hands on the poor man's skin.

"You did a good job, Vanessa," Jayne said, lowering the gun. "Finally."

Chapter Thirty-Eight

"How's the ass, Cole?" Vanessa asked, her voice soft in the darkness. They'd lain there in silence since Jayne and Buddy had escorted them back to the bedroom at gunpoint and tied them back to the four-poster.

Cole was in pain, the skin on his butt was on fire, and the muscle beneath throbbed like a bastard. However, he'd live through it, and Jayne had been thoughtful enough to instruct her husband to tie him face down on the bed to ease the discomfort. *Husband*—the word sounded peculiar in relation to Jayne Torrez. In all the years she'd worked on the show, she'd never once mentioned she was married.

"I'll be okay," he told her. "Don't blame yourself for what they made you do to me—you really had no other choice."

"I wasn't blaming myself, Cole." There was a hint of wry humor in Vanessa's tone. Cole turned his head on the pillow to face her, only just able to make out the outline of her body in the dark beside him.

"Thanks a bunch, Vanessa," Cole returned the tone; sharing a soupcon of humor with Vanessa, despite their situation, made him feel just a tad better. "You bruised the crap out of my ass, and you just don't care."

"I saved your balls, didn't I?" Vanessa stirred on the bed, the gentle motion of her body shifting the sheets a little.

Cole sensed she was facing him, even though he couldn't see much of her features in the pitch black. Buddy had drawn the blackout curtains across the huge window, and the only light in the room was a thin sliver of moonlight that snuck in through the gap between them. Closing his eyes, Cole imagined he could feel the warmth of Vanessa's body close to his, the soft caress of her breath against his cheek. At that moment, he'd have given anything to have her in his arms, her head heavy on his chest. "Maybe it would have been for the best if you hadn't," Cole mused.

It was his balls that had gotten him into the mess in the first place; it was his dumb libido that landed him with Skippy and *The Gentleman's Choice*, without either of which, life for Cole Gianni could have been so much different.

"You don't mean that." There was a lighthearted lilt to his costar's voice.

"I could have been in Hollywood by now," he told her. "I had plans to be a big action star when I came to America."

"You and a million others," Vanessa replied. "You should be grateful for what you've achieved, Cole. There's plenty out there who'd give their right arm to have what you have."

Cole tugged on the ropes binding him to the bed; the rough nylon dug into his flesh. "I can't imagine too many people wishing they were strapped to a bed in the middle of God knows where at the mercy of a pair of crazy people."

"I meant your success, Cole." Vanessa was feigning exasperation, and Cole hoped he'd raised a smile.

"Breaking into Hollywood is harder than they make it look in the movies," Cole went on. "For every Tom Cruise or Jennifer Lawrence, there are thousands of wannabe stars left by the side of the road. Tinseltown, we used to call it back home—that makes it sound so wonderful; like the streets are paved with gold or something."

"Is that why you came here? To find fame and make your fortune?" Vanessa asked.

"I know you think it's just one big fucking cliché." Cole sighed. "But a dream is a dream, and I wouldn't be me if I hadn't at least chased it." Of course, Cole had other reasons for fleeing his home country, but he figured he'd be better keeping those to himself. "I tried my damndest to get my big break, but the most I ever got were a handful of roles as an extra—background scenes, crowd shots, that sort of thing. The money was nowhere near enough to survive in LA, so I had to do *something*."

"Porn?"

"It was the only thing I could think of that didn't feel like I was turning my back on my goals—it was still acting, in a way. I thought it would bring the money in to buy me enough time to get noticed by the studios—even if it was only the small, independent ones to begin with. Then I met Skippy, and we created *The Gentleman's Choice*, and I thought we were onto something, that I'd finally found my stepping-stone to the big time."

"Is that still the dream? To be the next Dwayne Johnson?"

"I wanted to be the first Cole Gianni," Cole replied with sadness. "Instead, I'm known now as the guy who has sex on camera. There isn't a single studio that matters who will take me seriously now. Sure, I get offers, but they're nothing more than pathetic cameos to cash in on my *Gentleman's Choice* fame. I'm right there with the likes of John Holmes, Traci Lords, and Ron Jeremy."

"I'd hardly compare you with Ron Jeremy," Vanessa said. "Especially with what's come out about him recently—you've been the perfect gentleman, Cole."

There had been a time when Cole looked up to Ron; he'd even met him at the AVN Awards in Vegas one year. But, since his spectacular fall from grace, courtesy of the #MeToo movement, Ron Jeremy had become a dirty word in Cole's vocabulary. As it was, Cole was saddened enough to have found himself among the ranks of porn stars who'd tried—and failed—to transition into the mainstream.

"What about you, Vanessa?" Cole did what he did best and deflected the subject away from himself. "How the fuck did you wind up in all of this?"

"Well…" Cole detected some hesitance—as if Vanessa was keeping something from him—perhaps she wanted to tell him she loved him before it was too late? "I'm just a girl using what God gave her to make a little money and get by."

"I find that hard to believe," Cole said. "You're a smart one, Vanessa. You strike me as the kind of woman who could be anything she sets her mind to be. So, what you're doing on my seedy little porn show, I really don't know."

"Maybe it's my thing," Vanessa ventured. "Perhaps it was always my fantasy to star in an internet skin flick and then move onward and upward in the adult film industry?"

Cole doubted that very much. There was something about Vanessa Young that had piqued his interest, along with his libido, from their very first meeting; she had that *je ne sais quoi* about her, a definite intrigue that paired perfectly with her stunning good looks and sharp intelligence. Cole had begun *The Gentleman's Choice* adventure with her, hoping he might make a connection with Vanessa: get inside her head, nurture something special, and fall in love. Instead, his thoughts were crowded with fading hopes of actually surviving beyond the next few days.

"I hope you get what you wish for, Vanessa." Cole couldn't keep the gloom from his voice. "I really hope we both do."

Vanessa didn't reply.

Chapter Thirty-Nine

When Cole awoke, he was no longer tied to the four-post bed—he was in a different room entirely, lying naked on a bare concrete floor, and had a thick iron chain shackled to his ankle. Vanessa lay next to him, still sleeping, her bare flank rising and falling with each gentle snore. She was nude too, and had an identical restraint about her ankle. Both chains entwined as they snaked across the gray floor and were secured to a fat metal loop embedded in the concrete.

Looking around, Cole took in his Spartan surroundings, which were a stark contrast to the luxury of the bedroom. The bare-brick walls, devoid of any adornment, were broken only by a small arched door made of what looked like dark stained pinewood, and a small window close to the ceiling that streamed bright morning sunlight. From the height of the window and the angle of the sunlight, Cole deduced they were in a basement room.

The room itself housed only two bottles of spring water, a bucket, and a large-screen TV, which was propped up in one corner.

"Vanessa." Sitting up, ignoring the dull pain in his butt, Cole shuffled the short distance over to where Vanessa lay motionless; either Jayne had slipped something into their dinner the night before or she'd snuck into the bedroom while they were sleeping and drugged them both. "*Vanessa!*" Cole hissed and shook her by one bare shoulder.

"What the f—?" Vanessa snapped awake, her eyes opened wide, immediately aware. "Where are we, Cole?"

Cole shrugged. "My guess is the basement."

"Why?"

Cole looked over at the chains tethered to the floor and then to the bucket, which had a red striped tea cloth draped over it. He shuddered. "I'm sure Jayne will enlighten us soon enough."

Sitting herself up, Vanessa brought her knees up to her chest and hugged them, hiding her breasts from Cole's view. It made her look scared and vulnerable, and he tried his best not to stare.

The TV popped to life with a loud crackle.

"Oh, Jesus Christ, not more," Vanessa groaned as the TV's screen showed a dark-skinned girl tied to a St. Andrew's cross against a background of a black-painted brick wall. The girl was sobbing, begging for her life as Jayne's long, latex-covered fingers encircled her throat, and Buddy scuttled around filming her agony.

Cole recognized Omawumi immediately. She was the beautiful Nigerian girl he'd fallen for what seemed like a lifetime ago. So, this was how she had died?

Her ebony skin, from thighs to breasts, was crisscrossed with a myriad of thin red stripes, most likely created by a bamboo cane; Cole had seen enough BDSM during his time on *The Gentleman's Choice* to recognize which weapon made which marks. Only, in his experience, it had only ever been a handful at the most, and gentle ones at that—he always did his best to not break the skin.

Sadly for the poor Nigerian girl, Jayne and Buddy had made no such concessions: the cane had split her skin and bitten deep—so much so the raw pink of her parted flesh ran sticky with blood and the camera picked out the white of several of the girl's ribs.

"This is for you, Cole!" Jayne's maniacal smile filled the screen, her spittle flecking the lens with blurry spots. "You can't love her now!"

"You knew that girl?" Vanessa asked, turning away from Omawumi's final moments.

Cole nodded, unable to avert his eyes; the last time he'd seen Omawumi, she'd been in his arms as he struggled to find the words to tell her he'd fallen in love and hoped she felt the same. "She was a contestant."

"And Jayne killed her for that?"

"How was I to know how Jayne felt about me? She was six years ago, and she… *changed.*"

"You worked with her all this time and didn't recognize her?" Vanessa sounded incredulous, and Cole was forced to admit to himself it did sound strange. But Jayne had changed, and not just her hair color and face—she *must* have had work done on that.

"She's different," was all Cole could think of to say by means of defense. "And she wasn't batshit crazy back then—she killed all those girls because of me."

"There's more?" Vanessa hugged her knees tighter and wriggled away from Cole.

"Yeah." Admitting it out loud dug deep into Cole's conscience; had it not been for the stupid show, so many innocent lives could have been spared. "The first one was

Tracy Hickersley—she was one of our earliest contestants. You probably heard about her on the news."

Vanessa shook her head no, but something in her expression told Cole otherwise; Miss Young appeared to know more than she was letting on. Cole decided not to call her on that, as it was neither the time nor the place. "They tortured and killed her just like…" Cole pointed a trembling finger at the TV, where Omawumi had finally succumbed to Jayne; her ruined body slumped, suspended by her bloodied arms against the cross.

"And you just carried on like nothing had happened?"

Cole winced at Vanessa's accusatory tone and raised voice. "We had no idea they were connected until they left Mai Ling on the studio doorstep."

That revelation didn't alleviate Vanessa's anger any. "And you *still* went ahead with your show? With *me*!"

"I'm sorry, Vanessa," Cole offered; any warmth he'd felt—or *imagined* he'd felt—between them was no longer there.

"Save it, Cole," Vanessa growled. "You put everyone's safety behind ratings and money. You're one sick bastard, you know that?"

Over in the corner, the TV switched from Omawumi to a much younger Jayne and Buddy holding plastic bags over the heads of a young couple; they were expertly bound with white bondage rope and could barely even shuffle around in their death throes as they inflated and deflated the bags with their final breaths. Then, as they quit moving, the camera panned to an elderly man drenched in blood and suspended by his ankles from the ceiling of some dank, dark dungeon room. Jayne stalked around him as he wept, her stiletto knife clutched in one hand, the old man's dick and balls in the other.

"Oh, God, no…" Cole moaned as his stomach lurched and heaved up what remained of the night before's dinner.

Chapter Forty

They left Vanessa and Cole in the basement room until the light began to fade outside. No communication, no food, nothing, save for the looped scenes of torture and perversions on the TV in the corner. And, while the quiet isolation was almost unbearable, Vanessa had been grateful for the respite; it gave her some time to reconsider coming clean to Cole about her true identity and purpose for taking part on the show. She'd held back before through fear of changing the dynamic between them; she had to keep Cole strong and focused for if—*when*—they saw an opportunity to escape. Unconditional trust was paramount if they were to stand any chance of getting away with their lives, and Vanessa knew confessing she'd been lying to Cole all along might well damage that beyond all repair.

Unable to stomach seeing Omawumi's terrible demise at the hands of Buddy and Jayne, Cole threw the galvanized bucket at the TV on the third go-around. The screen shattered, sparks flew, and the basement room was silent.

Vanessa had feared retribution of some kind from Jayne as punishment for destroying the TV and interrupting the macabre show she was forcing upon them. Naked, cold, afraid, Vanessa had huddled into the corner opposite the dead TV and awaited her fate.

Nothing.

Either Jayne had not noticed Cole's action, she was away from the ranch, or she simply didn't care, but neither she nor her gimpy husband made an appearance until much later.

"*Up!*" Jayne commanded as she marched into the room, her heels echoing loudly on the cement floor.

She wore the same dom outfit as the day before; it looked like she'd had Buddy sit up most of the night polishing it. Jayne carried a long cattle prod, which she pointed at Cole by means of encouragement. The thing fizzed and crackled, and Vanessa smelled the unmistakable odor of ozone. The message was painfully clear: Jayne was just itching to try out her new toy. Buddy scurried in behind her, gun clutched in one chubby hand, a cattle prod identical to Jayne's in the other.

Vanessa struggled to her feet in unison with Cole. The prod was something new, and Vanessa wondered if they had discovered them around the ranch or had brought them along for their own amusement. Either way, they signified a potential change in circumstance: they were going to be untethered and moved.

Once Buddy unchained them, Vanessa and Cole were led up a flight of concrete stairs and into a mudroom just off the kitchen.

"Put those on." Jayne pointed her prod at the clothes laid out neatly on top of the washing machine; there was a black tuxedo—complete with red cummerbund and matching bow tie—and a short, electric blue cocktail dress. "Quickly." A hint of Jayne in her role as coach on the show flickered through; there was no room for arguing—all Vanessa and Cole could do was quietly comply.

Cole pulled on the black pants over his bruised ass—Jayne had eschewed underwear for both he and Vanessa—and then reached for the crisp white shirt, which took some effort to button up with trembling fingers.

As Vanessa plucked the slinky dress from the washer, she noted that, along with undergarments, her captors had not provided shoes of any kind. That reinforced her theory that she and Cole were to be taken somewhere on the ranch; bare feet would make any attempt at escape that much more difficult.

But not impossible.

Vanessa slipped the dress over her head and was not all that surprised to discover it hardly covered her body. It had a low cowl front that dipped below her navel, and the hem stopped above her mid-thigh; at least it was a step up from being naked—just.

"Could you help me with this?" Cole held out the tie to Jayne, his voice timid, embarrassed. "I never learned how to tie one of these things."

"I'm not your fucking lackey anymore, worm." Jayne sneered and jabbed her cattle prod into Cole's thigh. It buzzed loudly; Cole screamed and collapsed to the floor, his body twitching.

"Hey!" Vanessa stepped forward to put herself between the dominatrix and Cole. Buddy lifted up his prod and pointed at Vanessa's exposed belly with it.

Vanessa lifted up her hands in surrender but stood her ground. "Get up," Jayne barked at Cole. "She'll put the fucking tie on you."

A nod toward Vanessa.

Vanessa helped Cole up off the tiled floor; his bladder had let go when Jayne zapped him, so the front of his pants was dark and wet. Leaning him against the washing machine as the leg Jayne zapped was refusing to support is weight, Vanessa threaded the bow tie under his shirt collar and proceeded to tie it with expert ease. Of course, Jayne knew she could do that, as Vanessa had added "tie a bow tie" in the special skills section on her application for the show.

Tie tied, black jacket on, Cole was directed out through the mudroom door and into the dry dirt courtyard at the rear of the ranch house. Vanessa followed, with Buddy close behind, as they were led across to the stables and barn.

It was their first time outside, and Vanessa took the opportunity to assess her surroundings. Even though the light was fading fast as the sun dropped toward the horizon, she made out the vast acres of fields, a handful of trees, a sparse smattering of farm buildings way in the distance, and what looked to be a small dirt road snaking its way away from the ranch. It very much looked like they were still in Texas, although it was a hell of a big state, and Jayne could have transported them a long way while she and Cole were unconscious. Other than that, there was nothing at all Vanessa would consider helpful in the event of an escape— she couldn't even see where her captors had parked their car. If she and Cole had to make a run for it, there was no cover—they'd be hunted down in minutes. "In there." Jayne jabbed Cole in the back with her prod; mercifully, she didn't hit the button, but Cole winced at its touch.

The barn door was open, and the interior was brightly illuminated by twin strings of lights. Bales of hay were stacked almost to the roof, a small John Deere tractor and a pair of quad bikes were parked neatly in a corner, and pitchforks and shovels hung from iron wall hooks behind them. In the center of the barn, chained by her wrists to a low crossbeam with her back to Vanessa and Cole, was a young girl. Her pitiful crying was stifled by a red ball gag stuffed in her mouth and tied around her hairless head with a tight leather strap.

Scattered around the girl's feet, which touched the floor only by tiptoes, Vanessa saw the clumps of long, bleach-blonde hair mixed in with what was unmistakably dark tufts of pubic hair—Jayne and Buddy had shaved her.

"Welcome to your second date night," Jayne said with a twisted smile as she came to a halt beside the suspended girl. She poked her cattle prod into the girl's hip and spun her around—giving the girl a little jolt as she did so.

Vanessa cringed as the young girl squealed against the ball gag and her knees involuntarily lifted up toward her belly; her tiny breasts were dotted with blobs of stale blood, and there were a dozen or so hypodermic needles sticking in the soft flesh and skewering the nipples—Jayne and Buddy had clearly started on her.

For a second or so, the girl hung there, her arms strained, body shiny with sweat, and eyes rolled toward the back of her head; Vanessa's heart went out to her.

"For your Night Two date, you'll both have fun with your new toy." Jayne jabbed the prod at the young girl's rib cage just as her legs lowered, and she stirred back into awareness. "You first, Vanessa."

Striding over to the hay bales, Jayne retrieved a small whip no longer than two, maybe two and a half feet long. She handed it over to Vanessa, pressing its cool metal handle into her hands as if it were something truly special.

"It's an exact copy of the flagellum the Jesuit priests use to self-flagellate," Jayne told her. "It's designed to perform *cilice* with maximum efficiency—that's mortification of the flesh to us, Vanessa."

"I can't…" Vanessa stared with horror at the thing in her hands. It had a stainless-steel handle from which sprouted eight braided leather straps; each one had either a sharp metal hook or a short, spiked nail at its tip, their purpose painfully obvious.

"You *can*," Jayne insisted. "Back or front—it's your decision."

Whimpering, the young girl struggled against the chains that dug into her wrists, her bare toes scrabbling about in the dirt floor; it had all the appearance of a grotesquely comical dance.

Vanessa shook her head and held the whip out to Jayne. "No."

At that moment, Vanessa wanted no part of Jayne's sick games, no matter what the consequences might be. She stared the dominatrix straight in the eyes and thrust the whip at her naked breasts.

However, Vanessa's defiance was short-lived.

Buddy pressed his cattle prod hard into Vanessa's buttock, slipping its chilly metal end under the hem of her dress, and pumped ten thousand into her.

Vanessa's world exploded into a silver shower of light and the sensation of falling into an endless, stark-white hole. Her jolted brain barely registered she'd hit the ground, even as she breathed in the fine red dust and choked on it.

"Help her up," Vanessa heard a voice saying. It sounded far away and stirred up memories of the hotel rooftop.

Then, hands were on her, and she was back to her feet, the steel and leather whip back in her hands.

"*Action!*" Jayne said with a flourish of her prod and a step backward. Buddy pointed his camera at Vanessa and then panned to her intended victim.

"I'm so sorry," Vanessa said, trying her best not to look into the young girl's terrified eyes. "I'll try not to hurt you."

As soon as the words left Vanessa's mouth, she knew just how hollow they sounded.

Vanessa limped around the girl's suspended body—her left leg still numb from the shock Buddy had delivered—and stood facing her bare back. The girl's entire body tensed in anticipation of what was to come, her chest heaving as she sobbed.

The first strike of the whip barely left a mark, which angered Jayne. Vanessa had made the blow as soft as she could manage, but still the young girl's lower back was peppered with pinpricks of blood.

"Harder!" Jayne snapped and zapped Vanessa's ass with her prod.

Standing her ground, Vanessa refused to hit the floor; the jolt seemed less that time, the wave of dull pain somehow more *manageable*. Either Jayne had turned down the dial a tad or Vanessa was getting used to it. Breathing deep through her pain and anger, Vanessa stared down her tormentor. She knew there was no use even trying to resist Jayne's perverse demands, and it really would come down to the poor young girl or her and Cole—giving in to the dom meant buying time.

Disgusted with herself at giving into her selfish sense of self- preservation, Vanessa began to flog the young girl's back.

It took only a half-dozen lashes of the flagellum to make a complete mess of the girl's back. Angry, horizontal red welts patterned the delicate skin, while the nails and hooks on the straps had gouged out fingertip-sized chunks of flesh; her entire back, and the backs of her legs, were slick with blood. The young girl jerked and flinched and twisted and turned at each blow, desperately but hopelessly trying to get away from the agony of the whip as it destroyed her body.

Vanessa cried as she struck again and again and inwardly cursed Jayne each time she brought the girl back from unconsciousness with a whiff of the smelling salts she kept in her hand. She hated being complicit in Jayne's perverted pleasures and felt disgusted with herself for giving in to the woman's twisted demands; as Vanessa inflicted yet more pain on her victim, she promised herself she'd get revenge on Jayne, even if it killed her.

"Stop!" At Jayne's abrupt shout, Vanessa dropped the whip into the dirt, glad to have it out of her hand. "It's your turn, Cole." Jayne nudged the thing toward Cole with her foot. "Work on her front." That evil smile again; Vanessa's guts churned.

Cole picked up the whip and dusted it off against the leg of his tuxedo pants. He stood there for a moment or two, quietly contemplating the girl hanging from the beam with sadness in his eyes, and in that instant, Vanessa thought he might just throw down the whip and do his best to spare the girl.

But no.

Cole Gianni's self-preservation kicked in as resolutely as Vanessa's, and he swung the whip at the soft part of the girl's belly between her navel and badly shaven pudendum.

Vanessa turned away as whip smacked against flesh, and droplets of warm blood sprayed her face. The young girl's screams echoed through the barn's rafters as Cole struck her again and again. The whip's cruel hooks and spikes shredded the girl's flesh, ripped out the needles Jayne and Buddy had stuck into her breasts, and opened up her skin in ugly, bloodied tears. Jayne ensured the girl was awake to endure each and every one of Cole's strikes, and her muffled, pitiful pleas had Cole weeping as he whipped her.

Jayne finally put a stop to the torture when the young girl could no longer support her ruined body on her toes;

moaning softly and dripping blood into the dirt, she hung by her arms, legs limp.

"Come." Jayne indicated toward the barn door with her prod and ushered Vanessa and Cole away. Behind them, Buddy rested his camera upon a hay bale, pointed at the girl. He pulled out his gun and placed it next to the camera, along with the cattle prod, and picked up the whip from the ground where Cole had thrown it in disgust when Jayne called time. The sound of leather biting into flesh once again filled the barn; each strike, each weak yelp from the girl, hardened Vanessa's resolve to make damn sure Jayne and her husband got what they deserved.

No matter what.

Chapter Forty-One

J ayne guided them back into the house and up the sweeping staircase at gunpoint. All the while, she made sure to maintain a distance between herself and her captives, which ruled out Vanessa's thoughts of turning on the woman, disarming her, and putting a bullet into her sick little brain. Vanessa knew she had to bide her time—a sudden move then would give Jayne plenty of time to shoot both her and Cole. The mutiny would be over almost before it began.

At the end of the hallway, Jayne took them through an arched wooden door and into a purple-painted dungeon. Vanessa's attention went immediately to the huge painting of the couple on the black wall; as she'd suspected, the ranch wasn't Jayne's at all. Whoever the couple who owned the ranch house were, they were clearly BDSM aficionados and had enough money to indulge their tastes. The room housed every conceivable piece of equipment including some Vanessa had never even heard of.

"You'll be enjoying your final date in the dungeon." Jayne's emulation of the show's announcements was uncanny. "I've decided to bring things forward to make sure you're both fit and able to enjoy the activities I have planned. Vanessa, Cole, you'll both die in here tomorrow."

Vanessa's heart sank. She'd clung to the notion Jayne would stick to *The Gentleman's Choice* format, and she and Cole would have another three days and nights to make a bid for freedom. Vanessa was counting on Jayne and Buddy making at least one careless mistake in that time.

Maybe that was Jayne's thinking too?

"Sit." Jayne pushed Cole toward a mahogany, high-backed chair with her prod, giving him a quick jolt for good measure.

Cole grunted his protest and sat himself down on the chair's hard wooden seat.

"Do the honors, Vanessa?" Jayne's question was rhetorical. She pointed the gun and the prod to ensure compliance, and Vanessa set about securing Cole to the chair arms and legs by means of the thick leather straps and buckles.

Vanessa had recognized the queening chair the moment they'd walked into the dungeon room. Designed to hold a submissive in place, it had a large hole cut into the seat and was designed for scat play among other things. And for one dreadful moment, Vanessa pictured herself being forced by Jayne to lie beneath the chair and await Cole's waste.

Buddy walked in just as Vanessa finished strapping Cole into the chair. His gimp suit was flecked with blood and tiny gobbets of pink-red flesh, and he still had the blood-soaked whip clenched in his chubby fist. "What took you so long?" Jayne chastised her husband. "You were supposed to finish the job quickly, not slowly beat the girl to death—we don't have time for you to play with other people's toys, *worm*."

Buddy withered beneath his wife's harsh words, and Vanessa was sure she saw a flicker of resentment toward Jayne in the eyes behind the bloody mask. If he was the weak point of the duo, Vanessa could work with that; what man could resist feminine wiles turned in his direction, no matter how under the spell of a domineering wife he was?

"Make sure she doesn't move." Jayne pointed at Vanessa, then made her way across the room to where a mind-boggling array of BDSM toys were spread out upon a low stainless-steel table.

When Jayne swapped her cattle prod for a straight razor with a mother-of-pearl handle, Vanessa's blood ran cold.

"Where is it?" Jayne barked at Buddy as she strode back to the queening chair. "You were supposed to fetch it from the bathroom, worm."

"Yes, Mistress," Buddy simpered. He turned tail and scurried from the dungeon.

"Jayne…" Vanessa broke the loaded silence.

"*Mistress*."

"Sorry… Mistress." Vanessa kept her eyes downcast, not wishing to appear confrontational and anger the madwoman. "Please don't—"

"Don't *what*?" Jayne's tone sharpened. She opened up the razor, and its keen blade twinkled in the purple light.

"Don't hurt him."

"How dare you?" Jayne's temper flared, and her voice echoed loudly in the dungeon room. Quickly closing the gap between them, she hit Vanessa in the face.

Vanessa staggered backward. At first, she thought Jayne had slashed her cheek with the razor. Instinctively, Vanessa lifted a hand to her face, fully expecting to feel the wetness of blood there, but felt only hot skin she imagined to be reddening from the dominatrix's blow.

"*Never* address me unless I speak to you first, bitch!" Jayne moved in so close, Vanessa felt her nipples graze against the exposed skin between her own breasts.

Now was her chance.

Making a grab for Jayne's hand, Vanessa's fingers closed around the razor's handle.

Jayne jumped away, one hand in Vanessa's, her other reaching to the back of her corset, and in a split second, her gun was inches away from Vanessa's face.

Vanessa froze—her entire attention upon the Jayne's gun; she didn't even register Buddy's return to the dungeon room.

"Don't ever dare touch your mistress again," Jayne growled and yanked her hand away.

The razor's blade sliced Vanessa's fingers almost down to the bone, but she felt nothing other than a faint pulling; her heart pounded hard in her chest, and her mind whirled away as she prepared to die.

Then, as suddenly as it had appeared, the gun was gone; Jayne backed away to her place next to the queening chair.

With the spell broken, Vanessa felt the pain in her hand. Looking down, she watched, detached, as blood poured from the deep slices in each one of her fingers to splash onto the wood floor.

Jayne instructed Buddy to bandage up Vanessa's hand with whatever he could find in the bathroom's medicine cabinet. As it turned out, he managed to locate gauze, bandages, and tape and did a half-decent job of patching Vanessa up.

As soon as Buddy finished up and had his gun and cattle prod pointed at Vanessa, Jayne retrieved her prod from the low table and handed her the straight razor and a can of aloe-infused shaving foam.

"Shave him," she said.

Vanessa did as instructed, and when Cole's face was silky smooth, Jayne made her shave every hair off his head.

Chapter Forty-Two

Vanessa knew Cole felt terrible about what they'd made him do to her. Her long, raven-black hair had been—literally—her crowning glory, even though its color was out of a bottle.

"I'm sorry, Vanessa," he apologized again.

"Quit beating yourself up, Cole," Vanessa reassured him. Her cut fingers throbbed like hell—a sore reminder of how quickly priorities can change. "We have bigger things to worry about right now than my hair."

She was right, of course, painfully so.

After they'd shaved one another's heads at gunpoint, Cole and Vanessa had been forced into cages set in the shadow of the St. Andrew's cross. Vanessa was grateful that Jayne and Buddy hadn't insisted they share, as the barred cages were far too small for two occupants. Her cage was cramped with barely enough room to stretch out, and its smooth, steel floor was marked with a myriad of stains Vanessa didn't really want to think about.

"They're going to kill us," Cole said, matter of fact. "Unless we can figure a way out of here."

"Then we figure something out," Vanessa replied. She was surprised at just how well she and Cole were holding it all together—it was as if the time for panic was long over, and they had both synchronized into survival mode. She was experiencing a clarity she'd never known before and absolutely refused to believe Jayne's grim promise that they'd die in the dungeon.

Having said that, she'd yet to identify any potential way out—Jayne had obviously planned everything with her typical meticulous eye for detail and had her gimp husband running around like some chubby, subservient extension of herself. All it would take was one little mistake from either of them, and Vanessa was confident she'd have a shot at getting away. As a PI, she'd been in a scrape or two and had always managed to make her way out of them with little more than cuts and bruises to show for it. But it always relied upon someone making a simple mistake.

"If I could get the gun from the husband, we could overpower the both of them," Cole said.

Vanessa peered through the steel bars of her cage at him; he looked so small and vulnerable curled up in his own tiny prison. Cole Gianni was a tragic figure who'd lost his way on the quest for fame and fortune, and despite having found both, he'd still ended up empty—like some caged wild animal awaiting slaughter. It was that vulnerability that touched Vanessa's heart. She'd gotten to know Cole— the *real* Cole—and there was a genuine human being behind the macho façade and lascivious reputation, one she found herself falling for.

Although, Vanessa reminded herself, her feelings could just be a reaction to the extraordinary circumstances in which they'd found themselves—a twisted version of Stockholm syndrome perhaps? Or maybe even a simple case of two doomed souls connecting in adversity? All Vanessa could do was hope she'd live long enough to find out. "They'll make a mistake at some point." The tremble in Cole's voice told Vanessa he was not convinced of that fact. "They *have* to."

"We have to be ready for if… *when* they do, and act together."

"I guess it's safe to assume they'll be tying us to something in here?"

"Yeah." Vanessa looked around the dungeon room at the array of equipment. Cole was likely right, but which one would Jayne choose for her victims to endure in their final hours?

"They'll have to untie us from these first." Cole rattled the chains and cuffs that secured him inside his cage—Jayne had even added the indignity of an iron spreader bar that held his ankles three feet apart; she really was taking no chances. "Which means…"

"We may have a chance."

"Exactly."

Vanessa rested her head against the bars; the steel icy against her bald scalp, she hoped Cole was right.

Chapter Forty-Three

Cole had no idea how, but he managed to sleep, despite the discomfort of being shackled in a small steel cage with his legs forced apart.

"*Wake up!*" Jayne's strident voice assaulted his ears before he'd even had the chance to open his eyes. Then, a splash of icy cold water hit his body, and as Cole recoiled, he heard Vanessa receiving the same rude awakening.

"It's time for your final date, lovebirds," Jayne said as she unlocked first Vanessa's cage and then Cole's. "I hope you managed to say your fond goodbyes last night—because today will be your last day."

Cole wriggled headfirst from his cage, his progress hindered by his restraints. Jayne had her gimp husband help him and Vanessa to their feet and stand them side by side; Vanessa was barely recognizable sans hair and with her makeup all but rinsed away, and blood had seeped through the bandage on her hand.

Buddy then retrieved his ever-present camera and began to film.

Jayne took great delight in presenting Cole and Vanessa with the vicious array of torture instruments with which she was going to torment them. Parading each one before them, gun clasped in her hand, Jayne was clearly playing to the camera as if she had every intention of sharing Cole and Vanessa's demise with the general public.

"We have clamps for nipples, tongues, and genitals," Jayne explained, holding up a matching pair of tiny, serrated-toothed presses. "There are Wartenberg wheels, speculums, medical sounds, a violet wand—of course—and a whole range of butt plugs to test your mettle. There are also all the whips, crops, and paddles for us to try out. As you can see, our hosts are especially well-prepared for all kinds of fun."

Cole eyed each piece of BDSM equipment as Jayne presented it. He was familiar with all of them and had used most on the show at one time or another. He'd been on the receiving end of a multitude of whips and paddles on the BDSM date nights, but never at the hands of a madwoman with cruel, sadistic intent.

He'd seen her type before, though. They frequented the underground clubs he'd visited by means of research for *The Gentleman's Choice*, and he knew all too well the perverse pleasure they took in torturing their willing victims.

"Step forward, Vanessa." Jayne held the Violet Wand a half inch from Vanessa's belly. The tip of the wand sparked to life, and a tiny arc of electricity jumped from it to Vanessa's damp skin.

Cole could only look on helplessly as Vanessa screamed and jumped back, her chains rattling loudly.

"You'll have to be quicker than that." Jayne laughed, then aimed the wand at Vanessa's breast and zapped her once more. "We'll have our fun with you first—let your lover watch you die in agony. Buddy?"

"Whatever pleases you, Mistress," the gimp mumbled from behind his camera, his attention on Vanessa's pained expression and teary eyes.

"Stay still, Vanessa." Jayne picked up a small silver key from the top of Vanessa's cage and began unlocking her cuffs.

"No," Cole interrupted. "I want you to play with me first." He shuffled forward the best his spreader bar would allow, his eyes seeking Jayne's. "I've been waiting for this moment since I realized who you were, Jayne—since I discovered the *real* you."

Jayne quit fiddling with Vanessa's handcuffs and eyed Cole with suspicion. "You *really* want to die first?"

Cole flinched at Jayne's words; they sounded so cold, so *final*, spoken out loud. Nonetheless, he persevered with his attempt to win her over with what he reckoned she wanted to hear from him. "I'm the one you want, Jayne, not her." He gave Vanessa a dismissive glance as if she meant nothing to him at all. "And before I… before *we* play, I want you to know I never forgot our time together on the show. It was truly something special—my only regret is I never had the chance to make love to you."

"You didn't even know who I was in all the time I worked with you."

Jayne took a step toward Cole, Vanessa seemingly forgotten.

"How could I?" Cole furrowed his brow and gave her a sheepish grin. "You changed so much."

Jayne touched a hand to her face. Caressing her cheek, she replied, "I had work done, courtesy of my fiancé and his fists."

"I'm so sorry, Jayne." Cole shuffled a little closer. "You didn't deserve that at all."

Jayne shook her head. "No, I did not. But I don't regret my time with you on the show at all—we had fun."

"It was more than just fun for me. We *connected*, Jayne, and I can feel that connection still between us." Eye contact. A sincere smile. "Can you?"

"Yes," Jayne replied softly, and for a moment she was no longer the cruel, strict mistress—just a lost, lonely woman who had been terribly hurt.

"So why don't we have some fun now?" Cole pushed. "If this is going to be my final adventure, I can't think of anyone I'd rather spend it with." As he spoke, Cole was all too aware of Buddy and his damn camera hovering only a couple feet away while another man declared warm feelings for his wife.

Jayne put down the key, took hold of Cole's arm, and nodded toward the St. Andrew's cross. "Come," she said, and the dominatrix was back. Cole didn't dare believe his ruse had actually worked or that his acting was good enough to fool Jayne. It had been a long shot based upon Cole's understanding that women could be easily seduced by hearing just the right words at the right time—he mentally kicked himself for not having thought of it sooner. And Jayne had believed him because she *wanted* to believe him.

The short walk to the cross was awkward, to say the least. With the bar attached to his ankles by thick straps, the best Cole could do was waddle like a wounded penguin; under any other circumstance, he'd have found it amusing. All the while, Jayne kept her gun pointed at Cole's ribs; she may have succumbed to a little of his sweet talk, but she was wily enough to not trust him.

"Hold still," Jayne commanded as she bent down to release Cole's legs from the spreader, which dropped to the floor with a resounding clatter. Then, expertly and with one hand, she unfastened his handcuffs while Cole stared motionlessly down the barrel of her Sig.

Free from his restraints, Cole rubbed at his wrists; the cuffs had chafed the delicate skin there overnight, and they were awfully sore.

"This is *so* hot, Jayne," Cole whispered to the dominatrix as she lifted his right arm up and pressed it hard against the wooden cross. She then began fiddling with the strap, the silver buckle jingling in Cole's ear. "We should be doing this together, alone, not with your husband filming and *her* watching. And not at gunpoint, either."

Jayne paused—just a heartbeat or two—and Cole thought he was getting through to her on some level; maybe he would live to tell the tale after all.

"We'd be so good together—it's such a turn-on knowing you love all of this…" He looked around the dungeon room with an expression of awe as if he'd died and gone to BDSM heaven. "Just think of all the things we could explore together, all the other people we could have fun with—away from judging eyes."

Cole saw Jayne's nipples stiffen at his words—he'd definitely hit a nerve somewhere beneath the woman's madness.

"Film the girl." Jayne stared into Buddy's camera, which was less than three feet from her face. "Leave me to do this—I'll tell you when you can come back."

As Jayne's attention diverted to the gimp as he turned his camera to Vanessa, her gun wavered a tad and its muzzle no longer pointed at his face.

Cole took his chance.

A high kick to Jayne's hand and the gun flew from her fingers; the top of Cole's foot where it connected with the Sig's handle flared with pain. Jayne's head snapped back around to Cole, and he hit her with a vicious head-butt to the bridge of her nose.

Stunned, Jayne staggered back, then she tripped over her vertiginous shoes and hit the floor hard; her skull bounced off the ground with a dull *thunk*.

Buddy spun around, a look of abject shock on his face at seeing his wife out cold on the dungeon floor. Dropping the camera, he grabbed for the gun he had tucked in the waist of his latex pants, but before he could retrieve it, Cole had picked up the spreader bar and was on him.

It felt good to be back in control and even better to swing the steel bar into Buddy's gimp mask. Cole's arms jarred with the impact, and he felt Buddy's bones crunch as the bar smacked hard into his face. Buddy screamed out loud and clutched at his broken face as blood poured through his fingers, all thoughts of the gun forgotten. Taking no chances, Cole swung the bar again. It connected with the gimp's temple, and he keeled over sideways with a guttural grunt.

Cole dropped the bar as Buddy went down; already, Jayne was stirring—there was no time to lose. Grabbing the key from the foot of the St. Andrew's cross, Cole raced over to Vanessa and unlocked her cuffs and shackles.

With a backward glance at their captors, Cole took Vanessa's uninjured hand and led her from the dungeon room.

Chapter Forty-Four

"How could you let this happen?" Jayne shouted at her husband, taking no pleasure in watching him shrink away from her. He'd taken off his mask to allow the blood to drain out of it, and his face was a swollen, misshapen mess.

Jayne touched the tips of her fingers to her bruised nose; Cole had hit her hard but not enough to break the cartilage as far as she could make out. Even if it was broken, she had more pressing matters to attend to.

"We have to kill them both before they get out of the house," she said.

Buddy shrugged. "Where are they going to go, Mistress?" They don't even have clothes, and there's nothing for miles.

A thought struck Jayne. "Where did you leave the car keys?"

"In the kitchen," Buddy replied. "On the counter by the teakettle."

Jayne slapped his face hard. "*You left them out*?"

Buddy rubbed at his cheek, tears welling in his eyes. "I didn't think they'd be leaving the dungeon," he said, and Jayne knew he'd stopped short of blaming her for Cole and Vanessa's escape—he just wouldn't *dare*.

"You fucking idiot," Jayne growled as she plucked her gun up off the floor and strode out of the dungeon. "I'll look for them up here, you take the servant's stairs and go get those keys, *worm*. And take your camera; I don't want to waste the opportunity to grab some good footage when we track those two down."

"Yes, Mistress," she heard her husband say as she stalked along the hallway.

* * *

Cole led Vanessa down the stairs, the marble cold beneath his bare feet. He'd given a fleeting thought that perhaps they ought to find clothes, but what would have been the point? They'd been naked together since the evening before, and although Vanessa looked striking nude and shaven headed, any notions of seduction were furthest from his mind.

"We could make a run for it." Vanessa peered out through the dining room window at the vast expanse of nothingness beyond it.

"And how far do you think we'd get like this?" Cole replied. "We have to find their car."

"You know how to hotwire?"

Cole shook his head no. "Do you?"

"No. So we'll need to find the car keys as well."

"Shit," Cole swore beneath his breath. The house was huge and spread across two floors—one of which had Jayne and Buddy looking for them. It was like searching for the proverbial needle. "Okay, I'll go this way," he pointed to their left, "and you go that. Let's meet by the front door in five minutes."

"What if we don't find the keys in that time?"

"Then I guess we go with your plan and take our chances out there." Cole stared out through the window and wondered just how far they'd get, naked and against armed hunters. Ironically, it was like taking part in some perverse game show.

"Good luck." Vanessa threw her arms around Cole's neck and hugged him tight. Her damp skin against his felt so good, Cole didn't want their embrace to end.

And then Vanessa was gone, her bare feet padding across the travertine floor.

Cole made his way out through the door at the opposite end of the dining room and into the hallway beyond, with the hope it would lead to the kitchen; people *always* left their car keys in the kitchen, right? Behind him, Cole heard Jayne's raised voice, her obvious anger and frustration at having lost control of her game aimed at her gimp husband.

The hallway was long, straight, and had five identical white doors: a secondary, smaller dining room, a library, game room complete with a pink-topped pool table, an exercise room containing only a single rowing machine, and the huge kitchen, which looked to Cole more like one he'd expect to find in a country club hotel. And, through the window that spanned one entire wall, Cole saw the black Challenger. Naturally, Jayne had been cunning enough to tuck the car away at the rear of the house and away from curious eyes.

"Eureka!" Cole whispered to himself as, frantically, he began searching for the keys he was convinced Jayne and her husband would have left there.

Then, over by the stove, by the antique-style stovetop teakettle, Cole spotted the car keys. His heart leapt in his chest and for the first time since waking up in that godforsaken place tied to the four-poster, he allowed himself to truly believe he had a chance.

Cole darted across the kitchen, his reflection caught in countless stainless-steel surfaces, his focus on getting those Challenger keys in his hand.

"Stop right there, Cole," a voice split the silence in the kitchen.

Instinctively, Cole spun around to face the man he'd only heard speak a few times throughout his ordeal and even then, only to say *yes, Mistress*. The gimp was a couple feet away, and Cole realized it was the first time he'd seen him without the mask; the spreader bar had done a number on his face and left it bloody and twisted. He held the camera by his side, the red record light on, its lens pointing at Cole. In his other hand, Buddy Torrez held out the gun he kept in his latex waistband; clearly, he wasn't taking the chance of being caught off guard again.

It took Cole a few seconds to register where the guy had suddenly sprung from. He'd stepped out of a doorway in the kitchen wall that had been designed to blend invisibly with its surroundings. Of course, a big, posh ranch house would have servants' doors and likely a rabbit warren of passageways and staircases behind the walls, too. It was a way, copied from the old days, by which rich families allowed their help to move about the house unseen.

"Hey, Buddy," Cole held out his hands to show he was unarmed, helpless. "We just want to get out of here, that's all."

Buddy shook his head. "I can't let that happen."

"Because your mistress will be mad at you?" Cole said as he inched forward.

"Because you can't be allowed to live." Buddy sounded flat, emotionless, like someone who'd died inside.

"You don't have to listen to her, Buddy," Cole offered. "Just look at the trouble she's gotten you into. I'm guessing all *this* was her idea?"

"I exist to obey Mistress."

"And what do you get out of it?" Another inch toward the gimp, Cole forced himself to keep his eyes on Buddy's and away from the gun. "You kill for her, and she treats you like shit. You let her use you for what? Her sick idea of revenge? You're nothing more than her puppet, Buddy—and just look at what she's reduced you to. You love her, and she's still in love with me—she's made no secret about that to your fucking face. What kind of man are you, Buddy?" Cole knew his words were harsh, that they would bite deep with any man who loved his woman, but more so with poor Buddy. He also knew he could tip the balance between the two of them one of two ways: either Buddy would back down and see reason, or…

Cole didn't wish to even contemplate the second option.

"It's how I choose to live my life." A glimmer of doubt crossed Buddy's face, and Cole seized the advantage.

"You're in Texas, Buddy," he said. "When they catch you—and they will—you'll sit and rot on death row for ten, maybe fifteen years and then they'll fry you while a crowd stands outside Huntsville, cheering. Or you could quit now, let us go, and make a break from Jayne. You could be in Mexico in a few hours, somewhere the cops and *she* will never find you."

"I can't leave her." Buddy's tone was final. "I won't—"

Taking his chance, Cole lunged for the gun. As he grabbed Buddy's hand and pushed the gun to the side, it fired off two shots; the recoil jolted through his arm. Cole gasped as the bullets grazed the skin at the top of his thigh with a sting of hot metal; behind him, the oven's glass door shattered.

Holding on to Buddy's gun with all his strength, Cole heaved his body weight into the gimp's chest and pinned him against the kitchen wall. Grunting, winded, Buddy tried his best to wrench his hand free and frantically kicked out his legs as he did so.

Unfortunately for Cole, one of Buddy's flailing knees caught him square between the legs. Hard bone met with soft, unprotected balls, and Cole doubled over in agony. Buddy's gun connected with the top of Cole's head; Cole's vision blurred, and he collapsed at the gimp's feet.

"Please, no…" Cole groaned; his bare feet slipped on the smooth floor as he attempted to scoot himself away from Buddy.

Buddy lifted the gun, his face slack and expressionless as his eyes fixed on Cole's.

"Don't do this, Buddy," Cole pleaded. "You don't have to do what she—"

With no hint of emotion, Buddy Torrez popped the muzzle of his Sig into his mouth and pulled the trigger.

"*Shit*!" Cole froze as the top of Buddy's head exploded. Brain, blood, and splinters of skull splashed the ceiling as Buddy keeled forward; his body landed face-first onto Cole's legs.

Cole kicked Buddy's corpse away, freeing his legs, and got to his feet. From above, a gruesome rain of the gimp's blood and brains drip-dripped down onto Cole's back. No time to process, Cole's thoughts turned to Vanessa: she would be making her way to the front door, and Jayne would be hunting her, no doubt alerted by the sound of Buddy's gunshots.

"*Buddy*?" As if on cue, Jayne's voice rang through the house. Cole guessed she was somewhere by the staircase— if only he knew exactly where.

Taking care not to slip on the mess Buddy's suicide had created, Cole grabbed Buddy's gun from the floor, the car keys from the countertop, and made his way to the outside door. He prayed it wouldn't be locked when he got there.

It wasn't.

The warm morning air tasted like freedom. Cole gulped it down and made for the Challenger; he'd drive it around to the front of the house where Vanessa would hopefully be waiting. Moving as quickly as he could on shaking legs, Cole thumbed the fob; the car beeped twice and flashed its blinkers as the doors unlocked. A nervous glance over his shoulder let Cole know the coast was still clear—although his racing imagination told him Jayne would be hurrying to the kitchen with her gun at the ready. Cole clambered into the car and, gunning the engine, he cringed at the loud, throaty sound it made. There could be no doubt Jayne had heard it, and it would certainly have alerted her to where he was.

Slamming the Challenger into drive, Cole maneuvered it out of the small courtyard; following the line of the house, he drove around to the front. If Jayne was making her way to the kitchen at the rear, it was his best chance at getting Vanessa out safely.

The front door was closed when Cole pulled up in front of it in a thick cloud of red dust. It ran against his every instinct to get out of the car to go to Vanessa—what if she was lost inside the house, what if Jayne had caught up with her? What if he blew his only chance of escaping by going to find Vanessa? But what if he didn't and Jayne killed her? Would Cole Gianni be able to live with himself?

By means of compromise, Cole nudged the center of the steering wheel with the heel of his hand. The horn sounded, loud, startling in the warm, still air. He chanced it again—all he could hope for was that Vanessa was closer to the front door than her pursuer.

"Damn it," Cole growled and reached for the door handle; he was going to have to take a risk. For as much as he wanted to floor the gas and get the hell away from the ranch, Jayne, and the death, in his heart, Cole knew he couldn't leave Vanessa behind.

Cole scanned a full three-sixty before easing open the Challenger's door and stepping out onto the sun-scorched driveway. Keeping low and using the car for cover, he scooted around to the front door of the house, his senses hyperalert for any movement or sound from inside.

Reaching the door, twisting the knob, Cole pushed at it with his shoulder. He left out the breath he'd been holding as the door swung open and he was met by the cool rush of conditioned air.

Behind him, a movement, and Cole cursed himself for leaving Buddy's gun on the passenger seat—he'd forgotten the thing, a simple mistake that could cost him dearly.

Half in, half out of the doorway, Cole saw Jayne appear around the corner of the house. Gun held tight in her outstretched hand, she walked with a peculiar gait as if struggling in the dirt with her high-heeled shoes. "Vanessa!" Cole called out; the name bounced around the spacious entryway. "*Where the fuck are you*?!"

"Cole!" Shrill, grating, Jayne's voice carried across the front of the ranch house. "*Cole*!" She fired her gun into the air, and Cole pressed himself tight to the doorway.

"I'm here!" Vanessa appeared from beneath the staircase and ran toward him.

"She's coming!" Cole hissed.

Jayne fired off another shot, threw her masked face heavenward, and let out a loud, piercing scream.

Cole and Vanessa scrambled into the Challenger, and Cole hit the gas. The car lurched and Cole spun it around toward the long driveway; behind them, Jayne screamed as she ran toward the car, gun kicking in her hand with each shot she fired.

Suddenly, the car tilted to the left as both tires on that side blew out. Cole fought for control, but the wheel spun from his grip and the Challenger veered toward the fence.

More shots.

Bullets ripped through the car's bodywork, steam hissed up from beneath the hood, and the engine made a strangled grinding noise as it shuddered to a stop.

"*Fuck*!" Cole slammed his hands on the steering wheel as the car ground to a juddering halt.

"Cole!" Vanessa already had her door open and was clambering out; she left a wet, bloody handprint on the handle.

Jolted into action, Cole grabbed the gun and got out of the car. Crouched down by the car's side, Cole wondered if he had any chance of hitting Jayne if he returned fire. "The stables are our only chance," he said. Jayne was too far away for him to waste bullets in an ill-conceived shootout. "At least we can hide there until we figure out what the fuck we're going to do." As much as he tried, he couldn't keep the despondency from his tone. He'd thought they were home and dry in the car, and now things seemed more hopeless than ever.

"Or take a couple of horses?" Vanessa had both hands clasped to her side. Blood oozed between her fingers, soaking the bandage on her already wounded hand.

"You're hurt."

"Either she got a lucky shot in or it's shrapnel from the engine." Vanessa forced a pained smile. "I'll be okay."

"Can you make it to the barn?" Vanessa nodded.

Cole had his doubts, but they had no other choice. Jayne was gaining ground, her mask gone from her face, her stilettos kicked off—all game-playing and pretense was over.

They ran out from behind the car, the sun hot on their naked bodies, and toward the barn. Cole held out a hand for Vanessa to clasp, and he helped her along as they zigzagged to deny Jayne a clear shot—it was a trick Cole had picked up as an extra in some zombie B-movie a long time ago.

The rank stink of death in the barn was unbearable. The young girl still hung from the crossbeam; her flayed skin hung in tatters, and she was covered with fat, buzzing flies feeding on her black, congealed blood there and in the dirt below her feet.

Gagging, Cole ran by the girl's lifeless body; his memory replayed her screams that had filled the expansive barn the night before, and he was keen to be away from the ghoulish sight.

Behind them, Jayne fired off another shot as Cole and Vanessa disappeared into the relative gloom of the barn. It was as if she wanted them to know she was hot on their heels and there was nowhere to run.

Daring a glance behind them—Jayne was nowhere in sight, which concerned Cole more than seeing her crazy, gun-toting ass—Cole led Vanessa through to the stables beyond the barn, his mind fixed on grabbing a horse or two.

The smell in the stables was worse than in the barn; they were assaulted by the thick, cloying reek of rotten flesh and stale horseshit. Cole's stomach heaved and the acid burn of bile stabbed at his gullet.

"*Oh…*" Vanessa stopped dead in her tracks behind Cole; her sudden stop almost wrenched his shoulder from its socket. Letting go of Vanessa's hand, Cole turned around, expecting to see Jayne holding her by the throat with the gun to her temple.

Vanessa was doubled over, hands on her knees, heaving bile and blood onto the stable floor, the bleeding wound to her side forgotten.

There, lying together in the dirt, were the couple from the dungeon room portrait. They were both naked, and the man's leg appeared to have been ripped off. Someone, Buddy presumably, had pushed it tight up to the stump to give the semblance of remaining attached.

"We have to go, Vanessa," Cole urged, placing an arm about her bare, heaving shoulders. "I don't want us to end up like…"

A thick, black curtain of flies lifted up off the dead couple's bodies as Cole maneuvered Vanessa past. She buried her face into his shoulder as they skirted around the wide pool of dried blood and headed toward the stalls to the left that housed a half dozen horses.

"*Cole*!" Jayne's voice had the horses shifting skittishly. She was in the barn—time really was running out.

"Wait here." Cole sat Vanessa down on a hay bale in one of the unoccupied stalls; he placed the gun by her side. "I'm afraid I won't have time to saddle up."

Although Vanessa dismissed him with a flippant wave, Cole saw she was in pain. Her hands were once more clasped to the hole in her side, which pumped out thick rivulets of blood each time she moved. "I'll be okay. Just get us out of here, Cole."

Cole left Vanessa and crossed over to the first of the stalls. Pulling the bolt, he swung open the low door. The horse inside snorted and shifted nervously as it left its confines. Cole moved onto the next door, then the next, liberating the horses, all the while keeping one eye on the stable's main door for Jayne. She *had* to be there by now, which meant she was planning her next move.

At the penultimate stall, Cole slipped a rope around the horse's neck and led it out. The horse was calm, used to strangers, and it trotted alongside Cole quite happily as he guided it between its stable mates to where Vanessa was waiting for him.

"You good?" Cole pushed open the door to Vanessa's hiding place.

"Yeah." She eyed the horse with some suspicion, and Cole wished

he'd had time to put a saddle on it.

Cole helped Vanessa stand; her skin had taken on a worrisome pallor, and her left thigh was soaked with blood. She grimaced as she stood, leaning her weight into Cole's side for support.

"*No, you fucking don't!*" Jayne screamed as she burst through the stable door. She took aim at Cole and a shot rang out.

Panicked, the horses whinnied and jostled one another to get away from the noise; Cole felt the rope from his horse pull through his hands, the friction burning him, and his chosen animal ran to the far end of the stable with its companions.

Jayne let off another shot, and Cole felt hot pain in his calf muscle. Ignoring it, he dropped low and grabbed his gun from the hay bale. He pushed Vanessa to the ground as he did so—she went down with a pained squeal.

Cole crawled across to the stall door, poked his head and gun out, and returned fire at Jayne; there were only five bullets left in Buddy's magazine, and every one of them missed. Nonetheless, Jayne ran for cover in the tack room.

That bought Cole a little time.

Taking his chance, Cole stood up and ran toward the horses, desperately looking for the one with the rope around its neck.

Clustered at the far end of the stable, the horses had calmed down some; Cole reckoned they were used for hunting and were accustomed to the sound of gunshots. As he moved around them, he whispered and clucked his tongue to keep them calm.

Jayne stalked from the tack room and made her way across the stables with intent. A glance across at Cole told him she knew exactly where he was and that he was too far away to stop her.

"There you are, *bitch*," Jayne snarled, kicking open the stall door.

And, making sure Cole was watching, she aimed her gun at Vanessa. "No!" Cole stepped out from behind the horses.

Jayne turned to Cole, a crazy smile parting her lips. "I knew you'd want to play the hero, Cole." She aimed the gun at him, finger on the trigger.

Pursing his lips, Cole made a low hissing noise at the back of his throat.

The horses reared up, kicking, stomping, and ran away from Cole and toward Jayne.

She managed to fire off a few shots—felling one of the chestnut mares—before the animals were upon her, their terror fueled further by the sound of her gun. Pummeled by merciless hooves, Jayne went down amid a cloud of dust, her bloodcurdling cries rising above those of the horses as they trampled her in their frenzy.

As the horses stomped at Jayne's broken body, Cole returned to Vanessa—he couldn't wait for the animals to calm down; he didn't want to leave her alone.

"It's over." Cole scooped Vanessa up from the floor and brushed away the straw sticking to her face.

"Jayne?"

"It's *all* over," Cole reiterated. He placed a hand over hers on her wounded flank, felt the heat of her blood there; she was heavy in his arms. "I need to get you to a hospital."

"I think it's too late," Vanessa replied. "I lost a lot of blood, Cole."

"You're a fighter—you're not about to give up now, not after everything we've been through together…" Cole stopped short of telling Vanessa he loved her—he knew how he felt but couldn't be certain it wouldn't be their circumstance talking. Struggling against the pain in his lower leg, he got up and pulled Vanessa upright as he did so. "Cole," Vanessa said, "I have to tell you something…"

Cole guided Vanessa toward the stall's door. The horses, satisfied they'd eliminated the threat to their well-being, had calmed and sauntered back to the far end of the stable as if waiting to be let out into the fields beyond.

"I'm not exactly who you think I am—"

"And neither am I, Vanessa," Cole said as he all but carried her by Jayne Torrez's mangled body and back toward the barn. "Let's leave the confessions for another time, shall we?"

Vanessa fell quiet; the heat of the day welcomed them as they stepped out of the barn and made their way slowly toward the house. Whatever the future held for him, he knew in his heart it was one with Vanessa, and for the first time in his life, Cole Gianni felt he was free from *The Gentleman's Choice* and the damaged past that led him there.

About the Author

Blake Rudman enjoyed a former, successful career in executive management, building his own companies from the ground up.

Success or not, Blake's heart has always been in the written word, and the myriad ideas he spent much of his spare time jotting down in notebooks, Post-Its, and scraps of paper whenever the inspiration hit him.

Now a breakout author of five noir thriller novels – all to be published in 2023 – Blake's destiny of becoming a writer of some renown is well under way.

When he's not working diligently on his next novel, Blake spends quality time with his family and tropical fish.

Follow Blake's blog at: https://blakerudman.com
Facebook: @BRudmanThriller
Instagram: @BRudmanThriller
Twitter: @BRudmanThriller

For all Blake's books, visit him at:
www.hellboundbookspublishing.com/authorpage_rudman.html

Dark Beauty

Tessa and Kristin Morgan are identical twins, exquisitely beautiful, and have the world at their perfectly pedicured feet; they are also profoundly different beneath their stunning facades.

Tessa is the laser-focused academic with her eyes firmly fixed upon a career in neurology, while Kristin exploits her striking looks and undeniable power over men to carve out a single-minded path to fame and fortune as a model and actress; an ambition she also holds for her sister.

But, on the night of the pair's debut as top-tier models, and with a high-profile movie role in the bag, tragedy strikes the twins in the form of a cruel acid attack by an unknown assailant. Thus, a gruesome chain of events begins - one that leaves a trail of blood, death, and devastation behind both Tessa and Kristin.

As Tessa fights to rebuild her life and uncover the truth behind the attack, she finds herself getting closer and closer to an uncomfortable truth about her sister and her search for the truth turns into a nightmare struggle to stay alive.

Goodbye Stranger

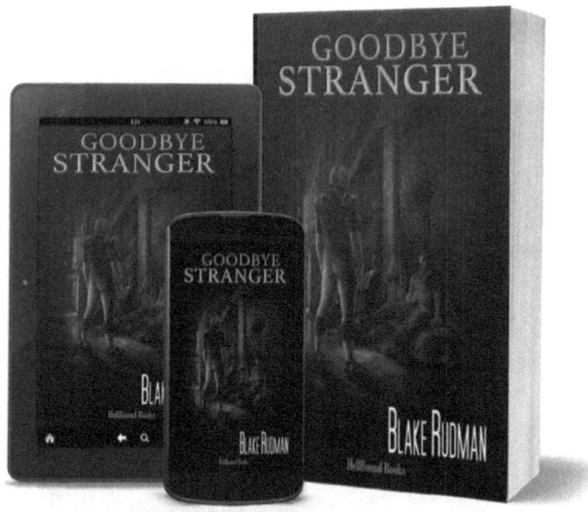

"As with *American Psycho*, Blake Rudman's *Goodbye Stranger* has a wealthy, successful man whose wonderful family life masks a much darker side. Throw in a once-trusting, increasingly suspicious wife, and the stage is set for twists and turns you'll never see coming!"

Danielle Harrington has the life many women envy: She's beautiful, rich, has two wonderful children, and is married to *the* Preston Harrington - the handsome, charismatic, retired quarterback who won two Super Bowls.

Unfortunately, something is very wrong with Preston. Having suffered more than his fair share of injuries and concussions, he becomes quiet, withdrawn, and distant. As Preston spends more time away from his family, Danielle begins suspect an affair without realizing her husband is involved in something much, much worse…

Following a series of tragic incidents and the return of an old nemesis from the past, things begin to spiral out of control for Danielle as Preston's dark side puts her and their children in terrible danger.

Redline

"If Lee Childs' Jack Reacher or Clive Cussler's Dirk Pitt tackled a terrorist scheme that utilized subliminal messaging to sow social and economic chaos on a global scale, it would look a lot like *Red Line.*"
Baltimore Police Detective Mitch Wilson wants a nice day out with his wife and son. Instead, they are all caught up in a catastrophic terrorist attack that has repercussions across the USA and triggers events that could alter the course of civilization.
Having lost everything, Mitch sets out to seek justice – and revenge and stumbles upon a global conspiracy.
On the other side of the world, renowned linguistic professor, Yasaman Karami, flees her native Iran for the freedom of the west; she holds one of the keys to defeating the terrorist organization.
Yasaman and Mitch's worlds collide as, alongside federal agents and allies, they race against the clock to hunt down the terrorist masterminds and prevent worldwide catastrophe.

Kutri

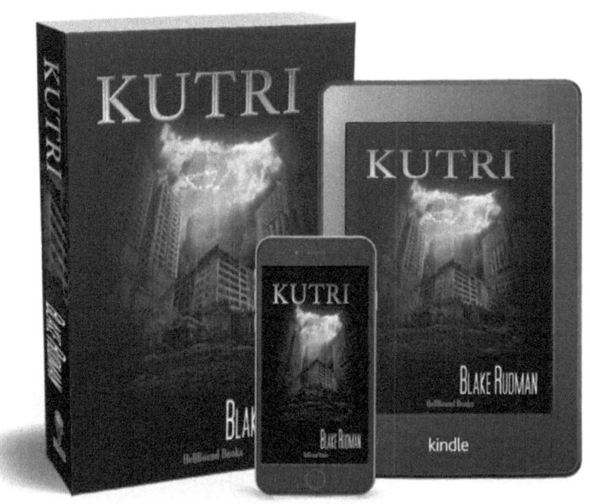

The Slow Plague killed billions of women and girls worldwide. The gender-targeting infection without cure drove the remaining, sparce female population into an insane supply and demand situation in which they are treated as valuable commodities.

Though their "market value" is high, paradoxically, women's rights take a nosedive as they have become more desirable than the most precious jewels. Women are objects avarice, awe, and worship – to be owned or won in high-stakes games.

Kutri Chandigarh, one such "prize" and a rare beauty, is shipped from her native India to Los Angeles, a shattered metropolis barricaded behind a radiation-repelling wall. Within the city stronghold, a bleak, broken society comprised mostly of men is mesmerized by the stupefying programs pumped out by Little Angel Studios: an endless parade of reality TV shows.

The studio's #1 hit is "Good Breeding", in which a bevy

of ethnically "pure" young women compete to marry a chosen suitor and produce a family in the spotlight of the public eye.

Like all women, Kutri has dreamed of wining the competition since her early childhood. But, when she arrives in LA and meets Jakob Freeman, her assigned matchmaker, the fantasy is turned on its head. It quickly twists into a horrific nightmare that extends far beyond Kutri and the man she chooses for herself.

As Kutri tries to escape the fate she once coveted, Jakob is swept up in events that threaten him body and soul and spark memories of a past he has deliberately tried to forget.

www.hellboundbookspublishing.com

Follow Blake's blog at: https://blakerudman.com
Facebook: @BRudmanThriller
Instagram: @BRudmanThriller
Twitter: @BRudmanThriller

For all Blake's books, visit him at:
www.hellboundbookspublishing.com/authorpage_rudman.html